THE ROCK

The Rock of Gibraltar has been a British Fortress and Colony for more than two hundred and fifty years; to all of us it has long been a symbol. As our last foothold on the Continent of Europe, as a bastion of British sea power, as the custodian of the entrance to the Mediterranean, it has always been a vital factor in British strategy. In the last war the fate of the Rock lay dangerously in the balance.

This fine novel by the author of *The Cruiser* is the story of Gibraltar in its most fateful years. From the first days of the war, the Rock became a vital pivot of the Mediterranean theatre. From the shelter of its harbour Force H, headed by the great battle-cruiser *Hood* and the carrier *Ark Royal*, sailed out to drive the Italian Navy from its own waters, to immobilize the French Fleet after the fall of France, to join the avenging hunt for the *Bismarck*, and, in the most suicidal convoy that ever sailed, to break the siege of Malta. From early in 1940 the Rock was under continuous threat by land should the Germans decide to swing through Spain, and by air from German bases in North Africa. She was as dangerously threatened by sabotage from within, for 10,000 Spanish workers crossed from Spain every morning to work in the Dockyard and crossed back again every night. But Gibraltar survived to garner and send forth the mightiest Armada the world had ever known. From the Rock was launched Operation Torch—the invasion of North Africa.

By the Same Author

THE FELTHAMS   THE YOUNGER FELTHAMS
GENTLEMAN IN PINK UNIFORM LADY IN THIN ARMOUR
GIRL IN THE LIMELIGHT   THE CRUISER

THE ROCK

A NOVEL

BY

WARREN TUTE

CASSELL & COMPANY LTD
LONDON

CASSELL & COMPANY LTD
37/38 St. Andrew's Hill, Queen Victoria Street
London, E.C.4
and at
31/34 George IV Bridge, Edinburgh
210 Queen Street, Melbourne
26/30 Clarence Street, Sydney
24 Wyndham Street, Auckland, New Zealand
1068 Broadview Avenue, Toronto 6
P.O. Box 275, Cape Town
P.O. Box 11190, Johannesburg
58 Pembroke Street, Port of Spain, Trinidad
Haroon Chambers, South Napier Road, Karachi
13/14 Ajmeri Gate Extension, New Delhi 1
15 Graham Road, Ballard Estate, Bombay 1
17 Chittaranjan Avenue, Calcutta 13
Macdonald House, Orchard Road, Singapore 9
P.O. Box 959, Accra, Ghana
Avenida 9 de Julho 1138, São Paulo
Galeria Güemes, Escritorio 454/59 Florida 165, Buenos Aires
Marne 5b, Mexico 5, D.F.
25 rue Henri Barbusse, Paris 5e
25 Ny Strandvej, Espergaerde, Denmark
Kauwlaan 17, The Hague
Bederstrasse 51, Zurich 2

PRINTED IN GREAT BRITAIN
BY EBENEZER BAYLIS AND SON, LTD., THE
TRINITY PRESS, WORCESTER AND LONDON
F.457.

AUTHOR'S PREFACE

THE Rock of Gibraltar is a very real place indeed. It stands in a strategic position at one of the world's focal points. It is a British Fortress and Colony and has been so continuously for over 250 years. Thus it can be seen that in a story about a definite place, such as Gibraltar, at a distinct time, such as the Second World War, there are many nice little traps awaiting a writer who thinks up imaginary characters and allows them to operate against such a background. Of these pitfalls perhaps the principal one is the fact that a number of events in this book did actually happen. That is why a disclaimer that *no real person* is being described has to be firmly made at the start and then underlined.

A writer doing this sort of story is in a tricky position. I visited Gibraltar many times when I was in the Navy. I have friends there now. *None of them* are in this book in any shape or form. In particular no reference to any actual person, whether past or present, holding an official appointment at Gibraltar is intended in any personal sense, but in describing a real place such as Gibraltar those who served on the Rock may feel themselves vulnerable and therefore I am most anxious to reassure them that *all* characters in this book are purely fictional. I have done my best to imagine fresh and entirely different personalities. If by accident I have unwittingly given offence, I hope it will be understood in this spirit. My object has been to tell part of the great story of Gibraltar at a particularly crucial period and to try and express my admiration for those who, physically and psychologically, have suffered and survived a siege.

The Rock of Gibraltar has always meant something very special to the British. It is now our only foothold on the continent of Europe. It has long been a symbol to us all. 'Safe as the Rock of Gibraltar' and similar phrases have entered our daily speech. It is one of the things we take for granted without knowing too much about it, but instinctively we feel that were the Rock of Gibraltar to be given up, then something really desperate would have happened to the British Commonwealth.

People who wield power in the world, particularly those like the British, who do so with responsibility, are never much loved. Yet the free world has plenty of reason to be grateful for Anglo-Saxon tenacity and common sense. Gibraltar well illustrates this process. Today Spain wants it back and since, geographically speaking, it is as much a part of Spain as Portland Bill is of England, logic is on the Spanish side. Moreover in Gibraltar the mother tongue is Spanish and there is scarcely a Gibraltarian who has not got a blood connection in Andalusia or elsewhere in Spain.

Yet, as against that, it is said that were a referendum to be taken in Gibraltar today on whether the Rock should remain British or be handed back to Spain, 120 per cent would vote for it to remain British—the odd twenty per cent voting twice. I believe this to be a rough statement of the truth, but it is not what you commonly read in the papers nor in well-argued, professorial books. The problem of Gibraltar will not yield to intellectual theorists manipulating the facts. Common sense goes on guard and our hackles rise. It may not be logical that the vast majority of Gibraltarians wish to remain British—but they do. And this, I am sure, goes far beyond politics, as it goes beyond the current situation in Spain, whether the régime happens to be a monarchy, a republic or a ramshackle, corrupt dictatorship on the look-out for any canard to distract attention.

Of course, common sense also decrees that should Spain become actively hostile to us, the military value of the Rock might well be negligible, but that is another story. As things have been, the Rock itself has long caught the imagination and affection of the British and most of us are secretly, if not openly, glad it is there—an oasis of freedom and decency in a desert of . . . well, we all know what.

In its long story the Rock seems always to have been under siege in one form or another. At present the siege is petty and economic: at the period of this book it was mostly psychological, the pressure arising from a very real threat that Germany would march into Spain as she had done into France. This period of threat rose to a peak at the time of the North African landings, when for a few short and astonishing days Gibraltar came under the American flag, when it was upon Gibraltar that what Sir Winston Churchill has called the Hinge of Fate was to turn. It is a sobering thing to reflect how different the story of the Second World War might have been without the Rock of Gibraltar.

I would like to thank my friends in Gibraltar for the help so freely given in the early stages of writing this book and at the same time dedicate this story to Gibraltar and to those number-less people who at one time or another have served on the Rock and who have thus come to know personally, as so many of us did, the process of tempering and endurance needed to survive a siege in any form it may take. Gibraltar deserves the best salute we can give it. I hope that behind the events of this story a glimpse can be caught of the peculiar essence of the Rock and of its tough, friendly, and intensely loyal inhabitants.

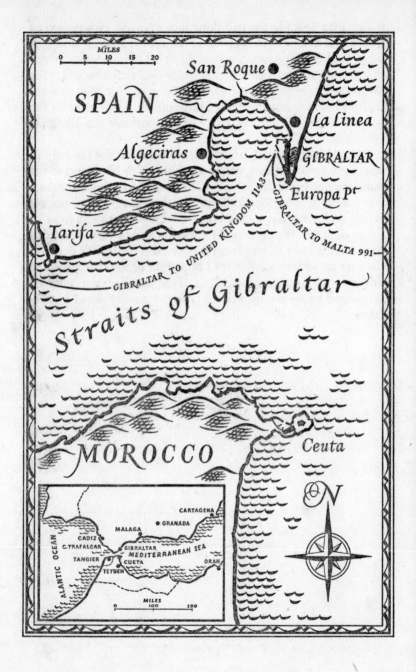

PART ONE

I

GIBRALTAR lay like a crouching animal, outlined mistily against the sun. Lieutenant-Commander Evers, pacing up and down the destroyer bridge to encourage his circulation, paused for a moment to look at the Rock. He had forgotten the impact it had. He thought about it vaguely as a lump of limestone at the bottom of Spain, a red dot on the map: he had forgotten the impressive mass of the Fortress as it first loomed up mysteriously out of the morning haze.

'Tarifa bearing 045 degrees, sir.'

Evers glanced at his First Lieutenant. Three days at sea had freshened him up, cleared away the bleariness which a spell of Pompey and harbour life did to young sea-going naval officers. Now his good humour and energy had reasserted themselves. Soon, he supposed, they would be starting the process all over again, beating up Gib. But this would only counterpoint the working-up period, the intensive drills and exercises which lay ahead. *Firesprite* and her flotilla were to be fully operational in a month's time. In June 1939 the pressure of coming events could already be felt. There was an urgency in the air. It was odd that their first job should be an almost lazy escorting of this aged P. and O. liner steaming so unexcitedly on their starboard quarter.

'I'm going below to have some breakfast, Number One. Keep an eye on the Rock and its new Governor and let me know if the Spaniards show any signs of life.'

'Aye, aye, sir.'

The First Lieutenant watched his Captain's angular face disappear. It struck him that, if Abraham Lincoln had ever arrayed himself as a Lieutenant-Commander, R.N., then he would have looked like David Evers lowering himself down the bridge ladder of one of H.M. Ships. But Evers was pretty much what Jimmy would have prescribed as a captain had he been given a chance. It was going to be all right. A happy ship and, God willing, a successful commission. He surveyed

[3]

the rest of the flotilla stationed ahead and astern of the old *Ranikapoor*. The new 'F' class destroyers had a businesslike look about them. Well—if a show had to be put on to induct the new Governor into his parish, then Jimmy Allendale supposed the 28th Destroyer Flotilla would rise to the occasion. In his private opinion it was a waste of time, but in any case they had to get out to Gib for their working-up. They might just as well arrive with a flourish.

Unconsciously imitating his Captain, he began pacing up and down the narrow bridge. It was pleasant to be able to do so again. There had been a heavy swell in the Bay of Biscay. *Firesprite* was evidently a good sea-boat, but even when destroyers are held down to a liner's economical speed they throw themselves about a good deal if there is any kind of sea running. Jimmy had been a sub in one of the old 'V' class destroyers. Compared with that, *Firesprite* was luxury, but there was no avoiding the essential elements of destroyer life, the thin, almost racing hull which gave you more speed than any other warship afloat, and its concomitant rolling, pitching and spray-drenched, sticky wetness. You couldn't have it both ways. Either you went for the ponderous, disciplined comfort of a battleship or cruiser, or you chose the more free-and-easy, stimulating adventurousness of destroyer and sloop. They were two distinct variants of service at sea. Jimmy Allendale had opted for small ships since his midshipman days. Now at twenty-five this was his first job as a Number One. He looked across at the Sub-Lieutenant gazing dreamily at Spain. So short a time ago he, too, had been an irresponsible sub-lieutenant. Now he was second-in-command of one of the Royal Navy's newest destroyers. Perhaps soon—especially if there was a war—he would have a command of his own. Life was very good for Jimmy Allendale at the moment.

By this time the sun was higher up over the Mediterranean and no longer silhouetted the Rock. They were two-thirds of the way through the Straits. Spain lay to port and Africa to starboard. The narrow stretch of water which the Rock dominated, that all-important neck giving on to the body of the inland sea—those cardinal Straits of Gibraltar were, at this narrowest point, only eight miles wide. There was always a lot of shipping hurrying east and west between the Pillars of Hercules. There were also ships crossing from north to south, between Spain and Morocco. It was a busy part of the world's seaways—a constricted place where special vigilance was necessary, where a number of important things could happen in a very short time. In that, too, lay the main significance of the Rock.

'Signalman!'

'Sir?'

'What's that steamer crossing our bows?'

Signalman Jones did not bother to look through his telescope. He had done a commission at Gibraltar before. He knew the shipping likely to be found in the Straits. He welcomed the opportunity of showing how valuable his experience was going to be.

'It's the morning ferry from Algeciras to Tangier, sir. She's dodging over to the African side to take advantage of the tide running west. When she comes back in the evening, she'll head down the centre of the Straits like us.'

'Ever been to Tangier?'

'No, sir.' Jones paused for a second and then ventured a remark. 'They say there's some very interesting Moorish relics in the Casbah.'

'So I hear—if you can get them to take off their yashmaks.'

Signalman Jones grinned. His instinct was to cap the remark but he was not yet sure how far he could go with his First Lieutenant. They had only been ten days in commission. A brand-new ship and a brand-new flotilla. Jimmy looked a bit of all right with his wide red face and curly black hair; he was certainly one of the boys and he could knock back the gin, as the Wardroom Steward had let it be known. Still it didn't pay to take risks at this stage of the game. They were going to see a lot of each other over the next two years. Jones had no wish to be known as familiar. That would never do—with his hook due at any moment now. So he contented himself with a grin and then, at that moment, a chain of small events began to take place almost simultaneously.

A string of bunting was hoisted by the Flotilla Leader, the Captain clambered back to the bridge, and as Jimmy turned to speak to him he noticed, with a sudden chill, black smoke pouring from the after-funnel straight down upon the *Ranikapoor*. Hell, he thought, that had to happen while the old man was below. He watched Evers make straight for the engine room voice-pipe. But before he could reach it, there was a whistle and the Chief's warm brogue could be heard all over the compass platform.

'I'm having a wee spot of bother with Number Two feed supply, sir. Permission to shut down Number Two boiler?'

'Very well. Let me know what the trouble is as soon as you can.' Evers turned to the First Lieutenant. 'How long have we been making smoke?'

'Only a few moments, sir. I just noticed it as you came back on the bridge.'

He's a little too eager, Evers thought; he answers too quickly. Perhaps responsibility will trim him down a bit in the next few months.

'We've got our pendants, sir.' Signalman Jones put in with appropriate sadness. To make smoke accidentally was not only a naval offence, it drew highly unwelcome attention upon the vessel concerned. To get your pendants was to have the misdemeanour registered by the Captain (D). Perhaps even explanations would have to be furnished. This was no way to approach Gibraltar after the thousand-mile voyage from England. Almost instinctively Evers looked across at the *Ranikapoor*, half-expecting the Governor-designate to be out on deck, brushing the smoke from his eyes. He smiled to himself. From his knowledge of Major-General Sir Giles Fortin, Baronet, D.S.O. and Bar, bachelor, and now about to be Governor of the Fortress and Colony of Gibraltar, he would expect the cold blue eyes to crease slightly into a smile and the mouth to harden in that extraordinary combination of understanding and will-power which had made the man what he was.

Allendale had followed his Captain's gaze. The smoke was now dying away and he, too, studied the old liner anxiously, as though some explosive reaction was to be expected from the personage they were escorting and whose ship they had just shrouded in smoke. It was an accident, but he had been in charge on the bridge when it happened. Any 'can' handed

[6]

down would be his. Jimmy had already a respect for Evers both as a man and as his commanding officer. In his vague, blundering way he felt he ought to say something to put matters right or at least to distract attention.

'Do you know anything about the new Big Noise, sir?' he asked, jerking his head at the *Ranikapoor*. Evers looked at him calmly for a moment and then smiled.

'As a matter of fact I do,' he answered. 'You see, the new Big Noise is my uncle.'

2

On board the *Ranikapoor*, Lieutenant Richard Seale, R.M., made his way along to the Governor's stateroom. The plaster cast on his back still made walking difficult and the superimposition on to this of Royal Marine full-dress uniform had been quite a feat. He knocked at the door and went in.

'We should be getting into Gibraltar in about half an hour, sir.'

'Good. The Captain has invited us up on the bridge. We may as well start the ball rolling from there.'

The Governor-designate finished buckling on his sword and examined the result in the mirror. The spectacle was magnificent but it seemed to leave him unmoved. Seale wondered if he should make some complimentary remark. He had only the sketchiest ideas of what was expected of an A.D.C. He shot a glance at His Cragginess—Seale's private name for this rocky-faced, blue-eyed, rather small man who for some unimaginable reason had selected him as his A.D.C. He decided it was safer to say nothing. Each time he met the Governor, Seale was for the moment unnerved by a feeling of awe and curiosity. So this was Fortin the Myth, the man who had known Lawrence in the desert, the severe lonely soldier, a 'freeman' of half a dozen Arab countries, the hero of that place Seale could never remember in Waziristan, which he had caused to surrender by calmly walking up to the gate through a hail of bullets, armed only with a swagger cane, Fortin the Mystic, the Man of God. What on earth am I doing in a job like this, Seale asked himself. I should be flying an aeroplane—getting ready for a war—not dancing attendance on a hero. At the thought of the word 'dance', his back gave him a tweak and he came out of his daydream to find the Governor looking at him from under his bushy eyebrows. It was a penetrating, under-standing look. It made Seale feel slightly uncomfortable, as though he were naked. He resented it. He felt guilty though he had nothing at all on his conscience. He had an absurd wish to hide, at the same time knowing perfectly well that there was nowhere anyone could hide from a look such as that. Well—as soon as that damned cast was off, he'd be back to the Fleet Air Arm like a flash.

'How's the back?'

'All right, sir, thank you. The strait-jacket gave me a bit of trouble with the belt.'

'You think you'll survive the poodle-faking? We're in for a good dose of it today.' The Governor smiled at him. 'How-ever, only a fool sees no point in ceremony. In a place like Gibraltar it's doubly important.'

The Governor walked up and down the stateroom as he talked. Seale envied the ease with which he wore the tight formal uniform. For a man who had spent so much of his life in the desert he seemed totally unconcerned by the restriction of full dress. He moved about as though in a well-fitting lounge suit.

'I've got the order of ceremony handy if you want another look at it, sir.'

'No, thanks. I know what should happen. I've no doubt it's a fairly simple piece of mechanism. If something goes wrong we'll have to adapt to it, that's all. But I don't suppose it will. They'll want to make a good impression on me. A lot of trouble will have been taken. That's as it should be. Of course they'll be curious to see what sort of figurehead the Colonial Office has managed to get out of the Army. I suppose they'll know something about me.' Seale was aware of being studied once again as the Governor spoke. He's looking at me, he thought, all the time he's looking at me inside. 'However, their knowledge of me is bound to be vague,' the Governor shrugged his shoulders, 'and probably romantic in a newspaper way. Some of them may know the facts. To most of them I'll merely be someone who's tinkered about with Arabs most of his life. They won't find out what sort of person I am till we're all past the Royal Salutes and the shaking of hands. That's our job for the day.'

'Yes, sir.'

'I suppose this appointment has rather taken you by surprise?'

'Well, yes, sir, it has.'

It was more than surprise; it smacked of magic. Briefly Seale thought about his days in the Fleet Air Arm. He'd been one of the first Royal Marine officers to become a pilot. 'Flying Bullocks?' his messmates had said. 'What next?' He'd paid no attention to the jeers, the incredulous scepticism which had accompanied his first airborne ventures. He'd proved it could be done. For the first time in history a Royal Marine officer had passed out of the flying course ahead of the regular entry. Three wonderful years. Then his crash, the broken back, the twisted broken legs, the muscular complications, the appalling loss of time at what, in his mid-twenties, he regarded as the prime of life. Six months of bed, hospital, convalescence, the taking-off of plaster casts, the opening-up, rebreaking and re-setting of bones. The growing probability of never flying again and the possibility that he might not even be fit for active service. The appalling, desolate feeling of uselessness which followed. Then one day, morosely limping about Eastney Barracks, the summons to the Commandant's office. 'They want to see you up in London, Dicky,' said his Colonel. 'They want to size you up for a job.' The journey to London to meet the Adjutant-General. The dismay at learning what the job was to be, offset only by the curiosity to know what 'Fortin of the Desert' would be like. His gradual acceptance of the new pattern of his life and now this climactic approach to the Rock.

'You see, Dicky,' the Governor went on and then shot him another arresting look, 'they do call you Dicky, don't they?'

'Yes, sir.'

'They' called you Dicky but surely not this bemedalled cragginess from Arabia? He smiled to himself. If his accident had taught him anything at all, it was to try and let things happen, accepting what life brought you. Even when it came to being addressed as Dicky by the King's new representative in the peninsular Fortress of Gibraltar.

'I've got an odd job to tackle here,' the Governor continued. 'One of its difficulties is that at first sight there's very little to be done. Elsewhere there's usually been plenty to do, but very little to do it with. Here the situation's reversed. A fortress has special problems. Gibraltar has special problems. Armed idleness is one thing with a Spanish civil war raging next door, quite another if a European war should break out. I won't go into that now. They're not overfond of me in Whitehall. They don't like independent eccentrics. However, they've appointed me here. I don't suppose I'll be popular. That doesn't matter to me personally. I've had some experience in making men do things they don't want to do. I can guess at the sort of people, the sort of set-up I shall find. Well—there are certain principles to abide by; for instance, that persuasion is better than force. That's where you come in. I don't know if there's been a Marine A.D.C. before. This is an experiment of mine—so I want you to prove me right. Gibraltar's in your regimental history; you're both a soldier and a sailor, so you can cultivate an equal ear for the two sides of my Service domain. Finally, so far as civilians are concerned, you have another asset: you're a Roman Catholic.'

'I don't see what that's got to do with it, sir.'

'Don't you, Dicky? Well, I expect you'll work it out over the next few months. Come on, let's go up on the bridge.'

3

A lot of trouble had certainly been taken to honour the new Governor's arrival in Gibraltar. Bunting hung everywhere, children jumped and yelled and waved their Union Jacks, roads had been closed to traffic, and from dawn, so it seemed to Grace Millingham, there had been the intermittent braying of bagpipes and the rat-tat-tat of drums. Now, as she sat in the special enclosure by the Ragged Staff steps where H.E. would land, she felt faded and out of key. Thank heavens, in another

[10]

hour it would all be over. Then lunch at home and perhaps a game of tennis in the afternoon.

The motor launch *Eliott*, containing the Governor and his A.D.C., had already left the *Ranikapoor*, preceded by the King's Harbour Master in his trim little launch. It was a balmy June day with a slight westerly breeze, sufficient to carry down the noise of buglers aboard H.M.S. *Cormorant*, the base ship at Gibraltar, sounding the alert as the *Eliott* passed. She glanced across at her husband, standing stiff and erect beside his Admiral, looking every inch of him a Flag-Lieutenant. It was any moment now. She turned to her sister sitting next to her.

'I don't see Heart Throb Number One anywhere about,' she said.

'Oh! Nicky wouldn't bother with a nonsense like this,' Rosita retorted. 'He's got better things to do with his time.'

'You mean that refugee, I suppose?'

'I do not,' Rosita snapped. 'I don't give a hoot who he's with.' And then to distract attention, she added quickly, 'I must say Boofles looks a dream in his cocked hat and all that gold lace.'

There was a twinge of jealousy in her sister's voice. Rosita was the only one in the family to refer to Lance by his hated nickname. She still resents me for marrying such a good-looking man, Grace thought, and wondered why. She considered Rosita to be far more attractive than herself. She could have the pick of the young Gibraltarians, if her mother wanted her to marry money, or perhaps the A.D.C. if Mother decided to try for another title. She wondered in passing what sort of man the new A.D.C. would be like. The last one had been a dud. She supposed that was why the family had made such a dead set at the Flag-Lieutenant. He was the next best thing. Charming, penniless, with a barony coming his way, and those really extraordinary good looks—Mother had worked it all out, weighed up the pros and cons and made her decision.

Now that Grace was married she was constantly surprised how little she had had to do with it. They had liked each other but that was all—and right from the start it had been out of her hands. Her mother had offered the bait in the form of the right parties at the right moment; she had got the young man on the hook for her elder, rather quiet daughter. He wasn't a Catholic, it's true, but what did that matter? The children would be. Day by day, week by week, as the stream of time ran on, Mother had played her bright shiny fish till, with a sudden jerk of which Lance was quite likely unconscious to this day, she had landed him flapping.

What had really been the bait? Herself or a share of the Barbarossa fortune? Certainly there was physical attraction, but without the wealth of one of the foremost Gibraltar families behind her, would Lance have given her a second look? Perhaps she would never know. Love? Well, that came later. That was a deeper thing. It grew out of marriage, the Church taught, a reward for obedience and duty and faith. Grace puckered her lips as she always did when her thoughts carried her down such dark alleys. She sighed. She had caught herself sighing a lot these days. She must stop. That way lay self-pity.

Well, well, it was early times yet. They had only been married eighteen months. Still, there hadn't been a child, the charm seemed to be a little cold and these moments of doubt and uneasiness had begun to recur more frequently than ever before. Perhaps it would change when Lance received another appointment away from Gibraltar. He was always fretting to get off to sea. One of these days that would happen—and then, perhaps, a new life would open for them both.

'Here they come!' said Rosita. There was a rustle of excitement as everyone stood up. Gibraltar was tensed and waiting for its new Governor. A touch on the button and the time-honoured ceremony would have begun. The *Eliott*, its bright-work gleaming, its canopy dazzling white, drew alongside the steps. Sailors with their boat-hooks stood rigid till the last moment and then with a few deft movements grappled the launch into the jetty. The coxswain saluted and His Excellency stepped ashore. As he did so the Guard of Honour gave the Royal Salute and at the same time the battery at King's Bastion began firing a salute of seventeen guns. The new Governor and Commander-in-Chief had arrived.

4

Major-General Sir Giles Fortin photographed the whole scene on to his mind as he took the first few steps from jetty to saluting-base. The old stone ramparts, now packed with people, the splashes of colour from uniforms and dresses, the hot dusty sunlight, and behind, towering up 1,300 feet, dominating himself and the whole ceremony, the huge grey bulk of the Rock itself.

In front of him the Guard of Honour in their kilts presented arms; to the right, the band slowly and, as it seemed, with a special emphasis began playing 'God Save the King'; to the left stood the line of important officials he would soon be meeting, the human material with which he would mainly be working over the next few years, the men and their wives who could make or ruin his governorship.

A part of him watched this ancient ceremony begin; another part watched his own reactions, watched to see that he made the right movements, would soon be shaking the right hands, saying the right things, and later signing the right papers; a third and more hidden part of him prayed. This was the only real part of the erect, impressive figure the world knew as General Fortin of Waziristan. This was the part in which the man himself strove to live, invisible to the world, alone with his God. 'Our Father which art in Heaven,' this part of him had said as he stepped ashore at Gibraltar. 'Hallowed be Thy Name, Thy Kingdom come, Thy Will be done—especially Thy Will be done, Father, on this tiny key-point of the earth, this Rock, this symbol of endurance and of siege—Thy Will be done on earth as it is in Heaven.'

It was a habit of his to meditate on particular phrases, sometimes even on words in the Lord's Prayer and the parables. They glowed like the heart of a fire in this third part of his being, they fed him silently with meaning, and gave to the outer parts, the personality enmeshed with life and its events, a significance and a light which the world could never comprehend. The world accepted him now as a man of destiny but it was Destiny itself with which he dealt on terms of respectful familiarity in this third and most intimate part of himself.

The Acting Governor, a Brigadier who was also the Deputy Fortress Commander, now stepped forward, shook hands and followed His Excellency as he inspected the Guard of Honour. Nothing wrong here, thought Fortin as he looked at the bronzed Highland faces, the gleaming brass and the blancoed leggings; and why should there be? This is what they're good at, what they've been trained to do. But—how would they be after four years of siege? Out of the corner of his eye he caught sight of the Rock mounting away into the sky. How many times had those sombre stones looked down on similar ceremonies, the outward and visible sign of an inner order, a disciplined way of life, and a decency which was in fact the backbone of British civilization. Fortin acknowledged the Captain of the Guard's salute and turned away. Their time would come: perhaps sooner than any of them thought. Followed by the Brigadier, he walked over to the short line of Very Important Gibraltar Personages. Three or four paces behind limped Dicky Seale.

'The Flag-Officer, Gibraltar, and Admiral-Superintendent of His Majesty's Dockyard, Rear-Admiral Barclay Calderwell.' It was a hell of a mouthful and the Brigadier managed to give it almost a ridiculous sound. Fortin's senses at once came alert. There's no love lost between these two, he thought, they hate each other's guts. He shook hands with the Admiral. A soft, sticky hand emanating from a large, hot, and flabby body which had evidently been poured with difficulty into its full-dress uniform. For some reason you never expected sailors to be obese. But perhaps that was what happened when you left the sea and took up a comfortable shore appointment, the last before you retired.

'I hope you had a good journey out,' the Admiral was saying. The tone was avuncular, almost condescending. 'I trust the Navy looked after you all right. I did ask the Admiralty to give you passage in one of H.M. Ships but I gather you preferred the greater comfort of the P. and O.'

'The important thing was to get here,' Fortin answered with the glint of a smile. Pomposity and vanity, he thought, entrenched in a tremendous self-esteem. But there must be qualities as well. You would have thought he had come out to

Gibraltar at the Admiral's behest. 'I did ask the Admiralty to give you passage. . . .' It was cheek of a schoolboy kind. The Admiral must feel very secure in his appointment, very sure of his powers. Well, we shall see, Fortin said to himself, we shall see.

'The Colonial Secretary,' the Brigadier was saying, 'Colonel Montague Bassett.'

Fortin found himself looking up into an autocratic, clean-cut face with a somewhat bushy moustache of the Rudyard Kipling type. A good, firm, businesslike handshake which suggested 'glad to make your acquaintance but don't waste too much of my time'. A certain amount of humour in the eyes, but Fortin had the impression that he might abruptly excuse himself, turn away and start doing something else. Bassett clearly had a picture of himself as a busy man, given to quick decisions but with a lot on his mind.

The last of the V.I.G.P.s was the Colonial Treasurer, a quiet rather meek-looking man in horn-rimmed glasses, of a smaller physique than Fortin himself, the sort of man often described as having a retiring disposition. Fortin made the appropriate conventional remarks and then returned to the other end of the line for the second round.

In affairs of state, precedence is a key factor. Locked up in precedence are countless struggles for power reaching back through the nation's history. Fortin was sensitive to its importance: indeed he had transposed this awareness to his great advantage in dealing with Arab sheikhs. He knew there was nothing accidental in the order in which things were done, people were introduced or ceremonies observed. He had a respect for ritual. The casual observer might see in this arrival at the Rock nothing but a mixture of official pomp and personal self-importance. Fortin knew otherwise. It was no accident that the Navy had precedence, was the Senior Service. It was no accident that the Governor was always a soldier on the Active List. It was no accident that prominent Gibraltarians would be waiting to meet him at Government House rather than here at the Ragged Staff steps. That was the order of things, their 'power-value' so to speak. Sometimes the balance of power would change; then, too, the order of precedence would reflect it.

The Admiral was introducing his Chief Staff-Officer (wrongly presented, as Fortin noted in passing, as 'My Chief of Staff'), his Secretary and Flag-Lieutenant. Here were the levels. Like looked across at and made its mark upon like. The Assistant Military Secretary in his own retinue would deal with the Admiral's Secretary, the A.D.C. with the Flag-Lieutenant.

'Lieutenant-Commander Millingham, our champion squash-player,' the Admiral had said as his Adonis of a Flag-Lieutenant shook hands—and then, as they turned away out of earshot, 'married a Rock Scorp.' No one except Fortin and Dicky Seale heard the tone of slight disdain in which this was said but upon both it made its separate impression. The Arab-trained intriguer in Fortin pricked up its ears, and in Lieutenant Richard Seale, R.M., there welled up the urgent desire to break out of his cast and kick the Admiral very, very hard upon his wide, fat arse.

5

Nicholas Pappadopoulos, Gibraltar's Heart Throb Number One, walked moodily down to the South Port Gate near the Trafalgar Cemetery, to take a look at the procession. He could have squeezed an invitation into any of the official stands or indeed into Government House itself had he wished. He did not so wish. If there had to be this ridiculous fuss, he preferred to be among Gibraltarians, among real people. In addition he had a quick way back to the office if he should need it in a hurry. But his reporter's instinct told him that nothing un-expected would happen today and already in his mind he was writing out with distaste a routine description of the new Governor's arrival and of his installation.

'After meeting principal officers of the Naval and Military Staffs, the Governor entered his car together with the Assistant Military Secretary and the A.D.C. and proceeded via the South Port Gate and Main Street to Government House. Large crowds were present to welcome the new Governor, including the wives of Naval, Military, Colonial and Dockyard officials and prominent citizens in a special enclosure, while the general public lined every point of vantage along the route.'

[16]

What was it all about? What made people turn out in their Sunday best to catch a glimpse of some stuffed shirt, emblem of rabid Imperialism, some gilded automaton who would only take away from the common people far more than he could ever give? Across the border in Spain, as Nicholas knew from first-hand experience, one of the most bitter civil wars in history had just come to an end. He had himself seen some of the atrocities, the women slit open from neck to crutch by Moorish bayonets, men choked to death with their own genitals, good loyal Republicans wrapped up alive in chains and thrown overboard to drown. He had seen a fair sample of man's bestial inhumanity to man. Well—the Fascists and the autocrats had come out on top. Here in Gibraltar there was another autocracy—more subtly dug in, but just as real. And here, on a calm, sunny day, the ruling hierarchy had decreed a ceremony to emphasize their vested interests.

No one should have gone. The whole downtrodden colony should have boycotted the event. Yet these dupes tumbled out of their slums and tenements merely to hear a band play and see a few uniforms strutting about. His mouth took on its habitual sour look. There was still a lot to be done before the workers came into their own.

'The route from Ragged Staff to Government House was kept by detachments of the Royal Navy, Royal Artillery, Royal Engineers and the 1st Battalion Welsh Guards, the detachments presenting arms as Major-General Sir Giles Fortin passed. Near Trafalgar Cemetery, Boy Scouts and Girl Guides were on parade.'

The whole thing sickened him. He'd throw his sub-editorship right back in the old man's face, he'd go back to France and the film business, he'd go anywhere provided it was outside this snobbish, smug, hated British Empire into which he had been born as a subject and in one part of which his father had so distinguished himself.

Yet, even as he formulated the idea, difficulties and objections rose in front of his eyes like a wall. Gibraltar had given him refuge—not that he was grateful. After all, he had a British passport and the right to enter the colony. He was a colonial himself. But they had taken him in and given him a

[17]

job. It was true that the sub-editorship of the Government-controlled *Gibraltar Gazette* did not rate very high in the salary scale. But it meant he could live. He did not have to write to Cyprus for money and get another of those hurt, un-understanding letters from his father. Fettered and confined as he was, he did have his own niche in the Rock and, to be honest, a freedom of a sort and a breathing-space to look around. Then, also, there was Myra. He turned back quickly to the job in hand.

'Outside Government House a Guard of Honour was mounted by the 2nd Battalion The Duke of Leicester's Light Infantry, which gave a Royal Salute as Sir Giles alighted from his car.'

Nicholas sniffed as he visualized the words in print. Personages never 'got out' of cars: they always 'alighted'. And why that huge gleaming Rolls-Royce? This was Gibraltar. A really democratic Governor would have chartered a gharry and trundled up to G.H. underneath the tassled canopy, seated upon the stuffed leather cushions, and to the clip-clop of horses' hooves. That was the style of Gibraltar, not a Rolls-Royce with the Royal Standard flying from a miniature flag-pole on the radiator. Huh!

'After inspecting the Guard of Honour, His Excellency entered Government House where His Honour the Chief Justice was presented. Members of the Executive Council, Heads of Naval, Military, Civil and Dockyard Departments were waiting in the hall, and a procession was formed to the Ball-room where deputations from representative bodies, Foreign Consuls, Justices of the Peace and Senior Officers of the Royal Navy, the Army, Colonial Service, H.M. Dockyard and prominent citizens had assembled.'

He knew it all. He knew it from Cyprus. There his father had been Chief Justice and was now a 'prominent citizen', a Knight of the British Empire, and thus blind to the simple fact, which so angered his son, that Cyprus was basically Greek and should be freed from bondage.

He knew in detail the machinery of Empire, the 'old boy frequency' by which a colony was governed. The window-dressing of wealthy natives—and how both Cypriots and

Gibraltarians hated that word—on the Executive Council, whose deliberations were unrecorded and secret; the solid front line of senior officers and officials and to one side in the shadows —but very intimately on the Governor's personal staff—the Defence Security Officer, the British Empire's equivalent of the Secret Police.

Perks and privileges for the ruling classes. Fifteen in a room for the poor-quality 'Scorps' whose Rock it was Nicholas Pappadopoulos burned with a sense of injustice as he thought about the scene now taking place in the ballroom of Government House. He could stand it no longer. Slipping out of the crowd, he made his way through the empty streets back to his room. Myra would be awake and wanting her coffee. There would be work to be planned. Work for the coming socialist revolution. There was also his piece to write up for the *Gazette*. He'd better get it in early today or the old man would be beefing again.

6

Inside the ballroom itself, with the throne on its raised dais at one end, its empty fireplace at the other, and dominated by huge portraits of Edward VII, Queen Alexandra and Queen Mary, the Royal Commission of Appointment was being read by the Clerk to the Executive Council. Despite the hot summer's day and the number of people in the room, the thick stone walls of the building that had once been a convent kept the temperature down. It might have been worse, Lance Millingham decided, as he ran a finger round his collar and tried by wriggling to stop the clip of his aiguilettes from cutting into his shoulder.

He edged over slightly to catch sight of himself in one of the mirrors in case his hair should have been disarranged or a smut have settled on his thin, elegant nose. He touched up a lock of his blond hair, but otherwise his appearance gave him its usual satisfaction. Looks were important. Whatever his other qualities and defects, no one could accuse him of not looking the part of a Flag-Lieutenant. Instinctively he glanced across at the A.D.C. No competition there. The creature looked thoroughly honest and dull. Fancy bringing a cripple to Gibraltar and a Royal Marine at that. Worthy, that was the word for him, Lance decided. Henceforth he would dub him conversationally as 'the worthy Seale'. That was it. Lieutenant R.M., the worthy Seale.

The Honourable Lancelot de Vere Millingham had learnt as a cadet that attack was generally the best form of defence. To hang a slightly disparaging label on a possible enemy had the double effect of establishing his own position and of discouraging casual remarks about his somewhat feminine good looks. If anyone was going to do the laughing, it had better be he and, aided by a certain ability to mimic, Lancelot was now adept at getting his blow in first.

Ever since he could remember, his almost alarming beauty had overshadowed every event in his life. At Dartmouth the mother of his then best friend had asked in passing who was the little cherub with the pink dimpled cheeks and the fair wavy hair. 'He's the boofullist little darling,' she had given it out and from then on his brother cadets had nicknamed him Boofles. People still called him Boofles to this day but usually behind his back. Indeed his sister-in-law, Rosita, was almost the only person who used that appellation to his face and as a matter of course. But then Rosita didn't care a damn for anyone, male or female. She had the personality and the looks to say exactly what she thought, even if it should be to the Governor himself. Why on earth does there have to be a sister? Lance said to himself for the thousandth time. Grace was a darling and a model wife but what a pair he and Rosita would have made. He fell into a daydream about her slender boyish figure, the small thrusting breasts, her almost lyrical legs. Now Grace had beautiful legs as well but she had a woman's seat and her bosom was full and rounded. Grace was already a woman and would soon be putting on weight in the Mediterranean way. Rosita was still a girl.

His Honour the Chief Justice was now administering the Oath of Allegiance and Office. The assembled company came to attention. Lance stood erect and firm, his left hand in its white kid glove drawing his sword in to his side, his cocked hat tucked under his left arm. As His Excellency assented to the

Oath, the battery at the King's Bastion fired another salute. The new Governor had been legally installed.

'The deed is done,' a voice whispered in his ear as they relaxed. 'O cursed spite that ever we were born to do it right.' Lance knew who it was without turning his head. Only Hobart, the Defence Security Officer, had this habit of adapting Shakespeare to his own purposes. Only Hobart, for that matter, could have slipped up behind him without attracting the slightest attention.

'We aren't through with it yet,' he answered. 'What about tennis this afternoon?'

'That's what I came to ask you. Can you manage three-thirty?'

'I think so. I'll have to ask the Admiral.'

'With or without?'

Lance thought about this for a moment. It would be social to take their wives: on the other hand Hobart and he were pretty evenly matched. Singles gave you a much better game.

'Just us, I think,' Lance decided. 'I'm not sure Grace isn't playing bridge.' He knew perfectly well she wasn't, but 'the girls' cluttered things up such a lot. A couple of men got on with the game so much better by themselves. 'Unless you think it's too rude . . .' he added, turning to look at Hobart. But the Defence Security Officer, Gibraltar's Own Herr Himmler, had already slipped away as unobtrusively as he had arrived. Now he was whispering to the A.D.C. and then suddenly he was in the limelight himself.

'The Keys to the Fortress of Gibraltar: His Majesty's Keys,' the Clerk to the Executive Council called out and, as if by magic, Hobart had produced the old Georgian keys, placed them on a purple cushion and handed them to the Deputy Fortress Commander, who in turn bore them to the Governor, who in turn gave them back to the Defence Security Officer. That ceremony done, the eminent Gibraltarians who were members of the Executive Council came forward for presentation to His Excellency, among them being Jaime Barbarossa, Lance's father-in-law.

7

The traditional offering of addresses of welcome meant that the end of the ceremony was near. Hobart watched with interest. These were the leaders of the civil community. These were the people taken all too often for granted by the Services, the key traders and professional men whose loyalty was paramount. Upon their co-operation and skill depended the successful working of Gibraltar as a commercial port. And upon their resources both Army and Navy depended, if not for essentials, then at any rate for most of the frills.

Perhaps of all people in the room Hobart enjoyed his life more keenly than anyone else. There were a number of reasons for this. He was virtually his own master. He was responsible to the Governor as Defence Security Officer for certain parts of his duty, but in the main it was with his headquarters in London with whom he dealt. He could come and go as he pleased. He had links in Tangier, Algeciras and Madrid. Thus, if at any time he wanted a trip away from the Rock, he had a legitimate excuse for taking it. This was open to abuse. No doubt other security officers in other parts of the world did take advantage of the job. To Hobart it was no temptation at all. This was because he derived the meaning in his life from two main sources—his wife and the study of people. The one he loved steadily and deeply and with astonishing pleasure: to the other he gave a passionate interest which rewarded him both as a man and as a security officer.

People, in fact, were the essence of his job. Hobart knew a good deal about human nature and a great deal more about the people at that moment in Government House. He never kidded himself he knew it all. One or two people, though, in their gold lace and well-starched uniform would have shivered with embarrassment had they realized that their secrets, their weaknesses, and some of the things they thought they'd got away with were most of them known to Major Atcheson Hobart as he sat smoking his pipe in the little office in Bomb House Lane.

Hobart had intense curiosity about people. There was nothing prurient in this. It was, in fact, much more the clinical attention of a doctor, which at one time he had wanted to be, than the routine inquiries of a police officer or the surface sensationalism of a well-trained reporter. Yet both those functions were bound up in his own. He liked people. He had a certain insight and he liked knowing what made them tick. He took pains to keep this well-disguised. People who knew they were under observation withdrew like snails under their shells. So Hobart used the gift he had been given, he put people at their ease, very rarely did he ask direct questions and then always as if it had no importance at all but was only said in passing. He was known as a light-hearted, almost frivolous person, who did very little work, attended innumerable parties and made the usual mocking fuss of his hangovers, had a cushy job and was mainly after a good time for himself.

They liked his American wife. She was alive and amusing in a sardonic way. She entertained with a flair and had two tough little boys of seven and five. Those who knew the Hobarts well relished the not infrequent panic that gripped the household when it was thought possible that a third little boy might be on the way. Atcheson would have liked it but Cornelia had declared herself dead-set against the whole goddam project and up to now the panic had been taken care of by the delayed and mysterious processes of time.

They were nice people, in the opinion of Gibraltar, and as a measure of Hobart's popularity, his delight in misquoting Shakespeare and the generally held absurdity of the whole idea of security, he had been nicknamed Himmlet, as the best combination of Himmler and Hamlet that could be devised. It was also a measure of the unreality of the British understanding of world affairs at that time that people would sometimes ask Hobart in joke where his thumbscrews were kept, whereas a few miles across the border in Spain these and other instruments of torture were in current use as they had been for centuries. Moreover, in the country of Franco's best friend, the concentration camp ovens were already in full blast. In the ordered decency of a British colony there was a touch of disbelief in such news. It seemed so remote from their everyday lives even if a European war did lie somewhere ahead. Hobart, however, was only too clearly aware of the dark forces and their secret representatives in the colony which, given a favourable opening, could overnight alter the scene.

He watched Jaime Barbarossa shaking hands with the Governor. There was a file on him in the office. Barbarossa was of Genoese extraction. He was the Gibraltar agent for one German and two Italian shipping lines. He had a brother who had gone with Franco to Madrid. His sister had married a Maltese Count. He himself had been educated at Downside and Oxford. A man in his middle fifties who had inherited a fortune from his father (the Merchant of Genoa, as Hobart called him) and had by this time trebled it. A man with an ambitious wife and two daughters, one of whom she had married off to the young Mr. Millingham, the other of whom kept an intermittent and well-disguised tryst with that young Cypriot, Pappadopoulos, on whom there was a considerably larger file and who in turn was sheltering a French Jewess who had fought at the barricades in Malaga and who carried a Communist Party card issued in Paris.

Yet all these people in different ways he respected and liked. It was one of Hobart's qualities that he almost never took sides. In one sense, of course, he was completely committed, but just as a good policeman has a large slice of the criminal in him, that sympathetic factor which alone gives entrance to the criminal's mind, so Hobart felt and understood the necessity for Jaime Barbarossa's diplomatic procedures, which the management of an internationally placed fortune required. He also understood the sense of injustice and idealism which burned in Pappadopoulos and the racial back-against-the-wall hatred which powered his girl friend and gave her piano playing in the Criterion Bar, where she had a temporary job, such fire and fury.

By this time the Chairman of the City Council, the Roman Catholic Bishop, the President of the Exchange Committee, the Vice-President of the Chamber of Commerce, the President of the Jewish Community and the District Organizer of the Transport and General Workers' Union had all and severally presented their Addresses of Welcome.

Hobart watched His Excellency for signs of wear and tear but found it almost impossible to gauge what he was thinking or feeling. No wonder the Arabs had given him their respect. He had the desert gift of inscrutability, yet at the same time made those he talked to feel that for the moment they were the centre of the world. There was a new power in the colony and that power was where it should be—on the throne as direct legate of His Majesty the King. There were going to be some healthy changes on the Rock. Hobart wondered how formal the Governor's answering address would be as the taut little figure with the bushy eyebrows and the ice-blue eyes stepped forward on the dais, pausing for a moment for complete quiet to come.

'Members of the City Council, my Lord Bishop, Gentlemen. I wish to thank you for the warm welcome you have given me in Gibraltar. Conventional addresses are one thing, spontaneous demonstrations by people in the streets, people whose leaders you are, and whose elected representatives you may one day be, are another. I am grateful for both of them.'

Crikey, thought Hobart, he's ringed a weak spot on the map the first time he's opened his mouth. 'Elected representatives' was not a very safe phrase in Gibraltar at that time where government was entirely autocratic.

'I am very conscious of the high honour His Majesty has done me in appointing me Governor of this historic City and Garrison. I intend, under God's guidance, to look after your interests to the best of my ability and at the same time keep the Rock in the state of armed readiness which the world situation demands. We are all of us speculating on whether a war will break out or not.' He paused for a moment and looked at the array of faces below him, then he continued: 'I think it will. . . .' There was an involuntary gasp from his audience and Hobart turned away to grin. This was something more than the formal drooling expected of a Governor. This was a fearless and highly controversial opinion which, coming from the throne, would be frowned on in London. Etiquette was being cracked right, left and centre, but there was a new feeling of life and energy in the air. Keep it up, old boy, he said to himself, there's going to be a lot of head-shaking over this and possibly a little waking-up as well.

'I know perfectly well,' the Governor continued, 'that this

[25]

is a formal occasion in which expressions of opinion have little place. I am sorry if I offend any of you by speaking in this way. However, it occurs to me that I may not see you all together like this for some little time. Gentlemen, in a very real sense, at this moment in time—we are Gibraltar. We have a number of tasks, vital to ourselves and vital to the British Empire. The first of these is to defend the Rock against any possible attack, the second is to provide the Royal Navy with the base it needs to maintain the freedom of the seas, the third is to look after ourselves. I would ask you to remember these aims as you go about your daily lives in the next few anxious months. Remember, too, that I am here both to lead you and to be at your service. In practical terms this means that I intend to be accessible to you—any or all of you from whatever station in life you may come—whenever you feel I can be of help. I hope you will accept this informal offer I make you now. In turn I shall count on your loyal support during my period of office. Thank you, gentlemen, let us now take off our full-dress armour and buckle down to the job in hand.'

There was a moment's complete silence, followed by a rather hesitant round of applause. His Excellency smiled and then, followed by Dicky Seale, strode quickly from the room. Hobart edged round to where he could see the Italian Consul's face. A bonfire had been lit all right this morning.

II

'OF course it's straight warmongering,' Nicholas Pappadopoulos said as he climbed into bed beside Myra Heisenberg, 'blatant, tactless, naïve. I had it out with the old man this evening.'

'Is he sending your cable?'

'He tore it up. Some editor isn't he? He maintains that what His Sainted Excellency says to oligarchs in Government House is a purely local and private affair. Fantastic, isn't it? Talk about freedom of the Press!'

'*Chéri*, this is a British colony. What do you expect?'

Myra was tired and worried. She was not in the mood for dialectic that night. She had just had eight hours hammering the piano at the Criterion Bar. She wanted to sleep. Besides, she'd just heard, privately, about the Barbarossa girl. It was time she moved on. Her work permit would soon have expired. She ought to get to Paris. Gibraltar was a dead-end so far as the Party was concerned. They'd never get anywhere as things were at present. She'd told them. Now that Spain had finally collapsed there was nothing useful she could do as an alien refugee in a Crown Colony. Why hadn't they sent her to Haifa as she'd repeatedly asked? There, at least, was work to be done. Gibraltar was not for her and they knew it.

'However, I got off a private cable to Duttle. The *Comrade* can use that sort of gaffe. If Fearless Freddy doesn't watch his step he'll be frigging his way back to the Desert. You'll see.'

'Bravo! Bis! bis!'

Myra lay on her back, her eyes closed. If only he'd cut out the yammer so she could get on to sleep. The schmo! No, that wasn't right. He'd been good to her. She was grateful in a way. She twined an arm round his neck and drew him towards her. To hell with Miss Barbarossa, she thought. Who does she think she is?

'Let's get through with the talk, darling, I'm tired.'

'Me, too.'

By a coincidence their hours were roughly the same. She came on at six in the evening and played through till two in the morning in one of those all-women bands for which Gibraltar was famous. He began his sub-editing at seven and if he was lucky put the paper to bed at about two-thirty. Very often when they finished working they were both wide awake. Then they'd drink a bottle of wine or cook up some food and stay talking till four and five in the morning. Those were the good nights. The nights when two eager bodies could do something to comfort each other for the disillusion and failure of those last three years in Spain, when the benison of sex released them for a little while from the oppressiveness, frustration and danger of the lives they had separately chosen to lead. Tonight, though, they were both of them tired, tonight he was making love in a mechanical, almost absent way.

'Tell me about Miss Barbarossa,' she murmured.

Instantly she felt him stiffen and pause.

'What do you mean?'

'You know what I mean,' she said lightly, 'the teen-ager with the money, the one who calls you Heart Throb Number One to her Yacht-Club friends—that is, when there's no one over twenty around.'

She felt him relax. So it *was* more serious than she thought. Mentally she shrugged her shoulders.

'You know how it is,' he said, 'she feels strangled to death in that tiled Barbarossa mansion. She's got romantic ideas about anyone who isn't an out-and-out Tory. Kid stuff. You know how it is.'

'Yes, darling, I know how it is.'

2

Elsewhere in Gibraltar other people were lying awake. In the Barbarossa mansion, though unknown to each other, sleep had deserted the entire household. It was a hot summer night. The Barbarossas' Gibraltar residence, built round a patio and turned in on itself in the Spanish style, despite its baby palm-trees and its fountain, was nevertheless in the heart of the city down by the Line Wall Road near the King's Bastion and thus subject to the heat and oppressiveness of a closely packed garrison town.

Jaime Barbarossa and his wife, in their separate rooms, both lay awake. Edie, who had a headache and an intermittent pain round her heart which she took to be indigestion, had turned on the light and was half-reading *Gone with the Wind* while her thoughts played round arrangements for the week-end.

Jaime who had been talking freight rates with a visiting Greek most of the evening found himself generally worried and disturbed. If the new Governor was right about a war, and Jaime felt certain he was, then his shipping interests were in for a thin time and especially those that began and ended at Genoa. If Hitler's greed continued Jaime could not see Mussolini sitting around waiting for German scraps. There would not be another Munich. Austria had gone in '38 and now Czecho-Slovakia this spring. Each time Hitler had achieved exactly what he wanted, had acquired exactly what he planned. It was unthinkable he should stop at this.

Once war broke out he could count on Spanish co-operation. Dictators talked the same language. There was probably an agreement already in existence. German infiltration in Spanish Morocco was high; there were German officers, German technicians all over southern Spain. Control of the Straits of Gibraltar was a prize the Fuehrer might easily claim in return for his aid in getting Franco to Madrid.

Just as the English had originally captured the Rock in the name of a foreign king, so now the Germans might well recapture it in the name of Spain. And Barbarossa had no doubt that the Rock would fall. The siege-cannons in General Eliott's day were one thing, the new Krupp guns at this moment being mounted in the hills behind Algeciras another. A day's bombardment and the dockyard would be useless. What then? And what about the civilian population? What about his estate at San Roque, across the border in Spain? Sometimes he thought his roots were really far more in that house than they were in Gibraltar.

His thoughts in their network of anxiety flitted here and there in the half-asleep, half-awake state he was in. Well, at least they had a man as Governor. A tough little businesslike man. Someone at home must be fully alive to the value of things for a man of Fortin's calibre to be sent to the Rock. At least Chamberlain wasn't going to give it away. Or was he? . . . was there another Munich in the offing?

On the other side of the patio Grace lay on her side, gazing moodily at the moon on the palm-tree outside their window. She was not sure if Lance was awake, nor did she care. . . . She had her back to him. They might just as well be sleeping in separate beds for all the interest he took in her. She sighed. Something had gone wrong and she did not know what it was. Lately he had displayed such pointed disinterest, she was beginning to wonder if all along the feelings he had shown her before were manufactured and false. Had her mother really tricked him into marriage? Or had he been genuinely fond of her and had it now gone cold? No, fondness was not the word for Lance. He had never been either tender or fond. Originally she had attracted him. But it was never as a lover. What was it then? As a mother? She shivered at the thought because instinct told her this was the likeliest thing. Even in the early days he would snuggle his head down on her breast and then go to sleep. It made her feel old. She wanted a lover and a husband, not a little boy who needed protection and comfort.

The first night had been disastrous for both of them. She had been a virgin and she was beginning to think he must have been too. Now they had been married eighteen months and matters were worse. He had no idea of arousing passion in a woman and apparently no desire to learn. His climax came almost at once. He would kiss her abruptly, half-ashamed, half-wanting to be liked. Then he would push himself away and go off to sleep. He left her semi-awake, unsatisfied, yearning, and he seemed utterly unaware of her basic needs as a woman. He thought only of himself and his wonderful looks.

A faint breeze stirred the palm leaves and a cloud obscured the moon. She drew the thin sheet over her shoulders and sighed. What could she do? The dislike she had felt for her mother since childhood now snarled itself up almost to the level of hatred. It was Mother's fault that she now lay sour and dry beside this husk of a man. It was Mother's ambition, Mother's energy and Mother's self-importance which always spilled over into other people's lives, corroding them drop by drop and day by day to her own remorseless will.

She suspected Lance's mother as well. The late Lady Pulborough would not have agreed to this marriage. Lance had been the only son and his mother had died during his first term at Dartmouth. Lance kept a photograph of her in his wallet. A large, erect woman with a leonine face. Not the sort of person who would have looked with favour on Lord Pulborough's heir marrying a Gibraltarian girl. And indeed her caste ideas lived on in Lance.

Well—the mothers had had their way, leaving the children to pick up the pieces. Her own mother had got her elder daughter safely married and, in the Catholic faith, that was final. As for Lance, the seeds of Lady Pulborough's snobbism had begun to sprout and take root. Over the last few months Grace had come to know that Lance was secretly ashamed of her and embarrassed by the 'Gibraltarianness' of her family. He tried to disguise it but she knew he felt awkward living in the Barbarossa household. In an unguarded moment he had even said that he wished the Admiral could have given them room at the Mount.

When the Fleet was in he was never at home, but playing squash or tennis with 'old ships' of his and afterwards going on board to dine. Very often he came back tiddly and Lance had almost as puritanical ideas on drink as he had on sex. He looked on indulgence in either as almost a capital loss, resulting in bleary eyes and a poor showing on the squash-court. She knew that when Lance allowed himself to drink too much— and there was never any problem about that aboard H.M. Ships—it meant there was something much more deeply wrong with him inside.

Another big sigh forced its way out and a tear trickled down her cheek slowly and saltily on to the pillow. At the other side of the bed Lance stirred uneasily.

'What's all the sighing about?'

She turned over and wriggled across, putting her head on his shoulder. She could feel him stiffening up. However he brought himself to pat her shoulder and say gently:

'What's the matter? Aren't you feeling well?'

She shook her head silently, unable to stop the tears.

'What is it, Grace? Is it something I've done?'

She clung to him desperately, pretending to herself that she didn't notice him shrinking away. Please God, please let me give him what he wants, what he needs, she prayed. She rested her cheek in the hollow of his shoulder above his tight, rigid chest.

'Why can't you sleep? Have you got a headache? Shall I get you an aspirin?'

To all three she shook her head vehemently, bringing her tears under control. Then she managed to say it shakily and hesitantly.

'Lance, why don't you love me any more? What have I done?'

'But I do love you, Grace. What an absurd idea to get into your head!'

'Do you, Lance, do you?'

'Well, of course I do. What a ninny you are! Just because we can't make love every night, doesn't mean I don't adore you in other ways.'

'Then kiss me, Lance.'

With a sinking heart, she noted the fractional pause while he tried to find a way out and then the effort with which he pressed his hard lips against her soft, yielding mouth, his unwilling body against her voluptuous, eager, burning breasts. It was no good. There was no meaning in anything they did. Reluctantly he began to go through the same old weary routine. She could stand it no more. Tearing herself away she buried her face in her own pillow on her own side of the bed.

'I can't bear it. I can't stand it any more,' she said with a moan, letting the emotion have its way. On the other side of the bed Lance remained stiff, hurt and resentful.

'There we go again! Sooner or later it always ends in hysterics. What do you want me to do, Grace? I just don't know what's got into you these days. It's getting worse and worse. And God knows what sort of shape I'll be in tomorrow. I don't often think of myself but you know quite well it's a heavy day. The destroyers are playing *Cormorant* at tennis and the

Admiral's got this huge cocktail party in the evening. I must say I can do without this sort of scene in the middle of the night. Do let's try and be adult about it. I'm doing the best that I can.'

But Grace said nothing. She lay on her stomach, her face deep in the pillow, her hands clutching and unclutching the sheets. Lance was quite right. There was nothing he could do. They were deep in an impasse, deep, deep, deep. Perhaps, as the Governor had said, there would be a war. A war. A war . . . gradually her breathing became more regular, the tears dried up and she fell asleep.

In the room next door Rosita had heard the quick rise and fall of their voices. That meant another row, another breakfast table with Lance's wooden face and Grace having a tray sent up to her room. If that was marriage then the longer she stayed clear of it the better. Mother was not going to foist *her* off on any effete Flag-Lieutenant or A.D.C. Though she had to admit that the new A.D.C. looked dreamy enough with his curly black hair and his limp. More of a man than Boofles whose masculinity, she supposed, was once more being put to the test next door. Boofles! One glance of encouragement and he'd be snatching a kiss every time Grace's back was turned, a nice messy state of affairs, the danger of which mercifully no one except herself was aware. Well, she could cope very easily with that. It was no hardship to her to smack a pretty young man like Boofles back into place. Rosita was the only one of her set quite unscared of Boofles' tongue and superior attitude. Indeed she had once gone so far as to mimic him in front of the Admiral himself. After that he had treated her with more respect.

But why was she wasting time even thinking of Boofles, when the touch of Nicky's lips was still radiant on her own? Now *there* was a man! She relived the tiny scene, all of her own devising, which had alone given meaning to the day. She, her girl friend Antonia, and two boy friends had been to the Theatre Royal to see a Carole Lombard film. The boy friends were Gibraltarians from a similar stratum to her own and were thus trusted to take the girls out without a chaperone. They had all met at the cinema. Rosita carried a couple of books

[33]

borrowed from the Garrison Library which was only about a hundred yards further down Governor's Parade. Next door to the library was the Garrison Printing Establishment and the *Gibraltar Gazette* office where Nicky would be working. She had waited until they were seated and the film had been on five minutes before whispering to her boy friend:

'Damn! I've forgotten these books of Mummy's. She'll be furious. I must get them in to the library before they close.'

'Can't they wait?'

'No.'

'Then I'll take them for you,' came the reluctant offer. But Rosita was already out of her seat.

'I know the girl who checks in the books,' she whispered. 'I may just catch her.'

She was gone before there was a chance of any further reply. Her heart was racing. The Garrison Library was shut as she had known it would be. She went directly into the *Gazette* office through the clatter of the tape-machine and the type-writers. Nicky had been staring at a piece of copy as though it was something infected. He was surprised and secretly pleased to see Rosita threading her way through the office to his desk. She waved the library books at him in their distinctive blue jackets so that other curious eyes in the office would know and not be suspicious of the reason for her visit. It had happened before. He got up and went with her on to the terrace between the dark Garrison Library and the *Gazette* office.

'I know it's after hours,' she said as casually as she could manage, 'but you once said there was a window you could open at the side.'

'You're quite a girl, aren't you?' he remarked, leading the way through a wooden gate to a deserted passage alongside the library. Then when they were alone and unobserved he took her in his arms and kissed her long and passionately on the lips. She let the books fall to the ground as she pressed her body in its thin summer dress hard against his. She could scarcely breathe, the feeling was so violent and rich.

'Oh! Nicky, Nicky,' she murmured, 'I love you.'

He said nothing but kissed her again, fondling the nipples of

[34]

her firm young breasts, stroking her back, drawing her closer, it seemed, all the time.

'When can I see you again?' she whispered. 'It's so hellishly difficult.'

He shrugged his shoulders.

'I have no keys to your world,' he said, 'your parents don't approve of my ideas at all.'

'I think I could get you a card for the Yacht Club. I know the secretary would stretch a point for me.'

'What good would that do?'

'At least we could meet without all this intrigue.'

He shrugged his shoulders again.

'Well, all right,' he said grudgingly. 'The Royal Gibraltar Yacht Club is hardly my line of country but, as you say, we could meet.'

Already his brain was alive in other directions. A card to the Yacht Club would certainly do no harm. It would strengthen his position and open up a new range of contacts and possibilities. And it was almost being forced down his throat. He kissed her again, her body quivering in his arms. Then he smacked her lightly on the bottom, picked up the books, and wiped the lipstick off his mouth with a handkerchief.

'Time you were getting back,' he said, 'and I've work to do too.'

She threw her arms round his neck and hugged him tight. Then taking the books and tossing her head, she walked straight back to the cinema, slipping into her seat as though nothing had happened.

'I was too late,' she said, 'she'd already gone. What have I missed in the film?'

3

The new Governor of Gibraltar lay awake on his camp-bed for another reason. He was halfway through one of his recurring attacks of malaria. Mercifully this was a mild one. With the quinine and the brandy and the firm control of himself which experience had brought, he could nowadays very nearly watch himself, detached, undergoing the process. By this time his temperature would be about 102—not even worth taking. The sheets and the mattress were soaked. Soon it would be dawn, the peak of it passed, the fever abating.

Some writer he had once read had called death an old friend. At times Fortin felt the same about malaria. They said it was with you for life, that after each outburst it returned to live in your marrow in a dormant state to be set in motion again by a change in temperature or some other such shock. It had certainly been with him for the last thirty years. Indeed Fortin tended to think that malaria was probably the main reason he'd been given Gibraltar. It was more temperate than the Persian Gulf and just far enough from Whitehall for comfort.

As he lay restlessly tossing and turning, he thought more about his appointment. Why had they sent him here? In peacetime Gibraltar was a social station. One of the biggest assets a Governor could bring to the appointment was a clever and capable wife. Fortin had never had and probably never would have a wife. In wartime—well, it was anyone's guess what would happen to the Rock. Air power had radically altered present-day warfare just as the submarine and the tank had done in the Great War for sea and land fighting.

Could Gibraltar be held if Spain joined the Axis powers in a total war? And if it were, if another great siege lay ahead comparable to the four brilliant years General Eliott had held the Rock a century and a half ago, what, if anything, was its value? Prestige? You couldn't dry-dock a warship on the prestige of the Union Jack fluttering over a lump of limestone. You had to have a complicated, articulated dockyard with power and a reliable labour force, sheltered from attack, not exposed to the full barrage of carefully hidden guns in the Algeciras hills a mere six miles away.

Deep in his fever it occurred to Fortin that those whose job was the strategy of the British Empire in another war had quite possibly already abandoned Gibraltar in their many alternative plans. If so, any siege became a useless piece of heroics. Perhaps that was all they thought he was worth. He had always sailed against the wind, always and instinctively chosen the difficult in preference to the obvious and the easy. In a deep and entirely personal humility he had felt all his life that God

[36]

was saving him for something, something hard and difficult which only he could do. This sense of destiny had removed from him any fear of death. Death in fact was something he looked forward to with pleasure and relief.

But first of all came the fulfilling of his duty, the working out of God's plan, never revealed in its entirety but sensed and obeyed in a different way at a different time, yet always with this overwhelming intimation of Fate. Your life was predetermined—inevitable—necessary for your spiritual growth. You attracted it to your being. It was small wonder that Fortin's hero had long been Gordon of Khartoum. It had even been said at one time that there was a physical resemblance, though no one would have called Chinese Gordon 'craggy'.

There was a knock at the door and Seale came in, nervously fiddling with the tassel of his dressing-gown.

'What is it?' Fortin asked angrily. He preferred to battle with his malaria alone.

'I wondered if you were all right, sir, if there's anything I can get you.'

'Nothing. I'm better alone.'

'Wouldn't you be more comfortable in the proper bed, sir?' It had seemed extraordinary to Seale that Fortin's first action on seeing his bedroom was to order the removal of the large gubernatorial bedstead and the erection near the window of his green canvas camp-bed with the sleeping-bag on top. Now Fortin was looking at him with those feverish, piercing eyes.

'I'm all right, Dicky, or I will be by breakfast. Go and get some sleep.'

'Well, sir. . . .'

'Do as I say. You'll have to get used to this sort of thing. It happens a lot.'

'Very well, sir. I'm there if there's anything you want.'

He closed the door and limped back to his own room, glaring down on the dark trees in the patio as he went. Poor old sod, he thought to himself, a go of malaria his very first night in Gibraltar. He climbed back into his bed. His spine and his legs ached and no doubt he'd have been better off on a hard bed himself. However, it would take more than a broken back and a malarial commander-in-chief to make Dicky

[37]

Seale give up a feather pillow and an interior-sprung mattress when a grateful Government had decreed that such was to be the sleeping equipment for an A.D.C. Fancy me, he murmured to himself as sleep overtook him, fancy me an A.D.C.!

4

Down in the destroyer pens on the North Mole of the harbour, H.M.S. *Firesprite* lay alongside what in the old days would have been called her 'chummy ship', H.M.S. *Forthright*, who in turn lay alongside the jetty. It was dawn. The water lapped gently against her freshly-painted hull. The sea-gulls were not yet awake. In a few moments 'reveille' would be sounded off and the ship's company would tousle out of their hammocks for their first day in harbour since leaving England. In a few moments feet would begin to ring out on metal decks, galley fires would be cooking breakfast, hammocks lashed up and stowed, hands fallen in and decks hosed down. Another naval day in a small new unit of His Majesty's Fleet would be ticking over in accordance with the King's Regulations and Admiralty Instructions.

For the moment, though, that unworldly twilight-in-reverse with its freshness, its coolth and its quietness held the west side of Gibraltar, which is where the town and the dockyard lie, in a kind of breathless expectancy—a daily expectancy which daily seemed to burn itself out in the glaring Mediterranean sun.

From his bunk David Evers scowled almost malevolently up at the Rock, the whole of its west side in deep shadow, the outline of its bulk haloed by the invisible sun. He had not slept well and this was extremely tedious. He had been exhausted, in fact his body had been aching for sleep after this first short passage he had made from England in command of his own ship. But he could not relax. This was an ability he knew he must acquire. Lesson one, in fact, in learning how to live with the responsibility for one of H.M. Ships and its complement of a hundred and eighty men always astride his shoulders. All captains must learn it—that is if they intend to stay in command. But for the present there was too much to worry about both in his public and his private lives, too much yet to be done that was cardinal to both, too much, to be honest, that he had yet to learn. Hence the troubled, uneasy night when it would have been natural and proper for him to have gone out like a light.

This was Saturday. The flotilla would begin their working-up practices in earnest on Monday. This afternoon he would play tennis, in the evening there was the Admiral's cocktail party at the Mount, perhaps afterwards he would beat it up at the Rock or the Bristol with some of the flotilla boys or other naval friends. On Sunday there had been talk of a picnic into Spain. The Civil War seemed very newly finished for that sort of thing—to loll about eating sandwiches where men had just been killing each other was odd, but he supposed he was thinking sentimentally. Or he might go sailing or he might bathe or he might get the loan of a horse—or even simply take a walk up the Rock and see how the apes were getting on. There was plenty of distraction to be had. He must write home to Pam. There were Saturday Rounds this morning. There would be Divisions on Sunday when Captain (D) had signified an intention of walking round his flotilla—otherwise the duty to be complied with was slight.

Yet now he was in command, the 'specific gravity' of his life had changed. He thought about his First Lieutenant and the casual, light-hearted way he could slip into his 'dog-robbers' and proceed on a 'run ashore'. David had been like that so short a time ago. Now he was playing another role. Now he was in command. As Commanding Officer of one of H.M. Ships he was technically freer, under fewer restrictions. Within limits the ship was there to serve his will. Within reason he could go ashore when he liked and return when he liked. As against that, however, his newness in command brought its own severe and unwritten discipline. Ashore or afloat he was still the Captain of one of H.M. Ships. Responsibility never left him, even when his body was asleep.

He gazed over at the City of Gibraltar, imagining the narrow, precipitous streets beginning to stir once more in the growing light, the eighteenth-century garrison houses in a kind of compressed confusion appearing to lean over towards one another

[39]

as children and grown-ups, dogs and chickens, all individually came to life, merging their distinctive noises, like separate instruments in an orchestra, into the general blur of Mediterranean noise.

There in the Old Convent with the arched porch and the view from Main Street through its entrance hall on to the cool patio, with its sentry outside stamping his beat to keep warm in the morning chill, there in some room successively occupied by the score or so of previous Governors, Uncle Giles would doubtless be asleep, his leathery face like an old boot on a cushion. He, too, would be fledging his wings on a new level of responsibility and suddenly it seemed to David as he lay in his bunk that it was seemly and appropriate for both of them to be there in Gibraltar at the start of what was to each a new step in their lives.

Siege was the essence of the Rock. You built things on rock to stand firm, whether a lighthouse, a church or a skyscraper. You burrowed into rock for safety against storm or foe. The Rock of Gibraltar symbolized something basic in the British character—an ability to endure in adversity, an ability to hang on till the storm was over.

This was exactly what happened to a man who changed his status as both David and his uncle had recently done. They were new people on a new level and the powers that wanted to drag them down, the giants of envy, jealousy and fear whose interest it was to make them fail, to make them give up in despair, would soon be assaulting their self-confidence with all the fury of worldly power. The siege in themselves would be on.

David's mother, who was General Fortin's sister, had had little of that urge to religion in her which so powered her brother but she had brought up her children to realize that life was a battleground, a place of continual strife where Good and Evil fought it out for the possession of man's soul. David did not know his uncle very well. But there was a link between them stronger than blood. They understood, in differing degrees, what life was about.

As the first strident notes of 'reveille' sounded out across the harbour, the Commanding Officer of H.M.S. *Firesprite* fell

into an uneasy slumber for the remaining hour of his night's
rest.

5

The first people to awake in the Hobart household were
Jonathan, seven, and Michael, five. They were under strict
orders not to disturb their parents before seven o'clock, but in
the summertime in Gibraltar, especially when you had a house
overlooking Rosia Bay, the little harbour where the *Victory*
had lain after Trafalgar, especially when there was a liner or a
warship entering or leaving the bay, especially when your beds
were on either side of a window through which there was so
much to be seen, it seemed to be a rotten swiz if you accidentally slept on after six. So there was usually an hour in which to
observe their part of Gibraltar coming to life, to listen to the
soldiers in the barracks near Scud Hill clattering about to the
sound of bugles, to watch Mrs. Gomez in the cottage below
cuffing her two little boys, letting out the chickens and beating
an old bit of carpet which Mummy said was surely swarming
with fleas. Then, when the cracked bell of a near-by church
banged out seven, Jonathan and his brother would both race
each other to their parents' room, tear open and slam doors,
jump into the big double-bed with Daddy on the right-hand
side and Mummy on the left, both pretending to be asleep,
both groaning at the noise and interruption from their two
vociferous sons, both to be breathlessly informed of the day's
events so far, both to be provoked to the limit of grown-up
endurance.

'Goddammitall,' their father would finally shout in his
bad imitation of their mother's New England accent, 'they
get to be more like the Dead-End Kids every day. What do
we have here? A couple of tough American gangsters?'

And their mother would retort in her imitation of an Oxford
accent.

'Saow sorry, aold boy, ai forgot it's such jolly, jolly bad form
to be alive. Children, children *desist*, I pray you.'

Then both children would scream with delight because
Mummy and Daddy would begin their age-old row about

[41]

which was better, American or British, in which both expressed surprise at having married the other and at having been given such odious children, or Daddy would insist on being called Father and would pretend to be a peppery English colonel, someone they called Colonel Blimp, and Mummy would do her Independent American Person, who wasn't going to be sat upon by any stiff-necked British Imperialist. Then Carmen would arrive with tea for Daddy and orange juice for Mummy and the children would snuggle down in the bed and pretend not to be there.

But Carmen, whose day had started an hour and a half earlier in a tiny mud-brick cottage, painted white, in La Línea de la Concepción, and who had come across the frontier in a rickety bus with her basket of eggs and tomatoes, and who would return in the evening with cigarettes or some metres of cloth hidden about her person, Carmen would indicate that Nanny was in the nursery and must not be kept waiting any longer and then Cornelia would say in her strong, rather rasping voice and the elementary Spanish which always made Hobart laugh:

'*Toma los niños*, Carmen, *y diga* Nanny to drown them both *en el baño. Pronto.*'

Then Carmen, whose uncle Pepe *had* been drowned in the Civil War trying to swim to Gibraltar across Algeciras Bay to escape from Franco's *Falangistas*, would grin and chirrup some unintelligible Andalusian Spanish at the lumps in the bed and then with encouragement from *el señor y la señora* would yank them out expertly and drag them protesting like pigs about to be slaughtered out of the room and into another day.

This Saturday morning in June 1939, the day after the new Governor had arrived, a mere three months before the Second World War, Atcheson Hobart put his arm round his wife's shoulders as soon as Carmen and the children had gone. Cornelia finished her orange juice, put down the glass and snuggled comfortably against her husband's rather hairy chest. This was one of the moments in the day which she most enjoyed. The Himmlet kissed her on the top of her corn-coloured hair.

'Tell me, Cornelia Hobart, tell me honestly and truly,' he

[42]

said, 'do you at this moment regret saying "yes" at a certain time eight years ago on a certain Bermuda beach to a certain question asked by a certain good-looking officer in a certain branch of the British Government Service?'

'Good looking?' said Cornelia scornfully. 'You should live so long . . .' but as she said it she hugged him with an affection which could only have been matured by eight years of a deepening love. She could never understand how all the time it seemed to get better. It went plain contrary to all she had ever expected, and indeed to the actual experience of most of her contemporaries from Newport, Rhode Island.

'I wonder how long they'll let us enjoy it,' said Hobart, his mind already beginning to involve itself with the coming day. As once more he kissed his wife's freesia-scented hair and then got out of bed, he remembered with distaste that at that moment he was the only person in Gibraltar aware that Hitler and Mussolini had arranged another meeting to which they had decided to bid the Caudillo of Spain.

6

Thus Gibraltar awoke and another week-end began. The warships in the harbour began to scrub decks and polish brightwork in preparation for Saturday Rounds. Over ten thousand properly documented Spanish workers crossed from La Línea and Algeciras for labour in the dockyard. Horses were being groomed for the afternoon's racing near Victoria Park, underneath the towering North Front. Other and more aged horses were being harnessed to draw the ancient gharries about the narrow streets of the town. Supplies of drink were being carted into the Yacht Club in readiness for Garrison Saturday and soon work would begin on the Sharpies and the Victories for the afternoon's racing in the Bay.

Up at the Colonial Hospital patients had long ago been washed and prepared for medical inspection. Down on the huge parade ground known as Europa Flats, at the southern end of the Rock, companies of soldiers in summer khaki were falling in to the rattle of rifle butts and the cursing of corporals. The Admiral was finishing his sausages and bacon, his car was at the door of the Mount and would soon be taking him down to the Dockyard Tower. A number of the seven hundred and sixty-five telephones in Gibraltar were being put into use as their owners finalized their week-end arrangements. An Imperial Airways flying-boat was circling the Rock before landing in the Bay. A small group of Barbary apes on the upper Rock were searching in their fur for fleas, whilst another of their number had just carried out a daring raid on the Chief Engineer's tomato plants and was now scaling his way back to the Queen's Road.

It was a calm summer's day with a south-westerly breeze freshening in the Bay. Conditions would be ideal for sailing that afternoon, the Deputy Fortress Commander considered, as he took a look at the harbour from the Line Wall Road before reluctantly burying himself in Fortress Headquarters for the morning. Eleven half-starved Republican refugees had crept into Gibraltar overnight—a grim reminder that only a few yards away in Spain there were other forces at work. There, anarchy, fratricide, and brutal oppression had torn a country to pieces, while the dictatorships of Germany, Italy and Russia had indulged in their clinical military experiments.

In Gibraltar that fine Saturday morning there were better things to be thought about than war. It was true that, under the initiative of the Chief Sapper's wife, a number of local ladies were being given elementary first-aid instruction. But this was something to be squeezed in at an odd moment during the week, at the reluctant sacrifice of an afternoon's bridge. The week-end was sacrosanct. The British week-end, that epitome of all that was best and worst in the British way of life, had Gibraltar in its grip. The British week-end, changeless and unchanging, except in outer detail, from Hong Kong to Trinidad, from Newfoundland to Mauritius, gradually took over possession of the Rock as the sun mounted south towards its zenith.

The work of the colony, some of it essential, some of it pointless, was locked away in safes and offices, armouries and dockyard stores. In 1939 the prestige of England was such that a mere handful of unarmed Gibraltarian Police in their 'London Bobby' uniforms, looking somehow quaint in the

Mediterranean sun, were sufficient to control the frontier into Spain. Nothing requiring official attention could happen over the week-end which could not easily be deferred until Monday morning. As inexorably as the passage of the sun across the sky, leisure, relaxation and sport took possession of the Rock. Uniforms were exchanged for flannels and shorts, just as later on the dinner-jacket would supersede them both. It was the pattern of garrison life in any British colony all over the world.

Creeping about the hills towards Ronda there were still desperate men, a rifle or a knife their only hope of survival, their days inevitably numbered now that the 'Reds' had lost the Civil War. From the shelter of their primitive caves, some of them could no doubt see Gibraltar—that taunt to Spanish pride as some might say, that paradise of decency and justice as it undoubtedly appeared to the thousands of refugees who had already sought asylum. Soon, no doubt, there would be German and Italian soldiers swarming over those hills constructing the roads and siting the guns. A little later, perhaps, the red flag with its black swastika inset would be hoisted where now the Union Jack fluttered gently in the breeze. The time of trial lay ahead. But in the meantime it was Saturday afternoon and the British were all at play.

III

THAT same Saturday morning in a Hampshire cottage Pam Evers was arguing with her mother, trying to suppress her annoyance.

'I've told you, Mummy, David agreed before he went off. If I could get a good let for the cottage, there's no reason why I shouldn't go out to Gibraltar. Well, I've got a tenant today.'

'But David's only going to be there a month.'

'How do you know? That's all the working-up is supposed to take but after that it's anyone's guess. They're supposed to be joining the Med Fleet but anything can happen—David said so himself.'

'The Med Fleet means Malta. I should have thought you'd have had enough of that to last you a lifetime.'

Pam had been taken to Malta at the age of one while her father had been Commander of a cruiser just before the Great War. They had stayed there throughout the war and then in the early 'thirties the family had returned to the island when her father did a commission in H.M.S. *St. Angelo*.

'For that matter I should have thought you'd have seen quite enough of Gib as well.'

Her father had also spent two years attached to the base ship at Gibraltar, the *Cormorant*. Pam frowned in irritation. Her mother was being difficult.

'Anyway I'm married, Mother, is it so very unreasonable to want to be with my husband?'

'There are times to be with your husband,' her mother said severely, 'and times to leave him alone—especially when he's just got his first destroyer command. I had to learn it with your father, and so will you.'

'The Navy's changed since you were a girl. Anyway, I've made up my mind.'

'I think you're just after a good time,' her mother went on. 'I don't think you consider David nearly enough. It's always what *you* want to do, how *you* want to spend the money.

You'll pay for that kind of attitude later on, dear, and then you'll be sorry.'

'Thank you, Mother, I can look after my own life perfectly well.'

It was always the same. Her mother always took David's side. It usually ended in tears and she hated the process. Why shouldn't she think of herself? Of course she was after a good time. Well, who wasn't? Good heavens above, you were only young once. The conversation in the garden pursued its familiar and well-worn track.

'It's a pity you haven't a family to take your mind off yourself a bit more,' her mother continued.

'Oh! really, Mummy, need you harp on it so? Anyway who wants to bring a child into a world like this? I can assure you I don't and neither does David.'

'I wouldn't be so sure about that. David'll soon get tired of being dragged round endless parties. He'll want to settle down and have a family.'

'Well, of course, if you know my husband better than I do myself. there's nothing more to be said.'

'I sometimes think I do.'

There she goes, on and on, Pam thought. Why can she never understand? Why can't she see that people are restless, strung-up, nervous these days? There might very well be a war. Her mother stood up and together they walked to the Austin Seven at the gate. Pam hated that car, hated the lack of money which had dogged her life, hated the threadbare existence which had befallen her parents on a mean naval pension and negligible private means.

'Then if you've settled about the cottage, when are you off?'

'If all goes well, about the middle of the week.' She hesitated as her mother got into the car. This was the part she dreaded, the humiliation she loathed. 'You see, Mummy, I'm actually terribly short of cash. I haven't quite got enough for the fare and I don't want to worry David unless I absolutely have to. I suppose Daddy couldn't make me an advance on my next half-year's allowance, could he?'

'But, darling, you've *had* an advance to buy that dressing-table and those worm-eaten chairs.'

'That doesn't count,' Pam said hotly. 'That isn't money *spent*. I mean, it went on capital assets: if we're really and absolutely broke, we could always sell them and get the money back. 1 was wondering if Daddy could let me have a little spending money.'

Her mother looked at her coolly.

'I'll ask him. But he's awfully hard-up at present. And you know what I feel—I think you ought to stay put for a while until we see what's going to happen. You could always let the cottage and come and live at home.'

'Yes, Mother.' She was twenty-six and they still treated her like a little girl. She would never get the money or she wouldn't get enough money. She felt like bursting into tears. She was profoundly depressed. She waved perfunctorily as the car turned the corner and walked back to the cottage. 'I'm *going* to get to Gibraltar or die in the attempt,' she told herself. As she reached the sitting-room the telephone rang. It was the house-agent from Havant.

'I'm afraid I've bad news. Mr. Anderson doesn't want to pay three-ten a week.'

'Would he take it for three pounds?'

'Probably. But I don't think you ought to come down. Wait a few days. The property market's affected by the news like everything else. Give me a little time and I'll get you three-ten a week.'

'I want it now. I'll accept three. Can you guarantee that?'

'I should think so. I'll call you back.'

Four threes were twelve. If she was away three months she'd get thirty-six pounds. That would certainly pay for her fare. Her spirits rose. She'd ring Cook's and get a berth on the *Calcutta*. And if she really ran short of money, she could always sell her ocelot coat. Anything—anything was better than being buried alive in Hampshire when David was at Gibraltar and she could be with him. She popped a couple of chocolates in her mouth, picked up *Vogue* and flopped down on the couch. Hippers hooray! It was going to be all right after all. She'd send David a cable after lunch. She had several friends in Gibraltar and after all David's uncle was Governor. It would not be too utterly boring.

Someone else had Gibraltar very much in the forefront of his mind that day, as he drove down from London for a week-end on the Hamble. That person was Sir Henry Patterson, the senior civil servant at the Colonial Office mainly responsible for Fortin's appointment. His wife had gone down the night before and this was just as well. Patterson had been later in starting than he intended and the reason lay on the front seat of the Lanchester as he drove. It was a copy of that morning's *Comrade* with its screaming headlines, 'Imperialist Governor Forecasts War. Gibraltar Bares Her Fangs.' The *Comrade* was not among the papers Patterson habitually read but his lively assistant had had it on top of the business awaiting his attention that morning. It had given him that odd twitch somewhere in the stomach which always heralded anxiety and doubt.

Had he been right to plug Fortin so hard? Could he not have made the most crashing misjudgment? The desert was one thing: Gibraltar another. Fortin had not been there a couple of hours before making headline news. 'Major-General Sir Giles (Waziristan) Fortin,' the *Comrade* had continued, 'the latest Tory lackey to be set in authority over an oppressed British colony, declared on landing this morning to take up the Governorship of Gibraltar, that war was inevitable. "I think war will come," this desert fire-eater declared to a select gathering of Gibraltar Imperialists in the Star Chamber of Government House. From his tone it was evident that the General would welcome the event. General Fortin, whose previous experience of colonial administration has consisted of bribing Arab chieftains in the Middle East, is Whitehall's new white hope in the key fortress of Gibraltar. Realists, if any, in the present Government must be fully aware that the military and naval value of the Rock, thanks to the aeroplane and the long-range gun, is now nil. However the principle of the British Empire remains unchanged. Once dominated, never given up. However futile the sacrifice, however useless a possession Gibraltar is proved, the Union Jack must continue to fly over an alien part of the world, no matter what the wishes of the local

[49]

inhabitants happen to be. General Fortin has the reputation of a strong, dictatorial personality. No doubt he is saying to himself, "The Rock Scorps will do as they're told." No doubt this explains the recent setting up of the Gibraltar Security Police Force, a Gestapo organization with the avowed object of denying the few civil rights that remain to the oppressed inhabitants of the Rock, who are no more British than General Franco himself. Let this new autocrat beware! He may find to his cost that a population in servitude, without electoral rights, without freedom, without hope, has other ways of expressing its will. There are enough Dictators in the world without fostering their growth in the British Empire itself.'

The same old thing, Patterson had thought as he put the paper to one side and proceeded with his morning's work. Yet, as always, there was a grain of truth in it all. The strategic value of the Rock *was* questionable: a Crown Colony *was* governed, it did not govern itself: any military governor of a fortress could scarcely be other than autocratic and one of the reasons why Patterson had lobbied so hard for Fortin's appointment was his ruthlessness.

Later that morning Patterson had rung up his opposite number in the War Office, the official without whose active support the appointment would never have been made.

'You've seen the *Comrade*, I take it. Our boy hasn't wasted much time.'

'Will there be a question in the House, do you think?'

'Your guess is as good as mine. Personally I think they've extracted the maximum sensation from what may have been a single casual aside. And anyway it may all be a lie. I'll send a copy of this article out to Gibraltar for the Governor's private comment. I won't recommend action this side.'

'Nor this side either,' said his colleague in the War Office, 'but I hope from now on he'll keep as mum as the desert sands —or some other situation will have to be found for his bonny personality. As a matter of fact,' he added as an afterthought, 'I should think he'll be unusually good with the local population. He never has liked the pomp and circumstance of the governing British abroad: his sympathies have usually been on the other side.'

'Let's hope they're not too revolutionary,' Patterson said. He belonged to the orthodox school of colonial administration. 'Festina lente' was a favourite precept of his. First things came first. The principal industry in Gibraltar was defence, with tourism, the bunkering, watering and provisioning of ships and the entrepôt trade all a long way behind. Gibraltar was primarily a fortress and in the ultimate analysis any civilian population was there only on sufferance. The Comrade wouldn't like that. Patterson was well aware that a position might easily come about where the presence of civilians was not only a luxury but a liability. In that event they would have to go. The Comrade would certainly hate that too.

It was easy to say that England should come to an arrangement with Spain about Gibraltar, altogether different when you tried to do something practical in the matter. No theory about Gibraltar, however nicely documented, however daintily argued from Oxford quadrangle or Devon cottage, could stand up to the impact of human nature on the spot. Franco knew that. Franco knew very well that Gibraltar directly and indirectly provided sustenance for at least 150,000 inhabitants of Andalusia fringed around the bay from La Línea to Algeciras. Franco was alive to the facts and so was Montague Bassett, the Colonial Secretary in Gibraltar, and the administrator upon whom Fortin would mainly have to rely when it came to civilian affairs and relations with Spain.

Patterson smiled as he thought of Monty Bassett today. He was a bit of an autocrat himself, accustomed with the last Governor to considerable independence. Well, now he'd have a very different cup of tea in front of him. Patterson remembered the great exception Bassett had taken to 'that book' about Gibraltar and especially to two sentences in it, one of which read: 'There is abundant proof of naval and military activity, but not of civil administrative effort,' and the other one of which went further: 'The position [in Gibraltar] hardly justifies that bland condescension with which English officials treat their neighbours on the Rock.' Bassett had wanted the author sued: well, now he would have to prove the real state of affairs in a quite different fashion to Fortin. And Patterson, deep in his heart, was doubtful if Bassett could do it. Fortin and he were somewhat alike but Fortin had the higher voltage.

3

Evers had just returned on board H.M.S. *Firesprite* after a hard game of tennis, when Pam's telegram arrived. He read it with a sense of dismay. He had left home barely a week ago and here she was already about to follow him to Gibraltar. He ran a bath and thought it over while his body relaxed. In another hour's time he would be at the Admiral's cocktail party at the Mount, a drink in one hand, inane conversation on his lips, glowing from the afternoon's exercise but very bored with this social manœuvre which could not be avoided. He would not remember a single thing the women had worn, whereas if Pam had been going she would proceed to talk about nothing else for the rest of the night. Clothes represented in her life what the Navy did in his. No, that was not quite fair. Perhaps they didn't rate altogether as high as that, but clothes, other women, money and 'things' were the basis on which her consciousness subsisted. A party of any kind was the breath of life: a dance on board the flag-ship a mountain peak and a dinner at Government House the zenith. David wondered in passing how social life in Gibraltar would pan out with Uncle Giles as Commander-in-Chief. From what he knew of his uncle, the bun circuit was in for a beating. Pam might not find Gibraltar quite the gay place she imagined.

He loved his wife. He knew, once she was here, that he would be proud of her, that she would embellish the scene. It would be pleasant to take her to parties, he enjoyed sleeping with her, generally speaking he liked having her around. But just at present he had a new ship and a raw ship's company. The flotilla had a task and that was to work up and become efficient with the minimum delay. This was a full-time job. Pam would only clutter things up. At a time like this it would be dangerous, perhaps even fatal, to divide his attention. David had a strong sense of duty. It was flexible, rarely dogmatic, and usually interpreted with tolerance and humour. But it was the steel backbone to everything he did. It governed his life.

As he dried himself, therefore, he found he was coming to a decision. He returned to his cabin, began dressing himself in the light-weight grey worsted which Pam had helped him to choose and then sat down at his desk to write out a cable. He must be careful of the wording. A sudden sense of doing something from a deeper part of himself, something almost fateful, assaulted him.

'Suggest you defer visit. No accommodation Gibraltar. Love David.'

That would do if he followed it up with a letter. Was it too curt? He thought of her opening the cable. She would hate it. She would throw herself into a crying rage. He tore up the piece of paper. Better let Fate take its course. Perhaps this was to be one of the trials in the desert he had thought about lying in bed that morning.

He brushed his hair, slipped on his jacket and reached for his hat. He was ready for the fray. Then he paused at the cabin-door and returned slowly to the desk. He sat down and made another attempt. How could he word it so that she wouldn't take offence?

'Practically never in harbour. Chances of seeing you slight. Suggest waiting till working-up period is over.'

That was very much worse. It sounded like a hell of a line-shoot. He clicked his tongue. Confound the girl: she was the daughter of a naval officer, brought up in a naval atmosphere: why couldn't she understand? He tore up the cable and started again.

'Gib overcrowded. Seatime high. Suggest not coming till after working-up period.'

That, too, went in the wastepaper-basket. He heard a knock at the door. It was his First Lieutenant.

'Are you walking up to the Mount, sir, or shall I get you a taxi?'

'I'll have to have a cab,' Evers replied, looking at his watch, 'you might ask the Captain of *Forthright* if he wants a lift.'

'Aye, aye, sir.'

Of the 28th Destroyer Flotilla only the Captains and Captain (D)'s staff had been invited. Presumably there would also be some chaps from the *Ramillies*, a fifteen-inch gun battleship, and the *Sussex*, one of the 'County' class cruisers also in Gibraltar at the time. A routine affair. David returned to his cable. By now all the benefit of the tennis had disappeared. He was as strained and tetchy as he had been that morning when he had run in six defaulters in quick succession as a result of Saturday Rounds. It was all eating into his time. He wanted to think about other things—not how to cable his wife without giving her offence. He took a turn up and down the cabin. He could waste no more time on this matter. He sat down and wrote.

'Hotels full. Much seatime ahead. Suggest you defer visit till after working-up period. Love David.'

He rang for his steward and sent him ashore straight away with the cable. It was done. There was now no further chance of changing his mind. He went down on deck with a sense of relief. The First Lieutenant was standing by the gangway. There was a taxi rattling along the North Mole towards the two ships, and over on *Forthright* he could see Bill Downey, her Captain, talking to his own First Lieutenant. He paused at the gangway to speak to Allendale.

'Not going ashore tonight, Number One?'

'No, sir. I've got the First Lieutenant of *Forthright* coming over to dine, and anyway it's the Sub's turn for a run.'

'Right. I don't suppose I'll be late.'

He stepped on the gangway. The Bos'n's Mate piped and the First Lieutenant saluted. The Captain of H.M.S. *Firesprite* was ashore.

'Do you know many people in Gib?' Downey asked as the ancient taxi made its way through the Waterport Gate, past Casemates and along Main Street, the garish, crowded Piccadilly of Gibraltar. Conversation was difficult since the driver drove on his brakes and kept beating the flat of his hand on the side panel to scare pedestrians out of the way.

'Millingham, the Flags, and I were the same Term,' David replied, 'and I know Allcot, the Torps of *Ramillies*. Otherwise I don't think I've any particular buddies. I haven't really had a look to see who's here yet.'

They passed the Roman Catholic Cathedral on the left, and a little further on, the Protestant Cathedral down on the right by the Bristol Hotel. Then, with its kilted sentry stamping away outside, the low bulk of Government House, giving on to Convent Place.

'I hear you've got influences in high places,' Downey remarked, jerking his thumb at Government House.

'None but the best,' said David. 'The Great Panjandrum himself.'

'What's he like?'

'Uncle Giles? I hardly know him. He's always been messing around in a desert ever since I was a tot. He's sort of mythical and remote—and rather tough: but he's a practical pongo. He'll know which end of a rifle the bullet comes out of and that's something these days.'

'They say he's got a Marine as an A.D.C. Funny sort of choice. I don't think I'd like to have a great clumsy Bullock crashing about my nice clean Government House.'

'I did a commission with him once. Dicky Seale, the A.D.C., I mean,' David said as they passed through the South Port Gate and began grinding up Mount Road towards the Rock Hotel, leaving the town of Gibraltar below and behind them. 'He's rather a bright one, or he was in those days. Then he went flying and bust himself up. Has to wear a corset or something to keep himself together in one piece.'

'Trust a Joey to do something stupid,' said Downey as the long white oblong of the Rock Hotel came and went on the left. 'What about a steak there after the party?'

'There's a dance on, I think. We'd need to be dressed. We might potter down to the Yacht Club, though. Anyway let's see how we feel. You may get off with a ravishing popsy.' Downey was still a bachelor and from most points of view an eligible one.

'I suppose now you're married such ideas never enter your head?'

'Hm!' said David, 'we'll let that one go.'

He did not like admitting, even to himself, how much he enjoyed being on his own again for a while: not having to worry and fuss about Pam being late, or forgetting something halfway to a party and having to go back, or feeling 'headachy' or despondent because her dress was antediluvian or the colour of her nails all wrong. She never kept these things to herself. She shared the full miseries of all her real and imagined disasters, all of them, in David's opinion, of an almost unbelievable triviality. She was very much a woman. Self-centred to a degree, the world was made to revolve round whatever concerned her at the time. She adored him, she said, and indeed David believed she really did but she never for a moment considered his point of view. She had only the vaguest idea of the problems and responsibilities which made up his day. For a naval officer's daughter she was oddly misinformed, apparently quite unaware of the pressures under which any naval officer has to conduct his life. She was a good though selfish lover, demanding attention the whole time, rarely giving him the peace which he sought, demanding, demanding, demanding. She would suck the energy out of him day and night if she could. When David withdrew in any way from her orbit, she began a childish petulance which, left to itself, soon blazed up into full-scale hysterical tears. She never felt secure something was always unfair or she thought herself owed. She could be envious and jealous by turns, and violently, stupidly possessive. He loved her very much, but it was sometimes a wonderful relief to be on his own.

The party was half in the garden and half in the house. The Mount, the residence of the senior naval officer at Gibraltar since 1797, had one of the best positions on the whole of the Rock. Originally built by a chief engineer who had lived in Gibraltar for forty-two years, from 1760 to 1802, the house itself had sober Georgian proportions adapted to that well-bred Colonial style which eighteenth-century England exported all over the world, from New England to the island of Corfu. There was no trace of Spanish or Moorish design. There was nothing Victorian, modern or vulgar. It was the sort of manor-house in Hampshire or Wiltshire which David dreamed he himself might one day possess. It faced due west and the sun was putting on one of its finest purple and orange displays as it sank down behind the Algeciras hills, setting them off in black, luminous relief. In the garden there were palm-trees and cactus, all of a dignified age. In fact the whole atmosphere of the Mount was of quiet, deep-rooted power expressing itself through the breeding and taste of a century and a half of uninterrupted aristocratic tradition.

It was not a large party. Allowing for last minute additions, there were probably not more than a hundred and twenty naval and dockyard officers, their wives, and a sprinkling of local talent. The Flag-Lieutenant was much in evidence. This sort of thing was child's play to Boofles. He did the job expertly and without drawing attention to himself. He was deft. Without fuss he saw that everyone was presented to the Admiral and Mrs. Calderwell, that the drinks flowed quick and strong at the beginning of the party and that, as the evening wore on, known heavy drinkers did not feel themselves stinted. He had charm and he used it. Shy, solitary people were whisked away with a smile and a joke into larger groups; star-turns such as the Superintending Electrical Engineer, whose hobby was shaggy dog stories, found themselves the centres of growing solar systems in different parts of the house, each with an audience, no rivals in close proximity.

The few eligible popsies, of whom Rosita was one, held court on their own: the younger wives formed another coterie, purposely kept away since the talk would almost certainly be of nannies and babies: arch-bores, where possible, were kept like sediment continuously on the move. The impulse in all this came from Fat Barclay, the Admiral whose Goering-like personality dominated the party, as indeed it dominated Gibraltar. Yet it was Millingham and Millingham alone who silently clapped his hands like Monsieur Fifi with his performing dogs, some of whom could be flattered, some of whom had to be stung into producing their acts, while others were hauled without compunction to one side of the arena, where their personal defects could not detract from the integrated glitter of the spectacle.

On these occasions Grace could not but admire her husband. It was a feminine quality, but he ran these affairs more efficiently than any woman could possibly have done. He was never still, never in one place more than a moment—yet he never gave the impression of rushing about. There was never a panic, never a fuss, even on that famous occasion when the matron of the Colonial Hospital had crumpled suddenly into a cactus bush,

[57]

pushed from behind, so it was said, by the Chief Medical Officer. The result was that people looked forward to these parties. They liked being asked up to the Mount. When first he had arrived in Gibraltar, Fat Barclay had told his Flag-Lieutenant: 'The Navy's the Senior Service and that's the way it's going to be in Gibraltar. *We're* going to run the show and the show's going to be good. When *I* entertain, people are going to enjoy themselves, people are going to remember where they are and who's giving the party. It's your job to get the thing moving.' Nobody liked Admiral Calderwell very much nor his drab of a wife but parties at the Mount were always a great success and the subject of conversation for days and sometimes weeks afterwards.

Tonight the object of the party was simple. As the Admiral had given it out to his staff—a new Governor had arrived: the Navy must meet him and he, the Navy, before anyone else. It was a pity His Excellency had no wife. Women could never resist the curiosity of seeing how the Admiral's wife ran a house like the Mount. A woman down in Government House would also want to see how things were done elsewhere in Gibraltar, size up the competition, gauge the style of the place. To a bachelor like Fortin, a cocktail party would be nothing but an irksome duty. General Fortin might happen to be a sociable man. From everything the Admiral had gleaned, however, the opposite was far more likely to be true and now that the party had been on for nearly three-quarters of an hour with no sign of the Governor showing up, Admiral Calderwell's face was clouded with worry. As always he cast around for someone to blame. His eye lighted on the Flag-Lieutenant, talking for the moment to that so-called local beauty of a wife of his. Ponderously the Admiral bellied across the lawn in his bluff, joking fashion. He addressed himself to Grace who relished his presence as little as he did hers.

'Well, Mrs. Millingham,' the Admiral said with a kind of forced jocularity, 'it looks as though the Flag-Lieutenant's fallen over again, doesn't it? We give a party for the Governor and the Flag-Lieutenant forgets to issue the invitation. Isn't that it, Millingham?' Then, without giving his victim a chance to interrupt, he went on, 'Flag-Lieutenants have much too good a time these days, don't you agree, Mrs. Millingham? What with tennis and pretty wives and a simple old dodderer like myself to look after—it's not such a bad life, is it? Ah! well, a good dose of seatime should soon get that out of the young gentleman's system—and I expect you'll be glad to get rid of him, too, for a while—isn't that so, Mrs. Millingham? Eh? Eh?'

Admiral Calderwell delighted to bombard his underlings beneath the guise of heavy-handed humour. Grace thought him a vulgar bully and never hesitated to say so to Lance. But Boofles was always surprisingly loyal. 'It's just his manner,' he would say, 'he's all right underneath. Remember, this is the end of the line for him: this is his last job before he retires.' Grace's private opinion was that Admiral Calderwell had spent far too much time on the Active List as it was.

'Isn't this H.E. arriving now?' said Grace, looking over the Admiral's shoulder. The Rolls-Royce with the Standard flying was sweeping up the long, curving drive. The Admiral grunted, gathered himself into motion and made for the front door, followed by Lance. No doubt he would blame her, thought Grace, for having spotted the guest of honour first. He could be unbelievably petty. Her glass was empty and she felt like a drink. She turned to see if there was anyone amusing she could talk to and in so doing bumped accidentally into a tall, blue-eyed man with lean features, hollows under his cheekbones, and good attractive hands. All this she took in at the speed of light, since suddenly the whole range of her instincts had come alert, and from previous experience Grace knew that her instincts worked at a far greater speed than either her thoughts or her emotions. She also noticed in this split fraction of a second that he was wearing a well-made grey worsted suit which somehow or other partnered the rather severe cut of his face.

'I beg your pardon,' he said, 'did I upset your drink?'

'No. It was my fault. I bumped into you.'

That was all they said. Two functional, social remarks—the sort of thing each had quite possibly said half a dozen times that evening already. Yet that was how it started and each of them knew it, though what they knew could never have been said nor, at that stage, defined. Both, however, were at a naval cocktail party halfway up the Rock of Gibraltar on a fine Saturday evening in June 1939: both had been brought up in the restrained, inhibited pattern of upper middle-class English life: both were married: both were clearly aware of their status and involvement in the outer world of that period, ticking itself away to another crisis ahead.

You read about love at first sight but if you suspected that it might be happening to yourself (which neither of them did) you quickly remembered who you were and where you were. But at this stage neither thought nor emotion had entered their relationship. Instinct had lit them up in a flash but the flash was gone. There had been a stab of recognition leaving behind a brief trace of magnetism between two human beings. Nothing more. Nothing to remark on or do anything about. Soon, too, that trace would have gone. Each would be as each had been before.

'Can I get you a drink?'

'Well—thank you, I'd love a martini.'

'I don't think we've met. My name's Evers: David Evers.'

'And mine is Grace Millingham. How do you do?'

They shook hands.

'Millingham. Is your husband the Flags?'

'Yes. Do you know him?'

'We were the same Term at Dartmouth. Hang on now. I'll go and get you that drink.'

Grace watched him as he made his unhurried way to the table where the drinks were being served. All round there was a buzz of excitement as the Governor arrived, then a general quietening down of the conversation. Grace knew that if she continued to gaze after him, as it were into the stream of the crowd's attention, she would become noticeable herself, so, like the rest, she fell to watching Fat Barclay and his angular wife greeting His Excellency, who looked oddly wrong in his plain clothes, and that nice limping A.D.C. But only a little of her attention was held by this outward scene. Inside she began furiously trying to order her thoughts and emotions. It was like an unexpected visit by Mademoiselle Gruener to her room at school—the same tumultuous feeling of having been taken by surprise, the same hopeless attempt to tidy up, the same instinctive urge to explain that if only she'd had five minutes' notice, the place would have been spick and span. On these occasions you had to hold hard on to something, you had to steady your thoughts and contain this dizzy feeling in the heart. A voice behind her whispered:

'All the world's a stage and Admirals and Generals rather awful players.'

It was Hobart, as usual materializing unobserved out of nothing, like a cat. But she was glad to find him there. They liked each other and here was the something familiar she needed to steady herself.

'Hallo, Himmlet. Where's Cornelia?'

'Caught up with some gentleman who drives a destroyer, as he puts it. A lot of Navy here tonight.'

Hobart was in the habit of making casual, off-hand remarks slightly out of context. You said, 'Yes', and then remembered that this was the Mount so of course there would be a lot of Navy present. The odd thing would have been to have found a lot of soldiers instead. You had the feeling all the time that Hobart was watching you from behind a mask, gently pulling your leg, seeing how alert you were.

'How did you wangle an invitation?' Grace asked. 'Didn't you see the notice—Pongos keep out?'

Hobart smiled at her indulgently.

'You don't think I play tennis with your husband simply for exercise, do you? I have to keep in with important people.' Then before she had a chance to react he went on, 'And what do *you* think of our new Governor? Cosy, Mrs. Prendergast says, and Mrs. Dawes feels he ought to have a nice comfortable wife. It isn't right, she says, for a man to live alone.'

'What *is* he like, Himmlet?'

Again Hobart looked at her with that veiled, ironic smile. It disturbed her not to know what he felt.

'You'd like him, I think. His nephew is just getting you a drink—or perhaps you know that already.'

For a second Grace had a giddy sensation that Hobart had seen right into her heart, that somehow or other she'd given away the whole game before it had even started. Then she pulled herself together. That was absurd.

[61]

'No, I didn't know,' she answered, 'we've only just met. But I suppose *you* knew that.'

They looked at each other and both of them laughed. He was a great favourite of hers.

'Grace, my darling,' said Hobart, 'I've always thought you madly attractive. Let's leave it at that.'

By this time Evers had reappeared with two drinks in his hand.

'Sorry I was so long. The protocol got in the way.'

He looked calmly at Hobart, waiting to be introduced.

'This is Commander Evans,' Grace said. 'It *is* Commander isn't it? Major Hobart.'

They shook hands.

'It's Lieutenant-Commander, as a matter of fact, and the name is *Evers*. David Evers.'

'Oh! look!' said Hobart, 'Mrs. Prendergast has spilt her lovely cocktail all down that hideous new dress.' Then, as Grace turned to look, he murmured in her ear, 'Be seeing you,' and slipped away unnoticed behind her back.

'Who was that?' David asked.

'The D.S.O. They're friends of ours.'

'I'm afraid D.S.O. only means Distinguished Service Order to me: what does it stand for in Gibraltar?'

'The Defence Security Officer. Our local Himmler—except that he doesn't take life quite so seriously.'

'Does anyone?' She found those blue eyes staring at her with a curious detachment.

'You mean—eat, drink and be merry for tomorrow we die?'

He waved vaguely at the darkening garden and the lights of Gibraltar below.

'Well, at any rate, the Ball on the eve of Waterloo—or am I being pompous?'

'I don't think so. Of course in a place like Gibraltar we all get absorbed in our own little lives. You come in from sea, from the outside world, and you notice it more.'

'Have you been here long?'

'I was born here. I'm Gibraltarian.'

She would have dreaded that question had Lance been there, dreaded the flinch he always suppressed, the dismay he tried

[62]

never to show because his wife was a 'native'. But with this one it was different.

'You must get pretty bored with nothing but the Army and the Navy around,' he said. 'My wife grew up quite a bit in Malta and she's always saying how you long to break out of the little circle of local Service life.'

So he was married. I wonder what she's like. Fluffy? Sensible? Silk? Tweeds? Comfortable? Exciting?

'Oh! it's not as bad as all that,' she heard herself saying. 'We live in Spain—well, I mean our real home's at San Roque. You must come and see us. Are you from *Ramillies*?'

'No. I've got a destroyer. The *Firesprite*. You must come and see *me*.'

It was absurd to feel as excited as this. She felt like a child on the fringe of a treat, tremulous, shaky, desperately afraid that something might happen to spoil it.

'We'd love to,' she said. When he smiled his eyes creased up but the rest of his face hardly moved. With Lance the face smiled but the eyes remained dead. It was never sincere. Or it never looked sincere.

'I was forgetting you were married,' he said, 'you look much too young.'

'Thank you.' There was nothing forced or artificial about him. It was all so natural, as though they had know each other for years. And that released her, too. With Lance she was always taut, always on guard.

'What on earth made you marry Boofles? Or has he kept that name a dark secret?' He spoke lightly: the casual interchange of equals. It could have been said with a far less pleasant significance. There was no trace of condescension in him. She almost clapped her hands in delight. Here was a young naval officer who actually wasn't a snob. She ignored the first part of the question.

'He kept it a secret from me,' she said, 'but my young sister found it out. You're not to use it against him.'

'From what I remember of Boofles he was quite capable of looking after himself.'

They glanced over at the group round the Governor. The Admiral glowing with self-satisfaction, Lance slightly bored, the new A.D.C. being talked at by Mrs. Calderwell, the Governor himself shaking hands with the Chief Engineer of the Dockyard and his Methodist wife. How odd that he made no mention of the fact that the Governor was his uncle. Was that modesty or false modesty?

'I hear the Governor's . . .' she began, and then stopped herself. It was for him to mention it, not her. Quickly she added, 'What's wrong with the A.D.C.?'

'Well, he's a Marine for a start. Isn't that enough?' That, too, could have been said with malice. It wasn't. I like you, Grace said to herself, I like you very much. For a moment or so she let herself wonder how he would be and then instantly, almost furtively, put it out of her mind. That would never do, never do at all. At the same moment she caught Lance's eye and rewarded him with an unusually spontaneous smile.

'I *like* Marines,' Grace said stoutly. 'Don't forget they're *our* Royal Marines: they're part of Gibraltar's history.'

'And you like Gibraltar?'

'I love it,' Grace said simply and sincerely. Then, out of habit defending herself from the snort of sneer with which Lance would have greeted the remark, 'Or does that sound sentimental?'

'Of course not. Why should it?'

'Lance always thinks it's a bit absurd to be proud of being born in a smelly old hole like Gibraltar.'

'Your husband's an ass. Come on, let's go and tell him so.'

Almost before she knew what was happening, she found herself being urged across to the Governor's group. This was most unorthodox. You didn't press yourself forward, you waited to be invited. As they came within range she saw a frown break on the Admiral's face, reflected almost at once on Lance's. She knew exactly what they were thinking. They would say she was presuming on her marriage, using her position to work herself into the limelight with some naval officer she'd met. It could have been and was legitimately said of her mother. It was the sort of 'dare' Rosita would have done. It would result in her own case in a snub either now or later, but at this moment she felt a new strength urging her from behind, an uprush of the spirit she had once upon a time briefly experienced before meeting Lance. Her individuality was no longer repressed. For a short time she no longer cared.

As they drew near, the frown on the Admiral's face deepened into a 'Keep Away' glare. If she opened her mouth at this point, an overt snub would be hurled at her head. From force of habit she quailed. Then something totally unexpected by the Admiral took place. The Governor caught sight of his nephew, excused himself from the people he was talking to, turned, and halted them in their tracks.

'David!'

'Sir!'

'I never knew you were here.'

'May I present Mrs. Millingham?'

The Governor bowed slightly and shook hands. Out of the corner of her eye, Grace saw the look on Fat Barclay's face turn to one of angry surprise. That damned Barbarossa family, he would be saying to himself, they get their fingers into every pie. By this time Lance had worked his way round to her side. He should have warned the Admiral. There'd be a can for that.

'I escorted Your Excellency,' David was saying with a straight face. 'That smart destroyer second from the left was mine.'

'Good! Dicky!' the Governor called over his shoulder. Seale, glad to be freed from Mrs. Calderwell, stumped up beside him. 'This is my nephew. He was part of my destroyer escort. Why wasn't I told?'

'I'm sorry, sir. I didn't know.'

'Well, see that he comes to luncheon tomorrow. Is your wife not here, David?'

'No, sir. We're at Gib to work up and what with the international situation and all that, I thought it better for Pam to wait for a while.'

So her name was Pam, Grace noted in passing, as she relished every moment of the scene. At this point the Admiral could stand it no longer. No one was going to steal the thunder at *his* party—whether they be relatives, Gibraltarians or pint-sized generals from the desert. Using his belly as a sort of battering-ram, he asserted his presence.

'I want to introduce the Chief Constructor of the Dockyard,'

[65]

he said, 'the Captain of *Ramillies* and the Captain (Destroyers).'

'Right,' said Fortin and turned away after a short concentrated look in turn at Grace, her husband and David. It was as though he was fixing them, as they then were at that moment in time, into his memory, and this in fact was exactly what he was doing.

'What's the name of your ship?' Seale whispered to David as he began following the Governor.

'*Firesprite*. We're down in the pens.'

'All right for twelve forty-five tomorrow? For one o'clock?'

'I'll put on a clean bib and tucker,' David said with a wink. 'Anyway it's Sunday.'

The Governor, his A.D.C., and the Admiral moved out of earshot. Grace shot an anxious look at her husband. David, too (it was already David in her mind), was looking at the Honourable Lancelot de Vere Millingham with his head slightly on one side as though weighing something up.

'Well, Evers,' Lance said with a slightly affected edge to his voice, 'this is an unexpected treat for old colonials like us. We were rivals at Dartmouth,' he added for Grace's benefit. 'Be careful of this one. He's not wearing that sheep's clothing for nothing.'

'If this is a wolf,' Grace said, 'I think he's rather a nice one.'

'There you are!' Lance said with a supercilious smile, 'five minutes with somebody else's wife and the home team's already out of the running.'

'You shouldn't neglect her, my dear Boofles. That's how the trouble always starts. Don't you read your *News of the World*?'

He could not know, nor could she, how ironic that remark would come to sound not so very much later. Now, however, there was a much more urgent problem confronting her. If she did nothing about it now—at this very moment—it was possible they might never see each other again except casually across another party such as this. She felt that something very precious to her, something quite impossible to define, was in danger of slipping through her fingers. Now was the time to act. She hated taking the initiative but now she knew she must do so.

'I thought Commander Evers might dine with us tonight,'

[66]

she said, noting the twitch of annoyance this produced in her husband, a twitch followed almost at once by his usual urbane smile and that powerful charm which so affected her mother. 'That is if we're all of us free,' she added as casually as possible. A very slight flicker in David's eyes, no more than a glint, told her what she wanted to know. He understands, she felt like shouting for joy, he understands.

'*I* can't manage it,' Lance said. 'I only wish I could. The Admiral's dining aboard *Ramillies*. A ghastly stag party. But I thought the parents were over in Spain. . . ?' He shot his wife a questioning look. Grace nodded.

'They'll be back at San Roque. I have to chaperone Rosita. That's my younger sister,' she added for David's benefit.

'Then why don't you come and have dinner with us?' David put in.

'Us?'

'Yes—Bill Downey, the Captain of *Forthright*, and I were going to the Yacht Club. That is, unless he'd got himself tied up with a . . . with a date of his own.'

He looked around and spotted Downey near a giant cactus doing his best to impress himself on a rather bored-looking girl. 'That's him over there in the blue suit. I'll just go and ask him what the form is—or have you sabbatical objections to your wife going out with another married man, Boofles?'

'On the contrary I'm delighted,' Lance said with apparent sincerity, but Grace knew he was acting. 'I hope you all have a jolly, spiffing, ripping old evening. If only I could slip the noose for one night, I'd be with you like a shot—but fat admirals are fat admirals and the noose is tight round my throat.'

'Well, then. . . ?' David said with a glance at Grace.

'Thank you, I'd love to.'

With an ill-suppressed smile she realized how much Fate was on her side at that moment. Everything had dropped into place. Everything.

'You don't happen to know who it is Bill Downey's working so hard at, do you?' David asked her.

'Yes,' she said with a radiant smile, 'it makes it very easy indeed. That's my sister, Rosita.'

[67]

Later in the relationship Grace returned to her memories of
that evening rather as a child goes back to a secret hiding-place
to count over its treasures. To her the early stages of the new
love which had begun that night not only remained always alive
but were instantly reachable by her whenever she wished. Invisible to the world, it glowed in the most secret part of herself.
David and the new love he brought into her life became steadily
more real as time and its attendant events closed in upon their
lives.

To outward eyes it had been a very ordinary evening. She,
Rosita, David and his friend Downey had all gone in her car
to the Yacht Club. It had been crowded and noisy. There had
been an exciting race among the 'Victories' that afternoon in
the Bay. Part of the Fleet was in, so there was an influx of
naval officers. Finally, it was Saturday night, when those not
away for the week-end naturally tended to foregather in lively
places such as the Yacht Club.

Lance had been in one of his trickiest moods as the party up
at the Mount wore on. Easy and charming on the outside, she
knew he was really resentful and petulant. With a practised
skill, intelligible only to Grace, he avoided them until the end
of the party. If she wanted her independence then she could
have it. But at a price he would make her pay later on. He
sensed a danger in this but it was his vanity not his jealousy
which now drove him on.

To be honest, she bored him: she bored him to the roots of
her black hair and her rich sensual body: she bored him but he
was not going to let her see it and he was not to be pitied. No
one made a fool out of Lance. She was still his wife. She might
be stupid and headstrong, she might have that element of the
tramp which Lance suspected in all Mediterranean peoples,
but from one point of view she only showed up his own
superiority. He might not have thought like this had he married an English aristocrat. But a Gibraltarian Catholic of
mixed Genoese-Spanish extraction, the daughter of a wealthy
trader in a British colony—oh! no, Lance said to himself, he
was not going to be out-manœuvred by her. He joked lightly

and easily as the party broke up but inside he was glowering with jealousy. He had never liked Evers since their cadet days at Dartmouth. He had resented him then and he resented him now, calmly taking his wife out to dinner, so to speak from under his nose.

Grace was glad to get away from the Mount. Later on she knew she would be 'punished', treated to a succession of Lance's exasperating and childish tricks, but she no longer cared. Even Rosita, whose mind revolved endlessly round the *Gibraltar Gazette* office where 'he' would just be getting down to an evening's work, even Rosita noticed that Boofles was unusually artificial and charming. 'What's up with the *prima donna?*' she whispered to Grace as they got into the car. 'Did no one notice the performance?'

But soon they had forgotten the party. Downey had had a liberal share of the Admiral's cocktails, made, so he maintained, of industrial alcohol and Ronuk. He brightened with every yard they drew nearer to proper pink gins. He had given up seriously trying with Rosita: early on he had classified her as U.P.—an 'Unmakable Popsy'—attractive but not to be had except via the altar. This did not worry him unduly: now he could get down to some serious drinking without any qualms.

There were friends and relatives of the Barbarossas at the Yacht Club, all of whom had to be introduced to Downey and Evers, to all of whom it was necessary to explain why Lance was not with them. Grace did this lightly and naturally, so that gossipy minds would have nothing to fasten on that night. Both Downey and Evers discovered 'old ships' and flotilla mates. Round followed round, in general only the men drinking. David was scarcely involved in the 'session' and Grace knew it. He would take his share in the rather hearty *bonhomie*, call his round whenever it seemed to be his turn, and then withdraw to one side, leaving the limelight to others who, luckily, were only too ready to take it. Grace realized he was doing this deliberately so that they could be together in their feeling. He would look at her and smile. They spoke very little but each was deeply, excitingly aware of the other. It was extraordinary how needless words were at this stage. Their hearts felt and their eyes expressed, briefly and privately to each other, the sense of wonder which had invaded them as the laughter and the Saturday evening life of the Yacht Club hummed all around them. But the wonder alternated with pain, with the chill of remembering that both were imprisoned by their lives, that what each so brilliantly felt must never be expressed, could never be fulfilled except at two other people's intolerable expense. The future did not bear thinking about. It was sufficient that they were alive, that their hearts had recognized each other, that they were standing together now in the hubbub and the buzz, silently knowing each other in understanding.

'Crippen?' said Rosita suddenly, 'I've forgotten Mother's library books. Give me the key of the car, Grace, and I'll pick them up now.'

'But the library's shut.'

'I have an arrangement with the librarian. She leaves them by one of the side windows. I won't be ten minutes.'

Grace handed her the keys of the car. It sounded genuine enough.

'Would you like me to come?'

'No, thank you, darling. I won't be a mo' and you know what Mummy's like if she hasn't her books.'

When she had gone, David remarked:

'She's very attractive. Is her future mapped out?'

'In broad outline. As mine was. She'll marry, of course, but possibly not the person Mother selects.'

David hesitated, giving her a flickering look. He was on tender skin.

'As you did?'

She nodded. There was nothing sentimental in that. How could there be? That was her life.

'Of course. My father has money. In Latin countries, amongst our sort of people, marriages are always arranged. Not as obviously as they once were. Perhaps with not quite the same Victorian brutality—but arranged they are nevertheless.'

'So one day you will be Lady Pulborough. Lance brings the title and you the money.'

'Oh! there's more to Lance than just a title,' she said, forcing herself to be loyal.

'I'm not getting at your husband,' he said quickly. 'I was thinking about your life. I suppose you'll have children and then the process will go on repeating itself through them.'

'That's more or less how it is.'

'Without rebellion on your part: without wanting anything different?'

Her heart ached as she looked at him. It wasn't quite fair of him to talk like that.

'My religion teaches that we have to accept what life brings us. It's all part of God's Will.'

'Thank heavens I'm not a Catholic.'

'But you're married,' she said with a mocking smile. 'Don't you regard the vows you took in your Church as sacred?'

He had looked at her with those blue, troubled eyes. Then his friend Downey had leant over and suggested another drink. The moment had passed and both of them were smiling again. Except that the ache in her heart was now fully reflected in his.

Later, when the Yacht Club closed, the four of them had gone on to the Royal to dance and watch the third-rate Spanish cabaret. She felt him somehow becoming reserved. He danced rather stiffly. She was disappointed in this but perhaps it was all to do with the evening's end, as though the parts of them that mattered had already said good night and gone their separate ways. Bill Downey, who had now got up a head of steam on pink gin, showed a desire to join in the cabaret and at this point Grace realized that just as she had started the evening, so now she must bring it to a close. Rosita had looked dreamily entranced from the moment of her return from the library (now who could it be at the Garrison Library? Grace thought, or was that merely a blind?) Grace sounded her out about going home and found her unexpectedly eager. Usually her younger sister had to be dragged away from a dance floor almost by the scruff of her neck. So the move was suggested by Grace, seconded by Rosita, acquiesced in by David and loudly and ineffectively resisted by Bill Downey who had begun to sing 'La Cucuracha' in opposition to the cabaret and who was temporarily winning.

They garaged the car, walked the few steps to the house near the King's Bastion, and then said good night. Grace asked

[71]

them in for a drink but they refused, wisely as it turned out since Lance had already returned and had gone up to bed. The farewell was formal except for an unspoken question from David's eyes and a veiled, acquiescent answer from Grace. This was noticed by Rosita, despite her own exhilarated state, and stored away in her mind for use on some future occasion. Bill Downey wanted to know who was in the house next door and whether they would respond to a serenade from the 28th Destroyer Flotilla. Then at that moment a gharry came clip-clopping by. David hailed it, and soon he and Downey were seated underneath the canopy in the cool night air, rumbling over the flagstones back to their ships.

IV

I T took the new Governor about a month to settle in and by
this time war was only six weeks away. From being a topic
of conversation, a theoretical event not really believed in,
the war had become something practical, something alive,
something which was daily altering the life of Gibraltar.

Seale was fascinated. To his surprise he found himself enjoying every minute of his day as A.D.C. The combination of
a coming emergency and a new man at the top provoked
effort and crisis in unending variety, and he was very much in
on it all. The new Governor was making things hum.

Fortin himself remained unshaken. He was beginning to see
what he wanted and once that stage was reached, as his A.D.C.
had good cause to know, decision, action, and fulfilment all
followed on in a natural order. Heads had already fallen. The
Chief Sapper had been promoted and removed. The Superintendent of the N.A.A.F.I. had gone. The Commissioner of
Lands and Works and the Superintending Civil Engineer of
the Dockyard were persuaded to ask for other appointments
and in the meantime had been hurried back to England on
leave. The A.A. defence of the Rock was drastically overhauled. New water restrictions came into force. The chand-
lering and repair of private yachts in H.M. Dockyard came to
a stop, to the disgruntlement of some members of the Yacht
Club. Offices and buildings were commandeered for Censorship, Contraband Control and a growing Intelligence and
Security section.

'There's an air of unreality,' Seale wrote home to his
mother, 'in almost all the socialities and relaxations which
used to make up life here on the Rock. You can't go on a
picnic nowadays, a fed-up R.E. Major told me yesterday,
without wondering if all your transport won't have been
pinched by the time you get back for some dark purpose connected with tunnelling or the restowage of gas-masks. H.E. is
shaking people out of their complacency. Most of them like it

and co-operate: a few of them don't. Those men—the die-hards and obstructionists—are marked men and they know it. As soon as H.E. has enough evidence the guillotine falls. Sometimes he doesn't even wait for the evidence. He's not popular with the red-tape merchants. People either admire him or they're afraid of him or they hate him in about equal proportions. One way or another I get it all. As for H.E. himself, he treats me as a mixture of slave and friend—rather more of the latter, I fancy, now that we know each other better. Luckily, Freddie Smallbones, the Assistant Military Secretary, is absolutely first-rate and has a strong sense of humour. We get on very well together. Generally speaking the Army accept me now that they're over their initial surprise and horror that a Royal Marine could actually have been chosen for this post.

'The weather is hot and I've managed to get in some bathing —though this plaster cast I'm in makes it little more than a paddle. We've had one Levanter—the damp, sticky wind from the east which covers the Rock in a haze and puts the humidity and people's tempers up. Otherwise the sun shines bright, the sky is blue, and almost anything can happen. I think it's really this which has transformed us all. For instance it's in no way fanciful to wonder if we won't wake up one of these days to find the square heads glaring at us from the Queen of Spain's chair. What may astonish the Master Race, however, is the hot reception awaiting them here, on, in, and from the Rock.

'Sometimes I almost wish it would happen. We can't stand by for ever and watch Hitler pick off countries whenever he thinks they're ripe. There are days when I'd give anything to be back in the Fleet Air Arm—or at least be at sea. I'd like to have a personal smack at the foe when the struggle begins. But the doctors are my warders and so far I've heard no jangle of keys about to open any prison doors. In the meantime I pound about Government House like a Court Chamberlain, with a certain power of access to the Throne (despite H.E.'s much advertised "open accessibility"), being lobbied, displaying tact on the one hand and a purposeful short temper on the other, incessantly phoning and organizing cars, dinner parties and sudden trips to unlikely places. When H.E. gets an idea in his head—for instance about siting a gun—he wants to find out all about it at once, go and see the place, surprise the local incumbents, the dust flies up in a tornado and when it settles again, the pattern is different. He is certainly getting people on their toes. The funny thing is that once over the initial jolt, they like it and feel glad it's happened. He reminds people of the aim and purpose of things, makes them feel a pride and a self-esteem in what is happening both in their own jobs and elsewhere in Gibraltar. He's a great one for making connections, for giving people a meaning. He reminds me of a good captain taking over a newly-commissioned ship: he drives everyone hard but he gives them a point to aim at, a reason for effort. Above everything else, he gets things done. There's a feeling that whatever else may be lacking, there's a Master in this particular household.'

There were other points of view. In the early days Fortin had confined himself to the Army, which he knew, while keeping an acute watch on the colonial administration and the Navy, which he did not. Both Bassett, the Colonial Secretary, and Admiral Calderwell down in the Dockyard were lulled into a false feeling of security. The famous Fortin of the Desert was all bark and no bite.

Then one day Fortin had got up early in the morning, had put on his oldest plain-clothes and, without telling anyone except Dicky Seale, had joined the stream of Spanish workmen pouring into the Dockyard at 7 a.m. He carried an old bag which might have been thought to contain his lunch but which actually concealed a large heavy stone. The police at the gate neither recognized him nor asked for a pass. In general every fourth or fifth labourer was tapped as he entered the Dockyard and had to show an identity card. Fortin watched this process and then adjusted his position in the queue. Once inside the Dockyard he made for the Tower. Most of the offices were locked or were being cleaned, but by some mischance the Admiral's Secretary's room was open and in the unlocked top drawer of his desk were six letters marked 'Confidential' and one marked 'Secret'. The Governor removed these, purloining a large O.H.M.S. envelope for the purpose. The safe at any rate was locked. Then, for the next hour and a half, he roamed the Dockyard, entering offices and stores without question, wrapping up the stone in a newspaper and carrying it unmolested into the tunnel under the Rock which led to the oil-tanks. The stone, he reckoned, was of a weight suitable to represent a bomb big enough to blow in the tunnel and perhaps set fire to the oil-tanks. Then, unchallenged and still unrecognized, he thumbed a lift in a lorry and slipped out of the Dockyard by the southern gate. Once back in Government House he wrote out a report of his raid and sent it, unofficially, to the Admiral and the Defence Security Officer, requesting their separate remarks.

The Admiral was furious. 'Damned interference.' 'Unheard-of behaviour from someone supposed to be the King's representative in a colony.' 'Practical joking at an undergraduate level'. These and more colourful epithets bounced about the Dockyard Tower as his chastened Secretary, a bored Lance and distressed senior officials of the Dockyard held a post-mortem on the foray. That it should be a soldier who had thus held up the Navy to scorn was bad enough; that it should be the Governor himself was outrageous. Fat Barclay seethed with humiliation and halfway through the morning stormed up to Government House to protest. Fortin heard him out, looking at him mildly.

'I'm sorry you take it that way, Admiral,' he said without rancour. 'I played this "dirty trick", as you call it, not to humiliate or laugh at the Navy. I wanted to find out how far a moderately determined foreign agent could get if he tried. It strikes me as very unfunny that the Rock of Gibraltar may suddenly blow up under our feet because of insufficient alertness.' He paused, looking coldly at the Flag-Officer in charge. 'Would you care to make an official matter of this? That's quite easy. Anyone who wants trouble can have it.'

He knew he had the Admiral where he wanted him. Fat Barclay valued this his last Active Service appointment far too much to jeopardize it for a storm in a teacup. He would bluster, protest, sail as near to the wind as veiled insult would allow, but Fortin knew he would do as he was told. This was a show of strength which the Admiral, who had been a natural bully all his life and who had, in one sense, bombasted his way to flag rank, was bound to lose and, moreover, knew he would lose.

'No, sir,' said Admiral Calderwell, 'I don't wish to make a mountain out of a molehill. I simply felt it wasn't quite playing the game.'

'It wasn't,' Fortin said curtly, 'and this isn't a game.'

'I feel perhaps you haven't confidence in me.'

The Admiral was certainly taking a risk.

'Do you, Admiral?'

The two men faced each other. Both pride and vanity—but mostly vanity—had been hurt on the one side: on the other there was a dislike bordering on contempt and as Fortin watched the emotion in himself, he knew it was leading him into dangerous places. There was no point in a show-down with the Admiral unless he wanted to be rid of him for good and all. This in itself—at the present critical juncture of world affairs—would be difficult and doubtful. Would a change on the eve of war be to the country's good?

'My duties and my jurisdiction are clearly defined,' the Admiral went on.

'Are you trying to teach me *my* job?' Fortin asked mildly.

'No, of course not. I'm merely asking——'

'I know what you're asking,' Fortin interrupted, 'and the answer is 'No'. So far as I am concerned no one on the Rock is infallible: no service or institution is sacrosanct. I intend to probe as I please. I will not keep out of your parish nor am I singling you out for special attention. If and when I no longer have confidence in you, Admiral, you may rest assured I shall take steps to inform you and to have you removed. In the meantime I suggest you trim your sails to the new wind now blowing—if you will allow me a nautical phrase. I have always had the utmost faith in the Navy's efficiency. I admire the Royal Navy. However, as long as I'm Governor, I shall continue to test you both officially and unofficially whenever I suspect or hear of a weakness. As I proved for myself this morning, the security of the Dockyard needs looking into—let's put it no more strongly than that. I suggest you do so right away. I've asked for your unofficial remarks on my un-official report. Perhaps you would care to give them to me at dinner tonight. I'll ask the Defence Security Officer as well if you like.'

But this was more than the Admiral could take.

'I'm sorry, sir, but I'm dining tonight—also unofficially—with the Governor of Algeciras. However I'll send in my report by the Dog Watches.'

'Why not bring it yourself?' said Fortin. 'I prefer to discuss these matters verbally to begin with.'

2

As Seale had written and the Admiral had personally discovered, Fortin was rapidly becoming Master in his own household. What others saw as disconnected events, Fortin treated as a continuous narrative. This was his story, his own particular pattern. To a small but exciting degree he found himself free to select what would or would not occur and a good part of Gibraltar's day resulted from the deliberate choice he exercised. The Rock, in one sense, was becoming his body and he was selecting the food of events on which to feed it.

He realized that this power of choice was tiny. A big event such as the coming war which was on a world scale would of course sweep up Gibraltar in its whirlwind orbit. Then Fortin and his colony would come under the restrictions and requirements—the laws, so to speak, of this big event. But within such happenings, and within Gibraltar itself, Fortin found himself not only making things happen but also choosing which part of his domain, which Service and, within that Service, which personalities would be made conscious to his attention.

Fortin had a strong sense of scale. And what was scale but a ladder of levels? The body was on one level, the brain—though contained in the body—on another. If Gibraltar had been given him as a body in one sense, then Fortin must learn to be the controlling brain in another, Like a growing child, finding itself endowed with strange powers, Fortin discovered, tried out and trained the muscles and the talents he had been given.

This had long been his philosophy. God had a plan. It was man's job to find out what that plan was and to do his best to obey it. If you did this honestly and sincerely, you were put through a severer testing than others more asleep in themselves.

On the other hand you were accorded a measure of divine protection. Like General Gordon, whom he had so admired as a boy, Fortin had a shrewd suspicion that nothing could happen to him till the job was done. Unless, of course, he indulged himself or proved a total failure. What the world saw as an almost reckless courage, Fortin knew as something much more curious and wonderful. God wanted something done. What was in God's mind Fortin did not presume to know but he believed that the job would be put in his way, that he had a duty towards it, that God would look after him reasonably until it was done and that, afterwards perhaps, he would be released from the bondage of the world which Fortin, like Gordon, saw only as an invisible prison.

Fortin knew that events always repeat. As it had been in the desert, so now he knew he would once again be tempted by power and by the other giants who had control of the world. The same great temptations recurred. Ambition had tortured him as a younger man. He saw it and laughed at it now. He could snap his fingers at his career in a way Admiral Calderwell could never understand. A fortune meant nothing to him. The money he needed had always been to hand and since he never spent anything on himself, the possession of money in quantity was pointless. Three other of the ruling giants could not touch him: he was envious of no one, jealous of no one, and impervious to self-pity. Man was put into the world to develop himself, to grow in spiritual stature, thus the difficulties one encountered in life were ideally designed to be struggled against and thereby lever oneself on to another level.

Only in one respect was he incomplete. Unlike General Gordon who feared and disliked women, Fortin was an unwilling celibate. His sexual urge had long been his Achilles' heel. It was for this reason that he had originally volunteered for the Persian Gulf and the self-discipline of the desert. Had he stayed in the western civilization in which he had grown up, he would have fallen and been submerged. He would never have been tempered in what was to him the hardest self-denial of all. The longing for women still gave him hell and since, so far as he knew, he was neither homosexual nor introverted, the only outlet for this powerful urge was to sublimate it. It was a potent fuel for the religious cast of his mind. He was aware, however, of some of the dangers it engendered. He could read *Rain* with a smile but also with complete understanding. He knew something of the tight-rope on which he walked.

The day might start on general principles, and Fortin made it his business to see that it did, but it soon got down to particulars. He loved a new problem, and if life did not always lay one in front of him on the breakfast table, he would in all probability seek one out for himself. His aim, in the early stages, was always to tackle a fresh idea, explore a new difficulty every day. He could have sat at his desk and the day would have come to him. To a certain extent, of course, this had to happen. He had letters to read and write, reports to approve, officials to see. He had said he would be accessible and little by little it became known that he was. Never before had so many Gibraltarians, prominent and not so prominent, 'dropped in' to Government House, to the distress and dismay of the Colonial Secretary. The Archdeacon, the Roman Catholic Bishop, the Editor of the *Gibraltar Gazette*, even a 'Trader on the High Seas' (the word 'smuggler' was frowned upon in Gibraltar) whom Hobart had mentioned—all took to sounding His Excellency on their more important problems 'if and when it was convenient'—and it usually was.

But after an hour or two of the office, he would throw all his papers at Freddie Smallbones, the Military Secretary, stride into Seale's sanctum and demand a breath of fresh air. Dicky, who was waiting for this moment, would either call an official car to the front door or, if Fortin was informally-minded, would lead the way down the backstairs to the courtyard behind Government House where he parked the second-hand Austin Ten he had bought. Perhaps there would be a visit to Eastern Beach to take a look at the race-course and visualize how it would look when the airstrip, then nothing but an idea, would have taken its place. Perhaps they would drive up past the waterworks and the catchments on which they depended, past the Moorish Castle, along the Queen's Road on the Upper Rock, stopping to feed biscuits to the apes and take in a bird's-eye view of the Dockyard and the Bay, returning by Windmill Hill Road and the new block of flats near Rosia Bay which were then being built. Sometimes they would look at a cruiser being dry-docked in the Prince of Wales Dock or—and these mornings were always the tops for Dicky Seale—they might take a flight in one of the Fleet Air Arm Walruses down by the slipway. One day they would surprise the N.A.A.F.I. staff at Ince's Hall, the Garrison's main canteen, on another call upon the Mother Superior of the Loretto Convent; on yet another the Garrison Library would be startled out of its morning calm.

Whatever part of Gibraltar had recently cropped up in reports or discussions, Fortin would always want to see it for himself—whether it was Colonial Hospital or Police Barracks, the Customs Shed at the Waterport or a new eruption of the underground earthwork defences the Spaniards were building on the neutral territory. He was coming to know Gibraltar intimately. Soon he would know it all.

3

As Sir John Patterson of the Colonial Office had forecast, Lieut.-Colonel Montague Bassett, D.S.O., C.M.G., the Colonial Secretary, was not enjoying himself at all. The previous Governor had been old and tired. He had arrived with a dragon of a wife. He had asked one thing of Gibraltar and that was peace. His wish had been granted. So far as the civil administration was concerned, Bassett ran Gibraltar like a purring machine, consulting with the Governor on the minimum number of occasions, putting on his desk only the formal, routine papers which His Excellency was required to sign by law.

Peace had certainly been provided. *Status quo* became the order of the day. The world slump had made colonial administrators wary of progress, especially those who had been temporary soldiers back in the Great War and who had spent most of their lives in Kenya and Nigeria. Bright new ideas from Gibraltar City Council had a short life in the Colonial Secretariat, where it was commonly believed that Bassett would send for his Number Two, hand him some proposal into which months of careful Gibraltarian thought had been poured and say, 'Choke that to death in four easy stages.' Whether this was grossly libellous or merely an understatement, the fact was that very little was done, the regulations were strictly observed and almost nothing went wrong. The immediate pre-war years were conservative in every sense of the word.

It was small wonder that Bassett had been so esteemed by the late Governor. His Excellency had never had such a quiet time in his life and when the dragon had contracted pneumonia and died, it was almost as though paradise had arrived on earth. In those days the Roman Catholic Bishop would not have dropped into Government House to discuss the gross over-crowding in the streets off City Mill Lane; the Jockey Club and the Mediterranean Racing Club had no uneasy thoughts about their next season's racing, and the Flag-Officer Gibraltar, reigned supreme at the Mount, confident that when his back was turned, no interfering soldier would be walking about his nice tidy Dockyard poking his nose into Lay Apart Stores.

Part of the trouble was that while Bassett respected Fortin as a man, he loathed his ideas. 'The shoemaker should stick to his last,' he was fond of saying. No doubt Fortin was a splendid general—what could he know of colonial administration? 'Heaven preserve us from amateurs,' became one of his daily prayers. Instead of running the show himself, as the real power behind the throne, he now found himself the negative opposition to the daily positive thrust which Fortin put into everything engaging his attention.

A new housing scheme up towards the Moorish Castle, one way traffic in the tortuous city streets, an amalgamation of the four different kinds of Gibraltar police—Bassett resisted them all. Since nearly all of them entailed the spending of money and since the Colonial Treasurer was entirely of Bassett's way of thinking, they were able to oppose and later on to block the majority of Fortin's proposals. They were on strong ground. With a clear conscience they could point to the regulations and claim that there was nothing personal in their veto. Money was the master. Gibraltar was in no sense a self-supporting colony: there was little industry and no agriculture at all. Gibraltar cost the Imperial Government money and the British Treasury was a Rock of Gibraltar itself when Colonial Governments besieged it for additional grants. After all, the

City of London had successfully applied the same principle to the Throne of England for nine hundred years: Fortin could scarcely expect to have it all his own way within a few weeks of arrival.

'I appreciate that Bassett is bound by the regulations,' Fortin wrote in a private note to Sir John Patterson, 'as any Colonial Secretary is in any British colony. I don't blame him for keeping me straight—indeed that's his job. However, it's in the use of discretion: in the attitude he has about getting things done with the few materials to hand that worries me. He's too stiff and unadaptable. And of course it's almost incredible to me that he can have been here through the greater part of the Spanish Civil War without bothering to learn the language. I am not asking to have him shifted yet—but should there be a bright young man due for another appointment please put him on ice for me. Or I could get along perfectly well with Bassett's assistant, Matheson, provided he can take on some local help.'

He knew this would put Patterson's back up; he knew it would not result in Bassett's immediate appointment elsewhere; he knew that from one point of view he was running the man down behind his back, but it was necessary to plant the seed. The old Governor had found Bassett a paragon and this was now a matter of record. Nothing that Fortin could do would alter that fact, nor had he the slightest wish to damage the man's reputation—he simply wanted him replaced by someone who could see the merits and possibilities in an idea, rather than the immediate snags.

Moreover it was through the Colonial Secretary that Spanish affairs reached the Governor. In the other direction, the relationship of Gibraltar to Spain also expressed itself in the main through the Colonial Secretariat. Bassett had certainly been impartial. The handling of refugees from the Civil War, the interning of warships and the continuing smooth use of a large Spanish labour force in the Dockyard all bore witness to that. But a new phase was opening up. The balance of power was altering. The stiff autocrat administering British impartiality to the refugees of a devastated nation would soon be as out of date as morning-coats and top hats. Soon the

British would be at war themselves. Soon Andalusia would be swarming with German and Italian technicians: Gibraltar itself under threat. A more wily, flexible brain was what was needed and Fortin determined to replace Bassett as soon as he could.

4

About Hobart there were no such qualms. Hobart had understanding, the one quality Bassett lacked. Hobart spoke excellent Spanish, he was a good mixer on any level, his working intelligence penetrated well under the surface, he had a sense of humour and he relished trickery and intrigue. Unlike the Admiral his retort to the Governor's security raid had not been a sulky protest. Instead he had burgled the Governor's private office, undetected and indeed without using his pass or being seen by anyone in the process. There he, too, found State papers of a 'Confidential' and 'Secret' marking which he took out of Fortin's desk. In doing this he risked losing his head and the daring lay not so much in the raid itself as in the reliance he placed on His Excellency's own sense of humour. He was by no means sure how Fortin would take it and when he had told Cornelia that evening she was horrified and immediately began to talk about packing and taking the first plane out.

But Fortin was furiously delighted. He gave Hobart the dressing-down he expected for the impertinence he had perpetrated, then immediately demanded to know how he had pulled off the raid. This Hobart showed him, together with an alternative he had worked out if the first had failed. From that day on no confidential papers of any kind were entrusted to locked drawers at Government House.

In other directions Hobart was of daily value to Fortin. Apart from security, Hobart knew a tremendous amount about Gibraltar, its inhabitants and the jobs they did, its visitors and what they were after. Fortin established a daily conference in the morning and encouraged him to look in for a glass of sherry or a cup of tea in the early evening. At these meetings Fortin insisted on informality. He treated Hobart as a friend, as indeed he was rapidly becoming. Each said what he thought. The Colonial Secretary, the Admiral and even the

[84]

Deputy Fortress Commander, a stiff and correct Brigadier, as crystallized in his military ideas as the Admiral was in Naval ones, would have been horrified at the way they and their affairs were kicked around at Government House by Fortin and Hobart with occasional help from Smallbones and Seale. It was a cabal in the making. Misused it could turn into a dangerous clique. Neither Fortin nor Hobart, however, had any intention of that.

The friendship had started from the very early days, in fact from the morning Sir John Patterson's letter had arrived with its cutting from the *Comrade*.

'Who would have cabled this home?' Fortin asked.

'A young Cypriot called Nicholas Pappadopoulos. A script-writer and journalist.'

'What's he doing here?'

'He fought for two years in Malaga and Madrid: he was caught by the Falange but escaped disguised as a priest, made his way down here and entered Gibraltar as a refugee.'

'What keeps him here?'

'He's got money. Or rather he could get money if he needed it: his father's a well-known Cypriot judge. He's intelligent, he's a British subject and he happened to arrive when the *Gazette* was looking for a new sub-editor. He seemed to hit it off with old Simonds, the Editor. He asked for him to be given a work permit and that was duly granted.'

'To a Communist?'

'He's not a Communist. His girl friend is, but her work permit expires next Tuesday. Then it's the boot for her. We can't discriminate against Pappadopoulos on political grounds. He knows that. They all know it. Except in rare cases I can only watch and report. I can't act.'

'Who's his girl friend?'

'The one I'm talking about is another refugee from the Spanish war. A German Jewess called Myra Heisenberg. Now has French nationality. I only found out about the Party card after the work permit was granted. As you know it's sometimes better to leave them where they are and check on their friends. Miss Heisenberg has helped us a lot. She's living with Pappadopoulos at the moment.'

'I'd like to have a look at this Pappadopoulos. How could that be arranged?'

'If you just want to see him, I suppose you and Seale could drop into the *Gazette* office one night on one of your surprise visits. You might rustle him out with his other girl friend, though, and that would be embarrassing in a number of ways.'

'He must be clever if he's living with two women at once.'

'He's not living with Miss Barbarossa,' Hobart said with a smile. 'It's a very, very private affair.'

'Except to you, it seems.'

'Ah! that's different, sir. People know my job doesn't let me gossip so they don't mind telling me things. Mama Barbarossa would be horrified if she learnt what her younger daughter's been up to. Madame has her eye firmly on the main chance. She married off Grace to a Flag-Lieutenant. I'm not sure the A.D.C. isn't marked down for Rosita. The only thing is Madame hasn't been very well of late. There hasn't been the energy there.'

'Does Dicky know his fate?'

Hobart grinned.

'I was going to keep it as a Christmas present. If he hasn't been hooked by then.'

'Suppose I ask Mr. Pappadopoulos up here to dinner?'

Hobart shook his head.

'You'd only horrify the snobs and you wouldn't get anywhere with Pappadopoulos. He'd merely laugh at you afterwards. He *believes* in what he's up to. It's his faith. You couldn't talk a Catholic out of the Pope's infallibility over a dinner table.'

'And what is he up to!'

'The destruction of what he hates. Colonialism. The British Empire.'

Fortin looked out of his window at the palm-trees in the patio.

'I don't see why we should harbour him here.'

'I can have him out tomorrow if you say the word, sir. There may be questions but you have the authority to deport anyone you think is subversive.'

'And young Mr. Pappadopoulos is?'

'He would be if he could—in certain circumstances. As things are he's harmless enough. I'd rather keep him where he is for the moment. There might be a bigger fish in the net one of these days.'

In his heart Fortin agreed with Hobart. It was sentimental to think you could frighten or persuade a man, when the force you were up against could move mountains. He tried to visualize Pappadopoulos. Why the chip on the shoulder? Why this hatred of the British Empire? Perhaps it had begun with the father, the powerful and successful Cypriot in a colony where to be successful meant seeing eye to eye with the British administration. He pictured a highly-strung child with that Greek hypersensitivity to arrogant foreigners engendered by five hundred years of Turkish rule. The growing boy's idealism continually battered as only idealism had been in the 'twenties and 'thirties. An alien casualty of the British Public School system, to which no doubt his father had been so eager to subject him. Then London University—the glamour of that militant socialism which was going to put the world to rights— the chance in Spain to do something practical about it—the disillusionment as he came into close contact with the realities of political power. And now Gibraltar. Fortin doodled on his blotter for a moment or so. He had seen much the same kind of thing in India and the Arab states. The warping of personality in its first impact with the world of power. He put down his pencil and looked up at the Defence Security Officer.

'All right, Hobart, he can stay for the present. If war breaks out we must think again. I wish there was some way of turning him round. He must have had the corners knocked off in Spain.'

'I think he did, sir. That's why I feel we ought to do nothing at the moment. He *might* change. It's possible. Once his eyes are open—if they're ever going to be—he could be a lot of use to us later on.'

5

By the end of July 1939 Fortin had established himself as a man respected and liked by the main Gibraltar families. Behind the British administration, as in other colonies of a similar size, stood a rich and locally powerful oligarchy. That Fortin was 'in' with the four or five faimlies who ran Gibraltar was due to two factors. One was his insight in appointing Jaime Barbarossa his Honorary A.D.C. The other, as Fortin had predicted on the passage out, was because Dicky Seale was a Roman Catholic. Encouraged by Fortin, his A.D.C. was at once taken up by the Barbarossas, the Gibertis, the Talgos and the Emerson-Lopez. He had been invited into their homes, cool shadowy houses nurturing wealth and power in seclusion, as no Protestant would ever have been. Indeed, in the early days, Seale's attendance at Mass was a more important factor in the restless Gibraltar scene than any number of formal meetings between the new Governor and the local *taipans*.

Hobart had remarked on this early on and had filled in the background of the oligarchy.

'The Barbarossas are shipping, coal and water—well, all of them are if you go into it deeply. It's only a matter of degree. The Gibertis are oil, coal and shipping. The eldest son runs the best garage in Gibraltar and the younger one has a warehouse full of American cigarettes, for trading on the high seas. The Talgos are food and drink wholesalers with interests in Seville and Jerez de la Frontera. The Emerson-Lopez have shares in the Rock, the Bristol and the Reina Cristina Hotel at Algeciras, they own parcels of land from Irish Town diagonally up to Governor's Parade and of course they're concerned in shipping and the trade in Main Street retail stores—as all of them are except for the shops owned by the Jews and Indians. Ninety per cent of the money in Gibraltar is held by the Catholic community. A Protestant trader wouldn't stand a chance. His troubles would start in the Customs and only Father O'Reilly could tell you where they'd end up—if they ever did.'

'Who's Father O'Reilly?'

'He's a very active Irish priest with a mop of red hair. Loves the liquor and is full of horse sense. The Bishop has to "rest" him from time to time but nothing can suppress him for long. He's got the run of Gibraltar from Casa Talgo to the Liberty Bar. Young girls are mad about him and so are their mothers. He cuts it pretty close but he keeps in with the fathers

[88]

because he knows how to make himself useful in dozens of under-cover ways. He and I help each other a lot. He fills the young men up with whisky, insults them and fires them with good ideas. He hates Cromwell, rages about the partition of Ireland, and is possibly the most completely loyal of His Majesty's subjects now on the Rock.'

A few days later Fortin asked his A.D.C. to bring Father O'Reilly to Government House. The meeting was more formal than Fortin had hoped and the red-haired priest oddly subdued. Afterwards Fortin asked why this was so. Seale hesitated and then said with a grin:

'He says it's a crying shame that there's a fine, upstanding, fighting man like Your Excellency supporting the devilish heresies of Martin Luther when the Holy Catholic Church is waiting to receive you with wide open arms.'

'H'm!' said Fortin and later on told Hobart the story.

'I'm afraid it's much more likely to be because you won't requisition that house in Devil's Gap Road for the Sanchez family, the one that belongs to the Garrison Library and hasn't been lived in for years because of the roof and the drains.'

'But I can't tell the Garrison Library Committee what to do. I know they're pretty well off but it's their property—it's their business entirely if they want to leave the house unlet and falling to pieces.'

'He says you could do it if you tried,' said Hobart with a twinkle.

'Did he, by heaven? He's got a nerve.'

'He's certainly got that.'

'And anyway who are the Sanchez family?'

'They lost their house in the widening of Picquet's Ramp. The replacement one the City Council found them isn't big enough for eleven children, two of them very pretty girls, and the *abuelo's* parrot. The Library Committee don't want to let them into the Devil's Gap house as it's going to lower the tone of the neighbourhood.'

'Hm!' said Fortin, thinking it over, 'in a few months' time there may not be a neighbourhood to lower the tone of.'

'Exactly,' Hobart agreed, 'and that's what Father O'Reilly asked me to tell you.' He smiled at Fortin, guessing what the

[89]

outcome would be. 'Perhaps if you had a word with old Simonds? He's for letting it anyway—it's only the die-hard element on the committee which won't hear of it, and they'd bow to your wishes.'

'I'll think it over,' Fortin said but he knew already that his mind was made up. The house would be requisitioned and Father O'Reilly would have his way. A remarkable man.

'Has Father O'Reilly met Mr. Pappadopoulos?' he asked Hobart as the latter was leaving the room.

'I don't know, sir. It's an idea. They might cancel each other out.'

Fortin looked at him from under his eyebrows in the penetrative way Hobart had learnt to beware of.

'But that's not altogether what we want, is it, Hobart? Don't they both have a place in your schemes?'

He smiled to show that he did not expect an answer and the D.S.O. left the room. As Hobart turned over the scene in bed that night, it occurred to him that Fortin was a far more tricky customer than Father O'Reilly suspected. He cushioned his head on his wife's shoulder and kissed her long slender neck with the freckles just behind the ears.

'There are more things in heaven and earth, Cornelia, than are dreamt of in your philosophy,' he murmured sleepily as her familiar hand began gently stroking his hair. That was something after all. Neither Fortin nor Father O'Reilly had a soft, lovable shoulder on which to lay all their troubles as they dropped off to sleep. Though that third Sanchez girl was a pretty hot little number, they said.

'What's so funny?' Cornelia asked.

'Oh! nothing,' he said. 'Just a passing idea.'

6

The duties required of an Honorary A.D.C. in Gibraltar were not strenuous, but as with the rest of his staff, Fortin encouraged Jaime Barbarossa to come and talk things over whenever he could. Fortin hated paper-work and this was another cause of distress to Bassett who tended to 'waffle' in speech but whose *forte* lay in the neat turning of civil service jargon. Barbarossa, however, was a businessman. Both the letters he wrote and the way he spoke impressed Fortin very much more than the autocratic pomposity emanating from the Colonial Secretariat.

Jaime Barbarossa accepted the appointment only under pressure. He was a busy man and, as things were, a worried one. The news from his brother in Madrid was disturbing; the Italian shipping line on which he relied for a large slice of his current earnings had decided, thanks to Mussolini, to be difficult; he had no son to follow him and take a little of the weight off his shoulders; he knew that something was wrong between Grace, whom he adored, and her husband; he felt uneasy about Rosita, sensing that the moment he or Edie relaxed their control, she would bolt or do something stupid, and to cap it all Edie herself was ill. The doctor had put her to bed and had told her mildly that the pain round her heart was caused by overstrain and too much smoking. To Jaime he broke the news that she had angina and that her heart was in an appalling condition.

When Fortin had sent for him, therefore, and asked him to be his Gibraltarian A.D.C. his instinct had been to refuse. The previous A.D.C.—an Emerson-Lopez—had decided to remove to New York where his affairs needed attention. It was an appropriate offer to make to Jaime. His friends and contemporaries at the Mediterranean Racing Club urged him to accept. He was 'one of them' and a man of sound good sense. Up to this time the voice of Gibraltar had not been strong in Government House circles. The previous A.D.C. had regarded the job as purely social. Jaime was equipped in every respect. He was already on the Executive Council, his son-in-law was Flag-Lieutenant up at the Mount, his brother was in with the ruling régime in Madrid, his sister was now a Maltese Contessa, he himself was a wealthy, educated man, quite capable, had the circumstances been different, of taking over the Governorship himself. His friends and associates wanted him to accept and, to clinch it, his friend Ramon Talgo offered him a partial merger with his own shipping agency representing one of the major British lines, together with the services of his nephew just down from Oxford.

So Jaime had accepted the post. The cabal, with the exception of Hobart, welcomed him to Government House. Hobart himself bore him no personal dislike. Jaime's loyalty had never been suspect, it was simply his connections which made Hobart query the appointment. Indeed Jaime himself had felt that his relations made him slightly vulnerable. He had therefore discussed his brother's position with the Governor.

'But that's exactly what I want,' Fortin had exclaimed. 'You'll be my ear to the ground in Madrid.'

Jaime had not mentioned the 'cousinage' in Milan and Genoa, two of whom were prominent Fascists, nor his Hamburg shipping friends, the Kreutzers. Both Hobart and Fortin had noted this omission, whether accidental or deliberate, as mildly interesting. But Jaime was a businessman. One of his cardinal principles had always been that the less other people knew of your affairs the better. It was certainly a principle on which his daughter, Rosita, was working unknown to her father.

After accepting the appointment, Jaime had gone straight home to Edie. She would be delighted. She had long had her eyes on Government House. She was lying in bed, the room as usual full of cigarette smoke.

'Doctor Gonzalez wants to keep me in bed over the weekend,' she had begun in her imperative way as soon as he entered the room. 'I told him it's absurd. I'm getting up tomorrow. I've got a lunch party at the Marquesa's on Saturday and we're expecting people for the day on Sunday at San Roque. I really can't be stuck here in Gibraltar in all this heat and idleness.'

'It's up to you,' Jaime said, knowing that opposition only strengthened her will. 'If you'll take it gently enough you might as well do what you want. We hire a doctor to give us professional advice: there's no law forcing us to take that advice.'

His wife looked at him narrowly.

'You're hiding something, Jimmy. You've got some bad news and you don't want me to know. What is it? I can always tell when you come in with that sleek, furtive look on your face.'

'I've certainly got some news. I don't know whether it's good or bad. The Governor's asked me to be his A.D.C. in place of Claudio.'

She clapped her hands and opened her arms to him.

'I knew it,' she said. 'This is my lucky season. I told you I had a little slam last Friday: then yesterday Mirabella Watkins went down with the measles so none of them can go to the Red Cross Ball—and now this. Well done, Jaime, well done.'

It was typical of Edie, he thought, to react as though she were the centre of the universe, as though the Governor had made this appointment solely to advance his wife's social career. She thought only of herself, yet did it so dynamically and with such a sweep that it seemed to increase her femininity and attractiveness. She assumed without a second's hesitation that everything he had achieved in his lifetime had been solely for her: indeed that she had been the cause of it, the inspiration, the reason why he made any effort at all. Rosita took after her mother, that's why they were always fighting like cats. Grace was a much more placid, unselfish character. She never fought back. She accepted her fate with the same ironical shrug of the shoulders as he had done all of his life. Edie called her tame, disappointing, dull—but there were never the tears from Grace that came in great headstrong gales from Rosita when she crossed swords with her mother.

'Of course I always thought it was something of a pointed insult to Gibraltar to send an unmarried Governor here,' Edie was saying. "After all there must be a woman at Government House.'

'Well,' Jaime said, kissing her on the forehead, 'it looks as though Government House has got what it needs—if you don't go counter to everything the doctor's suggested.'

She lit another cigarette and gazed into space. She had that calculating look in the eyes which, Jaime knew from experience, boded trouble.

'Do you know, dear,' she said, 'I believe I'll do as Dr. Gonzalez suggested. I'll put off the Marquesa and cancel our arrangements for Sunday. I'll get myself properly well. There's the Red Cross Ball on Wednesday next. I wasn't going to bother with it. But now . . . I think on Monday morning. . . .'

'You might as well enjoy it while the going's good,' Jaime remarked. 'My guess is there'll be a war as soon as the harvest's in.'

'The harvest, dear? What's that to do with it?' Edie said vaguely, her mind already snipping at invitation lists, rearranging seating plans, refusing favours in the way she herself had been for so long refused. Then the word 'war' made another connection in her mind, one much nearer home.

'Lance has put in another application for a sea-going appointment,' she said. 'I really do think it's unreasonable—especially now. Grace is very upset. It's beginning to look as though he simply wants to get away from his wife. Why don't you have a word with him, Jaime?'

'Having a word with someone' was Edie's infallible method of getting things exactly as she wanted them. This time, however, she was in for a shock.

'I wouldn't dream of it,' said Jaime. 'Most naval officers want to get back to sea. That's why they join the Navy. He's had a very good run for his money in Gibraltar—now it's high time he did a spell as a normal N.O. again.'

'Oh! Jimmy, how can you possibly talk like that? You know he and Grace are going through a difficult patch.'

'That's exactly what I mean. A little absence from each other may make their hearts grow fonder. I'm sorry, Edie, I won't lift a finger in the matter.'

From his tone of voice, Edie knew it was useless to pursue that particular course at that particular time. She sniffed gently to show her feelings.

'Well, at any rate I'm glad *you're* not a naval officer,' she said, 'simply aching to get away from his wife.'

'It's possible to do that,' said Jaime, 'without being a naval officer—if one wanted to, that is.'

He smiled at her and went out of the room, knowing that for one evening at least she would be blissfully happy.

V

GRACE was certainly upset, though not entirely for the reasons her mother assumed. But then her mother knew nothing of David. By now it was nearly August. The working-up period for the 28th Destroyer Flotilla was nearly completed. Soon David would be going away. So, too, would Lance and perhaps she would follow him back to England, especially if he got an appointment to the Home Fleet. Lance would pay lip service to the idea but she knew in her heart that he was tired of her and simply wanted to get away. She did not know what to do and, as usual, whenever there was a choice, indecision gripped her.

Yet was there a choice? She was married. That fact with its implicit duty went round and round in her brain like an un-ending worn-out gramophone record. She was trapped. Whatever happened she was married to Lance. She was mar-ried and Lance was married and David was married and David's wife was married.

In the early days she had tried simply to put it out of her mind. She had been taught to expect temptation. It set a value on marriage. Marriage was something to be struggled for. It need be no prison. She had once been in love with Lance: had admired and revered him: had been quickened by his reactions and interest in her. Originally they had wanted each other just as now a part of her was drawn, pleading in the dark, into con-tact with David Evers. Was this new attraction as much of an illusion as her feeling for Lance had turned out to be?

From the very beginning Lance had been jealous. As the gharry had taken David and his friend Downey off into the night, Grace had heard old Teresa locking and bolting the door behind them with a sense of returning to her dungeon. She had not expected to find Lance back so early but he had been in bed sulkily reading a book. She made herself go over and kiss him. There was no response. She knew that if she com-mented on this, she would lay herself open to one of his cutting remarks, so instead she said:

'You're back early. How was the dinner?'

'Ravishing as usual, thank you very much.'

He showed no inclination to talk. She knew he was eaten up with curiosity about her own evening but, having adopted this detached attitude, his pride kept him silent.

'We went to the Yacht Club,' she said as she began undressing, 'and then we looked in at the Royal.'

'Oh!'

'David's friend, Bill Downey, got a bit stinking and started to join in the cabaret, so we thought it was time to come home.'

'Rather early aren't you—for a night on the tiles? You *must* have been bored.'

She straightened up and looked at him.

'What's the matter, Lance? Didn't you want us to go out together?'

'What on earth gave you that idea? You're entirely free to do as you please. I'm delighted you went. Surely you know by now I'm the last person to stand in your way—or don't you?'

'For heaven's sake don't build it up into something it isn't,' she snapped. 'I don't racket around and I'm getting a little tired of these funny innuendoes.'

'I see Evers has made an impression. I hope *his* wife's as pleased about it as you are.'

He put down his book, turned away from her and pretended the conversation was over. But now Grace was angry herself. She resented having her evening ruined like this.

'What's happening to us, Lance? What have I done to make you behave like a bad-tempered little boy?'

'Must we discuss it now?'

'I will *not* be treated like this. If I had anything on my conscience, perhaps you'd be justified—but what have I done? What's gone wrong with us both?'

'Grace, please. I've had an exhausting day and I'd like to go to sleep.'

'Then you can damn well sleep by yourself,' she said, her hands shaking as she wrapped her dressing-gown round her and made for the door.

'What do you mean by that?' Lance countered sourly. 'Or are we in for some more Latin temperament?'

'I shall sleep in the corner room tonight. And tomorrow I'll have it made up for you.'

'You'll do no such thing. I'm not going to be made a laughing stock, thank you very much, in someone else's house. You can sleep in this bed, here, beside me.'

'This is *our* home,' said Grace, 'and it's time you came to your senses.'

She walked through the door, down the corridor and into the corner room with a sinking, sickening feeling at the bottom of her heart. If he followed her now, if he made the slightest move to say he was sorry, Grace knew she would collapse, she would do as he said, be his meek servant, accept his feeble love-making as if he were really the Adonis he thought himself: she would pay in humility for this outburst of independence and she would pay of her own free will, gladly, as a penance.

But Lance did not follow her along the passage: he turned out the light and went off to sleep. The moment had passed. The chance to heal the split at this—the first breaking of the skin— the first insertion of the thin edge of the wedge by life—had come and gone. With a grey feeling of fear at the possibilities now unfolding before her, she climbed into the strange, un-welcoming bed with a shiver of apprehension, not of the day to come but of the months and the years of loneliness now waiting to swallow her up.

2

Nothing so involved had taken place in David as he got back on board his ship. He was in a pleasant glow induced by alcohol and an attractive woman but he did not analyse his feelings. *Firesprite* was his home and this was more real to him than the Hampshire cottage, in which no doubt Pam would now be angrily in bed having received his cable. There had certainly been a great sympathy and understanding between Grace Millingham and himself but this initial meeting with her had fallen on a quite different place in David's being. He was frustrated neither in his career nor in his marriage. He certainly wished Pam was waiting for him now in his cabin, as he walked across the gangway and received his First Lieutenant's salute. But that in its turn was only a passing, fanciful thought. The

[97]

really important thing was that he was the Commanding Officer of one of His Majesty's Ships and that he was once more aboard that ship. He, David Evers, thirty-one years old and a lieutenant-commander in the zone for promotion.

The next day, therefore, after a sound night's sleep, the memory of Grace and her eyes came to him disturbingly for a moment on waking and was then put out of his mind. That morning Captain (D) walked round the flotilla expressing himself as very far from pleased with what he saw. Lunch with Uncle Giles had taken place, as directed, at Government House. He and Downey had played tennis in the Dog Watches and on the Monday morning both had conducted their ships to sea on the first phase of the stiff programme of working-up exercises for which they had come to Gibraltar.

From then on he thought more and more of the job he was doing and less and less of his wife or Grace Millingham. Day after day they would slip from the pens before the sun was over the Rock, glide out of harbour in a sleek, businesslike fashion, turn in the bay and then streak out to sea with that sudden urgency which only destroyers seem able to suggest. Then east into the Mediterranean for the full calibre shoots, the torpedo exercises, and the long series of seamanship tests known as 'Executive Drills'. Every department in *Firesprite*, as in the eight other ships of the flotilla, was exercised in turn, from the engine room with its 36,000 horse-power to the gunnery department with its four 4.7-inch guns. This was the same essential process undergone by all H.M. Ships newly commissioned, whether battleships or mine-sweepers, modified only in detail according to the type and size, by which freshly assorted sailors learn to settle down to their ship and work it efficiently as a man-of-war.

For Evers and for Allendale it was a sleepless, exasperating time. They had to drive their ship's company hard all day and then, at night, analyse one spasm of work and prepare themselves for the next. As always in the early days of a new commission both Captain and First Lieutenant learned a great deal that was strange, not only about the ship but also about themselves. Precedent and the King's Regulations were there to guide, but growth in responsibility depends upon a talent for teaching oneself. Each day Evers in command and Allendale as executive officer found new problems to solve, these problems becoming on the next stage down, matters of routine for the ship's company of the *Firesprite*. Both grew in initiative—that prime quality of the sea-going naval officer. Both changed. Both lost their early hesitancy and acquired a firmness of touch.

It was a period of grace, a work-shop time in which human material was being forged and tempered, when mistakes were expected but could still be remedied.

'It's consoling to remember that there are only a limited number of events which can take place at sea,' Evers remarked to his First Lieutenant one evening as they headed back to Gibraltar after a disastrous exhibition of seamanship in which both whalers had been lowered with their plugs out and had had to be baled out in full view of the flotilla. 'We seem to be getting them all. Some of them turn up in a new guise but they're the same old basic situations at bottom. The theme's in the good book but not all of the variations.'

'I think Leading-Seaman Sanderson knows most of them,' Allendale said morosely.

'What's it this time?'

'He's managed to jam the door of the Ready-Use Paint Store with Able-Seaman Rogers inside. They're now sawing off the hinges.'

Very often on their way back into harbour, with the Rock in silhouette against the setting sun, Allendale and Evers would hold an unofficial post-mortem on the day's work. It was a time when pride came to their aid. Whatever had gone wrong during the day, however abysmal the gunnery, however many submarine contacts they had missed, the sight of the 28th Destroyer Flotilla in line ahead, returning to the darkening Rock of Gibraltar, wheeling splendidly round Europa Point and then steaming proudly through the shipping in the bay, this naval spectacle of which they were part, never failed to inspire them. It restored their energies and helped to set the day's lapses into perspective. 'X' Gun might have had one of its celebrated jams. Their torpedoes might have 'porpoised', or wandered off casually as one of them did in the direction of Corsica. The wardroom might have been flooded, thanks to

[99]

an improperly closed scuttle and an emergency turn at speed. None of these mishaps could for long cloud over the growing *esprit de corps*, both in the ship and the flotilla—that deep, rewarding sense, given only after intensive hard work, of a number of intelligent, independent parts linked into a powerful and flexible unity called a Destroyer Flotilla.

Soon the teething troubles would be over—Evers noted with satisfaction that mistakes once made did not seem to recur—soon they would take the efficient working of their ship for granted, concentrating on whatever fleet task they were given: soon other destroyers would be built and brought into commission, undergoing the same experiences as themselves, making the 28th no longer the latest and best—but that had not yet happened and in July 1939 H.M.S. *Firesprite*, an 'F' class destroyer of 1,350 tons, was a proud member of a proud flotilla, the newest, most up-to-date destroyer flotilla of her type yet to be put into commission.

Over it all lay the growing uncertainties of the war which all of them now expected. These were vague and ill-defined, hanging over their consciousness like thunder-clouds over Mount Abyla on the African coast. What would a war do to them all? and where would it take them? It was coming, that was all you could be sure about, and Evers, reflecting about it in odd moments at sea, thanked Providence that he had been given command at exactly the right time. Whatever was to happen, at least he would be at sea and in command. How frustrating it must be for someone like Millingham, he thought, stuck ashore handing out tea and cakes at a time like this.

The thought of Millingham suggested Grace to his mind and Grace, who at each meeting seemed to enter deeper and deeper into his consciousness, in turn led almost guiltily to Pam from whom he had received not a word since sending his cable. He had duly written once a week but she had not replied. For a fortnight he had not been worried but now that it was nearly a month, he began to have a disturbed feeling at the back of his mind. He had eventually written to her mother to ask if anything was wrong—though he knew Pam would hate him for invoking her in their private affairs—but there had not so far been a reply.

Perhaps there would be that evening, he thought, as they returned to the pens. If not he must do something about it. Damn the girl! He loved her very much but he had enough to worry about without that sort of thing on top. It was unlike her to sulk for so long. Could she have run away? He put the idea from his mind. Either he would have heard from her mother or she, herself, with her love of the dramatic would have sent him a lurid telegram. That was what she had always threatened. 'When I go,' she had once told him, 'you'll hear all about it. No slinking out of the back door with a suitcase for me. When I give you up, darling, it will only be because you throw me out and if that happens I shall arrange for a rich lover with a Rolls-Royce and a representative of the *News of the World* to be present. You've got me, poppet, and you've got me for life.'

Perhaps she was punishing him for not letting her come out to Gibraltar. She was apt to do that sort of thing, feeling she was owed, working out an elaborate balance-sheet in her mind, taking some extraordinary action and telling him afterwards that it was all his fault. There was only one way to keep her happy and that was to be with her day and night. Whenever he found himself thinking along those lines, a sour, resentful feeling took possession of him. There was a conflict between the sort of person Pam was and the sort of life she was able to lead. It got neither of them anywhere and simply made for unhappiness. They should have had a family right at the start. Yet of all the girls he had ever known, Pam was the least maternal.

His premonition on the way into harbour proved to be true. There was a cable from her mother. 'Against best advice,' it read, 'Pam crewing in Yacht *Balthazar* to Gibraltar expected arrival August 4 via Bordeaux.' He put down the cable and stared out at the Rock. A feeling of blind rage overtook him. Was she quite out of her mind? Had she no sense of occasion? Had he not drummed into her head time and time again that if a war was coming, it would begin in August as the last one had done? And here she was traipsing off on the Valentine's yacht—with a wealthy, mad, irresponsible Irishman and his American wife whom they had met one year at Fowey, both of whom David disliked on principle. 'Expected arrival August 4.' A fine appropriate date! Serve her right if history repeated itself to the day. Still seething with anger he changed into plain-clothes and set off ashore. He felt like having a great deal to drink.

3

He walked to the Yacht Club. He liked stretching his legs after a cramped day on the bridge. He had always taken exercise of some kind in the Dog Watches since his cadet days. It released the knots of pressure and worry, which command of a destroyer set up in his mind. Now in addition there was this news about Pam. What could he do? Obviously nothing at this stage. There she was in the *Balthazar* and here he was in Gibraltar. If they arrived on time she would be here in two days. Where was she to stay? Certainly not in the yacht. It was a sizeable ketch but after a passage out from England couped up at close quarters with the Valentines and other unknowns, the sooner he took her out of that milieu the better. That she might be unfaithful to him never entered his mind. She was a one-man girl, or at any rate a girl with room only for one man at a time. But both the Valentines were as self-centred, in different ways, as Pam was herself. Sooner or later they would clash and a violent row would result. Then where was she to stay? He could not afford the Rock: the Bristol was full and other Gibraltar hotels grim and disagreeable. As he thought about this problem, his resentment came flooding back. He had enough on his hands without having to cast around for a home for his wife.

It was a busy evening at the Yacht Club. There were groups outside among the tubbed geraniums on the concrete terrace running down to the water, there was a group inside that had obviously spent the afternoon playing bridge and there were other clusters of people round the bar. *Forthright* had got in earlier from the day's exercises and Bill Downey was at the bar, limbering up with two other chaps from the flotilla. Hobart and Cornelia were there with Grace and Boofles: and even the younger sister, Rosita, talking to a dark, good-looking man with a cynical twist to his face. David made his way over to

Hobart's group. He saw Grace become aware of him and almost imperceptibly stiffen like a cat scenting danger. He saw Millingham's frown change to a supercilious cordiality. He saw Hobart's restless eye taking in the effect of his arrival and it was Hobart who welcomed him to the group.

'You've just missed Honourable Excellency the Uncle,' he said as David nodded and greeted the others; 'he and the A.D.C. went for a spin in the Admiral's Barge.'

'They went bathing,' Lance explained. 'I gather H.E. scorns the *hoi polloi* of Rosia Plage and since the launch *Eliott* has no engines at present, the Navy came to the rescue. You might say a gubernatorial immersion party took place in British territorial waters.'

'Fat Barclay as well? That must have been a sight.'

'The Admiral has been in Spain riding among the cork-trees with the Duke of Solterra.'

'Without his Flag-Lieutenant?'

'Surprising as it may seem, without his Flag-Lieutenant. Now, Captain Evers, give us the news from the great outside world. How was the sea? What is it like to *live*?'

'The sea has one more kedge anchor in it this evening than it had when the day started,' David said, talking to Lance but watching Grace out of the corner of his eye. She *was* pretty but not in the pinched-up, rather tricksy way that Pam was. She had a dark, even beauty and a strong animal magnetism he had scarcely noticed before. He could feel its pull on him now.

'Ah!' said Lance in his affected voice, 'carelessness with His Majesty's nautical stores is a crime punishable in Gibraltar with ten days' torture by paper-work. Describe on fifty forms the painful incident.'

'We simply threw the thing overboard,' David replied.

'Omitting to tie the other end of the string?'

'Exactly.'

'Tch! tch! tch!' Lance announced to the others. 'Guilty of not treasuring his anchors—just what the Admiral likes on a Monday morning.'

'In the meantime,' David said deciding to change the subject, 'I seem to have lost a wife.'

'Whose?' said Lance, quick as a flash.' Not your own, surely?'

David was aware of Hobart, Cornelia, Lance and Grace all looking at him with greater attention. Sensing the undertone Hobart immediately jumped in.

'How do you do it? I'm always trying to get rid of Cornelia. It never seems to work out.'

'The system is this,' David said after a long pull at his glass of Scotch. 'You first of all sail for a foreign clime such as Gibraltar. You then set up a world situation with the prospect of imminent war. Your wife suggests coming out and joining you. You cable back "No". You then pause for a week or two in silence, to discover in the meantime that your wife has joined a yacht as a member of the crew and is *en route* to the Rock via the Bay of Biscay and points south. Expected Time of Arrival of the party in question August the fourth.'

'Hm!' said Hobart, 'and what is the name of the yacht?'

'The *Balthazar*, owned by a rather fancy Irishman called Valentine.'

'Oh! you haven't lost her,' Hobart said with a laugh, 'she merely happens to be at Tangier.'

'What?'

'The *Balthazar's* a white schooner, isn't she? Or is it a ketch? Anyway I was over in Tangier this morning and I noticed her in the harbour. As a matter of fact I thought she was just putting to sea, but I didn't pay a lot of attention as my pilot had a rather choppy landing in his float-plane.'

Well, well, thought David, she might have cabled. Then he put the thought out of his mind. That kind of resentment got you nowhere at all. Instead the pendulum started swinging the other way and a part of him began to relish the humour of the situation.

'In that case,' he said, still aware of Grace's attention, 'I must do something about getting a room at a hotel. I expect she'll have had enough of the yacht.'

'Perhaps Valentine won't bring his boat in here at all,' Hobart said reflectively.

'Why not?'

'If the balloon goes up, it would certainly be immobilized and might possibly be requisitioned. If he's an Irishman, he mightn't like that very much.'

They all laughed at the thought and David bought another round. Already his irritation was going, transformed by the casual outlook of the others, the whisky and the friendliness he felt. Even Boofles seemed in a better mood.

'Well, I take my hat off to her,' Cornelia was saying. 'At the very least she had enterprise. We ought to catch up on that kind of trick, you and I, Grace. Why do we sit tamely at home, cooking and mending and you know what while our husbands have all the fun? Let's hitch ourselves to the first good-looking yachtsman we see and——'

'Yes?' said Hobart, 'and then?'

'Start cooking and mending and the rest of it all over again, I suppose,' Cornelia ended glumly. Then she winked at Grace, glanced at David and smiled. They liked each other. He had been to dinner two or three times at home and the children adored him. Grace watching them, wondered if either felt for the other anything of this inner turbulence which began the moment she set eyes on David. She studied Cornelia without envy or jealousy. She was one of her few non-Catholic friends. They admired each other and neither poached on the other's preserves. Grace discussed her private feelings with no one but she knew that Cornelia saw and understood the sort of trouble she was having with Lance.

'Any news of your new appointment?' Hobart asked Lance, who at once plunged into his practised satire of what took place on the receipt of an official submission in the Admiral's office. This was a moment when Grace knew she could speak to David without exciting suspicion. He had always been very careful and very good in the way he approached her. She wondered if he realized how grateful she was. She would not have supposed him much of a diplomat but he had a sense of when to speak and when to keep quiet. He had never embarrassed her on the few social occasions they had come into contact after that first astonishingly vivid meeting. He had taken pains to treat her very much as one of the crowd, never to talk to her straight away at any party, never to give Lance any opportunity to suspect their real feelings. Or rather her real feelings. She did not know how he felt. Yet from a sudden unexpected response, a slight movement of the head, a quick

[105]

light in the eye, she guessed that he still found her attractive. But whether it had any of this scorching fire which blazed up afresh and raced through her veins whenever she saw him, she did not know.

'How's your mother?' she heard him asking. Her mother's illness was always a safe conversational gambit.

'Just the same. If she does too much, she pays for it by having to stay in bed. She's not a very good patient, I'm afraid.'

'What will you do if Lance gets a sea-going appointment?'

'What any naval wife does. Wail at the bar until he returns. You know the principle—men must work and women must weep.'

It was not a very funny remark but it came out sharply and it made David smile. She was surprised and pleased. Through living with Lance, who protected himself behind a quick, sharp tongue and who always got his pointed reaction in first, she had found herself getting duller and duller, unwilling to compete. It was a pleasure to find she could still light up under the stimulus of male attention.

'Shall I ask her which bar?' Cornelia chipped in, 'so you can stick around?'

'Thank you,' David replied, 'I have a wailer of my own—over in Tangier.'

She looked at Cornelia with a touch of resentment. This was between David and herself. It called for quick action.

'If you're stumped for accommodation,' she said, 'we would be delighted to give your wife a bed either at San Roque or at Line Wall Road. After all, now Daddy's an A.D.C. and your uncle the Gov it's really just keeping it in the family, isn't it? I'll talk to mother tonight but I know she'll be delighted.'

'It's very kind of you.'

'And when she's through with the palaces and the caviare circuit,' Cornelia said, 'there's a spare room at Rosia Bay—very convenient for the bathing.'

'I'm confused by all this hospitality,' David said. When he really smiled he looked ten years younger. Her heart warmed to him in a sudden rush so that she had to fight hard not to throw her arms round his neck and kiss his bony, severe-looking features. At moments like these she had a longing to touch him, to feel his hard barrel of a chest against her own softness, to surrender to his strength and in so doing let him fulfil and be fulfilled, renew and be renewed. She tossed her head quickly as though she had dived badly into the sea and her eyes were full of salt-water. That way lay illusion and hopelessness, the prime carnal sin so roundly condemned by the Church, the broad, slippery slope to hell. As she came out of this giddy little daydream, she found both David and her husband looking at her, Hobart having gone to the bar for another round.

'I'm afraid I wasn't listening,' she said. 'What were you saying?'

'The gallant Commander was commenting on the world situation,' Lance said, 'and particularly as it seems to be affecting the 28th Destroyer Flotilla.'

'We should be joining the Med Fleet in a fortnight's time,' David went on, 'but there's a strong lower-deck buzz that the Home Fleet needs our support. The ship's company of *Firesprite* have in mind a patrol off Spithead as their principal role in the coming struggle. Perhaps you'll be joining us, Boofles. Or are you set on something larger and more luxurious?'

'When I get back to the Signal School,' Lance said airily, 'I shall shop around.'

'Quite so,' David agreed. 'At our age and in our delicate state of health, we can't afford to take just any old job. We have to be careful.'

'If you go,' Hobart asked as he handed round more drinks, 'who's going to look after the Rock?'

'There's always the *Cormorant*,' Lance said. 'When I get home I shall speak to the First Sea Lord. I'll ask him to spare you the *Hood* and a couple of battleships. Will that do?'

'Send us the *Ark Royal*,' Hobart said, unconsciously prophetic. 'I have a feeling that a few friendly aircraft in the vicinity of Gibraltar would buck us all up: though don't let the C.R.A. hear about this.'

'You pongos always go for the Christian names and initials,' David remarked. '*What* is C.R.A.?'

'The Commander, Royal Artillery,' Lance said, springing to attention and giving a terrific salute, 'the officer charged with the anti-aircraft defence of the Rock. Haven't you seen one

[107]

of his Guy Fawkes benefits? Remind me to get you a grand-stand seat out at Europa next Thursday night. Evening dress and tin helmets will be worn.'

One of the Club servants came up to Lance who excused himself and went to the phone. As he walked away Grace instinctively looked at David. She found him smiling at her. Again her heart seemed to turn over. He understood. But there was nothing she could say, with Hobart and Cornelia very much present, no way at that time of taking it further. There they both were, imprisoned by passing time, by the conventions, by the very responsibility with which they conducted themselves. It was as though her life was being lived for her by the intricate feminine machine in which it was trapped. For a moment the wild idea that she could burst out and run away took possession of her, run away and be free.

'If the war comes,' she said, looking out at the ships in the harbour, 'I wonder what will happen to us?'

'You'll be mobilized,' Hobart said.

'*I* shall?'

'All women will be, unless there are very small children to look after—men, women, boys, girls, cats, dogs—we shall need them all. Remember the Kitchener poster?' He pointed his forefinger straight at her. 'Your country needs you. This time if war comes everyone's going to be in it. Think of Guernica, think of Madrid and Barcelona—the way they were bombed from the air is the way it's going to be, only a hundred times worse. The Spanish Civil War was simply an experiment by the Germans and the Italians—and the Russians.'

'The trouble is,' David put in, 'that no one really knows what it's all about. I'll guarantee that not one sailor aboard *Firesprite* could tell you what we would be fighting for. They're in a daze. They don't like the way Hitler and Musso go on—but on the other hand, they say, look what they've done for their countries. They're strong and we're weak. Especially after Munich.'

'For the love of Mike,' Cornelia said, 'let's keep off Munich. If ever there was a conversation-stopper it's that word. Personally if war comes I intend running a shop.'

[108]

'Now that's interesting,' Hobart said, 'and quite new to me. What would you sell?'

'Candy.' She looked belligerently at her husband and then gave in. 'All right, then—sweets.'

'Will you go back to the States?' Grace asked.

'Not unless I'm made to by this mean old Security Man.' She looked at her husband affectionately. 'We don't see eye to eye about that sort of thing. I want to stay. He wants to get rid of us all.'

Lance returned, frowning importantly. He was very obviously the Flag-Lieutenant.

'The Admiral wants me up at the Mount,' he said; 'can you look after yourself for a bit?'

'I'll try,' said Grace. 'What shall we do about dinner?'

'We might have it here. I'll be back as soon as I can.'

'We'll look after her,' said Hobart, 'while you run Fat Barclay's bath for him or blow his nose or whatever it is flag-lieutenants do for their admirals at this time of day.'

'It's certainly not what you think,' said Lance and walked quickly away. He did not like being jeered at even though Hobart did it without malice. Grace, too, felt she ought to rally to her husband's aid.

'One of these days, Himmlet, someone's going to tell you a few home truths,' she said, 'you great, big, ugly bully.'

Cornelia linked her arm in her husband's and gave it a squeeze.

'It's only jealousy. Lance gave him such a hammering at tennis this afternoon. Come along, dear, I want a word with the Aldersons about next Tuesday—if you'll excuse us,' she said with a private little smile at Grace. They moved away, leaving Grace and David alone. Grace silently blessed her, yet at once fell into a dither. It was a magical opportunity yet now that they could say what they liked to each other, an awkwardness settled upon her. She did not know how to make the first move even though her heart cried out to communicate its feeling. She glanced at David and then unhappily at the floor. This was absurd. He looked as tongue-tied as she was. He cleared his throat and then said:

'I shouldn't say this, I know . . .' then he stopped. The pause grew in awkwardness and feeling.

[109]

'Go on,' she said softly, 'say what it was.'

He cleared his throat again and fiddled with his drink.

'It sounds so awful. But you do something desperate to me. I . . . I don't know how to put it.'

She was blushing scarlet, the back of her neck was on fire and her cheek-bones burned. She hadn't blushed like this for years. This was embarrassing, awful, not at all how it should be going.

'I don't know what it is,' he went on, 'except that I feel we know each other very well indeed. Almost too well.'

'What does that mean?'

She was still looking at the floor.

'I'm not sure except that it's a complication I know I don't want—and I'll bet you don't either—certainly not at this time or place. . . .' He stopped again, casting about in his mind for a way to express what he felt. 'We neither of us asked for this,' he faltered, 'but it's almost as if we belonged to each other—and of course that's quite absurd,' he went on at a gallop. 'I mean we're both happily married and you're a Catholic and—well, that's all there is to it. Why don't you say something? I feel an absolute fool.'

She looked up at him steadily in the eyes.

'You're not a fool,' she said, 'you're a good person. I feel it too. Very strongly.'

'Do you, Grace?'

'Yes, David, I do.'

It was the first time they had used each other's names. Again she studied the parquet flooring of the Yacht Club. All around the murmur of conversation, the occasional outburst of laughter continued. In the midst of the crowd they were quite alone.

'It's this extraordinary familiarity,' he went on. 'I feel I know you inside out—that I've always known you . . . and yet it's ridiculous. I mean you're Boofles' wife and that's about the real extent of my knowledge.'

She gave him a distressed, stricken look. She ached to touch him, to be in his arms, to be away somewhere by themselves. She managed an unhappy little smile, quite unable to put into words the depths of her feeling.

[110]

'It's a yearning, isn't it?' he said lamely. 'Oh! dear, isn't it awful when you can't say what you want to about anything at all.'

'Don't say any more,' Grace said in a low voice, 'and give me a cigarette. I don't want to burst into tears.'

She took a cigarette, trying to stop her hands trembling. It was a near thing. By the light of the match he saw that her eyes were wet and this had a numbing effect on them both. There *was* nothing to say.

'Let me get you another drink,' he said, taking her glass.

'Thanks.'

Out of the corner of his eye he saw Hobart and Cornelia coming back. Then something else happened which for a moment froze him rigid, as though he'd been struck by lightning. The door of the Yacht Club opened and Pam came in, followed by the Valentines and another couple he did not know. She was wearing black trousers, tight-cut over the hips, and a white shirt with a wide, extravagant collar. She looked round half-vaguely, half-petulantly, and then turned to say something to the Valentines. Her long fair hair had been bleached by the sun and her skin was a biscuit brown. There was no doubt she looked ravishingly attractive.

'Good Lord!' said David, half to himself, 'she's arrived.' Grace followed his gaze and with almost the same sense of shock knew at once who it was.

'Is that your wife?' she asked.

'Yes,' David said, 'that's Pam. Excuse me a minute.'

She watched him walk across to the group, she watched them kiss and hug each other, she watched him shaking hands with the rest of the party, all talking hard, all trying to say too much at once. Then she felt a hand in the crook of her elbow followed by a gentle squeeze. She looked round to find Hobart smiling at her and saying:

'I think we could all do with a very strong drink. Give me your glass.'

VI

OF all the polyglot refugee population then in Gibraltar, Nicholas Pappadopoulos was perhaps the most mixed-up and unhappy. This was no sudden condition in his life but in August 1939 it came boiling to a crisis. In fact the 22nd August 1939 was to date the worst day he could remember having endured in the whole of his troubled existence. It was a day of the maximum internal confusion, a day in which he felt sick at heart, a day when he could no longer put off a basic reassessment of the whole creed in which he had so far believed.

There were two reasons for this—both of them highly unpalatable. The day before, Molotov and von Ribbentrop had signed a non-aggression pact which had dumbfounded the world and especially the left wing *aficionados* to which Pappadopoulos belonged. The other item of news was personal but equally tedious and depressing—Rosita had informed him she thought she was pregnant.

Fortin had not been far out in imagining that the Cypriot background and English education had combined to turn a sensitive idealist into a thwarted young man full of hate. Despite a considerable individuality, Nicholas Pappadopoulos had long lived within the huge 'abstract calculation' of Communism and its paler sister in those despondent years of the late nineteen-thirties. He believed body and soul in socialism. The theory was fair and just, the world ripe for its application. The glowing sense of crusading for the betterment of those who could not better themselves fed upon hatred of rank and privilege, class in all its guises and the whole paraphernalia of the outmoded aristocratic idea.

When the Spanish Civil War had broken out, Nicholas saw it as a golden chance. Instead of talking he could do something practical at last. He abandoned the writing of 'quota quickies' for the British film industry and joined up in the International Brigade. This brought him almost immediately into close working contact with the Communist cells then taking over control of the Republican side. At first there had been no conflict of ideas. All means justified the end: the great incorruptible theory wrapped them all up like a cosy blanket. At last the workers of the world really were uniting to fight in one particular trouble spot and heroic death could be had at the barricades.

Then gradually an incident, a tiny doubt, an avoidable mistake nevertheless persisted in, began to form a pattern of distrust in his mind. He had never been a card-carrying Communist but he believed whole-heartedly in the soundness of Marxist philosophy. Now he saw this structure daily distorted to suit expediency and the Party line with a callousness which disturbed him. He saw a total indifference to human suffering provided that it was the Fascists who were suffering: he saw awkward but sincere objectors hurried away to the most dangerous parts of the front: he saw even the faintest opposition to the Party will ruthlessly suppressed however commonsensical the suggestion provoking it might have been. He saw how a murder was a Fascist atrocity if done by the Falange but an impartial necessity if done by the Republican side. The ideas of justice which had drawn him to the Left were constantly affronted and at times outraged. Only faith in the greater god of world socialism allowed him to continue working with the dehumanized intellectuals in whose company he now found himself. The dislike and contempt became mutual. Of a somewhat arrogant nature himself he did not enjoy coming up against the scorn of professional Communists and the Red Army cadres behind them.

By the time the Axis powers had prevailed and had got Franco to Madrid, Nicholas had had enough. He was still a militant socialist. Those ideas would never change but now he had seen a little of the real nature of Communism. He had been taught that Russia was the only truly socialist state in the world, the only place where the pure Marxist creed was put into daily use. This might still be so but he personally had begun to doubt it. He did not respect the Communists under whom he had worked. He was aware that like and dislike had nothing to do with Party discipline. He saw that there

[113]

had to be discipline. It was the blindness of its abuses which dismayed him.

So he had made his way, not with the tide to France but against it, through the Fascist hinterland, to Andalusia and Gibraltar. He needed time to think and to rest. Both Myra Heisenberg and the sub-editing job had arrived at opportune moments. It might seem a little absurd to have gone to Spain to fight for the world revolution and to have ended up as sub-editor of a small newspaper in the Colony of Gibraltar but Nicholas did not see it that way. It gave him an independence and Myra, whom he had known in Barcelona, was glad to share both his bed and the pause in their lives.

But Myra had returned to further work for the Party in France when her Gibraltar labour permit had not been renewed. Myra had urged him to come with her to Paris and then on to New York. One fight had failed: there were others to be started. But Nicholas's disillusionment had gone deeper than she suspected and when in addition she attacked, with understandable jealousy, the spontaneous love and admiration showered on him by Rosita, she only hastened her own departure. He did not love Rosita any more than he had loved Myra. One was practised and demanding, the other eager and inexperienced. But the bed was a solace. It helped to restore his self-esteem. It had its place. It was no longer the dazzling, shuddering adventure which Rosita had experienced that first afternoon, but the sexual worship she gave him, the satisfaction of having as a clandestine mistress the much-prized younger daughter of one of the Gibraltar oligarchs—all these different factors made up an agreeable state of affairs to Nicholas Pappadopoulos. It was a time of escape, a time of indulgence, a time when the hard facts both of life and of his political creed could be for the moment shelved.

Now, after a summer of personal relaxation against a background of mounting tension in world affairs, a double blow had fallen. Russia had finally betrayed him by coming to terms with Hitler. The Spanish Civil War might as well never have been fought. With Rosita the pendulum had abruptly swung from careless rapture to the most gnawing anxiety. An afternoon with the closed shutters and her young fervent body straining to his had been difficult to achieve but had paid off richly in pleasure to both of them. Now he dodged her every approach. He was not there when she slipped in anxiously to knock at his door in her jodhpurs or tennis clothes, dressed to simulate whatever it was she was supposed to be doing. He avoided the Yacht Club where she had got him a temporary membership. It was true that he still had to sit at his sub-editor's desk from seven-thirty onwards at night but now he had arranged advance warning of her arrival along the terrace of the Garrison Library and was able to be 'engaged with the Editor' until she could wait no longer and had gone. One session of agonized recrimination in the alley-way, where such a short time before their most passionate encounters had taken place, was enough to make him determined to disentangle himself at the earliest possible moment.

A part of him felt badly about Rosita and regretted the anxiety and distress she was suffering. He would help if he could. But it had been her fault in the first place that she was in the situation at all. She had made all of the running herself: he had warned her, he had never encouraged her, never once had he suggested a date nor asked her to come to his room. The more he thought back on it, the more obvious it became that she had practically forced herself on him. Well, he was sorry for her, but there was nothing he could do about it at all. She had had her pleasure and now she was paying the price. The Russian betrayal and now this local news formed a nice filthy bog of despair in his mind. Perhaps he should pack up and go: perhaps he should be moving elsewhere: but if a world war was coming what could he do? and where could he go? This was a time when he needed a friend. Unfortunately friendship was not a commodity he had bothered with very much. He felt very much alone.

2

The distress felt by Nicholas Pappadopoulos came nowhere near the inner turmoil in which the Barbarossa family viewed the onset of war. The Señora's heart condition had not improved and her activities were still restricted. Indeed, being

[115]

the wife of the Honorary A.D.C. had not worked out at all as expected.

The number of formal Government House functions had been drastically reduced and General Fortin had not made her as free of the place as she could have wished. Nor was this accidental. He had given it out publicly, and had even had his statement printed in the *Gazette*, that in view of the European crisis, as he called it, he wished the social life of Gibraltar curtailed in keeping with the situation. He had not defined exactly what this meant but had suggested that there were more important topics to think about than 'balls, parties and picnics'. To Edie this was almost a mortal blow and when, on top of it, her son-in-law had announced his imminent departure to Portsmouth for a short signal course prior to a sea-going appointment, it seemed as though her world was falling apart.

She knew nothing of the continuing panic in which her younger daughter had begun to live but she had scotched the idea of her going to England, should war break out, in order to join one of the women's Services. There was plenty to be done in Gibraltar. The right kind of volunteers were sought for the censorship organization then being set up. The naval authorities had let it be known that they needed suitable ladies down at the Dockyard Tower to cope with the vastly increased cypher traffic now already flowing into Gibraltar. There was always the Red Cross. The British Consul in Malaga, a friend of the family, had need of an assistant. Jaime's brother in Madrid could be relied on to find both accommodation and employment for Grace and Rosita should the distaff side of the family move to Madrid as Jaime had at one time been planning. No, she had made it clear, there could be no question of Rosita rushing off to England, and while her control over Grace was less direct, she made it equally plain that her duty, too, was to stay with her mother at San Roque or, if Spain looked like falling into Hitler's hands, then in the Line Wall House in Gibraltar.

'Requisition' was a word which had recently made its way into everyday speech and the threat of having to cede part of the house or take in strangers had suddenly hit them. Until then *la Señora* had not enjoyed having the Evers in their Gibraltar house. Despite the close Government House connection she could see little to commend either David, whom she regarded as a rather ordinary threadbare naval officer, or his frivolous scatter-brained wife. She had been surprised when Grace had invited them to stay. She was not impressed with either. Now, however, with requisitioning in the air, to have naval guests in the house had suddenly taken on new possibilities. Edie did not suppose that rationing would worry them much, but if it was to come then the bigger the household the better for them all. Her manner to Pam Evers thawed and instead of maintaining a discreet silence whenever the young woman suggested that she must soon move back to England or on to Malta (in that vague peacetime thinking, that was already so out of date), she urged her to stay for as long as she liked: indeed, she continued, until the war settled down and the whereabouts of her husband's flotilla was known—why not a job with the cypher organization at the Dockyard Tower? Everyone would have to make some kind of war effort.

Jaime Barbarossa watched his household as he watched his business, with anxiety and uncertainty, trying to see a daily way through the fog. He had taken a liking to David Evers. He admired him and privately wished he could have had a son-in-law of his kind rather than that fancy little snob Edie had chosen. But the dominant factor in his daily life was the speed with which events on a world scale pressed in on each other. Everything was in a state of flux. Shipping companies altered schedules and cancelled contracts. Staff was being called up. Soon Lance would have gone and so, too, would David Evers and his pretty young wife. He had privately counselled Grace to travel with her husband to England if she wished. Her first loyalty was to Lance and that must come before any natural concern for her mother. He had not told Edie. He knew her views only too well but the war would soon be changing them. He sensed more clearly than anyone in the household how the coming period of siege would strip away their lives to essentials.

Grace, too, though outwardly calm, spent her days rushing from meetings to farewell parties, her nights in a final attempt both to recapture the early love between Lance and herself and also to create something strong enough to carry them over the coming break. This was a total failure: he scarcely had power to arouse, let alone satisfy. Night by night her craving for simple physical love grew like a monstrous thirst. Moreover, to be aware that elsewhere in the house David was accomplishing only too well what Lance could not even bother to try filled her with a sickening envy. Until now envy and jealousy had rarely entered her consciousness. Now, however, as Lance turned his brown, beautiful back on her with a murmur and went off to sleep, she would lie for hours, her arms under her head, her naked body wracked with desire, watching the moon on its slow journey across the palm-trees of the patio, listening to her heart-beats and the irritating chirrup of the crickets.

However things were not as idyllic in the guest-room as Grace had imagined. The future bore down on the present, taking the edge off pleasure, unsettling their minds, disturbing the shortened tranquillity their love-making brought them. Pam was as insatiable as ever, unable to sleep, waking him with her ivy fingers as the whim took her. But now she was finding everything soured. She accused him of keeping his mind on other things. When they were in bed together, she was fond of telling him, other things should cease to exist.

But late in August 1939 the world unfortunately refused to respond to her specifically selfish ideas. The ship, the next day's exercises, the vaguely defined problems of the coming war could not be put out of mind by the touch of her clinging lips. This in turn made her angry. She accused him of thinking more of his ship than of herself and was paralysed with surprise when he blithely agreed. It was a shock. In periods of stress she was prepared to pay lip-service to the idea that other things could for a moment or two be more important than herself. When this was proved to be roundly true, she was horrified.

She had always resented the Navy except as a pretty pastime. Now she began to hate what it was doing to her life. She pointed out that she had not come all this way to Gibraltar to be neglected and put in the second place and when David told her frankly that it would have been better if she had not come at all, she was pained and hurt. She could not believe the Royal Navy to be her rival. She could not form the idea in her mind. She was prepared to suspect another woman but only in circumstances which she knew did not exist. In her private thoughts she esteemed her sexual prowess to such an extent that an unfaithful husband was inconceivable. It never occurred to her that David might begin to find her possessive and stupidly demanding. He would never look elsewhere. She knew she made David happy in bed, and that was the heart of the matter.

It was in Rosita's room, however, that confusion, disturbance, a sense of personal danger, panic, uncertainty, the breaking of familiar habits and patterns—in fact everything that the war would soon be doing to individuals all over the world—raged round and round. Elsewhere on the Rock, tired shopkeepers, drunken sailors and elderly maiden ladies might lie peacefully sleeping, digesting one day's experience and restoring their energies for the next. Not so Rosita. She could not sleep: she scarcely relaxed. She was trapped. She could see no way out and fear fed on her young consciousness like some lascivious old witch in a fairy tale.

To put a keener edge on her pain came the realization that her love for Nicky had been nothing but illusion. The burning adoration she had sought to express had been casually accepted and lightly returned, but now that she looked to him for help and support, for some sign that he cared about her condition, she realized that she was quite alone.

Her love changed to contempt. She began to hate him and to hate herself. The bland, exciting lover had proved under stress to be nothing but a callous coward. That she had actually run after him, had almost forced her virginal body into his arms, now made her as psychologically sick as she was physically so in the morning. The violence and war about to break out in a few days' time was mirrored in the turbulence of her being as she lay tossing and turning through the hot August nights.

3

Outwardly Gibraltar itself changed very little. Indeed Seale, who had taken to keeping a diary, remarked more than once on the ability of Gibraltar to absorb into its narrow, winding streets, its steeply rising ramps, noisy with life, a boat-load of tourists or the ship's companies of two battle-cruisers without in any way bursting at the seams. Indeed, in Seale's opinion, the presence of Royal Marines and sailors, in that order, gave the Rock a comfortably furnished appearance.

It was true that the officers and men now to be seen in unexpected quarters at all hours of the day and night, were more likely to be permanencies connected with the role Gibraltar would play in the war than transit visitors. 'Boom Defence', 'Contraband Control' and the 'Sea Transport Organization' were now as frequently in people's thoughts and on people's lips as the Gibraltar Cricket Club's Flannel Dances at the Pavilion or evening Band-Concerts from the terrace of the Garrison Library. The Annual Swimming Competition of Girl Guides might as usual take place at the Warrant Officers' and Senior N.C.O.'s Bathing Establishment, the Alameda Cinema might offer chairs in the summer evenings at fivepence a time to witness the 'wonderful, musical super-production, English Talking *Chu-Chin-Chow*, with Anna May Wong and George Robey' but the clientele viewing it would have Censorship or Swept Channels or the preparations of Torpedo Warheads very near the forefront of their minds.

'You ask me what Gibraltar is like,' Seale wrote home to his father, 'and whether it's changed since you and mother were here just after the Great War. Except for the Rock Hotel and a couple of big blocks of flats I shouldn't think you'd notice any difference at all. Perhaps there are one or two more Indian shops selling cheap scent and Japanese silk along Main Street. The gharries are still drawn by decrepit horses and leathery, smelly old drivers. The Universal, the Royal and the Trocadero Cafés are still full of beer-drinking sailors, and "Daily Concerts by Famous Orchestras composed of English and French Ladies" are still the rather dubious attraction. From the look of some of these ladies I should imagine they were here long before your visit and there is one of particular notoriety known as the "Manchester Cow" who bangs away at an ancient piano in a ghastly, tassellated dress.

' "Society" life still revolves round the horse—odd, really, when you visualize how cramped and cluttered up Gibraltar's total area of just over two square miles has become, the bulk of

[120]

which is, and of course always must be, the bare rock itself. But the Royal Calpe Hunt, which the Civil War in Spain nearly finished off for good, has been resuscitated (it is still across the border at Campamento but the money for it, as always, comes from Gib) and the race-course at North Front is still going strong.

'The apes still steal anything they can get their hands on and Freddy Smallbones, the Military Secretary, who considers he has proprietary rights on the Upper Rock, saw one of them making off with the blades of his windscreen-wiper: as there are no spares to be had on the Rock unless you are on very good terms with the Head Ape, Freddy gave chase. This resulted in a sprained ankle and some typical Gib exasperation. Just as Freddy was about to pounce on the ape, who had the blade in one hand and an orange in the other, the ape began to do something *very* curious with the blade to his brother or his sister (or possibly his grandmother). Anyway Freddy was so fascinated by this performance that he abandoned the blade, returning to the car just in time to see another ape make off with the filler cap of his petrol tank. There are dark stories that one of the garages has an arrangement with the apes and that you can buy back your stolen spare parts at a special price a few days later but I'm not sure this is true.

'Of course Gib *is* very full. Refugees are still coming in and although it's against the law to harbour them in secret, the fine is still only a shilling or two so that you get cases, such as Emilio Fernandez in today's paper. Emilio was charged with "knowingly harbouring a Spaniard, to wit Maria Teresa Pilar, not duly authorized to be in Gibraltar, between the 18th and 22nd June at his house in Willis Road, contrary to section 16 of the Aliens and Strangers Ordinance, Chapter 5". Nothing much to that, you would think, but the accused was further charged with allowing the said alien to be delivered of a child (it's difficult to see how ' could have prevented it) without having previously obtained the special sanction of H.E. the Governor. This was highly reprehensible as the brat will now have British nationality, but when the accused explained that he had committed this crime "for humanity's sake" the fine was four shillings and another problem was dumped in the

Welfare Officer's lap. However, refugees are no longer the problem they were a few months ago. For better or for worse Franco has Spain completely under control and unless Hitler invades the country (and us!) the wretched Spaniards are likely to have their hands full for the next few years just staying alive and repairing the damage.

'H.E. is in fine form and has not had another attack of malaria for over a month. The Admiral and the Colonial Secretary continue to be our principal pain in the neck, but both Brigadiers and the C.R.A. are a hundred per cent and an Air-Commodore is due to arrive any moment to advise about making an airstrip on the race-course at North Front. We're not sure how the Spaniards will react to that one. The Colonial Secretary holds that it doesn't matter a hoot what the Spaniards think and he may be right: they've certainly fortified their stretch of the neutral territory which they had no right to do—General Eliott's requirement after the Great Siege being that they should keep at a distance of a gun-shot from the Rock. Of course a gun-shot then and now are two different things, but at the moment they can pop out of their tiny Maginot Line defences within a few feet of the frontier.

'H.E.'s nephew—David Evers, the chap I once did a commission with in *Caradoc*, is here. He has command of *Firesprite*, one of the new "F" class destroyers. I've had a couple of days at sea with him to blow out the cobwebs and thoroughly enjoyed it. He looks a bit craggy, like his uncle, but he has a chocolate-box-pretty wife who came out to Gib in an Irishman's yacht—the Irishman, needless to say, took one look at Gib in its present mood and sailed on to the south of France as soon as he could. The Evers are staying with the Barbarossas (The father I told you about has now thawed out completely and treats me as a friend.) and I've had several meals with them. Madame is pretty good hell—social chatter and bridge most of the time and very much Queen of her Castle, but the two daughters are good value. The elder one, who made a curiously ill-assorted marriage with the Flag-Lieutenant, is quiet, dark, and in a Spanish way ravishingly beautiful. The younger one has the mother's fire and also has most of Gibraltar under thirty-five running after her. I asked H.E. if I could take her on as a gash secretary at Government House but I'm afraid he wouldn't wear that one—at least not yet. He says she's too like her mother and one of that calibre is enough. The truth is, I think, that H.E.'s just a tiny bit afraid of Madame. In fact he only lets her into G.H. because Jaime Barbarossa is such a touchstone in local affairs.

'Nobody quite knows what will happen if war does break out. The defences of the Rock are impressive but there's an awful lot of valuable dockyard exposed in a tempting position. H.E. is always saying that the English quality is an ability to improvise in the face of disaster but that the peacetime tendency is to sit back and do nothing until suddenly an emergency is on us and, as usual, we're caught with our trousers down. It's this attitude that he fights all the time. For instance he has astonished the Admiral with his enthusiasm for burrowing into the Rock. Air-raid shelters are going up—or rather going into all parts of the Rock—and H.E. is determined to build a whole bomb-proof H.Q. inside the Rock. (To me it's incredible that it doesn't already exist but there it is, it costs money and for one reason or another it's never been done.) You would think that here is a subject that everyone could be unanimous about. Not a bit of it. Red tape in the Dockyard, red tape in the supply side of the Army, so that if soldiers are told off for the work the necessary tools are not forthcoming, red tape about whose headquarters it would be (For instance access would be through the Dockyard but the Army would maintain it and provide the communications.) etc., etc., etc. I suppose the war will suddenly bring a sense of urgency into the game but at present H.E.'s terse expression and his energy are the only active factors operating on the spongy mass of parsimonious, penny-watching inertia which is what official Gibraltar looks like to me. As always it is the fear of the Treasury auditor which nips any initiative in the bud. Blood and sweat are cheap but money is not.

'It's Sunday morning and now it's time for church. The Royal Marine band from the First Cruiser Squadron will be playing in the Protestant Cathedral and as I went to early Mass, I shall attend the heretics in my official capacity as A.D.C. to the Governor. Then the Barbarossas have asked both H.E.

and the Admiral to lunch at their San Roque house and no doubt afterwards we shall go along the Malaga road and find somewhere to bathe. It would be a wonderful life, if there wasn't a war somewhere ahead. . . .'

4

Though neither was aware of it, Fortin and his A.D.C. went to the Cathedral service with much the same train of thought in their heads. Seale had been writing to his father; Fortin reading a letter written by one of his predecessors, a Lord Tyrawley, to Henry Fox in 1756. His Lordship in a different day and age had exactly mirrored Fortin's own conclusions on this the Sunday immediately prior to the outbreak of war.

His Lordship had written: 'You will find that I am not so thoroughly satisfied that Gibraltar is so formidable a place as the common cry thinks it; but that it would want time, money and ability in the distribution of both to make it so. That Gibraltar is the strongest town in the world, that one Englishman can beat three Frenchmen and that London Bridge is one of the seven wonders of the world are the natural prejudices of an English coffee-house politician. I am doing some little matters here that add, I think, to the strength of it; but much more ought to be done that I cannot take upon myself to work upon without orders. I really grow intolerably weary of Gibraltar, which is in all respects upon the most scandalous foot that ever town was, that pretends to call itself *une place de guerre*; though so exactly consistent with our notions of this sort of thing, that I assure myself it will never take any other form.'

Thanks to the aircraft and the long-range gun, Gibraltar was no longer the impregnable fortress that coffee-house politicians once let themselves believe. On the other hand, Fortin reflected as he walked into Queen Adelaide's Cathedral, neither could it any longer be said that Gibraltar was 'upon a scandalous foot'. The centuries-old tradition of profiteering and chicanery in essential supplies which dated back at least to the Great Siege had been broken long before his own advent as Governor. Of the two evil characteristics of the Rock which, in 1802, had so horrified the Duke of Kent, another of his predecessors, corruption in administration had vanished and alcoholic excess had been brought under control.

From his front-row pew Fortin could not watch the congregation as he was able to from his box in the King's Chapel at Government House. This was a pity. To Fortin who did his praying in private and quite probably with greater frequency than anyone else at that time in the squat, sunny Cathedral, a church service was a good chance to study and reflect upon the people he had been appointed to govern. He glanced round as the Royal Marine orchestra from the *Sussex* and the *Devonshire* struck up 'O Worship the King, All Glorious Above,' the congregation stood up and the service began. Perhaps alcohol was a more subtle foe than he had imagined. The ninety wine shops which had so distressed the Duke of Kent (and which had so contributed to the pockets of his many illustrious predecessors) had been drastically reduced. The bawdy houses had gone and to find forenoon drunkenness in the streets was now very rare. Yet the basic situation remained. Human beings continued to demand solace for their confinement in a fortress and the colossal boredom it engendered. If Garrison Saturday could be slept off or sailed away or exercised out of the system—the consumption of alcohol in Gibraltar yet remained fantastically high and one of the doctors at the Colonial Hospital had succumbed with D.T.s a mere week ago. If a real siege ever took place again, boredom and alcohol would be the two sore points to watch.

By this time the Dean was leading the general confession, the congregation murmuring it with that sort of shamefaced roar which the English bring to their official worship in church. 'We have left undone those things which we ought to have done and we have done those things which we ought not to have done. . . .' How apt and to the point it was on every level! Would there be a guilty stirring in one or two hearts that morning before it was altogether too late? Probably not: probably as usual life would flow on, time would pass and no effort would be made because of the conviction that it would all come right in the end. 'And grant O Most Merciful Father for His Sake, that we may hereafter live a godly, righteous and sober life to the glory of Thy Holy Name, Amen.' There it was—the prayer tidied up and put away, with God carrying the responsibility and expected to look after our interests. Fortin often wondered, human nature being what it was, why effort was so little stressed: 'O God, make speed to save us: O Lord make haste to help us.' It was all very well, he reflected, as the psalm and the lesson continued, to look to the Almighty for help and guidance in times of trouble. There was much to be done by oneself and for oneself. Once again the problems of Gibraltar threatened to rise up in his mind and swamp him.

To Fortin Gibraltar was like the Ark. If the flood came it might float for a while, but certainly not if there were leaks all over the vessel. It was his job to inspect the fabric and see that the leaks were stopped. He could ginger people up. He had done a certain amount already. But, somehow or other, the idea of doing something oneself had to catch on in each individual mind before an emergency broke over their heads, before the rains began pouring down, before it was all too late.

By now one of the chaplains from the Fleet had launched into the sermon. It was on the subject of loving one's neighbour, a plea for tolerance and for realizing that other people's faults, to which we so objected, were also there, in a disguised form, in ourselves. The content was good but the chaplain saw fit to rant and declaim with the gestures of a politician. It was what he took to be the technique of 'putting it across'. He gesticulated, thumped the pulpit, brought up his intonation at the end of a sentence, leant forward and whispered confidentially, then roared like a Hyde Park revivalist. It all added up to a performance. Fortin could not recall when he had heard anything so insincere. It revolted him. He had an eye for pretentiousness, snobbery and arrogance. They were bad enough in the social life in which he now found himself involved as Governor. In church, where sincerity and humility should walk hand-in-hand, they were intolerable and at one stage it was all he could do not to get up and walk out. It was the old, old English sin—the attitude that would eventually lose us the Empire—the really dangerous Pharisee outlook. He had seen it in India, he had seen it in Waziristan and the Persian Gulf, he was finding it here in Gibraltar. The Indians had said to him: 'The English have brought us justice and built us roads but they never let us become friends.' A century ago when the aristocratic idea was still held in respect, there had been outward arrogance, pride and disdain. Three disastrous wars had made such attitudes circumspect. The Crimea, South Africa and the Great War had each of them progressively discredited the powers of leadership assumed as a divine right by the English aristocracy. Officers had been brave but hopelessly inefficient and thus, in the end, absurd. Arrogance cannot for long stand the ridicule of fact. So by 1939 haughtiness had been driven underground except in people such as the Admiral and the Colonial Secretary, but the basic attitude remained. They must not show it—it was not good form—but the English continued to be sure in themselves that their way of life, their way of doing things, was superior to anything else. You did not say it, you simply lived it. You showed it by example. You were incorruptible and you could not modify. It was this fatal attitude which made it impossible to absorb or adapt to local populations and customs. A Gibraltarian girl might marry an Englishman; where was the English girl who would condescend to marry a Gibraltarian man?

The final hymn came and then the two verses of 'God Save the King'. This was the reward for those with a taste for spectacle. This was magnificent. The Royal Marine orchestra and the organ, for once surprisingly in time, the strong male voices of soldiers and sailors swelling in depth, the surge of what was perhaps the most moving and potent anthem in the world, the sunlight pouring into the Cathedral—all these ingredients led to an emotional catharsis which swept away the deficiencies of the sermon and which sent the congregation out into the square on a wave of good feeling and warm-heartedness.

The war lay exactly one week ahead.

5

The Barbarossa estate took up a great deal of the area between Campamento and San Roque, the house itself standing among cypress and eucalyptus trees on the top of a hillock. The walls were white, the arches Moorish in style, the windows covered by delicately wrought iron grilles and the front door studded with brass like a palace in Seville. As in Gibraltar, the house looked inward on to a patio which had a fountain and was filled with palm-trees and green shrubs. There were hand-painted tiles in the hall and in a number of rooms. Large, gloomy oil-paintings of notables and ancestors of the Barbarossa family hung on the walls. Highly polished Spanish oak was the principal motif in the furniture, though Jaime's mother had specialized in Louis Quinze, and Edie herself had continued in the same French vein. The atmosphere was cool, the style severely well-bred and in no way florid. It was a house for someone of culture and of means, typical of that Spanish colonial architecture which the *conquistadores* had dotted over the west coast of South America, California and Mexico.

The Admiral and Mrs. Calderwell had already arrived by the time the Governor and his A.D.C. came up the drive in the Rolls-Royce. The Military Governor of Algeciras would be half an hour late in the Spanish habit. Lady Hallerton-Glebe, who owned the estate next door, had been ten minutes early since, despite nearly forty years in Spain, she was totally unable to shake off the influence of her father's fetish for Greenwich Mean Time. The only other guests were David Evers and his pretty, sulky-looking wife.

Jaime Barbarossa conducted his guests to a small shaded terrace giving on to the garden and here sherry was served by a white-coated butler. Edie drew Fortin and the Admiral to a seat from which a view of the Rock could be had through a fringe of palm leaves and immediately began to talk about the Gibraltar Red Cross and the knitting schedule she had already inaugurated in anticipation of the war. It seemed that whatever else the Navy might lack, mittens, mufflers and balaclava helmets were going to be available in quantity by Christmas with, of course, the same articles in khaki, she added for Fortin's benefit, so that anti-aircraft guns' crews and others in exposed positions on the Rock would not be forgotten. It was a monologue rather than a conversation and neither Fortin nor the Admiral were called on to remark; indeed Fortin found the ceaseless running of her percussive voice oddly relaxing. He murmured encouragement, counterpointing an occasional grunt from the Admiral, and allowed his thoughts to play on the Barbarossa family, on Grace gravely talking to Dicky Seale, on Rosita gesticulating to his nephew, being watched in turn by Pam in desultory conversation with the Flag-Lieutenant.

It was a typical scene, outwardly of but little significance. A number of people linked by family or official duty were gathered together at a particular place and at a particular moment in time. They would chatter, consume a few drinks, eat, take coffee, smoke, and then go their several ways. Such events happened and were happening all over the world all along time. Yet during the coming week both his nephew and young Millingham would have left Gibraltar, possibly for ever. Change was very present in the air that day. The war was coming nearer and nearer. The war, in a sense, was already there.

The sun was now high over the Rock. That breathless 1,400-foot drop of the north face lay slightly in shadow. Fortin looked through the palm-tree fringe and, while his hostess continued to chirrup on, allowed his thoughts to wander where they chose. He was aware of a feeling he had not had since Waziristan when he had drawn together a collection of desert irregulars and almost miraculously turned them into an effective military force. It was a rare feeling, compounded of a sense of personal magnetism, of conscious possession, of pride, of responsibility, of being a centurion set under authority and of knowing, as that original centurion had known, the upper and the lower limits of his power, and of where he stood in relation to the Master whose help he sought.

Gibraltar, that huge commanding body of rock, shimmering now in the heat, its mass accentuated by tiny white sails in the bay; Gibraltar the fortress-colony, key to the Mediterranean, as the travel brochures had it, was his. Sitting there on the Barbarossas' veranda, Giles Fortin had a moment of knowing himself. He *was* Gibraltar. For a second or so he remained quite still in himself, a trifle surprised, his breath in suspense, without movement, conscious and aware. Then in a flash it had gone, there was a stir on the terrace and he found himself getting to his feet to shake hands with the Spanish General and his bosomy wife.

There were different feelings in David Evers as he sat down

[129]

at table next to Grace. He was as involved with his ship as his uncle was with Gibraltar. He, too, was aware of the swirl of the leaves, the uneasy movement of little things before the tornado of the coming war. He did not define it to himself. There it was and soon it would engulf them all. In the meantime he was far more disturbed at having to admit a failure to himself and in himself over Grace. Since Pam's arrival he had tried to push Grace out of his mind and to an extent had succeeded. Pam absorbed him as she always did when they were together. Between her and the ship, there was precious little time to brood about other things. That this should be so, seemed to be understood and accepted by Grace so that although they were all living under the same roof there was no trace of the intensity which earlier on had engulfed them both. It had withdrawn. Perhaps it had died; perhaps it was merely in hiding. David did not care so long as it remained powerless to hurt now that his wife was here.

As the days went by, he had been tricked into believing that 'the thing' between Grace and himself had been nothing but illusion, a passing mood, a state of emotion set up by a chance meeting, of no significance. He had got on with running his ship during the day and with making love to his wife at night. It was simple. From one point of view he had had a narrow shave: but Fate had allowed him to escape and life carried him on. In two days' time the flotilla would be leaving Gibraltar. His feelings for Grace and, he supposed, hers for him would be carried away into nothing with the passage of time. That was the cure. Turn the attention elsewhere and allow it to die.

But reality refused to fit into theory. You could avoid things: you could shut your eyes, but if you were honest you had to admit they were there. He had kept it from Pam. For a time, too, he had kept it from himself, but today as he sat next to Grace talking about bathing at Marbella and other peace-time trivialities, he knew with a sinking heart that nothing whatever had altered between them. Indeed there was nothing that either of them could do to change. Whatever it was that had drawn them together was still vibrantly there. She played with her wine-glass, listening to his rather terse quiet voice. Then suddenly she looked up at him sideways out of the corner of her eyes. In that one moment his heart turned over and both of them knew. Almost guiltily he looked across the table. Pam was listening with feigned attention to one of the Admiral's Hong Kong anecdotes. Her mind would be away on the dress being copied for her in a Gibraltar back-room, a dress which as usual would cost nearly double the money she had first asked if she could spend, a dress which would never be 'right' even when it had been altered and re-altered, a dress which would merely illustrate the frustrated dissatisfaction she felt with life. She needed a child, he thought. It was an easy and obvious remedy. That would alter her outlook. But she wouldn't agree. Not yet, she always said when they discussed it, not just yet with all this war nonsense in the air.

'Are you really going on Tuesday?' Grace asked softly, her fingers still twined round the stem of her glass.

'Yes. We're being attached to the Home Fleet. So it's Scapa, I suppose, instead of Malta.'

'And Pam?'

David looked at his wife for a moment or so before answering.

'I don't know. Go home, I imagine. She never plans far ahead. What about you? Is Lance taking you back to England?'

'Not with him. He's going by H.M. Ship. But I might follow on. It all depends. It's so difficult to see what's likely to happen. Who knows? If the war really does come, I wouldn't want to be far from Gibraltar. My roots are all here.'

'And Rosita? Any change there?'

Grace gave a quick glance to see if her mother was listening. But Edie was chattering in Spanish to the Governor of Algeciras about an eccentric duchess they both knew.

'She's determined to go to England. Mother won't hear of it.'

'In other words no change anywhere at all.'

'No change in anything important.' Then she added with a smile, 'How could there be?'

'Ah! well,' David said, 'anything can happen in a war.'

'Anything?'

'I think so. We just have to wait and see.'

'And if one doesn't want to do that?' she asked, looking at the table.

'One just waits and sees all the same.'

[131]

Two hours later David and Pam, Lance, Grace, Dicky Seale and Rosita lay on one of the secluded beaches near Estepona. They had bathed and sunbathed and bathed again. The Rock, though visible, seemed a long way away. They had reached that stage in the afternoon when the formalities of lunch and the necessities of polite conversation had long ago been exhausted. Soon the sun would be dipping down towards Algeciras, the tea things would be stacked into the picnic basket and they would be making their way back to Gibraltar. Another summer Sunday would have come and gone.

Each one lay on the hot sand following a private train of thought. The flies had been troublesome so that real relaxation was out of the question. The sun beat down, an occasional car could be heard on the road behind, the bare hills mounting up to Ronda had almost a violet tinge and Gibraltar, away to the right, showed up only as an indistinct shape in the heat haze of the late afternoon.

'This time next week,' Grace said with a glance at Dicky Seale, 'you'll be the only one left—of the men, that is. Are you still fretting to get away to sea?'

'A bit. Wouldn't you?' They liked each other though somehow she never seemed to get to know him very well.

Already the innocence of the first few weeks had disappeared. Already the job was having its effect. The 'Worthy Seale', Lance had called him to begin with, and later on he became known as the 'Keen Marine'. There was more to him than that, she decided as she studied the pushed-in features, the blue eyes and the black curly hair. He was nice but perhaps just a little intense, as though even here on the beach he might suddenly leap to attention and become the A.D.C. in his bathing-dress. She was so used to Lance's blasé attitude to the whole business of being a Flag-Lieutenant or A.D.C. that perhaps she had lost sight of the technical qualities which the job required no matter who carried it out.

'Yes,' she said after a pause, 'if I were a man, I suppose I'd want to be out and about in a war.'

'Pity the poor earthbound A.D.C.,' Dicky said ruefully.

'You can say that again,' Lance chipped in with feeling. 'Eighteen months of Fat Barclay in a place like Gib is enough for anyone's self-respect.'

That's for me, thought Grace, that sarcastic tone was a way of relieving himself of the pent-up frustration caused by herself. Although hardened to it by now, it still upset her a little, making her want to comfort him in some way she had not yet succeeded in discovering.

'I suppose we always want what we haven't got,' David commented from the other side. 'Your neighbour's back-garden is always better than your own.'

'What's the Keen Marine's verdict on that?' Lance inquired. 'On what?'

'On the prospect of sitting on your backside in Gibraltar waiting for something to happen.'

'I haven't much option. I was told yesterday they'll never pass me fit for flying again. So I suppose I might as well putter along as I am. And I've got no complaints about your Uncle Giles,' he said with a glance at David.

'Wait till you've done it as long as I have,' Lance said. 'It's not a very grown-up job.'

Grace laid a restraining hand on his arm but he drew away as though not wanting to be touched. Why was he always trying to prove himself such a man in the eyes of the world? She hated the way he gave himself away.

'I don't know why you gripe such a lot, Boofles,' David said, stifling an urge to say what he really thought; 'you've had a pretty good run for your money.'

'Being a Flag-Lieutenant isn't quite the same thing as having a command of your own.'

'Now, boys, no bickering on our last Sunday together,' Grace said quickly, noticing with a pang how Pam had instinctively snuggled up to her husband. That was how it ought to be between her and Lance. Instead there was simply the old familiar deadness they both knew so well. Something inside her, something she tried not to acknowledge, something sprang up to say she was glad he was going away. Something that hated him hoped he would go away and never return.

She tossed her head to free herself of the feeling. It was odd how the little reflected the big, how the strained relations which had suddenly arisen amongst them, symptomatic of what each one really thought, reflected the greater pressures in the world of late August 1939 when the skin of an uneasy peace was being stretched and tautened over the swelling, turbulent elements now coming to the surface like a boil about to burst.

'Saving your presence, Evers,' Lance said tartly, 'but you destroyer chaps do fancy yourselves a lot.'

'Oh! yes? How?'

'I don't know—there's a sort of inverted snobbery you all have about capital ships and clean cap covers. You seem to think there's some hidden merit in being sloppy and casual just because it isn't a very comfortable life. Well, I know anyone can poke Charley at me. All I have to do in my job is dress up and look pretty—on the other hand the main impression we get from small ships passing through Gib is that they'll go to any limits to dodge even the mildest pomp and ceremony. Or am I treading on very thin ice?'

'I don't think so,' David replied without heat. 'I don't think you know very much about destroyer life, that's all. It will be a pleasure to initiate you.'

'What does that mean?'

'I understand you're taking passage with us back to England.'

'Am I?' said Lance surprised, 'you're one up on me there.'

'So we shall be ready to receive you in your cocked hat, sword, tin trousers, epaulettes, aiguilettes, ribbons and bows. You'll be taking your turn watch-keeping and we don't want any under-dressed passengers in the Twenty-Eighth Destroyer Flotilla. Is that all right, Boofles?'

But Lance refused to answer directly. He gave a thoughtful look at David, at Pam, and then finally at Grace. Then he stood up and went over to the picnic basket with a pile of dirty plates.

'It's getting late,' he said, 'we ought to be on our way.'

David looked at Grace and shrugged his shoulders. Then picking up a towel he put it round his wife's shoulders and busied himself clearing up the picnic remains. Grace opened her compact and took a look at her tan. A sixth sense told her that Pam was watching her and that there was a new, uneasy quality in her attention.

VII

WAR was declared on Sunday 3rd September 1939. In Gibraltar the preceding week saw events both big and small, both public and private, tumbling into time as though Fate had turned on an invisible waterfall which swamped and swirled and carried away the familiar trappings, the comfort, and the quiet routines of peace.

Dormant powers held by the Governor for just such an emergency woke into life. Civilian freedom was abruptly curtailed. Government notices having the power of law poured out in the *Gibraltar Gazette*—an ordinance for water economy, decrees about the distribution and selling of food, a zoning of the Rock for its various purposes into 'Protected', 'Prohibited' and 'Restricted' areas. Identity cards made their appearance together with a flock of newly-posted sentries to examine them. Lights on the Upper Rock were shaded so as to be invisible from the sea. Espionage and sabotage became current words and at the conferences now convened almost daily at Government House between the Services and the Colonial Departments, conflicting demands were hammered out into regulations to be promulgated by the Governor in Executive Council—demands which tried to meet the convenience of the public but which invariably put that convenience a good long way behind the urgent necessity of hustling the fortress on to a war footing, of securing the Rock without further delay against assault and siege.

In the Dockyard a tremendous surge of activity took place. A battleship and a cruiser in dock for bottom-scraping and routine refits were speedily completed and made ready for sea. Noise and dust, both of them fair rule-of-thumb measures of activity in a colonial dockyard, grew in intensity. Riveting, air-compressors for tunnelling, the roar of flying-boat engines, the occasional clang of steel girder upon metal hull all forced themselves on the attention with a new urgency.

The Gibraltar Defence Force was mobilized and the seventy-seven members of the Special Constabulary, whose duties were counter-sabotage and the guarding of vulnerable points, were duly called up. Preparations were made for the taking of Naval Prizes on the high seas and the Jurisdiction of the Supreme Court in matters of Prize, conferred by Warrant of the Lords Commissioners of the Admiralty in 1899, was revived by proclamation of the Governor and Flag-Officer, Gibraltar.

As on a general so also on a personal plane, differences became noticeable. Lance Millingham's relief was an R.N.V.R. Lieutenant and the wavy stripes, together with the criss-cross ones of the R.N.R., now began to be seen about Gibraltar in quantity. Plain-clothes, in fact, progressively disappeared so that the Rock took on the appearance as well as the sound of a heavily fortified, heavily manned strong-point where soldiers, sailors and airmen were now the most important personages instead of the car-loads and gharry-loads of tourists with their cameras and dark glasses which had been such a feature of the scene but a short time ago.

2

For the Governor, the week and the new era it heralded began immediately on his return to Government House from Sunday luncheon with the Barbarossas. This had been shortly after 4 p.m. and Fortin was surprised to see his Military Secretary coming down the corridor to meet him, a cypher message in his hand.

'Hallo, Freddy, what are you doing here at this time of day on a Sunday?' Fortin asked. 'You're supposed to be sailing.'

'They want you back in London for a conference, sir,' the Military Secretary answered. 'I've been trying to get hold of Imperial Airways. There's a flying-boat due in tomorrow at seven, if that would be suitable. I don't know if you want to take anyone with you?'

'Hm!' said Fortin thoughtfully, returning the signal, 'let's have a look at the Short List and see how many birds we can kill with one stone.'

The 'Short List' was a private ladder of priorities which Fortin kept to himself but which very largely governed the amount of attention and pressure which any set of topics received. Once a problem got on to the Short List, it was never left alone until a solution or substantial progress towards it was made. 'When someone is both King and Prime Minister,' Fortin was fond of saying to his closest advisers, 'the job is to see that things are not hidden from you and when action is called for, make someone take it.' So the Short List came into being. It was revised every day and at times had been very far from short.

'Will you want to see the First Eleven before you go? The Brigadier's sailing. I gather the Admiral came back at the same time as you did. Colonel Bassett's at home.'

'Ask them to look in and see me when it's convenient to them. I want to see Hobart as well.'

'He's over in Tangier, sir.'

'Oh! yes, of course he is. Well then, get hold of Ferris, he'll do.'

Ferris was one of the bunch of young Army Intelligence officers who had recently arrived as the Himmlet's assistants. They had established themselves at Fortin's suggestion in the old stables behind Government House and their demands for equipment, telephones, facilities, had already upset cautious Army Supply authorities. In fact the cloak-and-dagger brigade with their airs of rather self-important mystery had gone some way towards losing the respect and esteem in Gibraltar which Hobart had built up for the job. All the Services were suddenly and violently expanding, there was a jockeying for position, a struggling for power within each particular Service, between recently called-up civilian and regular, between the various branches in a Service and between the Services themselves.

Fortin wondered why he and the Governor of Malta had both been thus unexpectedly summoned to London. Perhaps the war was now certain. Perhaps there were new aspects of the situation as it would be in the Mediterranean. Perhaps Mussolini, after all, was being prised away from Hitler. In any case Fortin had a personal problem to be settled which came near to putting everything else in the shade. A private note had come the day before from the Secretary of the Cabinet saying that the Regent of Iraq, the Amir Abdul Ilah, had asked for his services. 'The appointment is unspecified,' the note had continued, 'and no doubt this is how you would wish it. We are sure that the job and its location is right up your street and normally you would certainly be seconded to take it immediately, if you so wished. However, the Prime Minister feels that in the present emergency the importance of keeping open the Mediterranean overshadows everything else. The Cabinet is far from happy about Gibraltar and has decided that you are more necessary where you are. You are therefore to remain in your present appointment. I expect you will be disappointed and I am writing in this way to give you the opportunity of protesting, if you wish, or of raising the matter again.'

Here, almost before he had had time to turn it over in his mind, an opportunity had come for him to talk it over in London. There were a number of other things he would need to discuss.

3

The 28th Destroyer Flotilla, having worked up, having been inspected and passed by the Admiral as fully operational, having fuelled, stored and provisioned and being 'in all respects ready for sea', sailed from Gibraltar on the evening of Tuesday, 29th August 1939. It was a clear summer evening and a large party of friends and relations came down to the pens to see them off. Lance had already made his farewells. The previous night the Barbarossas had thrown a party for him at the Line Wall Road House. It was his mother-in-law's final splash so far as he was concerned. All the oligarchs were there—the Talgos, the Gibertis and the Emerson-Lopez. The Admiral had looked in: it was tedious of the Governor to have flown off to England that morning, but the two Brigadiers and the Air-Commodore had obliged. Then, on the lower levels, there were people such as the Hobarts, the A.D.C. and the Assistant Military Secretary, Jimmy Allendale from the *Firesprite*, Bill Downey from *Forthright* and various minor tennis- and squash-playing friends.

While most of the guests realized that the party was primarily a piece of exhibitionism from the Barbarossa family, it was still done with a splendid flourish on a peacetime scale which would soon be nothing but a memory. Lance's relief, a young barrister in the uniform of a lieutenant R.N.V.R. took it all blandly. He regarded himself as far more of a trained Signal Officer than a Flag-Lieutenant and he had already had the worst of a fall with Fat Barclay. He was calmly interested in watching the death throes of a social life he was determined to avoid as far as he could. Whether Edie sensed his disinterest as typical of the new order of things coming about in Gibraltar, or whether she merely resented anyone taking the place of her elegant son-in-law could not be determined but she was stiff and distant with the new Flag-Lieutenant. To Mrs. Barbarossa it would never be the new but always the old Gibraltar that mattered.

They had been asked aboard *Firesprite* to tea, but when the time drew near, Grace could scarcely make herself go. Her husband and the man she now knew she loved with her heart and soul were both leaving Gibraltar in the same ship on the eve of a war. She became more and more deeply depressed. Superstition plagued her with premonitions and doubts that she would ever see either of them again. She avoided Pam as much as she could. She had never liked her. She had tried to be casual and polite but now she could no longer stand the sight of that pretty, petulant face with the eyes seeming always to be turned inwards in a sort of dream. Jealousy and envy, for so long held at bay, now vied for possession of her and alternated in control. What had this empty, fussily pretty girl done to deserve a man like David? Because sarcasm and contempt were alien to her nature, she was astonished now to feel both of them in herself. The hidden bitterness of someone like Lance had always surprised her. To feel as she now did over Pam dismayed her. But she did not express it nor did she let herself brood. She had wisdom enough to fill the last two days with as much activity as possible.

But now as she sat in the tiny wardroom of *Firesprite* on the white canvas covers piped with blue, with Rosita on one side and Jimmy Allendale on the other, she felt so utterly woebegone she did not know where to turn. Across the Admiralty pattern carpet sat Cornelia Hobart on a settee with the

Himmlet perched on one arm. Lance was standing by the fireplace having naturally picked the most effective position in the room, Dicky Seale was crunched up in the corner, the only person in the wardroom thoroughly enjoying himself. MacGregor, the Lieutenant (E) in his white engine-room overalls and Mr. Clapp, the Gunner (T) both helped pass round the tea and cakes, formally sorry to be leaving Gibraltar, actually excited and eager to be going out on the job at last. The Sub-Lieutenant chattered eagerly to Rosita and as Grace looked round she realized with a sinking heart that David and Pam had slipped out of the wardroom and perhaps even now were kissing each other for the last time beside the bunk in his cabin. Her hand shook slightly and the tea spilled into the saucer. This was a dangerous condition and her instinct came to the rescue. She must force her attention on to something else. She made herself concentrate on Jimmy Allendale. She looked at him and then across at Dicky Seale. There was a slight resemblance between them. Both had curly black hair and rather wide, big-boned cheeks. Both were nice attractive young men in a conventional way. But whereas Dicky Seale was beginning to show the effects of Government House in a shrewdness of look and a wariness in reaction, Jimmy Allendale was still almost boyish in the light way in which he accepted responsibility, in the sureness of touch in what little Grace had seen of his dealings with the ship's company of *Firesprite*, in his knowledge of and contentment in his position as First Lieutenant of a new destroyer.

'Now that you're going,' she said, 'what's the real verdict on Gibraltar? Do you want to come back?'

'Yes please, ma'am,' he answered with a glance at her husband. Lance did not fit into any of this. He seemed oddly out of place in a destroyer wardroom and Grace noticed how careful all the ship's officers seemed to be when Lance was about. They did not trust him.

'I suppose even if you'd hated it, you wouldn't say so now.' Allendale grinned.

'Well, hardly,' he agreed, 'but Gib's a splendid place to work up from. It's the right size. You don't feel so lost as you do in Malta—even when the harbour's stuffed full of battlewagons and aircraft-carriers. There's still something intimate about the Rock. Or perhaps I'm romancing,' he added, and suddenly blushed, trying to cover this up by quickly taking her tea things and putting them down on the table. A pang of motherliness struck her as she watched him. He looked so very fresh and young, and somehow he knew it and was shamefaced about it. Perhaps that was why he drank so much. He had had a hideous hangover that morning—a not unknown feature of destroyer life—yet however hard he tried he could not disguise a boyishness and a charm. It was so ingenuous, so un-Mediterranean. Here in the south where boyhood turned almost overnight into a swaggering kind of aggressive virility, young men like Jimmy Allendale seemed possessed of an almost virginal innocence. In a funny way Lance had it too and perhaps it was that which made him so unsatisfactory as a lover. A Frenchman she had known had remarked that the idea of Peter Pan was unthinkable in the Mediterranean countries. No one accustomed to the sun could understand this Anglo-Saxon reluctance to grow up, which nevertheless, and even when struggled against—as it was in Jimmy Allendale—seemed to produce a superficial appeal and a charm for hot-blooded girls. It was only when you married one, she reflected bitterly, that you discovered how tedious an illusion it was. Yet, though she had been through it all with Lance, here she was attracted by the same quality in David's First Lieutenant. She cut off the train of thought abruptly. Perhaps the fact that he was David's First Lieutenant had something to do with it and also that in a few moment's time they would be sailing away into the sunset and out of her life.

This was only her third visit to the ship—and visits to warships were a normal part of Gibraltar life—but she felt oddly possessive about *Firesprite*, as though it were her ship. Here again she resented Pam. She failed to understand how uninterested and casual she could be about her husband's ship. Certainly the opposite was just as bad and an intense preoccupation just as undesirable, but Pam was purely and simply bored by it all. 'My father was in the Navy,' she had once said, 'and sometimes I think my mother was too. I think naval wives lose all sense of proportion, don't you?'

Grace had understood what she was fighting against. To a certain extent she had seen the danger herself with Lance and his absorption with the social side of the Navy. Yet the Navy itself was far more important. The Navy always won. The Navy had a nicely judged scale of rewards and now that Pam was up in her husband's cabin and that husband Captain of his own ship, envy gnawed at her. It suddenly occurred to her that Lance would always be a passenger. How absurd we all are, she told herself. She knew she was only concealing from herself the loneliness and pointlessness of life as it would be once the flotilla had sailed. It would not have been so bad had she thought Lance would miss her but there was no comfort to be had in that direction. She knew only too well that he was aching to get away both from Gibraltar and from herself and her family. As these thoughts went through her mind, she felt Hobart's eyes on her and looked up with a jerk. They smiled at each other and she had the sudden feeling that he saw right into her heart and that he understood.

A bos'n's pipe sounded out on the deck above followed by the order, 'Special sea dutymen close up to your stations. Hands fall in for leaving harbour.'

'I'm afraid you'll have to go ashore now,' Allendale was saying and then Hobart led the way up on deck. There David and Pam were standing beside the gangway. The sun was just dipping down over the hills behind Algeciras and there was a fresh breeze from the west. They all shook hands for the last time, she and Lance smiled at each other, rather as a sister might smile at a brother, then David's hand was in hers and she felt engulfed by emotion, scarcely able to look him in the eyes. But the others were all around. It was a public and formal little scene.

'We won't forget Gibraltar,' he was saying in rather too matter-of-fact a voice, 'so spare us a thought from time to time. Perhaps you could even send us a postcard care of the G.P.O., London. You know how grateful we are for everything you've done for us. . . .' We—we—when it was 'I' he meant. How demoralizing a farewell could be.

The words did not matter. Nothing mattered except the touch of his hand. That was all she would have of him for God

[142]

knows how long. There were tears in her eyes. He saw them and so did Rosita, who quickly and effectively came to her aid by dropping her handbag on the deck so that it spilled its contents in a kind of tinkling profusion. It was only a matter of seconds but it gave Grace the chance to recover herself, smile unhappily at David and then follow the others across on to *Forthright* and so down on to the jetty. 'Please write,' she had whispered so that only he could hear and he had nodded. She was afraid to say anything more in case her voice should give it all away.

Soon the brows were out and the hawsers slipped. Slowly the destroyers eased out of the pens one after another, as they had done so often over the past month, turned in the harbour and then made for the Bay. The stiff ranks of sailors in their white ducks, the figures on the bridge saluting as they passed the battleship alongside the detached mole, the white ensigns fluttering in the evening breeze—it was a familiar enough sight to Gibraltarians, yet tonight, because they would not be coming back, their departure was like a tolling bell in Grace's heart. She felt empty and lonely and very, very sad.

She and Rosita stood on the jetty, closer together in themselves than they had been for years. Next to them stood the Hobarts and then Dicky Seale and Pam a little further away. All the destroyers had now left harbour and were taking line-ahead formation in the Bay.

'What's *she* going to do?' Rosita whispered with a jerk of the eyes towards Pam. 'Why hasn't she made any plans? Is she just going to hang around?'

'What else can she do for the moment? The flotilla's supposed to be coming back to the Med. At least that's what David maintains. This returning to England is only a temporary thing.'

'Is it? Who knows?'

Grace looked up at the towering slopes of the Rock and then out at the flotilla, already dwarfed by distance as it headed for the Straits. Soon they would be no more than specks. Soon they would be out of sight.

'I don't think I want to leave Gibraltar,' Grace said slowly, 'if there really is going to be a war.'

[143]

'Well, I do,' Rosita retorted with a toss of the head. 'I'm going to England.' Grace shot her sister a sharp look. There was something more than defiance in that tone of voice.

'Mother won't let you,' she said.

'Mother may have to,' Rosita said, dropping her voice so that no one else could hear, 'I think I'm going to have a baby.'

Grace said nothing at all. She studied her sister for a moment, stunned by the news, then her eyes went back to the destroyers now turning out of the Bay of Gibraltar west into the setting sun. A few moments more and they would have gone. Everything in her world seemed to be falling apart. She touched her sister's arm affectionately and for the second time that evening her eyes filled with tears.

'Poor Ros,' she murmured. 'Poor all of us! How everything happens at once!'

They became aware of the Hobarts behind them.

'Come along now!' Hobart said with a brisk kindness, 'there's to be no muttering and no moist eyes on His Majesty's jetties. Let's console ourselves now at the Yacht Club and come and have dinner at home.'

He took Grace by one arm and Rosita by the other, squeezing them both. Then followed by Cornelia, Pam, and Dicky Seale they turned away from the Bay and began walking towards the town.

4

That night and for some time to come, it seemed to Grace that the house in the Line Wall Road was a void, a place suddenly abandoned by life. The empty tiled corridors, echoing to her footsteps, an open door giving on to the patio to reveal no one but old Teresa shuffling back to the storeroom, the quiet shadowy drawing-room—she looked round the familiar setting which she had known all her life, with an ache and a deep urge to escape. Like all illusions, this sense of emptiness and loss was sustained by the slenderest of facts. Lance and David had gone but Pam, Rosita and she still remained in the house.

Her mother had removed to San Roque to recover from the after-effects of the party but her father looked in each day for lunch and his siesta. The telephone continued to ring and young men with tennis racquets called as before for Rosita and indeed for all of them. Only at night, with no man in the house and herself a lonely chaperone to the other two, did the absence both of Lance and of David really strike home. Then the emptiness in the house seemed like a dramatic pause in a play, a kind of almost palpitating tension between opposites, when none of the characters said a word and the audience remained breathless and alert with expectancy.

In the news that Rosita had told her, there was certainly cause for a breathless expectancy. Now the fat was in the fire. Initially she had simply turned the fact over and over in her mind as they had all stood about that evening rather lost in the Yacht Club, while Hobart plied them with drinks and tried to stop them thinking of the little destroyer churning on into the night—west and north and away from them all.

The Hobarts were wonderful people. He and Cornelia had not only understood what Pam and she would be feeling— which was quite natural—they had also taken intelligent steps to cope with the situation. After a short session at the Yacht Club, they had all gone to the Hobart house at Rosia for pot-luck and then, almost against their wills, been whisked off to see a film. It was only when the three of them had returned to the empty house that Rosita had come along to her room, thrown herself across the bed and told her the whole story, as Grace, in turn, had admitted her real feelings over David. This in itself had been a relief of a kind and Grace reflected that it was years since she and Rosita had been so close together.

A couple of days later, when shopping in Main Street, she accidentally ran into Father O'Reilly and on the spur of the moment decided to enlist his help. She did this with a qualm. In her heart she neither respected nor very much liked the red-headed priest. He had made her too much aware of the very alive hot-blooded man beneath the habit.

She saw—and resented—how completely the Irish charm had overcome her mother and on one particular occasion had to put the good Father firmly in his place so far as illusions about herself were concerned. Nevertheless he was active and basically good. He could make rings round any Spanish priest in Gibraltar. Knocked flat by alcohol or the Bishop's disapproval, he promptly picked himself up and tried once again. He had an irrepressible sense of humour. He lived in the moment and he bore no malice. Moreover he was very much a man, and a man's outlook, a man's energy was what Grace felt was needed at that moment.

'Mother's at San Roque: Father's over in Algeciras: Ros and our guest, Pam Evers, will both be out—so come and have lunch at home,' she had suggested and over the *soles meunières*, which she knew he liked, she had put the problem to him obliquely and without mentioning names. But of course it was at once obvious to Father O'Reilly and his face clouded with anger.

'If I was Governor of this bedevilled lump of limestone,' he muttered, 'I'd have offered him up for export a long time ago.'

'Who?'

He looked at her a little sourly.

'Now it wouldn't be direct questions we'd either of us be asking at a time like this, would it, Grace?'

She smiled.

'No, Father, I see we understand each other better than I thought.'

'And what would Father O'Reilly be doing sitting in this house if he didn't understand the Barbarossa family from its bottom to its top? The trouble with you, Grace, has always been that you don't want to be understood. You go your own sweet way and the devil may care.'

'Do I, Father?' she said, quite unmoved. The picture of David at sea on the bridge of H.M.S. *Firesprite* suddenly arose very vividly in her mind, the bows of the destroyer plunging into the Atlantic rollers, the spray blowing over the bridge. Lance, too, would be there but somehow he didn't fit into the same picture. It wasn't his place. Perhaps Father O'Reilly was right; it was her own soul she should worry about a little bit more.

'I'll be thinking over the problem you've mentioned,' he said as he left the house after lunch. 'There'll be no easy solution. But this is no time for a wedding—however needed a wedding may be. . . .'

She watched him walk off towards the King's Bastion, the

sun beating down on his flat-domed hat, the dust swirling about him as a lorry passed full of sailors and kitbags, an old man on a donkey crossing himself on the other side of the street. They were testing the air-raid warning system down by the *Cormorant* and the noise of this mingled with the low siren zoom of an aircraft-carrier manoeuvring out in the Bay. There was work going on all around in Gibraltar despite the heat of the afternoon. It was certainly no time for a wedding. That same day the German Army invaded Poland. It was September 1st and although England and France did not come in till the 3rd, the Second World War itself had begun.

5

It was on the last Saturday of peace that Nicholas Pappado-poulos discovered a friend. He had now been for what seemed a lifetime in a trough of depression. He could not make up his mind what to do—whether to go or to stay. Day by day he woke up morose and moody. He hated this sour state and since he was temporarily without a mistress, he had taken to drinking steadily and to remaining in bed, often until it was time to go to the office. Because he wished to have nothing further to do with Rosita he avoided the Yacht Club, which he had never liked, and instead took his cognac among the Spanish workmen who frequented bars like 'El Tribuno' at the bottom end of Main Street near the Casemates.

This was one of the bars in which the Spanish labour force, which came over the frontier each day to work in the Dock-yard, would take its wine or beer or coffee while waiting for the buses back to La Línea. To begin with he was looked on with suspicion, but soon he became accepted as a regular and the Spaniards reverted to their principal interests, namely gambling which they argued about incessantly and with passion, and petty smuggling which they brooded about and for obvious reasons never mentioned at all.

On a normal Saturday the noon hooter would have seen the Dockyard empty itself and the rush back into Spain begin. On Saturday 2nd September, however, the emergency was fairly astride of Gibraltar, and Fat Barclay, in his capacity as

Admiral-Superintendent of the Dockyard, had authorized a change of routine and a freeing of the overtime regulations. Several of the Dockyard Departments, such as the foundry and the electrical repair shop had gone on to a shift basis. The pattern of labour, therefore, was changing and this in turn was reflected in a sparse attendance of the normal clientele of the Tribuno.

There was an alertness on the Rock, a restlessness and uncertainty, which was invading all the comfortable habits of a decade. Nicholas watched newly-landed military vehicles dashing about the streets in their self-important clouds of dust, he watched sailors, soldiers and airmen saluting their officers with a new pride and he watched the coming and going in the Tribuno Bar. He was involved, yet felt above it. This was not *his* emergency and if the war came, it would not be his war. As he happened to be in Gibraltar he could not but be swept up in its train but emotionally he was not to be shifted from his position of dully glowing hatred of the British Empire, its colonial hierarchy and its way of life.

As the cheap Spanish brandy scoured his throat and inflamed his stomach, he began noticing the stranger next to him at the bar, a man, he judged, in his early forties, with grey hair, eyes that darted very sharply about the room, and a somewhat dark and angry expression in the down-turned mouth. The stranger was drinking cognac and the contemptuous set of his mouth struck a similar note to his own mood of dislike and scorn.

They observed each other covertly through three cognacs and then an approach was made. Outside in Main Street a gharry and a huge military truck were disputing the right of way. As usual a crowd had collected, a row had begun, and soon a Gibraltarian policeman would be forced unwillingly to assert his authority. In the meantime a red-faced captain of the R.A.S.C. was swearing at the gharry-driver who replied with surly witticisms in Spanish which delighted the crowd but which infuriated the captain even more, since he could not understand a word. Then, when complete deadlock had been reached, the gharry horse relieved itself in a great steaming flood as if in silent comment upon the whole matter. At this point the stranger shot Nicholas a look and remarked:

'That horse is about the only one with the right ideas.' The voice had a Yorkshire accent and a gruff quality. Nicholas smiled briefly and answered:

'Have you just arrived in Gibraltar?'

'About a week ago.'

'Passing through?'

'Dockyard,' said the stranger, clamping shut his mouth as though that settled it all, then added as an afterthought, 'I'll be here for the duration, I shouldn't wonder, or until the Rock blows up.'

This was evidently meant as a sardonic joke but as Nicholas signed to the barman to fill up their glasses, his reporter's instincts came alert and he suddenly felt an interest stirring which he knew, from experience, would take him in unexpected directions.

'Is the Rock likely to do that?' he inquired.

'Aye, it could do,' said the other, 'if some of the cordite storage I've had a look at isn't improved.'

So he was to do with armament supply. Nicholas now felt all his faculties coming alive. He knew better than to arouse suspicion by asking obvious questions at the start. But here, right under his nose, was someone who might one day be of paramount use to the interests he intermittently served. He passed along the cognac and they raised their glasses to each other.

'My name's Pappadopoulos,' he said, 'and I'm sub-editor of the *Gibraltar Gazette*—but don't let that worry you.'

'My name's Boothroyd,' said the other, 'and it won't. I know about the *Gazette*. You're not allowed to criticize or comment in a Crown Colony. Isn't that so? You've to print Reuter's despatches and nowt else, isn't that it?'

'For one week in Gibraltar you know a lot.'

'Aye,' said Boothroyd, 'I do. We might happen to have mutual friends. Like someone called Zimmerman, for instance. Ever come across him in your travels?'

'The name's familiar but I can't place it for the moment,' Nicholas said with an expressionless face. Zimmerman had been a very active member of the same group he had been concerned with in London. By now his instincts were fully alert and as always this condition brought a practised caution. Mr. Boothroyd might easily be a stool-pigeon, an agent for the other side leading him on and on into a trap. He looked at him keenly but the verdict was neutral. He might be minded as Nicholas was himself or he might be merely pretending. At this stage it was impossible to tell. A voice in him said, 'Caution, caution, caution.'

'I have to go,' he said, deciding to keep the initiative, 'perhaps we'll be meeting again.'

'Happen we may,' said Boothroyd, apparently as unconcerned as Nicholas himself, 'in which case, no doubt, you'll be having one with me.'

They nodded briefly at each other and Nicholas quietly left the bar. Outside the sun beat down into the narrow streets. He suddenly felt he had a lot to think about and he needed a clear head. He decided to have an omelette and then go across into Spain to bathe.

6

England was officially at war at 9 a.m. on 3rd September. By this time the 28th Destroyer Flotilla had called in at Liverpool to fuel and discharge its passengers and had proceeded north to the Orkneys. Here, working out of Scapa as a screen for battleships of the Home Fleet, they patrolled towards the North Cape hoping to intercept a break-out of the *Scharnhorst* or *Gneisenau*.

Thus, for the first five days of the war *Firesprite* was at sea. Since leaving Gibraltar they had steamed nearly two thousand miles. They had packed away their white uniform and although it was mild weather, they were already glad of their blues. On the Sunday morning they all listened in silence to Chamberlain's weak voice on the radio announcing the news. There should have been relief, joy—at the very least a feeling of excitement. Instead there was a numbness amounting very nearly to apathy. It was an odd way to go to war. Yet at least they were at sea, at least they were doing the job for which they had all been trained, however much of an anticlimax the outbreak of war itself might seem to be.

David sat on his high stool on the bridge, his arms on the

coping, staring out at the grey northern sea, thinking back over the past week and beyond that over the whole of their working-up period at Gibraltar. There was so much to digest. No doubt, a voice in him said, there would now be ample time in which to get on with the digestion. No doubt they would soon be looking back on their month's exercising between the Pillars of Hercules as a period of peacetime ease and luxury. At present, though, it seemed extraordinary that a mere week ago he and Pam had been getting into the Barbarossas' second car at the Line Wall Road House and going to lunch at San Roque with the Governor, the Admiral, and the Military Governor of Algeciras. Now what? Though they had as yet seen no action, he had already become used to the comfortless sea-going routine of the *Firesprite* bridge, a few uneasy hours' sleep on his bunk, food that was rubbery, cocoa in the night watches and all the time the 'swift irresponsible motion' of a destroyer at sea. He had already forced himself, red-eyed and monosyllabic, up to and through one exhaustion barrier. He knew this was merely the start—the early tempering process—not the siege itself.

The idea of siege took his thoughts back to the Rock, to Pam and to Grace. Now that the war had really come, he supposed he must do something positive about Pam. He was always saying that sort of thing to himself: indeed it was an attitude he had been forced to adopt since they were first married and he had realized that a casual vagueness is one thing in a fiancée, quite another in a wife. He wondered what Pam would do if he himself took no further action at all. Get a job in Gibraltar? They were crying out for assistance and if she stayed with the Barbarossa family, which in every respect would be undesirable, then she would virtually be forced into some sort of war work. He had given her a cheque for her passage back to England but she was perfectly capable of spending it all on a set of new clothes. Then what would she do?

Jimmy Allendale came up on the bridge to ask if he would see two Requestmen and one Defaulter. The Chief reported that No. 2 dynamo which he had had to take off the board was now working normally again. The Sub-Lieutenant's station-keeping needed watching more carefully. The sea was choppy and the wind sang in the rigging. David's eyes were bloodshot with tiredness as he went down off the bridge behind his First Lieutenant: yet as he dealt with Requestmen and Defaulters in accordance with the King's Regulations and Admiralty Instructions, a picture of his pretty, feckless wife and behind her the grave, sensitive features of Grace arose in his mind. And behind them both, as if another picture was forming out of nothing in his mind, the Rock of Gibraltar obtruded itself, its top covered in Levanter mist, its town seething with life, the background to a period of vivid feeling and now some two thousand miles to the south.

7

General Fortin flew back to Gibraltar via Lisbon on the Saturday. His time had not been wasted. He had been briefed afresh by the Foreign Office, the War Office and the Admiralty. The politicians and the Colonial Office had both been unusually forthcoming. 'Gibraltar thrives upon the misfortunes of others,' the Secretary to the Cabinet had told him. 'Whenever there's trouble elsewhere in the world, the Rock grows in importance. This is one of those moments.'

This factor more than any other had occasioned his own return to Gibraltar and the other appointments which would soon be announced. The job had grown. There had been strong pressure, he gathered, to send him to Iraq. The Emir had been insistent. Fortin was certainly ideal for the job. He would probably have enjoyed it more and with mepacrin and attabrin to hand malaria would not have been as exhausting as it once was. He knew and had an affection for the Arabs he would be dealing with. But Gibraltar needed a strong man and an intelligent one. To Fortin personally it was the more difficult job and its responsibility was very much greater.

If Gibraltar were lost the Mediterranean might well be closed. It was assumed that Italy would support her Axis partner in a war and her present detachment, which Mussolini had just reaffirmed, was only to see how the initial dispositions would work out. With Gibraltar gone and a hostile Italy at her back, Malta would not long be able to survive. The Mediterranean was an enormous prize and Gibraltar was essential to its winning.

Within reason he had been given *carte blanche*. This in itself was a measure of the Rock's new status in the war. 'Gibraltar is essential to the Empire's survival,' the Prime Minister had told him in a five-minute interview. 'Whatever you need will be found somehow or other.'

So, although he had again been given the option of going to Iraq, he had chosen to stay in Gibraltar. The testing-time was ahead. The Foreign Office thought it more likely than not that Hitler would move into Spain. German infiltration into Spanish Morocco was at its peak. With both sides of the Straits of Gibraltar in German hands, an attack on the Rock would be certain. What happened then might well be crucial to the war and indeed to England herself.

The changing status of Gibraltar gave the Admiralty and the Colonial Office the excuse they needed to meet General Fortin's wishes. Fat Barclay was appointed Admiral-Superintendent of Rosyth Dockyard and Colonel Bassett made Governor of a small West Indian island. This had come about without direct pressure from Fortin but more because of a kind of Byzantine manœuvring undertaken by three senior civil servants in the Colonial Office, the War Office and the Admiralty. In this Patterson had taken the lead and he had been greatly helped by an understanding Naval Assistant to the First Sea Lord in whose purview came the appointment of flag and senior officers.

Fat Barclay was not only being replaced, the job itself was expanded and stepped up in intensity. Gibraltar was now to contain the Vice-Admiral Commanding the North Atlantic Station, a double-headed command, looking both west into the Atlantic and east into the Mediterranean, with responsibilities for convoys at a vital point between the United Kingdom and Malta and for an operational striking force composed of battle-cruisers, aircraft-carriers, cruisers and destroyers to be based on Gibraltar Dockyard. This force, soon to be known as 'Force H', although under the operational control of the Admiralty, would come to look on the Rock as its home. Gibraltar would be the bastion to which it would return for its fuel and supplies and which, in a crisis, it would materially support with its fifteen-inch guns and its fighter and reconnaissance aircraft.

On the Sunday morning that war was declared, therefore, His Excellency the Governor and Commander-in-Chief found himself for the moment poised on a pinnacle of power, with all the reins of a small empire in his hands, still conscious in his inner humility of being set under authority yet in his turn in absolute control of the levels below. Surrounded by his personal staff he listened in his study to the Prime Minister's broadcast. He had signed the 'Proclamation to the Fortress and Colony of Gibraltar'. It was quiet in the Old Convent and the small group round Fortin were quiet in themselves, each absorbed in thinking out the personal implications of the war. When the broadcast was over, there was a silence. The hot sunlight slanting down on the patio outside threw into contrast the cool shadows of the Governor's room: a few flies made a pattern of movement up by the vaulted ceiling: the deep note of a ship's siren recalled the harbour and the shipping for the time being immobilized in the Bay. At a sign from the Governor, Hobart switched off the radio and then looked round at the others.

'A moment of history calls for a rattling good banality,' he said, 'but I can't even think up a cliché.'

'I suppose everyone knows what we're fighting about,' Smallbones added, looking out at the patio, 'I'm not at all sure I do.'

'We may find out sooner than anyone expects,' Fortin said gravely. 'At all events I'm glad I've got this particular team around me at this particular time.' Then, since he realized that any form of mutual back-slapping has the effect of paralysing the self-conscious English, he went on quickly to Dicky Seale, 'Is that car of yours in working order again?'

'Yes, sir.'

'Is it capable of climbing up to the Queen's Road?'

'Yes, sir.'

'Good,' said Fortin handing a pile of papers to the Military Secretary, 'then I feel like a short spell on the Upper Rock to see how the apes are adapting themselves to the state of war. Back in about half an hour,' he said to the others as he left the room followed by the limping Seale. Gibraltar was at war.

PART TWO

VIII

TOWARDS Christmas, life in wartime Gibraltar had settled down to a recognizable pattern. The style and the rhythm had changed. Almost everyone on the Rock now had a job, even if it was only one of sorting and packing up comforts for the troops which, for instance, comprised Mrs. Barbarossa's war effort. Almost everyone wore uniform of one kind or another. Almost everyone had a turn of duty or a watch to keep, and essential jobs such as cyphering were manned round the clock. And it was always the job which came first, the job, the sacred job.

Grace had joined the naval cypher organization at the Dockyard Tower. In the early days they had all been grossly overworked. Even now that the Wrens were taking over and would soon outnumber the temporary civilian assistants, the volume of work kept them all at it hard. At times she was exhausted, coming off watch only to sleep and then eat and then go on watch again: at other times she could lift her head above it a little, but when she began to think about her life and the war, the pain and confusion returned and she was grateful when the time came round to submerge herself once more in the endless figures and strange naval jargon which they were made to reveal.

Generally speaking, the initial excitements of being at war had quickly faded. The first phase of slow anticlimax had begun. Hitler had not walked into Spain. Indeed, since Poland, he had not walked into anywhere and the 'phoney war' experts were saying that already he was in grave difficulties—the oil and the rubber were short and his continued inaction proved that Germany was more than half defeated. It was only a question of waiting. And in Gibraltar they could easily learn to do that.

Routine brought with it boredom. Life narrowed down. You took what you could get and you learnt, as never before, to queue and to wait. Perhaps one or two people understood that in order to be free you had voluntarily to drop down to the status of ants. Most people, however, simply accepted life as it came. Theirs not to reason why. They did their jobs and then escaped into private dreams of wife, home, children or whatever were the most powerful ingredients in their lives which were currently missing.

Gibraltar had its paradoxes, too. Though the harbour might be full of warships, though the Rock itself might be bristling with guns, no shot had yet been fired in anger and there was still horse-racing at the North Front. Indeed, although the race-course itself was so arranged that light planes could land and take off down its centre, the weight and efficiency of the A.A. barrage which the Rock could put up in the event of air attack, had caused the building of an airfield to be deferred. Fortin had accepted this under duress. He remained determined to have his aerodrome as soon as possible. He realized, though, that even had this been done, the necessary fighters to operate from it simply did not exist.

Life in Gibraltar, indeed, epitomized the bemused uncertainty, the apathy and inertia of that first winter of the war. Despite Poland, and before that Czecho-Slovakia and Austria, the Germans were still thought to be bluffing and Italy's continued neutrality abetted this idea. Whilst these notions were at no time held by Fortin or the other senior officers, it was the popular cry. No one wanted the war. No one knew what it was about. The Great War had begun as a tremendous emotional crusade. This new war was entered upon by ordinary people reluctantly and without any glowing sense of purpose, its symbol the shrug of the shoulders, its mood indifference.

So the autumn had gone on its way with the French Army safe and snug behind the Maginot forts and the British singing about how they were going to hang up the washing on the Siegfried Line but not in fact making any move to do so. To the man in the street the winter of the phoney war was a bewildering stalemate, and in Gibraltar itself the main problems, as Fortin had foreseen, would soon be boredom and drink.

The Spanish attitude was stiffening as the pro-German officers of the Spanish Army began to exploit their position of authority. Indeed the army was still the only real power in

Spain after the ravages of the Civil War, and the fact that the majority of its officers admired and modelled themselves on the German Army—and naturally thought that Germany would win the war—became more and more insistent in the Intelligence reports which Hobart compiled.

Only at sea was the war at full force, as it had been from 3rd September when, on that very first day, the liner *Athenia* had been torpedoed in the Atlantic and unrestricted U-boat warfare began.

The Royal Navy, alone of the three Services, was in a dominant position *vis-à-vis* the enemy. That the Allies still had command of the seas became clear from the start. Winston was back at the Admiralty and the Silent Service had a superb leader delighting to speak out richly when the occasion demanded.

All over the world, at any given moment, two thousand ships under the British flag alone are sailing the high seas. In the autumn of 1939, and after a short interruption while the convoy system was brought into force, those two thousand ships continued to arrive at and sail from the United Kingdom as a matter of routine. The contrast in Gibraltar, therefore, was intense. The Navy and the Merchant Service were flat out and liable to be in action the moment they cleared the Boom Defence. The two other Services perforce had to sit about in a state of preparedness while in the meantime nothing whatever happened.

Once again it was the sea which succoured Gibraltar. Before, the fortress had looked at least with one eye towards Spain for its life blood; now, thanks to the continuing flow of ships in the Bay, the inhabitants and the garrison could and did rely on replenishment by sea. With command of the sea, there never was nor would there ever be any effective method in Spanish hands of starving out the Rock. There it was and there it would remain. Only a full-scale military attack could change its status.

2

Against this background of war routine, however, other events moved to a climax. The first of these was Rosita.

There was now no doubt at all that she was going to have a baby though this was still not obvious to casual eyes. Indeed, even now that she was over four months gone, only Grace and Father O'Reilly were in the know, but soon the fat would be in the fire. The Almighty had withheld the miscarriage which in the early days all three had secretly prayed for, and strangely enough Rosita had regained inside herself the feeling for Nicholas which had originally caused all the trouble. But now it had been purified. Now it had matured from a raging uncontrollable passion into an undemanding love.

To begin with she had been appalled at herself and her situation from which she could see no escape. She went deep down into a valley of fear, of hatred and of violence. For a time she could not bear the thought of him. She loathed him and had been deeply hurt by his indifference to her fate. Then, somehow, as if suddenly she had straightened up to something, the fears, the disgrace and the pain dropped away. A miraculous calm possessed her and a detachment came. Paying for her folly as she had done with hours, days, and weeks of tearing anxiety, she had in some way reached another state of consciousness where the values were different. She had disgraced her family and she was deeply sorry. But it was her own life she was living and it was she who would bear the baby. She resisted no longer. She made her confession: in her heart she was penitent and this new state released into her being an understanding and a compassion which, from its taste, was worth all the suffering she had already endured and all the pain which still lay ahead. She began to change in herself, no longer blaming Nicholas, no longer even blaming herself, but simply seeing that life had brought her a great disaster which, through being accepted, had miraculously given her a goodness and a strength. Faith and a sweetness came to her aid and the arrogant, self-loving girl yielded to the new, understanding woman. She was ready to face up to it all alone.

Only Grace was aware of this change, and since she had, under a different stimulus, been through a like crisis over Lance, for the first time in their lives the two sisters came together, recognizing each other as neighbours in their invisible selves and as friends. Indeed, the fact that they had each other to lean on, the fact that each understood, gave them both a new strength, helping each one to bear the other's burdens.

In the meantime Father O'Reilly had taken the bull by the horns and had gone to see Nicholas Pappadopoulos. The blood of a long line of Irish fighters in Father O 'Reilly fired him with anger and a hatred of all that Nicholas Pappadopoulos stood for, in materiality and the anti-Christ. He knew he must attack and he sensed an advantage in taking the gentleman by surprise. He had not approached him, therefore, either in his room or in the Tribuno Bar. Instead he went along one evening to the offices of the *Gibraltar Gazette* and brushing aside all opposition had sailed in like an angry prize-fighter. He marched up to the sub-editor's desk and glared into the Cypriot's eyes. Nicholas Pappadopoulos took this calmly enough.

'What can I do for you?' he asked. He had long disliked and scorned the whole mealy-mouthed tribe. He had a contempt for the Catholic faith and the corruption he had seen in Spain had in no way changed his basic Marxist outlook on religion and the priesthood.

'I want a short talk with you.'

'Sorry, I'm busy. Some other time.'

'Not too busy for me. You know who I am.'

'I know who you are.'

For a moment or so they faced each other in the noisy office as the tape-machine clattered away and the typewriters clicked.

'Very well,' Nicholas said in the end, 'I'll give you five minutes. Come into the Editor's room.'

The machine noise could still be heard in the inner office but at least it was unnecessary to raise one's voice. Nicholas studied his visitor intently. He had had something to do with this kind of militant priest in the Spanish Civil War, and he knew the sort of trouble they could make. Bastards, all of them. Yet this one had a good reputation in Gibraltar. This one was at least a man.

'Well?'

'What are you proposing to do about Miss Barbarossa?'

'What's that to do with you?'

'She needs help. She needs your support.' He paused to control his feelings and to find the words to express exactly

TR—F*

what he intended. 'I dislike saying this—but she needs your love—if you're capable of such an emotion.'

'I still ask what is it to do with you?'

'I'm her adviser.'

A weary sneer came into Nicholas's face.

'I thought the confessional was secret.'

'There'll be nothing secret about what's going to happen in a few months' time.'

'Have you come here to threaten me?'

'I've come here prepared for a lot of things. One of them might be to give you such a hiding you'll be a hospital case for months.'

'And where would that get either of us, Father?'

'Into serious trouble, I've no doubt. But I shall survive.'

'You've made a mistake. I got used to being knocked about in the Spanish war. You'll have to try another line of attack.'

Then suddenly at the same moment the essential absurdity of the scene struck them both and both of them smiled. There was a pause as they looked at each other. Outside, the office hummed, and outside that the war. To Nicholas the proportions began changing. Everything changed in time. He had always fought it before but now he began to be ashamed.

'Well, anyway she loves you,' said Father O'Reilly in a more gentle tone of voice. Then he turned to go out. 'You'd be a fool to throw it away. And you're not a fool.'

'The mother would never accept me.'

'You wouldn't be marrying the mother.'

He looked down at the desk, lost in his thoughts. When he looked up Father O'Reilly had gone. He felt tired and depressed. As always, he supposed he would have to compromise in the end. He had never wanted to be married. Yet of all the women he had had in his life, Rosita was the only one he still found himself respecting. There was something else here, something other than the repetitive physical expression of sex.

Wearily he got up and went back to his desk. He still had three hours' work to be done.

3

This skirmish had taken place in September when the

impact of the war was still overwhelming and personal problems, however fundamental, were dwarfed by the newness of the world events then taking place.

Rosita made no move towards him of any kind, nor did she run away to England as she had so blithely forecast and which she could so easily have done. Acceptance of her fate was surprising and it acted as a leaven. She was working with the censorship organization and, like Grace, had submerged herself in the routine, waiting to see what would happen in a curiously detached fashion.

It was odd. It was almost as though the more reason she had for anxiety, the more detached she became. This disinvolvement in turn affected Nicholas in some invisible way. He had expected to have to resist, to have a shot-gun at his back in some way or another, and if the worst came to the worst, he had been prepared to chuck up the job and go back to England.

Instead he found the opposite happening. He found himself wanting the girl, intrigued by the way she was taking it, drawn towards her of his own free will in a way in which force would have been useless. His basic ideas had not changed and he was not going to subscribe to any Catholic nonsense, but as the days and weeks went by he came to accept the idea of marrying Rosita, if she would have him.

So, late in October, he had suddenly come to a decision. He made a date to take her dancing at the Rock Hotel, with Grace and Dicky Seale as chaperones. Already the pattern of wartime relaxation was established and the formality had largely gone out of invitations to dine and dance. Indeed, since everyone was in uniform and uniform was in a sense its own guarantee of discipline and self-control, the chaperone idea was on the way out.

But Nicholas Pappadopoulos wore no uniform and he was intelligent about getting things done. Once he had decided to try and marry Rosita, he saw he must be clever in not setting up unnecessary opposition to his plans. So he rang up Grace, took her into his confidence and asked for her help. From then on, he considered, the machine was in gear and it was only a question of driving it right.

Grace and Dicky Seale were by this time old friends. They

did things together without tension and each liked the other. There was but little sexual feeling between them yet both felt that without much trouble there very soon could be. Grace drew on his cheerfulness and his unsnobbish shrewdness over the people and the problems that passed through Government House. He, in turn, enjoyed her company, liked her personality and the way she dressed, and thought her, in addition, full of good sense. She spoke both from intuition and experience; she had temper and he respected the way she dealt with her life which, now that that ass Millingham had gone, seemed to have become firmer and more sure of itself. They talked to each other with the licence of friends and when Grace had asked him to come on the Pappadopoulos party, he had retorted:

'I can't think of anyone whose company I'd less enjoy.'

'Rosey's mad about him—and *I* want your support.'

'Why doesn't he bog off back to Cyprus? Nobody wants him here.'

'Rosita does. She'll probably marry him if he asks her and he'll probably ask her tonight.'

'*What?* She must be mad.'

'She's not mad, Dicky. She loves him and you're not to breathe a word of this to a single soul. Promise? And you're to be as nice to him as you possibly can. It's important to Rosey.'

'But he's—he's a—well, you know what he is,' Seale spluttered. 'He's got Regulation 18B hanging over his head.'

'Haven't we all?' Grace answered tartly.

'He hasn't a friend on the Rock. And do you know why? Because one of these days he'll stick a knife in your back. Hobart's always on the point of getting him thrown out for good.'

'Dicky, *please*,' Grace said, 'I just want your help.'

'Well, all right,' he said a bit sulkily, 'I'll come, but it sounds like the waste of a perfectly good evening to me.'

So the evening had come and gone. The Rock Hotel dinner-dances had long been a suitable public setting for the expression of private ideas without attracting undue attention. Between two people on the dance floor anything or nothing might be in process of happening. Nicholas, well plied with wine, had put the question to Rosita while they danced late in the evening and had been genuinely shocked when she squeezed his shoulder and said 'No'.

'But why not?' he asked, astonished. In thinking out all the snags and troubles there would be he had taken her consent as a foregone conclusion. She leant back and looked at his face as they danced. He excited her as he always had done. She yearned for him and now that they were dancing it was more difficult than ever to keep a clear head. Yet she had paid for a kind of tranquillity and she was not going to throw it lightly away.

'You don't *really* want me,' she eventually said. 'You don't want to be married. You're being forced into this simply because we made a ghastly mistake.'

'But I do love you,' he said, still astonished at her refusal and hating the banality of the phrase.

'Do you, Nicky? I wonder.'

'But . . . what are you going to do? You can't just sit here and have the baby as though. . . .'

'I shan't, Nicky. I shall tell my father and he'll be very angry indeed but he'll help me. I shall go either to Tangier or to Madrid or possibly to England. At least—I think I might.'

A short time ago he would have been secretly glad to have heard her talk in this way. It would have let him out. Now he was equally surprised to discover he felt angry and hurt. This was his baby and he had a right to be its father, if he wanted to be.

'I suppose I'm up against the Barbarossa vanity,' he said after a pause, 'the good old Rock pride.'

'You've left it a little late,' she answered slowly, spacing out the words so that each seemed set in its own reflective pause. 'You ran away. You left it all on my shoulders. You blamed *me* for being so careless, so you shrugged it off and let me stew in my own juice. I was terrified, Nicky. You can't have any idea of what I've been through. My parents still don't know. My mother is quite capable of throwing me out in the street. I've had to face all that alone.'

'I'm sorry,' he muttered, 'I really am sorry.'

It was almost the first time he had ever said such a thing in his life.

'And you *knew* all that,' she went on relentlessly, 'you're sensitive and very aware; you *knew* what I was going through and you deliberately turned your back on it all.'

She spoke unemotionally and without resentment. The detachment she had gained made it almost seem as if it was someone else's story she was discussing. She felt him stiffen in her arms.

'I'll go and see your father tomorrow,' he said. She made no answer at all. Across the floor Grace trudged round with Dicky Seale whose limp made dancing a sort of slow, drawn-out hiccup. She caught Grace's eyes and held them for a moment. Then her mouth formed a troubled little smile, and her eyes filled with tears. She looked quickly away.

'God!' said Nicholas Pappadopoulos, 'what a mess it all is!'

4

Jaime Barbarossa, in agreement with most of official Gibraltar, found the new Admiral a vast improvement on Fat Barclay. Indeed Vice-Admiral Sir John Vickerson, K.C.B., D.S.O., proved to be a contrast in every respect. To begin with, there was a new and very much closer liaison with Government House. He and Fortin saw eye to eye both in the flexibility with which they dealt with their daily administrative problems and also in the growing, changing possibilities which an attack and siege of the Rock would entail.

Vickerson was a Lowland Scot and he had the same unsmiling, terse approach which characterized Fortin. He had a sense of values and a sense of humour but both were in the lean, disciplined Puritan tradition. Fat Barclay's expansive, shallow and insincere *bonhomie* had been swept away with the peace. Now the Vice-Admiral Commanding the North Atlantic Station with its greatly increased responsibilities was an ex-navigator with a sharp brain, a quick grasp of essentials and almost no tolerance whatever for fools or stupidities.

Moreover Lady Vickerson had not come out to Gibraltar, so that the Mount, like Government House, had become a bachelor establishment. When Edie heard this, her eyes lit up and she visualized herself in charge of the social arrangements at the Mount, rather as she had once hoped to be at Government House. Unfortunately for her, however, the new Admiral had as little use for 'poodle-faking' as the Governor. Their minds were on the war and on little else. Thus Edie found that 'her' Gibraltar progressively shrank with the passing weeks so that even by the first Christmas of the war, it was no more than a shadow of its former self.

More and more she consoled herself with Red Cross work in the mornings and with bridge in the afternoons. She still had her daughters with her, but since they now had jobs she saw as little of them as she did of Jaime, and the idea of removing in dudgeon to Madrid grew more and more attractive in her mind. But with this escape plan also grew the realization that there was something seriously wrong with her heart.

Jaime knew what was wrong with her heart and he knew there was the danger of a seizure at any time. It was, since he still loved his wife, the first of his worries and worry was something which seemed to him to have increased a thousandfold with the war.

All the old, comfortable, convenient routines had one by one been broken up. Week after week the staff in his shipping office disappeared either into uniform or into jobs more directly concerned with the war. The expense of maintaining the San Roque house weighed more and more heavily on his resources and he began seriously to think of selling it up and withdrawing into Gibraltar. Italian liners continued to call at Gibraltar but the traffic had dropped to a fraction of what it was and the difficulties brought about by Mussolini's belligerent neutrality caused more expense than profit.

Nor was there comfort to be had from his brother in Madrid. Each bulletin he received—each visit he paid him—convinced Jaime that Franco was only waiting for the right moment, for the best terms he could get out of Hitler, before opening up a corridor for German troops to Gibraltar and the entrance to the Mediterranean. The outlook was sombre and try as he might he could not stop brooding about what was likely to happen.

But human nature is an odd paradox, he reflected, a few moments before Nicholas Pappadopoulos arrived to see him in his office. When there is no hope to be had from the world the resignation and the trust in God which his religion taught brought a peace of mind not attainable in more normal times. Responsibility, the only burden laid upon man which the animals do not share, diminished in some strange way the more terrible the outward situation became. He and Fortin had lunched with the new Admiral and the conversation had turned on the British character during what was soon to be known as the 'twilight war'.

'For some reason I can never understand,' the Admiral had said, 'the tide always has to go against us before we come to our senses. It takes a full-scale disaster to wake us all up. We bumble on improvising like amateurs—dodging the issue—actually taking pride in our monstrous inefficiency. That's why we're always out of date at the start of a war. That's why it took Mons and Ypres and the Somme to show us that a pair of wire-clippers and a gas-mask were of more practical use than a sabre and a horse.'

Fortin had agreed.

'I've actually had it said to me that the professional is all very well but in some way he's not to be trusted. Politicians never take our advice until it's much too late. Look at the combined staff headquarters under the Rock! It should be ready *now*. The idea's old enough. Instead—because it needs money it's always been deferred. Well—it's pure chance that Gibraltar hasn't been under attack already.'

'Then you reckon we've not yet had our disaster?' Jaime asked.

'What disaster?' snapped the Admiral. ''We haven't even been pricked.'

The memory of this conversation came back to him as he sat behind his desk in the office in Irish Town looking at young Mr. Pappadopoulos and wondering what he was going to say. He did not have long to wait.

'I want your permission to marry Rosita,' Nicholas said, his nervousness making him more abrupt than ever. In spite of the scowl which had driven a big tram-line between the eyebrows, there was no doubt that he was a magnetic young man. For the moment, though, Jaime was so surprised he said nothing, merely studying the dark features and the strained, slightly shifty expression. He came to the conclusion that there was something there he would always distrust.

'Well,' he said eventually, 'that's a surprise. Does my daughter want to marry you?'

'I think so.'

'Good heavens above, haven't you asked her?'

'Of course,' Nicholas said, looking at the floor, 'but she thinks she's being forced into it.'

'I don't understand.'

'You see, I'm afraid we were lovers . . .' he tailed off lamely and a long silence ensued. There seemed nothing to say. The flies buzzed, and outside in the street two Spanish women argued in hard, passionate voices. The hoof of a horse could be heard as it shifted position on the tarmac, children shouted in the distance, and the almost inevitable siren boomed from the bay. Edie mustn't be told, Jaime kept repeating to himself, Edie must never know. Whatever else happens it must be kept from Edie. He looked with disgust at the Cypriot sitting forward in the worn leather armchair. In his heart he could have murdered him then. What could have possessed her? Why did she do it? And at the same time the glaring realization came that his daughter was a stranger to him, that he simply did not know her in reality at all.

'You don't appear to be in any way sorry,' he said eventually in a hard voice.

'It's our affair,' Nicholas answered gruffly, 'I'm sorry to cause you trouble but it's *our* affair.'

'In that case why come to me?'

Nicholas shrugged his shoulders.

'Because you're her father: because we love each other: because I think we ought to get married quite apart from the obvious reasons.'

'I've never heard anything so cool and calculated—and disgusting, in all my life.'

'I knew it would be a shock. I'm sorry about that—but our lives are still our own. I can look after Rosita and she belongs far more in my world than in yours.'

'Never in my life have I heard such insolence,' Jaime spluttered. For a moment rage blinded him and only his strong habitual self-control prevented him from expressing it in violence.

'I have to be blunt,' Nicholas said, 'because that's what I believe. I know you and Mrs. Barbarossa will never accept me—and there's nothing I can do about that. I won't change your point of view and you can't alter mine.' He shrugged his shoulders again. 'Well, now we're in this particular situation and something has to be done.'

'Something has to be done?' Jaime rasped. 'Good God Almighty, I could have you jailed for what you've done.'

'I don't think you could,' Nicholas said quietly, 'and I don't advise you to try.'

They faced each other in anger for a moment or so; then it passed and Jaime regained his composure. The young man was right from one point of view: there was the situation and something must be done about it.

'I must talk first to Rosita,' Jaime said. 'Perhaps you'll come and see me tomorrow.'

'Perhaps,' Nicholas said.

He rose to his feet and went to the door. Then he paused and turned back for a moment.

'We all have to fight for what we believe,' he said, 'and what we each believe happens to be different. My father would be just as angry as you are—and perhaps that's why this thing has happened at all.' Then with a cool nod, he slipped out of the door.

Well, thought Jaime, of all the nerve! Of all the colossal, bare-faced, humiliating nerve! Like a colossus awakening from sleep, his pride began to be aroused. What had the Admiral said at lunch? It took a first-class disaster to bring us fully to our senses. He smiled grimly, drumming his fingers on the desk. He certainly had a personal disaster fairly and squarely facing him now.

5

Among the few real friends she had in Gibraltar, Grace put the Hobarts a clear first. They were not grand people and they were not well-off. But in their unsentimental affection for each other, in the joy their children gave them, in the goodness and understanding and gaiety which seemed to permeate the house at Rosia Bay, they were unique.

They had seen her engaged and married, they had watched her marriage go silently to pieces, they had noticed the impact of David and later, when his wife had arrived, they had unostentatiously moved into the foreground and become active when activity on someone else's part was clearly required. Now that both her husband and David had gone and Pam had returned to England to join the Wrens, they saw Grace learning to be alone once more and without putting it into words, they showed by their actions that they understood. The cliché of being a 'rock of strength' fitted admirably. Indeed, around Hobart and Cornelia there was a rock-like quality which had become symbolic to Grace. They were people to whom she instinctively turned when tired or under stress, and in some magic way, they fed her and restored her strength.

The evening of the day Nicholas saw her father, Grace had been asked round to the Hobarts for dinner. She had come off watch at four o'clock in the afternoon and after shopping in Main Street had reached home to find Rosita and her father, both pale and tense, in the middle of a scene of recrimination and reproach. Her mother was still at the Club playing bridge and Rosita had been summoned from the Censorship at her father's urgent request. She took one look at her sister's wooden face and at her father's exasperated stance and decided that she would have to plunge in herself.

'I gather you know all about this disgraceful state of affairs,' her father began and when she nodded and went over to her sister. 'I suppose it's natural you should both stick together. . . .'

'It's not a conspiracy,' Grace put in quickly, 'it's common sense. You didn't expect her to shout it from the house-tops, did you?'

'You should have told me before,' their father said. 'Haven't I always warned you to do things ahead of life—to take some sort of step in a crisis before you have to, before your hand is forced and you've no option?'

'There's not much she could have done,' Grace said, 'when

[171]

you think it out. She could have run away to England, but she didn't do that. She could have done a number of silly, even dangerous things. She didn't. The point is what's to be done now?'

'Your mother will never agree to the marriage. I can't say he's my idea of a husband for you either.'

'She loves him, Father.'

'Love?' Jaime said with a touch of anger. 'Love means responsibility: love means sacrifice and denying yourself: the sort of love that matters has to discipline itself—or are you talking of animal love?'

'That's a horrible thing to say.'

'It strikes me some rather horrible things have been done.'

Quite silently the tears welled out of Rosita's eyes as she looked at the floor. Grace went over and put her arm round her shoulder. Then she spoke out as she had never done before.

'As long as I'm in this house,' she began, 'I'm not going to stand on one side and see Mother wreck Rosey's life as she wrecked mine. Mother's always wanted the wrong things.'

'We won't discuss your mother now.'

'Excuse me, Father, but we will. Mother—and you, if it comes to that—plotted my marriage to Lance and at the right moment made it almost impossible for him not to propose. Mother's a snob. It didn't matter whether Lance would make me a good husband or not, whether he really loved me or I him—the fact that one day he would be Lord Pulborough and I his Lady was the beginning and end of it all for Mother. Well, she got what she wanted over me—and she isn't going to over Rosita.'

Jaime did not react for the moment. He was frankly a little surprised. Never before had his authority been questioned in this way. He had never thought of his quiet elder daughter as resentful—in this their religion had helped with its teaching of acceptance and resignation—yet now, in her sister's crisis, as though a door had been opened on to a dark cavern, lurking half-seen in the shadows, her real feelings about Edie and the life into which she had been born began to move uneasily. He looked at her with a new reserve.

[172]

'That's a curious way to speak to me, Grace.'

She looked at him unafraid. Before, she would always have been slightly diffident, would have cowered imperceptibly at the severity of his tone. His authority in the home had always been absolute.

'A whole lot of things are changing, Father. We have to bring ourselves up to date. We have to face the truth in ourselves once in a while.'

'I didn't realize you and Lance . . .' Jaime began and found himself full in the glare of her long-repressed anger.

'Oh! yes, you did, Father,' Grace interrupted curtly, 'you never thought much of Lance from the start. But you let Mother talk you into it and now it's too late. You put away your instinct, you made a nice little human sacrifice of me and Mother got what she wanted. So long as Mother gets what she wants it doesn't matter about anyone else.'

She heard the click of the door too late. Their mother had bustled into the room in her usual way, taking off her gloves, removing her hat and absorbing the scene out of the corners of her eyes.

'What doesn't matter, dear?' she asked briskly, 'and why is my Rosey crying?'

'Because your Rosey . . .' Grace began and then stopped. This was all wrong. It was Rosey and Rosey alone who mattered.

'Well, what is it?' their mother said. 'If it's that green brocade dress again, I've told you once and for all. . . .'

'It isn't anything to do with a dress, Mother,' Grace began and then in the next five minutes the story was out. Their mother rose to the situation like a general faced with a sudden enemy break-through. If there had been a shock, she showed no trace of it at all. She had looked first at her nails, then into the middle distance.

'She'd better go to England,' she said. 'I'll write to Cousin Flora at Beckenham.' Cousin Flora was a poor relation married to an accountant in a gasworks. She was always up Edie's sleeve for an emergency where publicity was not required.

'I don't think so,' Rosita said quietly. 'I think I'll marry Nicholas.'

[173]

Since the issue had now been brought to a head, their mother's tactics were to avoid it for the present.

'I think you'll do nothing at all,' she said, 'until your father and I have talked things over.' And on this remark she picked up her hat and gloves and went out of the room, followed by Jaime. Rosita and Grace looked at each other.

'Now the war really has begun,' Grace said, 'but remember what happened to me . . . there's no real need to give in. It's *your* life you have to think about. Mother isn't the only person on the Rock who can stand a long siege.'

Later that night she told the Hobarts the whole story.

'I can quite see your parents' point of view,' Hobart remarked. 'Out of all possibles on the Rock, Nicholas Pappadopoulos rates a good bottom.'

'I don't like him either,' Grace said, 'but my sister loves him and that's all that really matters.'

'How long will that go on for,' Cornelia asked, 'once the family throw her out into the snow?'

'She might be the making of him.'

'They may find themselves leaving the Rock in a hurry,' Hobart observed, 'he has some very questionable friends.'

'You're always saying that. What does it mean?'

'Exactly what I said. He keeps odd company.'

'Such as?'

'Now, Grace darling,' Hobart said with a smile, 'you don't expect me to tell you, do you?'

There, for the time being, it was left.

6

'Rumour is one thing, facts another,' the Governor had said to Jaime when the latter had so far violated his own instincts as to discuss Rosita and Nicholas a few evenings later. 'You know, as well as I do, that any repressive action I take will have to be justified later. Whatever we suspect, Pappadopoulos has a blameless record in Gibraltar and he's first-rate at his job. If I throw him out, there may well be a question in the House. I have the powers but I can't use them on vague suspicion. I'm sorry. I wish I could help.'

Fortin looked coolly at his Honorary A.D.C., at the urbane head of grey hair and the tired, responsible eyes. A good man with a lot on his plate, he mused, principally that wife of his. Proud, certainly, but no doubt it was the wife who mainly disliked the idea of this marriage. When all was said and done the young Cypriot came from a similar family in another colony—indeed the standing of Judge Pappadopoulos in Cyprus was, if anything, higher than that of the Barbarossas in Gibraltar. It would be the wife, Fortin concluded, with that inflexible, entrenched snobbery she exhibited wherever the Rock oligarchy was concerned—that outlook and that state of affairs which could be abolished, he reflected sardonically, by a single stroke of the pen.

The Evacuation Plan, the organization needed to remove all the women and children from Gibraltar ahead of a German attack, was already in existence. He had but to sign it and the niceties of whether Miss Barbarossa was marrying above or below her station would be swept away in a few short hours as a cup of water disappears in a torrent. Indeed, the thought of this small domestic event when lined up alongside the problems he had already had to consider that day brought a wry smile to his lips.

Yet as he watched Jaime Barbarossa walk stiffly to the door, another voice inside him pointed out that everything had its own place and that on each separate rung of the ladder an event had its own importance and value. There were microcosms and macrocosms. To Jaime Barbarossa the marriage of that strip of a girl was a more important problem than the disposal of Fat Barclay and Montague Bassett had been to Fortin. It was where a man habitually put the feeling of himself that determined the quality and characteristics of that man. As the door closed behind Jaime Barbarossa, Fortin thought for a moment of his own celibate life—from one point of view so empty, from another so free of the encumbrances which, for instance, were currently consuming his Gibraltarian A.D.C. For everything there was a price, even for an efficient wife and two elegant daughters.

Fortin remembered back thirty years to his own brief, ill-starred engagement. It still touched a sensitive place in his

[175]

being. He and Mary had been as much in love as it was possible to be, but right from the start it had come up against the stiff social machinery of the day. She had wanted to be Lady Fortin and to take her place in society. She had wanted him to use the Army as an expendable career, virtually a hobby. Fortin knew he could never continue to pay that particular price. His essential nature had taken him to India and the Persian Gulf, not into Edwardian salons, just as Mary's had taken her into marriage with the man who had once been his best friend, who was in addition a Peer of the Realm and who had been able to give Mary the things she had decided she needed.

Fortin opened the drawer of his desk, took out his bottle of quinine tablets and dosed himself. The rainy season was on them with its quickly changing temperatures and at this moment the damp mist of a Levanter was creeping round the corners of Government House bringing with it a mid-December shiver. The last Levanter had touched off his malaria again and he did not intend to be caught this time.

Apart from malaria, Gilbraltar illnesses were something to beware of. His eye caught a paragraph of Richard Ford's book open on his desk. He was writing of Gibraltar in the Napoleonic wars, yet to a degree it still applied to this day, '. . . the Gibraltar fever, about which doctors have disagreed so much, the patients dying in the meanwhile, is nurtured in Hebrew dirt, fed by want of circulation of air and offensive sewers at low tide. It is called into fatal activity by autumnal atmospheric peculiarity.'

It must have been the typhus, he thought, yet as he turned it over in his mind it struck him that there were other diseases equally as fatal, which the unnatural conditions of Gibraltar brought into sharp focus. There were the diseases of the mind and of the soul, the diseases which flourished on maladjustments between human beings. Jaime Barbarossa, his daughter and the unwanted son-in-law-to-be. The arrogance of the late and unlamented Colonial Secretary, the lazy selfishness of the departed Admiral Calderwell, the misunderstandings and meannesses which arise when a stress such as war is put upon ordinary people.

The war was contracting their lives: already he had had to

put Spain out of bounds to service personnel below officer's rank. Thus the brothels of La Línea could no longer assuage in some measure the needs of sailors and soldiers unable to sleep with their wives. At this stage it was scarcely a problem but with more and more servicemen pouring into Gibraltar, with steadily diminishing amenities and with the over-activity of naval life in contrast with the comparative idleness of garrison life—there were problems lurking very close at hand which would make the difficulties of Miss Barbarossa and Mr. Pappadopoulos of very small import. Let them get married, he said to himself, and to hell with the mother, to hell with the political doubts the young Cypriot aroused. Everything was in a state of flux and new proportions had to be found.

As Fortin went down to dinner and as Jaime told his wife of the Governor's refusal to help behind the scenes, the first reports of the Battle of the River Plate on the other side of the Atlantic were coming through. In England the first magnetic mine to be recovered and dismantled intact was yielding up its last secrets. David Evers and the 28th Destroyer Flotilla were at sea on a northern patrol. In France movement had died down on the Western Front while King George VI had just returned from a visit to the British Expeditionary Force. Italy remained sulkily on the fence, Russia had re-declared her neutrality and had then promptly invaded Finland to find herself expelled from the League of Nations for her pains.

In Gibraltar the Jockey Club and the Mediterranean Racing Club had both held their Autumn Meetings, the Gunners' Concert Party had taken over the Theatre Royal, *The Lady Vanishes* was showing at the R.N. Cinema and the Gibraltar Needlework Guild had thrown open their annual exhibition.

Such then was the general and particular state of affairs the night that Rosita decided to marry Nicholas Pappadopoulos in direct contravention of her parents' will and in the full knowledge that her mother would henceforth forbid her the house.

[177]

IX

H.M.S. *Firesprite*, H.M.S. *Forthright* and two other ships of the 28th Flotilla spent Christmas of 1939 at sea, forming the anti-submarine screen for a battleship and two cruisers of the Home Fleet on a dark, cold, ill-weathered patrol from the Shetlands to Norway.

To David Evers, on Christmas Day 1939, Gibraltar seemed like the memory of another life. His physical existence was now bounded by the cramped destroyer bridge, the tall chair on which he would sit hour after hour staring at the leaden-coloured sea and listening to the clicking of the gyro-compass repeater, and the occasional couple of hours asleep in his cabin below. At times it seemed as though he was a machine watching a machine: at others as though he was slightly above it observing it all revolving down there below him.

He was coming to know his own mechanism very well indeed. He was learning how to overload the human apparatus without wearing it to a standstill, he was finding out how to be clever about periods of fatigue which before the war would have rendered him useless. He was teaching himself how to relax within an outer framework of vigilance. He was continually sounding the depths of his reserves of energy, discovering how his brain, as dark and sodden as the winter sea, could be fired into new activity by a variety of self-given shocks so that a real emergency would never catch him napping.

He thought a lot about Pam and more often still about Grace in Gibraltar. Pam had returned to England in the first fortnight of the war, had joined the Wrens and was now a Third Officer cyphering at Kirkwall in the Orkneys. This was far from being an ideal arrangement for either of them.

Ever since the battleship *Royal Oak* had been sunk at anchor inside the protected harbour of Scapa by a German submarine, the main body of the Home Fleet had used Loch Ewe on the west coast of Scotland and, after November, Rosyth and the Firth of Forth. Work was proceeding at top speed on the boom, block-ships and A.A. Defence of Scapa Flow, but in the meantime the Fleet's dump of 130,000 tons of oil was used only for refuelling destroyers. Since the pumping aboard of oil fuel is virtually a matter of moments and the destroyers were hurried out to sea again as soon as possible, David and Pam found themselves frequently within a few miles of each other yet unable to meet. This exasperated them both and Pam had put in for transfer to Rosyth. One of the early lessons of the war, however, was that Wrens were made for the Navy and not vice versa. A transfer took time and very often by the time it took place the need for it had passed. Such conditions, therefore, had resulted in their seeing each other only twice in the first four months of the war.

Mail is perhaps ultimately the most essential food a sea-going sailor needs in wartime. David realized with twinges of guilty regret that it was Grace's letters and hers alone that he looked forward to receiving. Grace put her heart into the letters she wrote under the shadow of the Rock and sent off care of G.P.O. London: in Pam's school-girl scrawl there was only a curious deadness so that they seemed like the epistles children were made to write home from school. This same reluctant dutiful flavour was to be found in the correspondence between Lance Millingham, now serving in a cruiser, and his wife.

There was certainly plenty of time at sea, during that long first winter of the war, for reflection about themselves and their destiny. The odd boiler-clean or an attack of 'condenseritis' to which the ship's 36,000 horse-power engines were especially prone became almost the only respite they could anticipate. Yet there was nothing unwilling in their response to this drain on their energy. It was their job and they were proud to be doing it instead of sitting like the pongos halfway up the Rock of Gibraltar trying to keep the apes from pinching the ammunition—which was the picture Leading Signalman Jones, for example, carried of military duties at the port where they had worked up.

They groused and they moaned, but none of them would have swapped places with the other Services nor indeed with the 'plush-lined brotherhood' of the cruisers and battleships and aircraft-carriers they spent so much of their lives protecting. 'To hell with the *Nelson*, the *Hood* and the *Warspite*,' they chanted, 'the whole flipping Navy depends on the *Firesprite*.' That was their traditional, undefeatable answer to filthy weather and red-eyed exhaustion and even, with a few qualifying adjectives, to Christmas Day at sea with the Northern Patrol.

2

While *Firesprite* was thrashing the northern Atlantic that winter, no one on board guessed that their real destiny was always to be interwoven with Gibraltar, but late in January 1940 a practical link was forged.

'We've been adopted,' the Sub remarked, tossing over the letter in the wardroom to the First Lieutenant, 'so someone wants us after all—even if it's only the Gibraltar War Comforts Committee.' In a destroyer the Sub-Lieutenant deals with the correspondence and *Firesprite* now had a very new R.N.V.R. sub, an ex-garage proprietor, who had joined shortly before Christmas and had been almost continuously sea-sick ever since.

When the letter arrived, they had put into Scapa to refuel, David had gone ashore for a couple of hours to see Pam and everyone on board was exhausted after a ten days' patrol to the east of Iceland. Jimmy looked at the letter. It was signed Edith Barbarossa. That, he supposed, would be the mother. Already the Gibraltar hierarchy was indistinct in his mind. So much had happened since. He knew the Captain received regular letters with Gibraltar postmarks and he suspected that something was up between him and the elder daughter, but Jimmy Allendale was not unduly curious. Of the Barbarossa family he only remembered Rosita with clarity, and that because, in his mind, she was typical of the sort of colonial society girl from whom it was a relief to escape. A hostage having once been offered to the social life required of a naval officer, Jimmy Allendale's lusty tastes had taken him to the cafés and clubs of Main Street and across into murky La Línea for what the gunner called a 'drop of the real McCoy'.

'Show that letter to the Captain,' he told the Sub, 'and draft a reply thanking them and asking for a regular supply of—I don't know: what do we want?'

'Popsies,' put in the Surgeon-Lieutenant whose medical student days were only just at an end. This remark was greeted with a weary groan in the destroyer wardroom. A few draughty hours in Scapa were enough to convince the ship's company of *Firesprite* that women were out of their lives for ever. Even the gag about the Orkneys being full of 'Wrens in fur coats' which was what sheep were called on the Stokers' Mess-deck, now failed to raise even a smile.

'Better ask the Coxswain, I suppose,' said Jimmy. 'Perhaps if we put in for enough mittens and balaclava helmets, they'll send us south to pick them up.'

David returned to the ship a few minutes before they were due to sail. He glanced through the mail, pausing for a moment over the letter from the Gibraltar W.C. Committee, as the Sub had labelled it. Up in his cabin there was an unopened letter from Grace but for the moment it would have to wait. He had to get the ship back to sea and his mind was full of the meeting with Pam which had just taken place.

A restless, disturbed two hours together in the back room of a Kirkwall café, Pam in her neat Wren uniform and he grey with fatigue. He had thought himself too tired for any depth of feeling but the sight of the wife he had once loved so much and who now so obviously needed him threw open a door on to a void of emotion he had no wish to explore.

Everything was wrong with her life, she told him, the work she had to do, the other Wren officers, all of whom she disliked, the endless dark winter in the Orkneys, the fact that she needed her husband. She had sat in the café looking at the floor, crying without noise or fuss and it had twisted his heart. He did not want her but her plight moved him and she was still his wife. 'I miss you so terribly,' she had said in a low voice and without looking at him. 'I never thought it would be as empty as this.' He had tried to comfort her but there was nothing effective he could do. You could never counterfeit a feeling. He did not want her but the compassion in his heart was almost more than he could bear. She had never been quite like this before. She would have said she missed him but it would have been perfunctory and only partially true. Now she was like a lost child, absorbed in her grief. He had sat looking at her, his hand over hers, and behind her bowed head he had seen for a moment Grace's troubled eyes looking at him gravely, alive with understanding and a compassion of her own.

Sick at heart and appalled at his helplessness, he had talked encouragingly of her transfer to Rosyth, of enduring this trial which must in the nature of things have an end, of hope, of affection and of better times ahead. But he did not really believe what he was saying and her pointlessness and the lack of meaning in her life defeated the small positiveness he could muster. It was her life and she had to use it or throw it away. They were losing their common ground. He felt unable to reach her. She was turned inwards on to her own misery and despair. Sadly he had kissed her good-bye and had returned to the ship.

3

He did not open Grace's letter till they had been a night at sea. This was in the nature of a discipline—even of a punishment of himself—a tiny form of asceticism, the private pitifulness of which only he himself was aware.

During this time he had gone over and over in his mind the possibilities with Pam that perhaps had been missed, the mistakes that perhaps had been made. During long hours on the bridge he had brooded a great deal about destiny in general and his own in particular. Like his Uncle Giles, David believed that there was a pattern and a purpose in the life your being attracted. But you had to see what it was. You could use life for your own spiritual growth once you knew how, thus turning even apparent disasters to advantage. There was a way, but it had to be found. The great religions and the looser philosophies all pointed in a single direction once you became aware of the language they spoke. But you could know that and still not be able to do anything about it. You had to learn how to wait.

That was all very well in a general sense. What was his own particular pattern and purpose? Here he was at thirty-two, a lieutenant-commander in the zone for promotion, with eighteen years' service behind him since entering Dartmouth as a cadet of fourteen; with a pretty, sad wife from whom he was now diverging; with Grace whom he knew to be another part of his life fifteen hundred miles away to the south. He had a command of his own, a father who was a doctor, a brother in the Army and an uncle Governor of Gibraltar. A war was in progress and himself as much in it as it was possible to be and yet with it all a sense of incompleteness, doubt, and the suspicion lurking in his mind that somewhere or other he had lost the way. Had he caught it from Pam? Was her present unhappiness a reflection of something missing in himself?

Luckily for the present there was nothing to be done, no choice to be exercised. There was the ship, the sea and the war. That in a way was a mercy. The ship, the sea and the war allowed very little time for personal worries. Yet the two hours he had so recently been through with Pam reminded him uneasily that perhaps in himself he was running away. To put a thing out of your mind was one thing, to dispose of it for good another. At sea an excuse could always be found for stopping a train of thought. Perhaps it would be wiser to think it all out and not leave one's personal problems to settle themselves as so many of his ship's company were doing. Through the night he slept, went up on the bridge, slept and went on the bridge again. The dawn came, iron-grey and cold, his frame of mind remaining the same. He went down to his cabin to shave and when that was done, he opened Grace's letter as the ship rolled and pitched in the foaming sea off Cape Wrath.

'My dear David,' she began and then at once plunged into the centre of the thing without wasting time on preliminaries. 'I was utterly miserable reading between the lines about your last meeting with Pam and, as she's now installed at Scapa, I suppose you'll have seen her again by the time this arrives. My heart bleeds for you both—as it has done lately for myself—especially (and I know this is just self-pity but I can't help it) when Lance's Christmas present came—a leather-bound diary with the family crest embossed on the front which might have been ordered by his late and unlamented mother or indeed by

[183]

my own. But nothing personal: not even a handkerchief: even one of the funny little messages he once used to write would have been something—but no, Lance regards me as part of the furniture which he cannot dispose of—a rather dull, dowdy piece he would like to put out of his house but dare not. And us? What are we to do, David, you and I? Jog along as we are at present? Tell our respective spouses—and if so what? I mustn't add to your troubles. Don't ever let me do that, even accidentally, but shouldn't we bring it out in the open for the sake of honesty and conscience? You were quite right, my dear, when you said the two main snags were Pam's love for you and my religion: perhaps Pam's love for herself would be more accurate, with you as a sort of mirror to her vanity—or has she changed since leaving Gibraltar? I don't suppose she has underneath any more than I have or you have or Lance has.

'Now that Rosita is married and forbidden the house, the tumult and the shouting have died down a little. Father O'Reilly has been doing his best to patch things up, but Mother says she will never forgive and Father, while not talking so violently, simply dislikes Nicholas and says he stands for everything he has fought against all his life. So you can imagine how happy things are at Line Wall Road. The San Roque house has been put on a "care and maintenance" basis since Father says we are broke and anyway he prefers us to be within the protective domain of the Rock. This really suits Mother, only she won't admit it. She bustles about with her Red Cross committees (and it was her idea for Gibraltar to "adopt" *Firesprite* and other ships of your flotilla), she plays bridge and she still goes racing on Wednesday and Saturday afternoons. There is talk of turning the race-course into an aerodrome but the vested interests are against it to a man. As you know I'm mad about horses, too, but I sometimes wonder if we aren't still just playing at the war down here. Two merchant ships from one of the last convoys were torpedoed off Cape Trafalgar but somehow or other didn't sink. They limped in here on a Saturday afternoon when everyone was at the races. I suppose the garrison needs its amusements like everyone else—but I must say I find it a bit gruesome that ambulances with the dead and the dying should be held up by crowds of race-goers on their way from the North Front. I suppose something happens to one's sense of proportion in wartime.

'There are times when I wonder if it's "our" war at all. I know it's *your* war all right—you're in it up to the neck—but here nothing dramatic ever happens except at sea. Gib is a complete backwater now that the early glamour of being at war has worn off. In fact the only siege taking place here is by that monster, Boredom. We were discussing it last night when Dicky Seale and I had dinner with the Hobarts. (She *has* started another baby and alternates between fury at the Himmlet and pleasure: I think she *really* wanted another one all along.) Atcheson was saying that the high-ups are already worried at a sort of jealousy which is brewing between the Army and the Navy. I think the River Plate action brought it to a head. The Navy has all the fun (fun!), the excitement and the glamour. The Army practises its air-raid barrage (but no hostile plane has been anywhere near), tunnels away into the Rock making headquarters which will probably never be used, and otherwise worries about its E.N.S.A. shows and its sacred amenities. Perhaps this is a very short-sighted view but envy and jealousy do funny things and when a couple of gunners and two merchant seamen got into a fight last week because the soldiers were accused of sitting on their backsides having a cosy time while sailors drowned bringing them their comforts— your uncle took notice and there have been high-level conferences at Government House to "butter up the pongos" as the Admiral's Secretary puts it. Meanwhile the fruit machine still rattles away in the cellar of the Bristol, the Rock Hotel still runs its Saturday night dinner-dances and Benny still presides benevolently over the Yacht Club bar. Algeciras is supposed to be riddled with German spies but the Reina Cristina still advertises a twelve-peseta lunch which a surprising number of people from Gibraltar manage to get across and eat. I'm still at the Tower working away at my figures though more and more Wrens are arriving and they say we shall soon be out of a job. I look across at the pens and long hopelessly to see *Firesprite* tied up there as she used to be. It's a dream, I know, but try and surprise us one of these days. Mother and Father still speak of you both as the ideal guests—so even in an outward

[185]

conventional way you know where your home is here. I can't tell you how I ache to see you again. But perhaps you know already how it is. . . .'

David put down the letter and looked out of his scuttle for a moment at the troubled sea. There was a whistle from the voice-pipe to the bridge, followed by Jimmy Allendale's voice.

'Captain, sir, *Forthright's* flying her contact pendant close up. There's nothing yet from our own Asdic.'

'Right,' said David as he folded the letter and put away Gibraltar from his thoughts, 'I'll be up right away.'

4

The four months of April, May, June, and July 1940 are perhaps the most extraordinary the western world has yet seen. Denmark and Norway fell on 9th April: a month later the assault on Holland, Belgium and France began: by the end of June England stood entirely alone awaiting invasion. It began to look as though anything could happen and during the forty days from the 10th May, which comprised the heart of the period, almost everything did. When France fell it seemed as if there could be no further disasters and life would continue from then on in a minor key.

In Gibraltar the idea that war was something which could be superimposed, albeit uncomfortably, on to ordinary peace-time life continued through the Norwegian campaign. In March and April, Italian liners such as the *Rex*, *Vulvania* and *Conte di Savoia* still called in at the Rock on their way to New York. Indeed there had been quite a stir when Hobart had had Herr Fritz von Opel, the German car-magnate, removed from the *Conte di Savoia* for a thorough investigation of his luggage. According to international law, it was asked, was this quite the thing?

The *Gibraltar Gazette* carried advertisements urging service-men to spend their leave in French Morocco, visiting the Marrakech and southern Morocco Fair, and while British soldiers were dying in the snows of Norway, day trips to Tangier at ten shillings a head were still being run by the S.S. *Gibel Dersa*, Noel Coward came and went, Charles Laughton could

[186]

be seen in the film, *Jamaica Inn*, the Jockey Club held its Charity Meeting. Ladies like Edith Barbarossa still devoted their mornings to Red Cross activity and their afternoons to bridge. Imperial Airways had died giving birth to a set of initials and permission had just been granted by Franco for British aircraft to fly over Spain *en route* to Lisbon which was the European terminal of the Pan-American Clipper service across the Atlantic. The war was a bore: prices were going up and things were in short supply: but Hitler was running out of oil, they said, and there was always the Maginot Line. One of these days he'd come a cropper and the whole Nazi façade would be shown up as a gigantic bluff, even the blitzkrieg into Poland and Norway being seen for what they were, mere flashes in the pan.

Such then was life in Gibraltar when Grace opened the Admiralty telegram announcing that Lance was 'Missing presumed dead'. She put it down and stared out at the patio, her feelings and thoughts at first unfocused. She had had a letter from him only that morning and although to be at sea in wartime at all was dangerous, it had never occurred to her seriously that he might be killed. He wasn't the type. Now that he had been, her first sensations were of surprise and uncertainty.

Then pity and a sense of guilt followed on quickly and a desire to be very quiet in herself. She slipped out of the house and walked up to the Roman Catholic Cathedral. There was no service in progress and she could be still and reflect by herself. She lit a candle and prayed for his soul, as sincerely and responsibly as she could, but try as she might her heart remained unmoved. This is my husband, she told herself, the man I married in the sight of God. I ought to feel: yet I don't. I feel nothing at all. What has happened to me? Why am I numb? Perhaps it was a dangerous sense of release, perhaps all along she had secretly wanted to be free. Perhaps in some awful way she had been the cause of his death.

She tucked herself away behind a pillar, staring at the altar and wondering back on her life. She was all right as long as she directed her attention. Whenever she relaxed, however, David's grave face and those deep steady eyes rose up in her mind. Instinctively she dodged it, yet perhaps her feeling for David was the root cause of it all. She felt about him all right. Sometimes simply forming his name would bring the tears to her eyes, yet it was something given, something unasked and above all something she knew to be more deeply real than anything she had ever experienced.

What then? We are here to learn, her religion decreed, to learn and to accept. Not to do as we like, not to covet your neighbour's husband, nor his ox, nor his ass, nor anything that was his. Well, if Lance were dead—and how odd it was that inside herself she had no means of knowing—then perhaps it was a first step on the long journey to freedom. Perhaps. . . .

When she left the Cathedral she took a gharry out to Rosia Bay and the Hobart's house. Soon there would be no more gharries in Gibraltar or rather no horses to pull them, but to-night, with a gentle wind from the west and the sun setting in a riot of colour over the Algeciras hills, she found the slow clip-clop of the trotting horse immensely soothing, the evening air cool on her cheeks. So Lance was missing, presumed dead! Suppose, though, he wasn't. Suppose the presumption were false? The ancient gharry passed through the South Port Gate with Charles V's thick stone wall stretching away up the Rock into the dusk, the Trafalgar Cemetery quiet and deserted on the left.

It was then that she admitted to herself that even if Lance happened still to be alive, she would never live with him again. She shivered slightly. She had never faced it so directly before. The horse eased to a walk up Scud Hill, the dockyard clatter to the right softened in the balmy air. Whether it was self-pity or whether it was a sense of fate, she felt the tears welling up in her eyes and knowing that she would soon be among friends she made no effort to stop them.

Ten minutes later she was in the Hobarts' comfortable, rather shabby sitting-room with Jonathan and Michael playing a tug-of-war over her knees, with Cornelia's warm American voice oddly comforting and with Hobart, as glad to see her as his wife, mixing the drinks and chattering banalities until the children could be sent off to bed.

Elsewhere in Gibraltar Mrs. Pappadopoulos cooked supper for her husband and prepared for the imminent birth of her baby. A great change had occurred in her life. From being a frivolous, idle girl accustomed to all the trappings of wealth, she was now learning what it was like to be ostracized, to have little money and less comfort and to live with a man whose bitterness and hatred seemed to warp everything he touched, in spite of all she could do to sweeten their lives.

Nothing had turned out quite as she had expected. She had not believed her parents would do as they had threatened and forbid her the house. They had done so and her one subsequent experience of breezing in uninvited had cured her of ever doing it again. Her friends, too, had drifted away in ones or twos. This had really hurt, yet in a way she could not blame them. To begin with they had made an effort with Nicholas, often against the opposition of their own parents, but since he never bothered with them in return and indeed went out of his way to show his disdain for their futile lives and the things they enjoyed doing, they tended to put 'the Cypriot *ménage*' at the bottom of their invitation list.

Alone, together, and in bed, it was as though the outer world no longer existed and there were days in which they did not get up but simply remained at rest with each other, their lives bounded by the bed and the tawdry room, the child that would soon be born stirring and kicking in her womb, their naked bodies expressing an affection and a tenderness which vanished with the putting-on of clothes and the aggressive technique they were finding it necessary to adopt with their outer lives.

To shopkeepers and other tenants in the block she was and always would be a Barbarossa, a lady and distinct from them in class and upbringing. Nicholas hated it and for a time humiliated her whenever he could. But he was powerless to change it. He himself was of breeding but he was from another place. They would never accept him, just as the Indian and Jewish traders kept their foothold in Gibraltar but little else. Moreover his raging hatred of injustice, as symbolized by British colonial rule, in no way endeared him to the people he was hoping to rouse. He struck the note but there was no response. It was, indeed, only among the conscript other ranks of the Army, the R.A.F. and the Navy, drawn into the war from industrial slums, that the sour dissatisfaction with privilege and the aristocratic idea provided the right soil for the militant socialism and class warfare he burned to preach.

She still worked in the censorship and he at the sub-editing job. Indeed, except for living together in the same room, their lives were as separate as they always had been. He was not a man who made friends and the changing acquaintances she had met in the early days did not attract her. They all had an axe to grind and after one or two meetings became as boring to her as her puppy friends were to him.

So after a time they gave up the attempt to mingle their worlds and he took to spending longer and longer in the Tribuno Bar with bloody-minded Air Force corporals and in odd meetings with the elusive Mr. Boothroyd about which she knew nothing at all. She went regularly to Mass and occasionally to confession, she saw Grace as often as she could and Father O'Reilly did what he could with Jaime and her mother, but he did not expect results, he told her, until the baby was born and Edie thus became a grandmother.

There was almost no self-pity in her make-up and this was just as well since she was finding her life and the world in which it was set just as puzzling as Grace had done when, after marrying the man her mother had chosen and with all the weight of social approval behind it, the relationship had none the less headed straight for the rocks. What was out of key? Was it herself—or Grace—or the Barbarossa family? She looked through the window at the darkening Rock. The six o'clock news had talked of the withdrawal from Namsos. The King and Government of Norway had landed safely in the United Kingdom. Despite the announcer's brisk, professional cheerfulness and the suggestion that all was for the best of all possible worlds, the end of resistance in Norway was now in sight. It was a fateful time to be bringing a child into the world.

The door of the flat opened and Nicholas appeared, half an hour late for his supper. He had obviously had a heavy session at the Tribuno bar.

6

Though Rosita did not know it, Nicholas had been else-where before visiting the Tribuno, and this habit was one of the tensions driving him to plunge more and more deeply into alcohol as time went on. He did this unconsciously. Had he stopped to think about his drinking a host of different reasons would have presented themselves all disguising the central fact which he avoided ever admitting—the fact that his political ideas, the drift of the war and the personal failures of his life were breeding in him a deep despair. Even the attraction he felt for Rosita and the odd fact that unlike any other woman he had lived with she did not pall, could not assuage this deep inexpressible ache at the pit of his heart.

The meetings with Boothroyd both fed his state of mind and gave it reason to continue. They were highly secret. Boothroyd, the bluff Yorkshireman in the Naval Armament Supply Service, saw to it that they never met twice running in the same place and that if curiosity should be aroused there was a valid reason for them to be together.

Boothroyd was the core and centre of the secret organization he had been sent to Gibraltar to create. Nicholas had assumed him to be a Communist but now he was not so sure. He could well be receiving money from a number of sources and his loyalties were never declared. All that Nicholas knew was that he had come to dispose of Gibraltar one way or another—and that such a result was by no means the fantastic impossibility it appeared at first sight. In any case he had been so successful in keeping all that side of his life secret that not even Hobart realized his identity. The inner core of his organization was very small. It consisted of himself, a clerk in the Naval Store Department, a Police Sub-Inspector and a Sergeant in the Army Education Corps. They met very seldom but from each member a small net was thrown out, the smaller reflecting the greater, the outer the inner. These separate webs were not known to each other and apparently they operated independently. Hobart knew of some of them but the source from which they renewed their strength remained hidden.

Nicholas was not a Communist. After the Spanish Civil

War he had become wary of their methods. Yet their power fascinated him. They were effective. They knew what they wanted and they had an unusual determination in getting it. The end was what mattered and since all means were subordinate to this, the Communist idea was in itself an antidote to half-hearted frustration. Once committed, doubt and an aimless drifting were banished and one of the qualities which drew him to Boothroyd was the latter's singleness of purpose and his obvious strength. But was he a Communist or was he simply a well-trained agent or was he both?

Whatever Boothroyd knew of Nicholas and his background was never revealed. Yet he knew about his Spanish adventure. He knew of his guarded attitude to the Communist Party. In fact he evidently knew quite a lot. He made no attempt to involve him directly. Perhaps, Nicholas thought, he was considered to be a fellow-traveller which in a great many senses he was. But as Boothroyd himself had once remarked—a fellow-traveller need not always be travelling. A time would come. That he was anti-colonial was enough. The job would come later. Now that Hitler and Stalin were in compact, the joint directive was to disrupt, sabotage, and destroy the Allies' war effort. The war at that time was described by the Left as an 'Imperialist and Capitalist crime against humanity'. Since this accorded with Nicholas's loathing of the British Empire, it was easy for him to co-operate with Boothroyd. Nicholas had a sense of fatalism much as Fortin had about the Rock and his role as Governor. Possibly behind it all, these were two sides of the same thing. To the one it was part of a crusade: to the other treachery.

7

Over it all lay the greater destiny of the war. Both Fortin and the Admiral shared the premonition, expressed by Churchill in the House of Commons, that the Norwegian campaign was but a prelude to a much greater thrust. In the week immediately preceding the 10th May 1940, Fortin had been on a semi-official visit to Seville and Madrid. He returned to Gibraltar grimly aware that there was a cold wind from the north blowing across the Sierras and that it would very soon be buffeting the Rock.

'My Spanish wasn't good enough to take in all the niceties,' he told the Defence Committee when he returned, 'but the interpreters filled in the gaps. The Ambassador told me that civilian Germans and Italians were pouring into the country. Well—that's no news, of course. The point is that the numbers have suddenly jumped. "Technicians and experts"—that covers almost anyone the enemy want to send down here. Work on the Tarifa fortifications was intensified as from a week ago and so was work on the military road to Ronda. The Spaniards I met in Sevilla and Madrid were studiously polite and courteous —but Norway hasn't done our reputation any good and even the Anglophiles don't think it will be long before Gibraltar is in the limelight. Franco is supposed to have worked out a formula with the Fuehrer by which Spain gets more than she gives.' He shrugged his shoulders. 'We can each have our own opinion on that. My view is that once the Germans are in, they're in, and there's nothing the Spaniards will be able to do about it. So it looks as though we may well have to evacuate the women and children to Morocco and put Plan P into operation in one continuous action. The Evacuation Committee, therefore, is to go into high gear. If the balloon goes up there are to be no exceptions of any kind. Only fighting men are to remain on the Rock. I've the feeling there's going to be much less time than we think. Poland, Denmark and Norway have shown us how quickly the enemy moves. I don't intend we should be caught with our trousers down.'

'If we evacuate before an attack begins, there's going to be great hardship, sir,' the Colonial Secretary interjected, 'especially among the older people. Some of them won't be budged off the Rock except by force. Some of them have never set foot outside Gibraltar the whole of their lives—not even into Spain.'

'We've been through all that. Force will have to be used.'

'And the fine for evasion?'

'What was recommended?'

'Fifty pounds.'

'Make it a hundred,' snapped Fortin.

[193]

'Done,' said the Colonial Secretary and got a laugh. Fortin smiled briefly: old Bassett would have made much heavier weather of it than this young man who looked more of a subaltern than an experienced colonial administrator. He was lucky with his team, there was no doubt about that.

'What about the beer?' said the Admiral. 'Every time Force H comes back into harbour all I hear are complaints about the beer. With Línea out of bounds and the beer undrinkable I won't answer for the Navy.'

'Seconded for the Army,' said the General and the Air-Commodore nodded in agreement.

'I took that up with the Ambassador, too,' said Fortin. 'I'm afraid he confirmed what we know already. The only breweries capable of giving us what we want in the quantities we need are owned and operated by Germans. The Treasury won't let us trade with the enemy.'

'Then the Treasury can roll up its sleeves and deal with some thirsty disgruntled sailors.'

'The Ambassador understands the position,' Fortin said. 'We all think the beer's more important than the money—so the beer is somehow or other going to be produced: only I hope no awkward questions will be asked.'

The Admiral looked across at him, his eyes wrinkled appreciatively.

'I think we can handle any awkward questions all right. We've got the *Hood* and the *Ark Royal* on our side down at the South Mole.'

Fortin turned to the Deputy Fortress Commander.

'How is the demise of the race-course being taken?'

'Philosophically. I've promised the Sports Committee they can go on using the football ground until aircraft actually dislodge them. The Victoria Gardens are going to be missed this summer, especially the tall trees near the neutral ground. They've been levelled to about a hundred yards from the road.'

'A lot of things are going to be missed this summer,' Fortin said reflectively and looked round at the Admiral, the General, the Air-Commodore and the Colonial Secretary as though he was going to miss them personally. Here, in their characteristic attitudes at the conference table, were the heads which would inevitably fall should anything happen to the Rock. These were the four human pillars on whom, under the Governor, the defence of the Rock relied. But there was a fifth factor to take into consideration nowadays. As he had pondered the course of the war so far, it had emerged over the months more and more into the forefront of his mind. It was the interior softening up of the victim which preceded a German blitz—that was the new factor one had to watch. On the spur of the moment he decided to bring it up, there and then.

'Both in Seville and Madrid,' he remarked, 'I thought a lot about that Norwegian chap—Quisling. I think we take it too much for granted that the fifth column can't happen here. Franco's alive to it well enough in Spain on his own account. I wouldn't be surprised if he slyly adapted the idea for his own purposes and tried to apply it here. Remember he wants Gibraltar quite apart from anything the Germans can do. I think the Defence Security Officer ought to attend our meetings. Treachery seems to have moved to another position in this war. The Germans are using it deliberately as a military weapon. So are the Russians. It's no good manning strong points and frontiers if the microbe is already working away inside. That's why I'd like Hobart to sit in on all our deliberations. He may have some bright ideas.'

The Committee nodded its assent but Fortin's train of thought was picked up by the Admiral and taken on further.

'It seems to me, when I put on my dockyard hat, that morale is going to be much more of a problem than any of us think. Not'—he emphasized the word and then paused before going on—'not if the crisis comes but if it doesn't. We talk about morale vaguely and as the C.-in-C. has just said we take it for granted. At sea that's all right. In a way the job does it for you: but ashore in a dockyard there isn't the danger, there isn't the discipline, there isn't the glamour. I don't know what we can do about it and I certainly don't want any more earnest committees of knitting ladies and welfare officers cluttering up the Dockyard Tower. The point is this. As a nation we usually assume that if no disaster happens then everything's all right. Here in Gibraltar in May 1940 I'm not so sure. There's a sense of injustice and disaffection lurking in the shadows.'

'Are you talking of Gibraltarians, Spaniards or what?' Fortin asked. The Admiral thought for a moment before answering.

'The sea-going sailor has always had a veiled contempt for dockyard types—bolshie mateys and so on. For one thing he's under discipline and they aren't, so things get done at sea whereas sometimes they don't ashore. From the sailor's point of view dockyard workers get paid more, they do less work and they can sleep at home every night. So there's a mixture of pride and envy at every point where the worlds come into contact. I'll exclude the Spanish labour force. That's another world on its own. All things considered I think they're amazingly loyal to us and I imagine even the Generalissimo may stub his toe on that one. It's the subordinate, white-collar Gibraltarians—the clerks and storehousemen and their British equivalents both in and out of uniform that are going to be the real headache. There's a class-resentment I haven't come across before—much more among the British conscripts than the Gibraltarians, to be fair. This isn't a crusade like the Great War was—there's a surliness, an apathy—a bloody-mindedness at the Petty Officer level which you never get at sea except in a very unhappy ship. That's where our trouble is going to be—if there' going to be any trouble at all.'

'If that's what the Admiral feels,' the General said dryly, 'when the Navy gets the pick of the bunch, he ought to come up to Europa Flats one day and see what's been wished on the poor old Army.'

The Admiral glinted.

'I don't precisely expect a mutiny down in the Dockyard,' he said crisply, 'I'm talking of something I occasionally see out of the corner of my eye. It doesn't keep me awake at night. But, like the C.-in-C. feels about Major Quisling, I sometimes wonder.'

X

A**t** least once a day Fortin gave silent thanks for the team
that had gathered around him and he did so especially
on the 10th May, the first day of the forty in the European wilderness, the day the Germans fell upon Holland,
Belgium and France, the day Churchill became Prime Minister,
the day when the first of the catastrophic shocks which was to
arouse the British Empire to its full fighting fury was given.

There was what Seale had once described as a 'dry friendship' between Fortin and Admiral Vickerson. This was based
on a mutual respect, experience and a kind of salty recognition
of each other's foibles. The Vice-Admiral Commanding the
North Atlantic knew with relish that Fortin of Waziristan
longed to take a hand in running the Atlantic. The Governor
and Commander-in-Chief, Gibraltar, was aware that Vickerson, who had got his D.S.O. at Zeebrugge, enjoyed trying to
impose Royal Naval technique and control on the running of
the Rock, its garrison, its air-defence and its relationship with
Spain. But whereas Fat Barclay would have been activated by
a personal vanity and pomposity, Vickerson's pride in the
Royal Navy went deeper and so did his awareness of limits.
He knew he could 'let the Governor in' without weakening
his position as a local nautical sovereign and equally Fortin
had taken to mentioning obliquely some of his political and
administrative problems and allowing the Admiral to develop
and express an opinion without feeling that the Admiral was
ever going to tell him how to run the Rock. Each respected
the other's integrity.

In May 1940 the Naval Operations Room had become to
Fortin the most fascinating place in Gibraltar. This was because shipping in the Atlantic and the Mediterranean was in
constant movement, the dotting of U-boats and the intermittent threat from German pocket-battleships altered the
picture from hour to hour, and finally because Force H,
Admiral Somerville's striking force, consisting usually of a

battle-cruiser, an aircraft-carrier, cruisers and destroyers, was now based upon Gibraltar.

Sometimes he would drive down to the Dockyard with Seale or Hobart, at other times, if the pressure of work allowed, he would walk. His pleasure in walking, however, was vitiated by the ceaseless saluting and springing to attention of sentries which his appearance provoked. It was only on the Upper Rock that, except for the apes and an occasional security patrol, he could enjoy the privacy and solitude which at one time he got from the desert.

On the evening of the 10th he and Hobart walked down to the Dockyard together. Hobart had just returned from an abortive plain-clothes expedition to a contact near Cape Trafalgar. This entailed taking the Cadiz road through Tarifa and Vejer. It was a journey he had made a countless number of times but that afternoon he had found that a whole maze of new restrictions, passes and *permisos* had been imposed. At each check-point he had had to invoke the highest authority in order to get through at all. There were new faces in the Customs and the friendly smiles had disappeared. On the highway itself it struck him that the *Guardia Civil* had been doubled and ordered to exercise more authority.

When at last he had reached the cottage, the fisherman he sought was 'away', the family strangely hostile. Hobart was the last person to over-value or to panic but the signs were unquestionably ominous. As Fortin had felt on his trip to Seville and Madrid, he had come back to Gibraltar most uneasy. Something was cooking up and it did not take a great deal of gumption to guess what it was likely to be.

The six o'clock B.B.C. news stunned and shocked. The Allied front line had ceased to exist. A disaster in depth had begun. In London Churchill was seeing the King and taking over the high office to which destiny had brought him, while elsewhere in the world maps were being redrawn and new assessments made, soon to be as out of date as the Maginot Line. Grace was decyphering a spate of messages down at the Tower, the same messages that Pam Evers was decyphering in far-distant Rosyth. The 28th Destroyer Flotilla was ferrying troops to Norway for a final stand, Boothroyd and Nicholas in a little bar off Engineer's Lane were raising their glasses in a silent toast, while Fortin and Hobart set off for the Naval Operations Room to see what the Navy was up to and were thus accidentally very close at hand when the first serious piece of sabotage in the Dockyard took place.

2

To blow up something in Gibraltar is both easier and more difficult than at first sight appears. At least ten thousand Spaniards, men and women, come across the border to work in Gibraltar every day. They bring chickens, eggs and vegetables to sell and they return with cloth and tobacco smuggled past the corrupt Spanish customs officers. So with a modicum of luck it is comparatively easy to bring a bomb or the components of a bomb into Gibraltar.

On the other hand, to assemble that bomb and to place it in the right position is exceedingly difficult. Space on the Rock is at a premium, the Dockyard is not big and the town perpetually overcrowded. There are eyes watching wherever you go. For a Spanish workman to slip out of the Dockyard, assemble his bomb in privacy and bring it back was almost impossible. For him to place it unobserved where it mattered, a triumph.

Yet this is what someone or some organization had achieved. As Fortin and Hobart reached the Dockyard Tower, a loud explosion occurred in the direction of the Graving Dock. This was followed by a rising sheet of flame and the roar of a second explosion. For a moment Fortin and Hobart remained paralysed in thought, looking at each other. It could be an accident, it could be deliberate, it could be the prelude to something much worse.

'Sounds like one of the oil-tanks,' Hobart said, flagging a car as it passed. This was, in fact, exactly what it turned out to be. Two basins down from where they were lay Coaling Island, a wharf built out into the harbour with coal dumps on it and nowadays oil-tanks and fuelling equipment. It was down towards the Yacht Club and outside the main Dockyard itself. Rattling along in their requisitioned car and overtaken at one point by the dockyard fire-engine, they made their way straight to Coaling Island, wondering what sort of disaster would meet their eyes when they got there, Hobart's mind racing over his short list of suspects capable of such a job, Fortin wondering if this was the signal for a fifth-column rising in the port such as the Germans had organized in Narvik, or whether it presaged an early attack on the Rock.

By the time they reached the scene of the explosion, one oil-tank was burning fiercely and there were subsidiary fires among oil-drums on the jetty. The explosion had torn up pipes and there was a chaos of twisted metal, silhouetted against the heart of the blaze. A sloop which had been alongside and whose bridge-plating was scorched and distorted had already rigged a couple of hoses and these were playing on the fire in two small and ineffective streams. The dockyard fire-engines had arrived and these were soon joined by the City Council Brigade in force. These made no attempt to put out the fire already burning but instead concentrated on preserving the other tanks on the jetty. If the one tank could burn itself out and the damage be confined, there was little danger to ships in the harbour. However the heat from the blaze was such that if the wind grew in force there might well be other explosions. Fortin looked at the *Hood* lying across the harbour at the South Mole. The world's largest warship was having a very special firework display put on for its benefit.

The Admiral arrived and Fortin went over to talk to him. Hobart was already away with two sergeants and a young Intelligence officer who had appeared out of the blue and Dicky Seale, as if by instinct, had homed on to the Coaling Jetty. Gradually the fire came under control and from out of the wreckage a badly charred corpse was extracted. Fortin watched it being dragged clear, watched it put on a stretcher and carried to an ambulance. Then, his mind still occupied with the implications and possibilities which might lie behind this explosion, he returned to Government House. The period of threat to Gibraltar had begun with a bang.

3

Two other occurrences on a personal scale took place in

Gibraltar that night. Rosita began her labour and Edith Barbarossa suffered a seizure. Each, as it happened, was quite alone when the event overtook them. How strange it was, thought Grace, who became at once involved with both of them, that they should be within a few hundred yards of each other yet inaccessible. The war might well have kept them thousands of miles apart, yet it was not the war but pride which divided them.

It began for Rosita at about eight-thirty at night when Nicholas had gone to the office. She had not seen him all day. He had got up about lunchtime in one of his silent, brooding moods and had gone out. She resented these absences more and more the nearer her time came. It was typical somehow. Now she knew he didn't really care.

She had expected him back for his evening meal but he had not shown up and then there had been the explosion which the neighbours were all chattering about in Spanish. She had prepared herself for what was to happen often enough in her mind. Yet when it began it took her by surprise and it frightened her. She rang Grace from the telephone in the shop across the street but Grace had not returned home. It was damnably public and she hated it although now everyone knew her story and accepted her. She rang the cypher office in the Dockyard but Grace was not on watch. She rang the Yacht Club without success. She rang Nicholas at the *Gibraltar Gazette* office but the line was continuously engaged. She sat down among the sacks of corn and dried peas and the smell of carbolic soap and paraffin as a spasm of pain shook her again. Then Señora Gaturrez who ran the shop realized what was happening and sent her youngest boy as fast as his legs could carry him to Father O'Reilly's lodgings. But Father O'Reilly was across in La Línea and not expected back till later that night. Then suddenly Rosita remembered the Hobarts, rang them and with a sense of boundless relief heard Cornelia saying:

'Why, surely she's here! Do you want to speak to her?'

Twenty minutes later Grace was in her room talking to her calmly about the day's happenings and especially the explosion which was now almost certainly thought to be sabotage. The pains came and went. When they came she wanted to be alone

[201]

and when they went she was grateful to have Grace in the room. Dr. Gonzalez, the Barbarossa family doctor, was summoned by Grace and a little later the nurse arrived. Both of them implied that Rosita had panicked, saying they would return nearer the time. At that point, Grace too, came to a decision as she sat in the dingy, depressing bedroom which was now her sister's home. This stupid ridiculous feud had gone on long enough.

'I'm going to take you back home with me,' she said as if she had seen something clearly after a long period of confusion. 'You just can't have it here: you're coming home where you can be properly looked after. I don't care what Nicholas feels or says—he should have taken better care of you all along. I'll see Mother doesn't bully you. In fact if she opens her mouth then I go, too, and for good—and if that happens Cornelia will take us in, she's already offered. But Mother isn't really like that. . . .' She paused as though she was explaining their mother to a stranger. 'She'd be appalled if she saw you in all this. So get your bits and pieces together. I'll dash home, warn Teresa, get the car and be back in a jiffy.'

Rosita looked at the floor as the pain started again.

'I don't think it matters very much,' she said, 'I should have gone to the hospital as Dr. Gonzalez suggested. Will you try and ring Nicholas again?'

But in Gibraltar news travels fast and somehow or other Nicholas had already been told. As Grace reached the door he came storming in. He had clearly been drinking and his face was grey and puffy. He paid no attention to Grace.

'I hear it's started,' he said to Rosita. "Why didn't you let me know?'

She did not answer but simply looked at him mutely. Instead Grace said:

'She tried. The line was engaged. And you were out all day. You never came back for supper.'

He turned on her harshly.

'You'd better keep out of this.'

'I'm taking Rosita home. It's time someone looked after her for a change.'

'You'll do no such thing. She's my wife and she has her

baby here in this room in this bed. I want no Barbarossa interference—do you understand? Rosita is *my wife*, understand?'

Grace stood her ground calmly.

'Then you should look after your wife—or do you consider that leaving her at midday and not coming back till the
early hours is how a girl about to have her first baby should be
treated?'

Nicholas frowned and his mouth set hard. All the bitterness
and hatred in him flashed angrily from his eyes.

'I have a job to do—or does that fact elude you? There's a
war on. Perhaps you've heard? The German break-through
has begun. There are big changes for all of us happening *now*
at this moment. In a couple of months it'll all be over. We
shall have been beaten—and there'll be no more Gibraltar, no
more British Empire. I love my wife but there *are* other things.
Tonight the Rock nearly blew up. One way and another,
Mrs. Millingham, it's been a day. Now shut up and get out.'
His voice had risen to an almost hysterical yell. Grace looked at
him with a very active dislike. But she tried to keep her reason,
to keep it calm.

'You seem to think you're the only person in Gibraltar
who's had "a day". I don't need to be told there's a war on—
especially by you, Nicholas. I heard the explosion too. I
heard the news on the B.B.C. I've also done a cypher watch.
You don't have to tell me it's been a day. It still doesn't excuse
you for leaving Rosita all this time.'

He strode over and for a moment she thought he was going
to strike her. Instead he took her by the shoulders and shook
her hard.

'Now get this once and for all,' he said, through his teeth,
'you, your father and that goddam, stuck-up, snobbish cow of
a mother of yours. I am perfectly capable of running my own
life and that of my wife. Not only that—I intend to do so.
Don't come round here again unless you're invited. Understand?'

So saying he opened the door and half-pushed, half-threw
her out on the landing. For a moment or so she stood still,
recovering from the shock, the slam of the door reverberating
in her ears, still feeling the grip of his hands on her shoulders,

wondering what she should do. Then as she started down the stairs the door opened again and Rosita appeared, leaning for a moment against the door-post and then walking slowly to the head of the stairs.

'Wait for me, Grace. I'm coming too.'

4

The two sisters arrived at the Line Wall Road house just as Dr. Gonzalez was leaving. Their mother's attack and Rosita's decision to come home were thus conveyed and understood in a matter of moments. Having been 'a day' it was evidently going to be 'a night' as well and Dr. Gonzalez had another emergency call. Their mother had been bending down to pick something up and suddenly it was upon her. Perhaps she would recover: perhaps there would be another one within hours: perhaps it would be years, it was impossible to say. There would certainly be another one, of that alone one could be completely sure.

He said he would be back as soon as he could and then he looked hard at Rosita and told her she was going to be all right, wasn't she? and she would remember what he had told her, wouldn't she? Dr. Gonzalez was an old man and very fond of the Barbarossa girls whom he had helped into the world. He thought the parents' attitude inhuman and a little absurd. Well, there it was . . . he did not enjoy a night like this.

Rosita nodded and thanked him and smiled with that extraordinary innocence which still filled his old heart with wonder. Then he had gone off into the night and together they had climbed up to their mother's room. Jaime was in a chair near the bed staring at his unconscious wife. He had been warned for so long that this was what might happen, had imagined he was fully prepared: yet now he found himself stunned. Rosita went and kissed him on the forehead and then was herself overtaken by a spasm of pain. Grace beckoned her father and together they went out on to the veranda overlooking the patio where she explained what had happened. The old servant Teresa was told to prepare Rosita's room but this she had already begun to do the moment she had seen the two señoritas arrive. Doña Rosita had always been her favourite. Now she was home again and the baby would be born in the family house. People died and people were born and at such moments Teresa came into her own. She understood. So with frequent darts into the señora's room to see if consciousness had returned, the old servant bustled about making things ready for the baby's arrival.

'I think we both need a drink,' said Jaime to his elder daughter. 'When are you next on watch?'

'At midnight.'

'Can't you get a relief?'

Grace looked at her father, a little surprised he should ask such a thing.

'I expect so,' she said, 'but I shan't. This isn't a time to start getting out of things.'

'I thought of sending you all to Pepe in Madrid if the evacuation begins.'

'Is that likely?'

'Very. I don't suppose Hitler will stop at the Pyrenees.'

'If the Germans go into Spain, that's not going to be very healthy for people with British passports, is it?'

'Pepe can fix all that. He can get you Spanish papers. At least you'd be safe and you can't stay here.'

'I don't want to be Spanish,' said Grace. 'I'd rather sink with the ship.'

'That's being sentimental, Grace. In any case they won't let any women stay here at all. You know that.'

'What about the Wrens?'

'You're not a Wren.'

'Then I'll go back to England,' said Grace, 'and become one.'

'And who is to look after your mother?'

There it was—the prison again. The family responsibility, Mother. She felt a wave of exhaustion sweep over her and the prospect of the middle watch in the cypher office became more and more grim. At that moment David's face rose up in her thoughts and she became filled with a desperately tender feeling. In imagination she longed to put her head on his shoulder and stay in his arms. Instead, David was somewhere in the North Sea, German Panzer Divisions were racing through

Holland and Belgium, a bomb had exploded in Gibraltar that evening, her mother had had a stroke and her sister was having a baby. She stood up and put down her glass. It was time to go down to the Dockyard and do her watch.

'I don't know who's to look after Mother,' she said. 'I'll try and think something out in the morning. But I'm not going to run away to Tangier or Madrid. Not even for Mother; not even for you. We weren't born on the Rock of Gibraltar for nothing . . . or were we?'

5

For a few moments after Rosita had walked out of the flat, Nicholas stood looking at the bed and wondering what he should do. He felt far from well. One instinct urged him to run after the sisters and plead he was sorry, another pulled him in the opposite direction suggesting that he had already made too many concessions, that if that was the way her self-will was driving her then she had better be left to go it alone. This was the instinct which finally came out on top. Or perhaps it was his overpowering resentment backed by a feeling of unease he had caught from Boothroyd and stoked up by the steady drinking he had indulged in all day.

He walked about the room picking things up and putting them down in an aimless fashion, humming a tuneless tune. He was sorry she had gone. He knew he was to blame yet in a way he felt glad: he had to get back to the office—the great crises then happening kept forcing themselves back on his attention—yet, half-pickled in alcohol as he was, he needed a break. He wanted to throw himself down on the bed and sleep, yet his brain was on fire—the world was on fire and life itself in a state of heaving flux, like some vast negress in labour. Soon Germany would have won the war and, in alliance with her, Soviet Russia—that was the important thing.

Ideologically it had been a shock—that pact—but now he was beginning to see what a smart move it had really been. Soon there would be enormous changes in the world: the British Empire would make its exit and a workers' state, based on equality, grow in its place. He took a deep breath and sighed. He must get back to his tiny sector of the struggle, sitting in that newspaper office pretending to be something he wasn't, waiting, waiting.

Then once again his thoughts went back to Rosita, her young, restless, exciting body when they had been lovers and now this slow, heavy creature on the edge of birth who had just walked out of his room and quite possibly out of his life. Yet had she? They were married. She was a Gibraltarian and if Nicholas had learnt anything at all about people who live on Rocks, it was their wily toughness of will, like a plant rooted in a crevice which clings there however fierce the subsequent storms may be. Well—they would see. She was still his wife.

He trudged back to the clattering office next to the Garrison Library and went on with his work. He wanted very badly to know how much damage had been done that afternoon down on Coaling Island but his press-card had been of no use against the Security cordon thrown round the place, and when he had griped to the old man about being a civilian in a uniformed world, he had been told that the authorities would supply the facts and also say how much or how little was to be published. He badly wanted to check up with Boothroyd on the success or otherwise of the evening's work—but he dare not make any move to excite the slightest interest in people whose job it was to watch others and to report. His own foothold on the Rock was precarious. He did not underestimate Hobart and the forces he controlled. It needed but one false step, and he would be out in an instant, quite possibly on his way to prison.

The trouble was that he was a person torn in himself. Deep in the drink he could sometimes see things with an appalling clarity. Where had it all gone wrong? Could he not come to terms with the ogre he was fighting? With his loathing of the privilege and position standing behind the Barbarossas, he could not forget that he came from such a family himself. Rosita was a strand of his own personal background. By his neglect and by his behaviour tonight he had done a violence to himself. This reflection, as he snipped and pasted and pencilled, took him even more subtly towards despair.

About 2.30 a.m. Hobart crept into bed exhausted. He had examined, re-examined and examined again the wreckage of the oil-tank, the few bits of the bomb mechanism which had been found, the body of Ramón Maria Domingo, the Spanish fitter who had been killed and burnt when it happened; he had visited ships in the vicinity, he had studied the records of the Dockyard Police on duty, he had instigated a search which would continue all night of every similar installation and vulnerable point in the Dockyard in case this bomb should have a replica elsewhere.

He had never let up for six gruelling hours, which had come after a troubled day, and at the end of it he had had to go to the Governor and report that he had not found a single clue of the slightest significance. A bomb had been brought into the Dockyard, placed in position and exploded according to plan and he had no idea at all as to who had done it nor how it had been achieved. This failure, more than anything else, had consumed his energy. There were dark powers at work bent on the destruction of Gibraltar, and it was Hobart's job to know them and to contain or deflect them. Tonight he had failed. This was the first manifestation of an organized plot on any scale and it had come at a crucial time.

He felt Cornelia's arm steal round his neck and draw him gently towards her. He sighed gratefully and kissed her shoulder. What did it matter so long as Cornelia was there to come back to—soft, wonderful, adorable Cornelia with the gentle touch of her fingers stroking away the tensions of the day? Yet soon she would have to go: soon there would be no wife and family to come back to at night. Soon Gibraltar would be as spartan as a man-of-war, and this comfortable love from which he must emerge, perhaps in an hour, perhaps at dawn, to face another crisis and another day would soon be nothing but a memory. He gave another sigh and then like a little boy nestling against her breast dropped, deep, deep, down into sleep.

Six days after Churchill became Prime Minister, the Governor of Gibraltar announced the 'Great Evacuation'. To begin with it was to be on a voluntary scale and in this sense Government Notice No. 73 read merely as a presage, a hint, almost a tip in advance. It urged those who could to make their own arrangements ahead of the main evacuation. There was no panic in the sober wording but, set against a background of what was happening in France, of what was likely to happen in Spain, and of what could then happen to the Rock itself, it brought people to their senses with a round turn.

These were the days when the B.B.C. announcers and Lord Haw-Haw from Berlin had the world on their lips. All over the globe people had been scalded by the news. In Gibraltar there was no one it did not touch. People were transported out of their everyday selves—wives, children, businesses, sports—all the different cogs in the machinery of life continued to turn but almost automatically. The consciousness of everyone on the Rock became riveted on what was to happen to Gibraltar and to themselves. There was a sense of the coming Flood but where was the Ark? The Rock itself had been their refuge up to now—but perhaps the Rock was becoming an ark for something less tangible than its ordinary inhabitants—perhaps it was to be the citadel for a last stand in Europe of British power, the single foothold on a continent going dark. If so, then there could be no place for passengers of any kind but only for fighting men.

Such was certainly the idea in Fortin's mind. He had had another bad dose of malaria and after the fever his brain was unusually clear. The decision to evacuate was not his, though his timing would have been the same. The War Cabinet in London, to which Gibraltar was but a pawn on the board, considered the Rock as it considered Malta, Cyprus, Suez and Aden, and the decision to evacuate civilians from both Gibraltar and Aden was connected with the likelihood of Italy coming into the war, with the thinning-out of traffic in the Mediterranean and with the re-routing of homeward-bound shipping from Aden round the Cape of Good Hope.

Four days later the tempo changed and use of the word 'Forthwith' told the Colony that the crisis was on them. Government Notice No. 78 read that 'His Excellency has received instructions from the War Cabinet that, owing to the international situation, this evacuation should take place forthwith.' From that moment on the great upheaval had begun.

'We can look for some trouble,' Fortin told his Defence Committee. 'It's not going to be easy. We're going to have to tear women and children out of their homes and no one likes that. The three Services are to give all the practical help they can to the City Council and Evacuation Committee. When the ships arrive and the physical move begins, there are going to be dodgers of every kind. Now I want this clearly understood down to the very lowest ranks. However high feeling may run, the operation goes through. I've already received letters saying I'm worse than Hitler, that I'm sticking a bayonet into family life, that I'm offending against God's Holy Law—and who's going to feed the cat and the parrot? I don't suppose the troops will enjoy it much. They'll enjoy what's ahead even less.' For a moment a vision of hand-to-hand fighting in the rubble of a devastated Main Street arose in his mind. That could be happening in a matter of days. Already there were gruesome reports of the slaughter of refugees on French roads. There was still a little time—a very little time—to ensure that in Gibraltar at least there would be no mangled women and children to distract and dismay.

'There must be a firm touch at all levels. In fact the leadership the colony expects of us. The Bishop has promised me all the help he can give and he's staying behind himself. I want the first looter or thief publicly strung up as an example—in fact whoever first steps out of line can rely on the maximum severity of punishment. I'm also prepared to revive a technique with prophets of woe and doom employed by General Eliott in the Great Siege. He smacked them into gaol till the period of their prophecy expired, then he flogged them and let them go. The incidence of prophecy—I think Whitehall would call it—dropped to an infinitesimal amount. I'll back you to the limit of the regulations and if need be beyond.' He paused

[210]

and looked round the ring of grave faces, then added under his breath, 'If there's time to hear any prophecies, that is.'

There was a short pause, then the Admiral said dryly:

'Before being clapped into irons myself, I'd like to ask a question. We're shipping all these women and children to Tangier and French Morocco. What happens to them if France collapses? They can hardly stay on in Morocco.'

'If France is occupied,' Fortin replied, 'I should hope the French would fight on from another part of their Empire as we shall if the Germans invade England. One of those places would undoubtedly be Morocco. If the Germans come into Spain and take over Spanish Morocco then I suppose we'll have to send our people elsewhere—perhaps to the West Indies. But that's unlikely. I imagine the French would be much more minded to take over the Spanish zone and unite the whole of North Africa.'

'Hm!' said the Admiral, 'I wonder.'

The Colonial Secretary spoke up.

'There's a point to be remembered about Gibraltarians. They're accustomed to living at close quarters here on the Rock. They need to be kept together—especially if there isn't any work for them to do in Morocco. That's why if we send them to England they'll probably have to be housed in one of the large suburban hotels or blocks of flats in London. A lot of them only speak Spanish.'

Fortin brought the discussion back to the matter in hand.

'If that happens,' he said, 'it's a problem for the Imperial Government—not us. Our task is to get them out of Gibraltar with the minimum fuss and disruption—and the maximum speed.'

8

So it began. All over the Rock, in every home from the Battery Major's married quarters up by Ince's Farm to the meanest hovel down by the small ship-repairing yards at the North End, from Europa Flats to Catalan Bay, wives were preparing to say good-bye to the familiar things, to separate from home and husband, neither of which they might ever see again. Young children cried, not understanding the invisible rupture that was taking place, older children were fobbed off with vague stories of the need to run away from the wicked Germans with their bombs, in not a few households ineffective decisions to hang on until dragged out of the house by force were taken—though the resisters all knew in their hearts that it was hopeless.

Everywhere the process was the same though its detailed expression took on a different form. The hours raced, as soon they would drag. Muddle, frayed tempers, the inability to select the most precious things and contain them in a suitcase, doubt about the future, poverty, the sudden yearning to cling to each other which besets people who have taken one another for granted over a number of years—all swirled up into a funnel of distress and despair.

Death in a thousand different shapes lay about the homes of Gibraltar late in May 1940 and the priests, trying to encourage, to drive out the devil of hopelessness and restore a faith in something higher, were no more than pin-points of light in the darkening night. Their words helped for a while but it was a human wife who was going and a human man who was to be left. The solace of religion could scarcely allay the domestic miseries of this cleavage caused by the war.

Only the bachelor soldiers, sailors and airmen remained untouched by the blight, yet they too knew what it was like. Memory of leaving their own homes in England, now about to be blitzed from the air, gave them a sympathy for the Gibraltarians to whom the process of going abroad was so utterly strange. The rough good-nature of the British fighting man, in many ways the gentlest soldier in the world, came to the rescue of the Latin temperament beset by hysteria. This enforced evacuation gave to even the youngest soldier fresh from a weeping mother in a Yorkshire slum the chance to rise above the situation in himself and with his understanding, clumsy humour and warm-hearted smile make a contribution far beyond his normal capacity to people deep in distress. It was a moving sight and Fortin, with Seale stumping about at his side, found himself caught up in the emotion of it as the most hardened republican will be caught by the majesty and hidden meaning of a coronation.

[212]

Jaime Barbarossa, too, was deeply concerned. He had been co-opted by the City Council Committee which organized the evacuation and thus found himself day after day confronted by new variations of hardship and distress. The little back-street shop run by an aged widow, the young mother whose husband had a girl friend in La Línea, the boat-builder of seventy with a half-finished boat on the stocks, the gharry-driver whose horse was to be slaughtered—each problem had a desperate reality to the person concerned yet the evacuation called for quick and ruthless decisions. Behind the City Council stood the Governor, representing the will of the British Empire. Over them all hung the threat of attack and siege. The closing down of a limekiln, the loss of a bakery, the abandoning of a tiny sweet factory had to be seen not in personal terms but against the dropping of bombs and the trundling of tanks which the old Rock might soon be witnessing.

Hobart and the Barbarossa family both had evacuation questions of their own, though they differed in scale. Hobart had to find accommodation on a ship going to the United States, whereas for Jaime the problem was to decide where his wife and daughters should go. Edie was still a bedridden invalid. Her strength was coming back slowly but she would always need attention and at this particular moment an invalid was the last person to have around the house in Gibraltar.

Then there was Rosita. She was a full-scale problem in herself alone. She had duly given birth to a daughter. Even before the child was born Nicholas had been demanding her return to the flat and backing this up with threats of enticement actions against the Barbarossa family. To begin with, Rosita had been much too exhausted to care. She had been over twenty-four hours in labour and the birth itself was unusually difficult. She could not be moved and at first the doctors decreed that no one was to see her.

This did not stop Nicholas for a single moment. He continued to make a fuss, even threatening to force his way in with police help. So Jaime, who had a full range of other troubles on his mind, had climbed down and had given instructions that Nicholas might come when he could. But the problem of where she was to go now was upon them. Go she must, in common with every other dependent woman, but where?

Only Grace, for the moment, had a reprieve and that because of her job. A boatload of R.N.V.R. cypher officers was reputed to be *en route* but until they arrived, Grace and the other voluntary workers could not be spared. Indeed the volume of cyphering was such that they all 'mucked in' to do a bit extra on top of their normal watches. The retreat of the British Expeditionary Force was producing a swamp of signals. Dunkirk had begun.

XI

W HILE Gibraltar was absorbed with one evacuation, 'Gibraltar's Very Own Destroyer Flotilla' and in particular H.M.S. *Firesprite* and H.M.S. *Forthright* were heavily engaged with another at Dunkirk. Following close upon the Norwegian campaign the rescue of the British Army seemed to form a climax to that first period of intensive war at sea.

Three destroyers from the flotilla had been lost in Norwegian waters and *Firesprite* herself had had her fo'c'sle buckled by a near miss. They had experienced the length and breadth of the Norwegian campaign. They had ferried troops into Narvik and a few weeks later had ferried them out again. They had narrowly missed being sunk when the cruisers *Southampton* and *Glasgow* were dive-bombed. They had themselves been cease-lessly attacked from the air and had suffered the repeated dis-tress of picking up survivors from other destroyers.

Though Norway herself was abandoned, though the Royal Navy had lost an aircraft-carrier, two cruisers, a sloop and nine destroyers, though sixteen more warships had been damaged, the German Fleet's effective strength in June 1940 had been reduced to three cruisers and four destroyers. Until repairs, therefore, could be made to the *Scharnhorst*, the *Gneisenau* and the pocket-battleships, the enemy's threat at sea consisted only of the submarine. Only of the submarine? The threat was enough. The Germans had all but won the First World War with the submarine: they stood an equal if not a better chance in the Second.

Already, by the time of Dunkirk, David Evers and his ship's company were taut and lean and matured in war. They had spent the winter convoying merchant ships across the Atlantic or patrolling in northern waters. In Norway they had func-tioned as part of the Fleet operating as an anti-submarine shield for battleships, cruisers or aircraft-carriers. Now they were doing a ferry-boat job nosing into Dunkirk harbour or in-shore to the beaches where the long snaking lines of exhausted soldiers stood with the sea up to their chests, patiently waiting as the bombs fell and an armada of over 800 boats, ranging from Dutch *schuits* to Thames pleasure-launches, relentlessly came and went, came and went until either the boats were sunk or the evacuation had been completed.

Altogether, during the Dunkirk period, *Firesprite* made twenty-five return journeys from Dover to Dunkirk pausing only to disembark the troops and to take on fuel and food. In this operation she was but one of thirty-nine destroyers. The climax came on the night of 2nd-3rd June when *Firesprite*, *Forthright*, nine other destroyers and fourteen minesweepers, went into what was left of Dunkirk harbour at night and brought off the rearguard of 4,000 British troops together with something like 20,000 French and Allied troops. This was the heaviest haul they had made and although Dunkirk was to hold out for another day, although Operation Dynamo was not to be officially closed till the afternoon of 4th June, it was *Firesprite's* last journey. Long overdue for a boiler-clean she had been ordered to Portsmouth where she would be docked for a few days of blessed rest.

That night as they tore down the channel, although both David and Jimmy were smudgy with exhaustion, a feeling that Dunkirk was over and that they had miraculously escaped gave them an elation they had not experienced for months. Neither of them would put it into words. Sailors are innately superstitious. To have commented on their luck, even by inference, in not sharing the fate of six of their sister ships sunk and nineteen damaged, would be tantamount to inviting a stray torpedo or a lurking mine. So far they had come through unscathed but until the ship was safely docked they could only too easily be caught off their guard on the last lap.

It was a calm, almost windless night. They had discussed the prospect of leave. Pam would be coming to London and Jimmy was going home to Somerset.

'Where I shall sleep, eat, drink beer at the local, eat, sleep and drink more beer at the local,' he said with a light in his eye. Everyone at sea sooner or later acquired a picture of the ideal leave down to the smallest detail, evolved during the long night-watches.

'And molest the local girls, I suppose,' David remarked dryly.

'Not on my own doorstep. I've learnt that lesson. Anyway the local girls are all Red Cross nurses or away in the Services.'

'Aren't you going to get married, Jimmy?'

Before he would have glibly answered in half a dozen different ways that he supposed eventually he would marry but that in the meantime he intended enjoying himself first. Now to David's surprise he turned the question back on himself.

'I don't know. Is it such a good idea?'

David hesitated.

'It has its rewards.' To his surprise he found himself on the defensive. Was this a feeling of guilt over Grace? How could he dare advise when his own life was so confused?

'They look pretty thin to me. Unless it's too much sea-time in H.M. Ships. Or too many girl friends. I don't know. It's all very well at present. But what happens later on? I don't see how you can be an N.O. and happily married. As I see it, to get anywhere with a marriage you've got to live with your wife. Otherwise something goes wrong.'

He peered at his Captain in the darkness trying to catch his expression. 'Or am I treading on thin ice?' he added and immediately regretted it. David stared at the sea, his arms on the bridge coping. He ignored the personal note in his First Lieutenant's question.

'Any marriage is pretty well always on thin ice,' he answered. 'I think possibly you're right. It used to be Their Lordships' settled policy to discourage N.O.s from marrying. And perhaps they were right. It's a dedicated job—the sea. The trouble is we all want to have our cake and eat it. I used to think coming home from sea would be a perpetual second honeymoon. Well—sometimes it is. More often it's a disaster from beginning to end. Women need a lot of attention, you know.'

There were questions about Pam which Jimmy longed to ask. He had always thought her a wildly attractive girl and at the same time quite unsuited to the severe, self-disciplined ruggedness of his Captain. Observing it from the outside, as he had done at Gibraltar and at momentary intervals since, he could not see how such a marriage could possibly work. He

[217]

supposed she must be splendid in bed but otherwise she seemed so vague and unfocused.

'I suppose I'll get married in the end,' he said moodily, 'simply because I don't want to be a gin-soaked old bachelor—but I can't say the prospect pleases.'

'You never know,' David said, 'we're all of us different. You marry to complete yourself. That's the theory. You can't make it happen to order but perhaps you'll be lucky. When you meet her, though, you'll know her all right. That's one of the rules of the game.'

But it was not of Pam he was thinking and even as he spoke the hopelessness of trying to rationalize one's heart brought back the sadness of it all. The feeling of being in prison returned and as he left the bridge for half an hour's sleep, he felt suddenly a hundred times more tired. He knew that he was trapped beyond hope of rescue. He would never be free.

'Well, anyway,' he remarked as he disappeared down the ladder, 'it's an academic question at present. We have this little war to take care of first.'

2

Though the British Expeditionary Force had been rescued from Dunkirk, the threat period in Gibraltar was only just beginning. 'We must be very careful,' Churchill had said in his famous speech to the Commons, 'not to assign to this deliverance the attributes of a victory. Wars are not won by evacuations.' By the time this speech was made the first boatloads of Gibraltar evacuees had reached Casablanca after thirteen hours of discomfort and danger. Their reception by the French was far from warm.

The French, even in Morocco, had been hypnotized by the German success and the speed with which France was crumbling into total collapse. The shock had knocked the fight out of them and they were in no mood to welcome the women and children of Gibraltar with their pitiful belongings upon whom became focused the resentment, the subtle jealousies, and the humiliation which the disasters in France were provoking and from which the English had so prudently escaped.

Jaime Barbarossa had still not taken a decision about his own family but he knew it could not be delayed more than a day or two longer. The crisis was upon them. There could be no escape. 'We shall not flag or fail,' Churchill had said. 'We shall go on to the end. We shall fight in France, we shall fight in the seas and oceans, we shall fight with growing confidence and growing strength in the air, we shall defend our island whatever the cost may be.'

All that could certainly be applied to Gibraltar. There would be no evacuation from England and none from the Rock: in that context they became interchangeable symbols. 'We shall fight on the beaches, we shall fight on the landing-grounds, we shall fight in the fields and in the streets, we shall fight in the hills, we shall never surrender.' Jaime had read and re-read the words of that tremendous speech which set alight the blaze of British defiance for the next eighteen months. He could visualize what it implied for Gibraltar.

There were only three possible alternatives to people under siege—death, enslavement or victory. England herself might be invaded and subjugated but Gibraltar, as part of 'our Empire beyond the seas, armed and guarded by the British Fleet, would carry on the struggle, until in God's good time, the New World with all its power and might steps forth to the rescue and the liberation of the Old.'

The night Jaime made his decision was hot and oppressive and as he walked home from Government House through the narrow streets, they seemed unusually full of noise and bustle. Jeeps had not yet made their appearance but military trucks and staff cars were always dashing about the Rock giving the town a dusty restlessness. Work on the airstrip had begun and at the same time the new Command H.Q. beneath the Rock were being excavated, the scree from which was being dumped into the Bay near the frontier and which would eventually form the hard base to the runway when it was extended west into the sea. So there was a constant procession of trucks filled and empty from dawn till dusk through the streets of Gibraltar. Because of petrol-rationing, civilian cars were less and less apparent but the sudden swerving roar of motor-cycle despatch-riders and the ubiquitous red-capped Military Police each contributed an ingredient to wartime Gibraltar which made the clip-clop of gharries and the leisurely evening *paseo* through Main Street the memories of another age.

It was only a short walk to the Line Wall Road and on a sudden impulse Jaime decided to stretch his legs. He would climb up towards the Devil's Gap Road and, by exercising his body, perhaps order his thoughts. He turned up into Governor's Parade, up the alley way to the left of the Garrison Library, up past Lorez' Ramp and Prince Edward Road to an outcrop of the Rock where he could rest and look down on the town and the harbour. The houses between which he had made his way were strangely silent. It was as though the children and their chattering mothers had never been there and already a ghostly quality lurked about the shuttered windows, set in their evening shadows. It gave Jaime the feeling that the siege had already begun.

What was he to do with Edie and Rosita? That morning he had had an anxious letter from his sister in Malta. The Italian faction there was making trouble: if and when Italy came into the war—and this, in fact, lay only three days ahead—then they expected the Dockyard to be bombed straight away. There had been a chance for his sister and her husband to take refuge in America but both had decided to stay 'with the same uneasy feeling at heart,' she had written, 'which no doubt you have in Gibraltar. But at least we are an island whereas you have Spain to contend with'.

Two days previously he had all but settled for Tangier. Then his brother had sent him word from Madrid that Franco intended to take over the International Zone at an opportune moment. If that proved to be so, British passports would not be of much value in Tangier. That left Madrid, Lisbon or England—and after Dunkirk it seemed very foolish to send anyone home for safety. Moreover Edie would now always need a nurse and attention.

There was his cousin in Baltimore. Asylum there had already been offered and Mrs. Hobart was willing to take charge of the invalid for the Atlantic crossing. Yet somehow such a distant exile went against the grain. The same thing that kept his sister and her husband in Malta operated now on

Jaime, even though to send his wife well out of harm's way was no more than elementary common sense. Sitting on a parapet looking down on the violet shadows thrown by the setting sun, Jaime was aware of the invisible pressures which, well-disguised, run human nature and which can only be felt for what they are in moments of crisis. He realized then that Edie did not have long to live and that to be comparatively near her at the end of her life was more important than asylum across the sea.

Later that evening he called his two daughters to his study to tell them his decision. But Grace and Rosita had a surprise in store for him.

'We can't put off your mother's move any longer,' he began. 'I've gone through every possibility as thoroughly as I can and I've talked it over with the experts. All things considered Madrid seems to be the most sensible place for you to go. Pepe will look after you all and even if the Germans come there's not likely to be any fighting around Madrid—if there's going to be any fighting at all.' He stopped abruptly and looked across at Grace. 'You don't agree? Why not?'

'It's too far away: there's no petrol and very little food in Spain.'

'Well, then, what do you suggest?'

Grace glanced at her sister for support and then took a breath.

'We think we ought to open up San Roque and stick it out there.'

'My dear girl, you know what would happen if Gibraltar is besieged?'

'We know that, Father—but if the Rock is attacked then the outlook is pretty thin for you, isn't it?'

'We're not talking about me.'

'Well of course you come into it,' Grace said with a touch of her mother's impatience. 'We all know Mother hasn't got long. You want to see as much of her as you can.'

'And I've got Nicholas to agree,' Rosita put in.

'To hell with Nicholas,' Jaime said irritably.

'Let's keep personalities out of this,' Grace said quickly. 'I've talked to Hobart and he's going to get me written on to

[221]

the dockyard rota—as soon as the voluntary cypherers are disposed of—I'll nominally be a cleaner or something and I can come across every day.'

'If the Germans come down into Spain, you and the house can both be written off.'

'I'm not so sure.'

'Well I am,' Jaime said briefly, 'and I know a little more about Spanish gun-emplacements than you do.'

But, from his tone of voice, Grace knew that he was playing for time, that he was secretly delighted that the proposal had come from his daughters, that this solution was really what he wanted himself in his heart and that he was more than half won over to the idea. She did not interrupt him now but let him develop all the objections to the scheme. Then at the right moment she produced her ace of trumps.

'Anyway,' she said, 'I've discussed it unofficially with the Governor. He said that if we could talk you into it, he would raise no official objection—in fact, all things considered, he gave it his active support. In a few weeks' time, he said, there may well be prisoners of war escaping over the Pyrenees—the house may well have its uses before it gets blown to smithereens. And after all, Father, it's *our* lives that are really at stake. If Ros and I feel the same way about it. . . .' She paused and looked critically at her father.

But Jaime's opposition had been conquered by a stronger emotion. With unusual awkwardness he took out his handkerchief and blew his nose. For so long there had been so great a barrier of stiffness and formality between him and his children. Now in a flash it had vanished. His heart was filled with an almost guilty gratitude. It was his duty to send them well out of harm's way but now the problem had been resolved and he knew he would bow to their will. He looked up to find Grace's arm round his shoulders and her smiling dark eyes close to his. She looked over his forehead to Rosita and spoke briskly in a way that reminded him very much of Edie when she had been a girl.

'Better get out the brandy,' she said. 'Father's starting to blub.'

3

Hobart had managed to get berths for Cornelia and the children on an American Export Line cargo boat running to Philadelphia. From the moment this was settled till the moment he left the ship with Cornelia and the children waving from the deck and he, himself, waving back from the tender, their lives had seemed to be a long drawn-out agony of parting.

'I know we've been lucky up to now,' he said as they clung together in bed the last night before she sailed, 'but it isn't much help.' Cornelia kissed him and began crying again: the third baby was now well on the way but none of the sickness she had endured came anywhere near this deep, primal ache for him which only his presence, only his arms about her, only the touch of his familiar body on hers could assuage. Both realized that their going away from each other was the commonest wartime experience. There was nothing unique in the sacrifice they were forced to make. Everyone had to say goodbye at one time or another. Everything came to an end.

'You'll write all the time, won't you?' he said, pressing her hard to him, 'all day and every day without ever stopping, won't you? And you'll take ceaseless, unending photographs of the children, won't you? And you'll think of the old Rock of Gibraltar from time to time—say once a month—with your old man, dusty, frustrated and part-worn, stamping about it and wanting his wife?'

'You'll make out fine,' Cornelia forced herself to say, 'you haven't a care in the world—you leave all that to me: it's typical of a man, isn't it? To leave the woman to cope with two children with another one on the way.'

'Nobody asked you to have another one.'

'I suppose it was nothing to do with you?'

'I sometimes wonder. There's a promiscuous streak in your nature. Your mother warned me.'

'Well,' said Cornelia with a brave show of tartness, 'while I'm washing my promiscuous nappies in Newport, Rhode Island, I can console myself that you will be investigating the red-light areas of La Línea and Tangier, in line of duty of course,' she paused, then it overcame her again and she squeezed him desperately, fighting the tears. 'It isn't any use, darling,' she cried. 'I don't know how I'm going to be without you. I need you so badly.'

The house at Rosia Bay with the dark green shutters, the cream walls with the brown inlaid tiles, the veranda, the high wall and the palm-trees would soon be no more than a memory, a photograph in a clutch of snaps, to Cornelia and, for that matter, to Hobart. He was giving up his married quarters. When Cornelia went he would move into a single room in the office in Bomb House Lane and to a certain extent this decision helped him over the parting. He could not be returning night after night to an empty house, trying not to remember how the door would open and she would suddenly be there in his arms, an innocent loving girl for all their nine years of married life. Carmen and the nanny were desolate. Carmen would be found another job and the nanny was returning to England, but to them, too, it was the end of a particularly happy life and in the meantime they moved about the house packing and clearing up as though under sentence of death.

It was a time of hasty farewells to friends and associates although by now most of the wives had gone. Grace was in and out of the house during the last few days. She and Cornelia had an understanding of each other based on affection and respect. Neither woman defined this too clearly but there was a trust and a latitude in the limits which their feminine instincts normally applied.

When Cornelia asked Grace to look after Hobart, she did not express even to herself exactly what that meant, yet she knew that, however interpreted, her husband would be safe in Grace's hands even if one morning they should happen to wake up in the same bed. She did not phrase it like that to herself but both Grace and she knew what it was to love, they knew the experience of giving and to give in love without thought of oneself is never, afterwards, to be quite the same. She knew more about this than Grace did but the potentiality was there and she had seen it come very near to flowering over David. Yearning and sacrifice were in it and these two qualities made a nonsense of the narrow morality which confined their ordinary lives. She had no wish whatever for Hobart and Grace to have an affair, but she loved her husband so much that in the loneliness which lay ahead she hoped Grace would understand him too and be kind.

So, on 10th June 1940—a fine hot summer's day—Cornelia, Jonathan and Michael sailed away to the west in the S.S. *Dallas Exporter*, across the Atlantic to the busy port of Philadelphia, and then on to a white clap-board house in Newport, Rhode Island, to Coca-cola, American schooling and the relaxed life of a great country still untouched by the war. As the ship headed for the Straits Hobart landed back at the Waterport, a feeling of numbness and a gnawing, hideous loneliness in his heart. He had sent his car away and now he began walking back to the office. The Rock shimmered in the heat, towering above him, as it seemed today, in a wholly malignant way. Just as he reached the Waterport Gate, Dicky Seale clattered up in his decrepit Austin.

'The bastards are in Paris,' he said briefly. 'Hop in. I have orders from the old man to take you to the Yacht Club and apply some very strong drink.'

4

Four days afterwards Franco put Spanish troops into Tangier in the name of the Sultan. The Spanish attitude was stiffening, and there were sombre conclusions to be drawn in Gibraltar. By now only women doing essential jobs were left in the fortress. There were still too many of them about for Fortin's liking but for the moment he had to rest content with the tightening up that had been done. The aftermath of Dunkirk and the fall of France, now imminent, were both to affect Gibraltar but in what way was not yet clear.

There was now a curfew on the Rock from eleven-thirty at night till five-thirty in the morning. Life was narrowing down. British bank-notes were withdrawn, special Gibraltar ones being issued in their place. Exit permits for anyone leaving the Rock were made necessary and day visitors to Spain were now compelled to 'sign off' in a book at Four Corners or the Waterport.

Across the border the Spanish authorities countered restriction with restriction, ban with ban, and it was clear that the British influence was to be strictly contained within a contracting perimeter. Work on the Tarifa guns dominating the Straits of Gibraltar was now at high pressure: a secret airstrip was being levelled in a valley alongside the new military road to Ronda, being built by Republican prisoners under gruelling German supervision. Even Hobart found himself less and less able to penetrate where he wanted by any of the half-dozen different methods he had previously employed. It became clear that Gibraltar was being progressively sealed off from the mainland. The feeling in the air was ominous.

In one sense, however, the presence of a large Spanish labour force working daily in the Dockyard guaranteed a margin of time should the Rock be attacked. Hobart calculated that if the flow of workers from La Línea dried up to a trickle or stopped entirely then the Rock was 'for it' in twenty-four to forty-eight hours. The human tide across the frontier, therefore, was closely watched and Fortin caused a half-hourly report to be made to him personally each morning by the frontier guards. Other people listened for the clangour of dockyard noise to begin and when it did, breathed freely again.

But no rule of thumb could allay Fortin's restlessness for long. The vigil had begun. Like the captain of a ship at sea, Fortin never allowed himself to become absorbed for too long in detailed administration. He would put an impulse into any problem needing his attention and then delegate it as soon as he could. Metaphorically he was always striding the bridge keeping a look-out through Intelligence reports, visitors from Spain and the various straws in the wind which he had marked down as significant. Sentries and look-outs in the lonely places of the Rock would suddenly be surprised in the middle of the night to find the Governor at their side. The shock of such unexpected visitations kept people on their toes. It reminded them that the security of the Rock itself might well depend upon the alertness of a single sentry.

There was no pomp or ceremony about these visits. Alone or with Seale or Hobart, he would go where his instinct took him. Wherever that was he would usually stay long enough to see the job through the eyes of the man doing it. In this way and almost as an accidental by-product the personal esteem in which the Governor was held rose to new heights. Fortin was good at names and he took a genuine interest in the men he talked with: they in turn rewarded him by speaking their minds as freely as they felt, so that for a time there was a closer bond between General and Private than between the Private and his own Sergeant.

The day Pétain capitulated to the Germans, the wanderlust got Fortin out of bed at about five in the morning. He dressed, left a message for Seale and then walked through the empty streets past Casemates, past the old palm-trees and the sloping stone ramparts, over what had once been a moat, down past the huddle of small factories at North End, most of them doomed by the airstrip, out to Four Corners and the frontier to Spain.

The first bus-loads of workers were just rolling through and from a vantage point near the immigration shed he watched the buses queuing up for inspection. Presently the Town Inspector—the head Customs and Excise official in Gibraltar—came and stood beside him watching the procession. They were old 'early-morning friends'. Fortin had done this many times before so that his presence excited no particular self-consciousness and the immigration, police and Army personnel on duty at the frontier did their routine tapping and searching as though unobserved.

Animated by the same ideas as Fortin, the Town Inspector made no scheduled appearance but also turned up unexpectedly, ready for any harvest which the element of surprise might garner him. Fortin liked him. He relished the tang of his outlook and, as with Hobart, appreciated his professional insight into human nature. The Town Inspector had a long memory. His experiences both as a boy smuggler and now on the side of authority made excellent hearing and some of his contacts in Spain had proved invaluable to Hobart and the security team.

Today neither he nor Fortin felt like talking. The collapse of France was such an overwhelming disaster that it forced itself into even the most concentrated attention. It was there, hanging over the Rock like a Levanter cloud: it was there in the deep, early-morning shadow lying over the town as yet scarcely awake: it was there in the trundling rickety buses bringing the unsmiling Spanish to their daily work in the fortress.

They watched the buses draw up one by one at the gate. They watched the cursory inspection, the nod to the driver, the grinding of gears and the passing on to the next one. No wonder it had been possible to smuggle in the bomb that had blown up the oil-tank on Coaling Island. To check on more than a tiny percentage of the ten to twelve thousand coming into Gibraltar each day would have meant intolerable delays. There was no option. So much simply had to be left in the hands of Fate.

'If you were the German General charged with the capture of Gibraltar,' Fortin suddenly remarked, 'how would you get your shock-troops into the fortress without firing a shot?'

'Aha!' said the Town Inspector, 'nothing easier than that! I'd pack them into these buses, most of them out of sight on the floor, a few dressed as peasant women so as not to give the game away before reaching the frontier. I'd send two buses ahead filled with normal workers, my other buses in a queue behind—just as they are now. I'd let the first two buses be inspected in the normal way then as they move on, we—that is the whole caravan behind would close up, become solid as it were, and keep moving instead of stopping at the gates. I reckon at least four bus-loads could be through before the dull British realized what was happening. One bus I'd detail to turn back and take the frontier from behind, the rest—well, they'd be in the fortress, wouldn't they, sir?'

Fortin saw that they would only too clearly and the Town Inspector had simply made a picture of an idea which had for long been dodging about in his mind. From that day on no bus crossed the frontier gates loaded. The passengers, from then on, were made to get out: the empty bus was searched and passed through and the passengers rejoined it after walking through the control points. At the end of the war the Town Inspector received a decoration for general services rendered.

The removal of the distaff side of the Barbarossa family to San Roque released Nicholas and at the same time added to his frustration. It released him in so far that he was now quite on his own. To reach San Roque he had to walk or take the infrequent bus. He had to be back in Gibraltar by 7 p.m. His father-in-law did not offer lifts in his car—at least not in the outward direction—and Nicholas was too proud to ask. Nor did Rosita seem especially anxious to see him. He was now free to drink all day and every day, if he chose, and this he began to do. It all seemed very unfair.

Moreover he had had a row with Boothroyd whose attitude to the fall of France was one of poorly concealed pleasure. Nobody liked the Nazis but they were doing Russia's work at no cost to the Party and the collapse of one of the major capitalist-imperialist powers was an important gain. In one sense Nicholas felt this too, but he had worked in France, he was fond of the country and the people, and once again he found himself in substantial opposition to the Party line. This he had been unwise enough to tell Boothroyd one afternoon when deep in the brandy. The result had been a continuing excommunication which at first he had taken defiantly but which soon began to disturb him. More than ever he found himself living in a no-man's-land of the soul, in which the only stout staff to lean on was the copious supply of duty-free brandy at three shillings a bottle.

Rosita, too, had withdrawn into herself. Her life had become the baby and to this she devoted herself single-mindedly. She did not think about the war. If the Germans came, they came. She felt no personal responsibility for the state of affairs which surrounded her and the family. When she thought about Nicholas she disposed of the twinge in her heart by remembering his utter uncontrollability when they had been living together. She must either submit or go her own way and she had chosen the latter.

Sometimes in the middle of the night she would wake up and begin to cry, she did not really know why. Then it would pass. In the early morning the baby would awaken and need to be fed: another day would come and go: Mother would have to be read to and cheered up: the house looked after and the marketing done. The war came into everything, of course, but there was no need to brood about it.

Grace, too, had adapted her life to the new conditions with fair success. The cyphering job at the Tower had come to an end and she had got a dockyard 'comforts-and-welfare' job in its place. This entailed sorting, listing, packing and delivering 'retail' consignments of balaclava helmets, mittens, games and books to visiting warships and especially to the little ships on exposed jobs such as mine-sweepers where living conditions were primitive. Whilst cyphering she had got used to being well informed about the war and this she missed to begin with. However there were compensations. She was in much closer contact with the sea-going Navy and she soon began to enjoy dealing with sailors very much more than wrestling with 'corrupt cyphering' and tedious Admiralty messages about mine-fields in the Western Approaches. She could keep an eye on the Line Wall Road house: perhaps she would see her father at lunch and she was allowed sufficient petrol to make the journey to and from San Roque once a day.

Two days after the French Armistice had been signed, sixteen days after Paris was occupied and a bare three weeks after Dunkirk, Grace drove into Gibraltar as usual, past Campamento, through La Línea, across the frontier, past the aerodrome which seemed to creep nearer and nearer the international road each day, then on into the noisy clamour of the town and the Dockyard. She could not get the suffering of France out of her head: it seemed to make a nonsense of everything else. It had had a deeply emotional impact and however hard she tried to direct her attention elsewhere, her thoughts drew back to the hopelessness of the situation. Somewhere in herself she had the disquieting suspicion that the war was already lost.

It all seemed unreal, set as it was against the hot summer's day, the dusty heat of the Dockyard, the racket of drills and riveters. What did all this activity amount to now that France had ceased to exist and the invasion of England was surely imminent? They would fight, of course. But what would actually happen when the Germans were in the streets of

[230]

England as they now were in Paris? The Italians had already begun heavy raiding on Malta: soon it would be Gibraltar's turn. But bombs were one thing: what happened when the Germans were here in the streets?

Absorbed in these thoughts Grace was therefore quite unprepared for two events which deeply affected her life. She had read somewhere that the big things in life have a habit of showing up when your back is turned and certainly when she found a postcard on her desk addressed in familiar writing, she did not immediately 'come to' since her thoughts were still on Paris and her friends who were there. Then, as if she had had a slap on the face, she came to her senses. The handwriting was Lance's and the postcard was from Oflag XIX, Germany, where he was a prisoner of war. She sat down stunned. He was still alive. Her husband was alive and a prisoner of war in German hands.

Somehow it seemed a keener and more cruel blow than she had ever experienced. Instinctively her heart went out to David and as his features arose in her mind, she felt sick and immensely weighed down. Now there was no hope in any direction.

For a long time she sat still at her desk mechanically dealing with the papers that were brought in and taken away. The inevitable cup of tea which she hated but which is a ritual in any British office was put in front of her by the tired old dockyard hand who was their general factotum in the 'Comforts Office'. She looked at his grey, bent head as he shuffled out. He should have gone with the others but he had had no dependants and he had volunteered to stay. Yet his heart was not in the war. He had simply wanted to stay in Gibraltar. What chance would he have if the Germans came? With a bitter taste in the mouth she startled herself by saying aloud, 'I wish they *would* come.'

'I beg your pardon, miss?'

She looked at the old man, for the moment bemused, and then refound herself.

'I was thinking I wish the Germans *would* attack the Rock—then we could get on and finish the job.'

'Yes, miss.'

It was his duty to agree but she knew he did not in reality. He was a frightened old man, hoping as most people did, that the war would pass him by.

'What would you do if the Germans were here, José?'

'Bring them tea, I suppose, miss,' José said with surprising honesty. 'If any of us are still alive, that is.'

He trudged out and Grace returned to her thoughts. Outside, a dockyard engine shunted some trucks with a clatter and a Spanish fuss, the driver and the shunter shouting contradictory orders at each other. Two sea-gulls sat on the lip of a roof serenely bored. The mid-morning light struck in, hard and bright, and there was a smell of oil and steam from a near-by engineering shed. It was all familiar and it was where she had chosen to be: she was part of the Rock and the Rock part of her. But today on her desk lay a letter from Lance, her husband. It connected her with other worlds. It was one of the unseen chains binding her life.

The telephone rang. Hobart's warm voice sounded in her ear. At once she was lifted in herself. That voice was like a hand reaching down from above. It reminded her, with a tender feeling in the heart, of the wonder of friendship and of how close it lay to her sorrows and distresses.

'I've some news for you,' he said, 'that is, if you don't know it already.'

'This is a day for news. I've just had a postcard from Lance.'

'A postcard?'

From the astonished tone of Hobart's voice, Grace could picture him just stopping in time from saying, 'How has he managed to get through from the other world?'

'He's alive. He's a P.O.W. in Germany.'

'Good heavens!' said Hobart, 'what really extraordinary timing!'

'You mean the Admiralty might have let me know first?'

'Well—that—certainly. . . .' He paused as though feeling for the words, 'I . . . I'll be at the Yacht Club about twelve-thirty if you feel like a drink.'

'That wasn't what you rang up to say, was it?'

'No.'

'Then what is your news? Something about Cornelia?'

'No,' Hobart replied. 'I was going to say that if you look out of your office window in a north-westerly direction—towards the pens—you might see something to your advantage—but perhaps, all things considered. . . .'

'No!' she almost shouted with excitement, 'it isn't true—it can't be true. . . .' She dropped the telephone on to the desk and rushed to the window. Across the harbour four destroyers were manœuvring into their berths. It was too far away to see their names or their numbers but their shape was very familiar. She went back to the telephone, her heart almost in her mouth.

'This isn't some awful practical joke, is it?' she asked.

'No,' said Hobart, 'as far as I know what is left of Gibraltar's Very Own Destroyer Flotilla is back with us this morning and also, as far as I know, Lieutenant-Commander Evers is still in command of one of them. Will you be at the Yacht Club? Or shall I come round and pick you up now? We could go round to the pens and see them berth. . . .'

'Yes, yes, come at once. Oh! Lord,' she wailed, 'what am I to do?'

'Do?' said the voice at the other end of the line, 'what can any of us do?'

XII

WITH the arrival at Gibraltar of Force H, of which *Firesprite* and what was left of the 28th Flotilla now formed part, the war furnace in the Mediterranean began to heat up. Gibraltar was the door to this furnace. From the sheltering Rock, over the next two and a half years, convoys were sailed to beleaguered Malta. It was from the Rock that the Italians found the war turned uncomfortably upon themselves, from Gibraltar that the French Fleet was destroyed and the North African invasion launched.

But at the end of June 1940 neither David nor indeed any of the ship's company of *Firesprite* had an inkling of what was to come. They had watched the welcome solidity of the Rock draw nearer with a feeling of having come home. It had been sufficiently surprising to find themselves ordered to Gibraltar as part of Force H. No one knew what lay ahead and David, sitting endlessly on the bridge of his destroyer, tried to put the future and especially Grace out of his thoughts. Perhaps she would not even be there. No one aboard *Firesprite* knew about the evacuation except that it had long been a possibility. Anything might have happened. At least the Rock itself was still there.

Instead he studied the magnificent lines of the battle-cruiser *Hood*, the flat-topped bulk of the *Ark Royal* and the proportioned, lesser might of the cruiser *Sheffield* with her twelve six-inch guns. These ships were the heart of Admiral Somerville's striking force and together with the battle-scarred 8th Destroyer Flotilla made up one of the most exclusive naval 'clubs' it was possible to join. Only four ships of the 28th Flotilla remained after Norway and Dunkirk and of these David was now the senior. Under the overall command of the Captain (D), David was thus responsible for a half flotilla of the 'F' class whenever they worked together, and unknown to him a recommendation had been put in for him to be given the acting rank of Commander. Next in seniority stood Bill Downey in *Forthright*, still their nearest and dearest.

An hour later they had passed through the boom, the big ships securing along the South Mole, the destroyers packing neatly into the pens at the north end of the harbour. Gibraltar looked quite unaltered, as indeed it was outwardly, since they had sailed away nine months before. The same heat haze over the Dockyard, the same dark clusters of trees scaling up the Rock, interspersed with bare concreted patches where the precious rain was caught and piped away into storage-tanks, the same abrupt drop of 1,400 feet at the North Front, the same landmarks standing out of the body of the Rock such as the Moorish Castle and the white oblong Rock Hotel. It all looked friendly and familiar, as Jimmy remarked, when he came up on the bridge after seeing the ship secured.

For a moment he and David stood with their backs to the jetty looking up at the Rock. They were both very tired. No doubt they would soon be once more at sea. But at this moment the long dark winter, Iceland and Scapa Flow, the horrors of Norway and Dunkirk fell into the shadows and they were once more in the summer sun. The four ships that were left of Gibraltar's Very Own Destroyer Flotilla were back where they belonged.

As David and Jimmy climbed down from the bridge a nondescript military staff car drew up alongside the ship and Hobart got out, followed by Grace. She had caught sight of the familiar lanky body clambering down the ladder. Her heart leapt and she yelled out his name. But he did not hear in the general noise going on all around them and the only people who paid attention were the berthing party and some dockyard officials waiting for the brows to be properly secured before going on board.

'Easy, old dear,' Hobart murmured as she began to run along the jetty, 'remember your cool British reserve.'

'To hell with the British,' Grace retorted, 'I'm just a madly excited old Scorp with a boy friend in from the sea.'

'That's what I mean,' said Hobart. 'It's lucky the *Gazette* doesn't run a gossip column.'

'Oh! come on, Stuffy,' Grace said, her eyes shining, 'I don't care. I'm so happy.'

'We'll soon put a stop to that,' Hobart said squeezing her

arm, then drawing attention to himself he bellowed through cupped hands, 'Hey! *Firesprite!* Remember us?'

David stopped, turned and walked to the guard-rail. He looked at Grace and she at him. For a moment or so no other people existed in the whole wide world and suddenly it was no longer necessary to shout. Jimmy Allendale had waved and gone on to the quarter-deck to receive the officials now walking up the gangway. David stood there smiling and looking down at his two dear friends on the jetty.

'Hallo, Grace. Hallo, Hobart—it's good to see you again. Come aboard and have a drink. It's been rather a thirsty trip.'

They went on board and down to the wardroom. There they met old friends such as Jimmy Allendale and the Chief and made new ones such as the two R.N.V.R. Subs and the Doctor. Grace was in a ferment as she looked round the little wardroom with its leather armchairs, its mahogany hatch to the pantry and the hideous Admiralty-pattern carpet on the deck. There was almost a queue to talk. Questions and answers were fired into the stream of conversation with an impatient delight. Outside and all around the work of the ship went on. She wanted to run across, throw her arms round David's neck and hug him hard but somehow or other she managed to sit tight where she was. Jimmy Allendale showed an unexpected pleasure at her presence on board and the better-looking of the two Subs made the opening moves in what the others called his 'Number Four A Routine Romantic Approach' in the belief that she was Mrs. Hobart. It was light-hearted, there was work to be done but everyone was for the moment relaxed and happy.

When a ship changes its working-base, there is a great deal of ordinary administrative detail to attend to. The mail came aboard and David was constantly breaking off to read signals or see ratings outside in the cabin flat. But now that they had been in commission nearly a year, the naval machine ran smoothly with no more than a nod, an assent or a brief, intelligent order.

After about twenty minutes Dicky Seale was ushered into the wardroom, his Royal Marine uniform oddly incongruous in the tiny mess, bearing a summons to luncheon at Government House.

'For some reason I can't think,' he added, darting a glance at Grace, 'Colonel Hobart and Mrs. Millingham are also commanded to appear.'

She longed to see David alone: she wanted to tell him the news about Lance: she wanted simply to feel his arms around her: she wanted somehow or other to express physically the tenderness and love which suffused her heart. But the situation did not develop in the way she wanted. Instead the Captain of *Firesprite* was summoned to a staff meeting aboard the *Hood* and was soon speeding across the harbour in a motor-boat, while Grace was returned by Hobart to her office and Seale, with other invitations to deliver, had also gone on his way. It was a paradox of the war, she reflected ruefully as she made a pretence of doing some work, that something you very much wanted was always placed just a little way out of your reach. But quite what it was she yearned for she did not define.

2

The time was indeed out of joint for personal affairs. The tragic summer and autumn of 1940 contained so many world crises that individual pathos and joy seemed to dwindle in importance. On 1st July the Pétain Government moved to Vichy, from which town it blackened the name and soul of France till the end of the war, and on that same day Force H at Gibraltar received an Admiralty signal warning them to prepare for Operation Catapult on 3rd July.

'Operation Catapult' was the immobilizing, the taking over or the destruction of the French Fleet all over the world. The Prime Minister referred to this as a hateful decision, the most unnatural and painful in which he had ever been concerned. In Gibraltar it was a horrible time. Until a few days previously France had been our gallant and respected ally. Now the officers and men of Force H were to be ordered to fire on their comrades for reasons which the brain could comprehend but the heart could not.

Ruthlessness is not an English quality and there was strong

opposition, within the bounds of discipline, to Operation Catapult from the Admiralty staff, who framed the orders, all the way down to the Captain of H.M.S. *Firesprite* which was one of the ships which would bring the action about. No one liked it nor the unclean feeling it engendered.

But the will of the nation was expressing itself. There were clear heads at the top and England, now in hourly danger of invasion, was at bay. It was dirty work but it was ordered and it had to be done. Such was the train of thought going through David's mind at the briefing conference on board the flagship, to which, surprisingly enough, his uncle was invited. This was a mark both of the personal esteem in which Fortin was held and of the close roping together at the highest levels of the Navy, Army, Air Force and civilian in Gibraltar's life. The petty back-biting days of Fat Barclay's term of office were far away in the past. It was now made visibly clear that they were all in it together.

The conference, which was at night, took place in the Admiral's Day cabin on board the *Hood*. Apart from the Admiral and his staff, there were present the Captains, the Navigating and the Gunnery officers of the battleships *Valiant* and *Resolution*, the aircraft-carrier *Ark Royal*, the cruisers *Sheffield* and *Antigone* and eleven destroyers. A remarkable collection of talent, Fortin considered, as he looked round the crowded cabin. He caught sight of his nephew, grave and weathered. Weathered or seasoned they all were. Indeed there was not a smiling face in the whole collection. The job they were going to have to do lay heavy upon them. Written orders had already been issued and these they now had in their hands. They were all highly experienced, highly trained naval officers. They could visualize only too clearly what lay ahead.

The Admiral held up a pink cypher form and now began to speak. 'I have received the following signal from the Admiralty,' he said in sombre tones, 'It reads: "You are charged with one of the most disagreeable and difficult tasks that a British Admiral has ever been faced with, but we have complete confidence in you and rely on you to carry it out relentlessly." The signal is addressed to me personally: its import is for all of us here and for the ships we command. I want you to know that the distaste and reluctance we all feel for what is about to be done has been put as forcefully as possible to the Admiralty and the Prime Minister. Now the decision has been taken and our feelings have no further place in the matter. The job is fairly and squarely in our hands and I intend it to be done with thoroughness. In the last three months the tide has gone badly against us. Our forces have been thrown out of Norway and thrown out of France. It is more likely than not that England herself will be invaded. His Excellency the Governor knows only too well what is at stake here from the point of view of Gibraltar. Gibraltar can expect the most vicious retaliation for what we are going to do. The bulk of the civilian population has been given asylum in French Morocco: one can only imagine what their position may be if we take French lives in Oran, Algiers and Dakar. With time to negotiate and persuade, perhaps we could achieve what is necessary without the use of force. But there is no time. We sail at dawn tomorrow in accordance with the orders you already hold. . . .'

As the Admiral continued and the various specialist officers dilated on the detailed action which was planned, Fortin allowed his thoughts to continue along the lines suggested by the Admiral. Retaliation was now only a few hours away. So far as air attack on the Rock was concerned, he was not unduly worried. The A.A. barrage was formidable and the French air forces in Algeria and Morocco dispirited and weak. Vindictiveness was a poor fuel for fighting men. He did not fear the French Air Force. France had consumed herself with her fatal defensive attitude and a late spite was no substitute for staunchness and a national self-respect. But what of Gibraltar's women and children?

The Gestapo might not yet be in Morocco but they could move fast and one invaluable way of sapping Gibraltarian morale would be to persecute the dependents of those who were left behind on the Rock. It was the Nazi technique, the lever employed by any effective Terror. The Jews had known it in Germany before the war, it would soon be operating in France and all the occupied countries, Stalin used it in Russia. It was a process unknown to the British for centuries. They could only imagine what it was like. But imagination and experience were two different things. The slow poison could be made to work here in Gibraltar if the Germans acted quickly enough. They must be got out of Morocco, Fortin decided, even if the French did not immediately throw them out. The women and children, the aged and infirm must be got out as soon as possible and sent somewhere else.

The conference came to an end, the naval officers breaking up into groups and talking among themselves. Fortin knew the majority by sight. His nephew was talking to Trevesham, the Captain of *Antigone*, the 'Leander' class cruiser they had been with in Norway. The post-Captain on the Admiral's staff who had been Naval Attaché in Paris and who was to try and negotiate with the French Admiral the following day was in the same group and Fortin joined them after he had thanked the Admiral and wished him luck. This was not a formal occasion and there was no standing around in order of seniority waiting for important personages to go. There was an eve-of-battle tingle in the atmosphere and for a second Fortin was carried back in memory to the desert fort where he had first learned the anatomy of war, the practised technical thinking, the calculated courage which was needed and, as always, the unknown unknowable gap into which entered what Fortin called the Will of God. He knew no fighting man who was not aware, at the crisis point, of this strange 'nothingness' as one of the ingredients of battle, the vacuum area where Fate could move and something new could be mysteriously created within the framework of life. Now on board the *Hood*, the world's greatest warship, on the eve of a dire moment of history, among these loosely assembled groups of captains and specialist naval officers, Fortin felt very vividly aware of the invisible Presence. As he took a farewell look at the faces, some of which might never come back, he wondered which of this grave attractive gathering felt as he did. Perhaps none of them did: perhaps they would phrase it another way: perhaps it was something they would rediscover only when battle was joined. He wished David luck and left. *Firesprite* had been chosen to take the negotiators into the harbour of Oran for the parley if the French would agree. He wondered if he would see his nephew again.

The Admiral saw him over the side and down to his waiting car. But Fortin felt like walking, and sending the car on ahead he began to pace along the shadowy mole past the great gaunt ships that would so soon be in action in another place. It was a hot, oppressive night and the lights of Gibraltar seemed to accentuate, with their small man-made twinkle, the dark, brooding vastness of the Rock, the symbol at this anxious time of something indestructible and firm against which the storm must, please God, break itself and disintegrate. He left the Dockyard by the South Gate and walked along Rosia Road overlooking the dry-docks and the harbour. Then, quickening his pace, he left the Navy to get on with it and in his thoughts turned away to other things. Dawn was a mere six hours away. It was just possible that by the following evening Gibraltar would be filled with the French Fleet.

3

So at 04.30, on 3rd July 1940, Force H sailed for Oran. Though David had returned straight on board his ship and had had nearly five hours' sleep, he felt the same mood of mysterious anticipation which seemed to hang about the Rock as ships were cleared away for sea. In the dawn light and the windless, oily silence that pervaded the harbour, there was a ghostly quality in the sailors working about the fo'c'sles, securing sea-boats and letting go hawsers as if they were all automata in some sinister ballet.

David had made innumerable dawn sailings before but today he felt especially tense. The huge 42,000-ton *Hood* eased away from the jetty, turned in the harbour and then led the battleships *Valiant* and *Resolution*, the *Ark Royal* and the two cruisers through the gate in the boom and out into the Bay. The destroyers, as their protective screen, had already preceded them and now swept ahead of the big ships for any lurking submarines.

In San Roque Grace lay sleepless. As dawn broke some instinct prompted her to get up, go to her window and look towards Gibraltar. In the dim light she could scarcely distinguish more than that warships were going to sea. She did not know if David would be among them but she sent up a prayer for him in any case as the dark shapes moved away towards the mouth of the Bay. At the same time the German Intelligence Organization was naming and counting the ships that had put to sea. Hobart had once shaken Fortin by repeating a favourite boast of German Intelligence in Algeciras. Such a close watch was kept on Gibraltar, they claimed, that it was known in Berlin what the Governor was having for breakfast an hour before he had it. Breakfast food was scarcely what interested the Germans, but as a pointer to what else might be gleaned it was only too likely to be true. So the enemy would know that Force H was at sea. Its destination, though, remained a secret. Only David and the other captains who turned their ships to the east, shivering in the coolness of the dawn, could visualize in detail what might lie ahead.

At the same moment, at Portsmouth and Plymouth, units of the French Navy were taken over in great strength and without opposition except in the giant submarine, the *Surcouf* where two naval officers and a leading-seaman were killed. At that same moment Malta was being bombed by Italian aircraft, German reinforcements were landing in Jersey and Guernsey, R.A.F. bombers were returning home from the marshalling yards of Hamm, and the Italian water pipe-line between Bardia and Capuzzo was being cut by a British desert patrol.

The light grew and soon it was another clear, Mediterranean day. The British squadron forged on to the east, breakfast was cooked and eaten, 'Action Stations' sounded off and at about 9.30 a.m. Force H lay off the low cliffs of Oran. The tragedy had begun.

Once in position *Firesprite* was ordered to close the *Hood* and the Captain, who was to negotiate with the French Admiral, came aboard. David then set course for the harbour mouth and with French acquiescence entered the port, as it appeared with every French gun that was visible trained upon them.

The four-ringed Captain who now stood beside David on the bridge was in possession of a long, carefully worded communiqué from the British Government demanding action on one of four alternatives. These were that the French Fleet should either sail with the British and continue the fight against th e Germans and Italians or that the ships should be sailed with reduced crews to a British port, the crews being repatriated at the earliest moment, or that they should be sailed to a port in the French West Indies such as Martinique and there be immobilized or—and here the blunt Anglo-Saxon will-power broke surface—they should be sunk by the French within six hours. The fifth alternative, which was that the Royal Navy would sink their ships for them, was again dressed up in slightly more tactful terms, the actual phrase being '. . . I have the orders of His Majesty's Government to use whatever force may be necessary to prevent your ships from falling into German or Italian hands.' Behind that wording, however, stood a direct order from the Admiralty to the Vice-Admiral Commanding Force H saying that '. . . if the French will not accept any of your alternatives, they are to be destroyed.'

It was to be a long day. To begin with the Captain was refused an interview with Admiral Gensoul on board the French flagship *Dunkerque*. This rebuff had the effect on David of making *Firesprite* shrink to the size of a picket boat under his feet. He looked round the harbour identifying various units of the French Fleet, all of them monstrous in size compared with *Firesprite*. There were the battleships *Bretagne* and *Provence*, and the two enormous battle-cruisers *Strasbourg* and *Dunkerque*, He could count three light cruisers, at least eight destroyers, and five submarines. He felt like a Pekinese in among a lot of bloodhounds.

However *Firesprite* was an important communication link between the French and the British. As such, sitting there in the middle of Oran harbour, she was privileged. But it was not much good having some delicate proposals on a piece of paper if the French were not going to discuss them. Further instructions were sought of the *Hood*, and *Firesprite* was then told to deliver the communiqué in writing to the French Admiral. The motor-boat was lowered and Jimmy Allendale set off for the *Dunkerque*. Having suffered a frigid and what in normal circumstances would have been an unacceptably humiliating reception, he contrived to deliver the historic demand to a French lieutenant on board the battle-cruiser. He then lay off awaiting a reply.

[243]

After what seemed like a half-century of delay, Admiral Gensoul had *Firesprite's* boat called alongside and a written reply was sent to Vice-Admiral Somerville via *Firesprite*. Here a deadly pride was at work with the French Navy firmly in its maw. 'Under no circumstances,' Admiral Gensoul answered, 'will French warships be allowed to fall intact into German or Italian hands.' He added that force would be met by force.

As the day wore on it seemed to David that a quietness and a hush fell over Oran, the equivalent in the full light of day of that brooding 'otherness' which last night had possessed Gibraltar. Movement in the harbour appeared to have ceased and attention now played, to the exclusion of everything else, on the *Dunkerque*, on his own tiny ship and on the great battle squadron almost lazily patrolling outside. Back and forth flew the messages between Admiral Gensoul and the French Admiralty, between Admiral Somerville and the British Admiralty, between the *Hood* and the *Firesprite*, between the *Firesprite* and the *Dunkerque*. Pride was to win the day and exact the violence it sought. The agonized reluctance to fire on the French was again made plain to the Admiralty. Again a direct order was received: 'French ships must comply with our terms or sink themselves or be sunk by you before dark.'

At 4.15 p.m. the British Captain was allowed on board the French flagship to see Admiral Gensoul. Although this was what he had been trying to do all day, it was already too late. The French Admiralty had twice been consulted. Admiral Darlan had withheld from the Council of Ministers what was perhaps the most acceptable of the British proposals—namely that the Fleet should sail to Martinique for immobilization—and as a result the fate of Oran was sealed.

Knowing, as both sides did, what was now likely to happen, the British Captain left the *Dunkerque* and rejoined *Firesprite*. Then, wondering if they might not be speeded on their way by a farewell shot up the stern, David set off with all speed for the *Hood* and the main body of Force H. After disembarking the Captain, *Firesprite* took up her proper station with the Force on an anti-submarine patrol.

At five fifty-four the bombardment began. For ten minutes the fifteen-inch guns of the *Hood*, *Valiant* and *Resolution* poured shells on the French Fleet and the coast defences. The French returned the fire and began putting to sea. In so doing only the *Strasbourg* escaped and she was torpedoed by aircraft from the *Ark Royal* before reaching Toulon. Of the other heavy ships, the old *Bretagne* was blown up, the *Provence* was beached and the *Dunkerque* ran aground while trying to escape.

Then, as darkness came and sick at heart at what they had been forced to do, the British Squadron returned to Gibraltar. There were the two new, nearly completed battleships at Casablanca and Dakar—the *Jean Bart* and the *Richelieu* yet to be dealt with—but next time the will and temper of the British would no longer be in doubt. Next time there would be no day-long parley in the hot Mediterranean sun. For a few short, tragic days the French and the Royal Navies were actively at war.

4

Retaliation came, as expected, the following night. Gibraltar had its first air-raid in earnest when, instead of friendly aircraft milling around the Rock and the firing off of blank ammunition, a blackout was swiftly imposed and a very lively A.A. barrage put up. When it happened Fortin was on the Upper Rock having an after-dinner prowl with Seale along the Queen's Road. It had been a long and exhausting day, in which the many different reactions to the destruction of the French Fleet had each to be judged and considered. Before turning in, therefore, he had felt like some fresh air and this was coupled with a wish to get somewhere high up out of Gibraltar. The Queen's Road runs through one of the treed areas of the Rock and they were thus both sheltered and in an excellent position to watch what happened.

The blackout was sudden and effective, the barrage deafening and the sweep of the searchlights spectacular. Fortin wondered in what strength the raid would be. If it was nothing more than a token retaliation by the French, then the grim realities of Oran would have been seen in their proper light and at least partially accepted. If it was in strength then it would presage a good deal worse to come when the Germans gained effective control over Morocco. Seale fetched their tin hats from the car and then they stood under a tree on a small promontory watching the display.

'I shouldn't like to be at the receiving end of this lot,' Seale remarked, visualizing as he spoke how Gibraltar would look to a bomber pilot. Now that he knew he would never fly again, the nostalgia for it was worse. Fortin grunted. He was not in a conversational mood. He felt ill-at-ease in himself. The Colonial Secretary, Hobart and Barbarossa had each separately come and told him there was unrest in the town. The men were worrying about their dependents in Morocco. He had brooded about it most of the day and now that this might well be the first of a series of night air-raids, the question of Gibraltar's morale had moved up to first place on the Short List.

Whatever needed to be done about the women and children of Gibraltar was a War Cabinet decision and Fortin knew well enough that it must take its place in the queue—but what was required of him as Governor in the meantime? Soft, comforting words at a time like this were apt to become nothing but irritants. Hobart said there were trouble-makers in the Dockyard. Gibraltarians were not public-school Englishmen trained to keep a stiff upper lip in times of adversity. They were excitable and depressed, they felt rather than thought, were easily prone to violence and then bitterly sorry. He knew he had had them with him up to now, he did not want to lose them at this point through blindness or an insufficiency of understanding.

'I can only hear three of them, sir,' Seale was saying, 'and they don't seem to want to come very near.' The barrage was now continuous and must surely be a formidable deterrent, Fortin considered, to a disaffected French pilot from Lyautey or Maison Blanche. Perhaps they would go back and tell the others how unhealthy it was to fly over Gibraltar at night.

'Ah! there's one!' Seale shouted, pointing out over the bay. Caught in the searchlights the aircraft was diving towards the ships in the harbour into what seemed a hail of tracer shells. There was at any rate one Frenchman who didn't give a damn.

Down in the city the air-raid shelters were full. Nicholas stood near the door of the one in the centre of Governor's Parade. He had learnt to respect aerial bombing in the Spanish war and the reaction of taking cover was now automatic. To the inhabitants of Gibraltar, however, this was a new experience. He listened to their emotional grumbling, to their uninformed prejudices, to their ill-expressed resentment, to the play of that childish and sometimes charming Mediterranean instability which was their nature. Boothroyd was right. These southerners were far more easily preyed upon by fear and uncontrollable panic than the stolid Anglo-Saxon soldiers and sailors some of whom were also in the shelter.

They chirruped and whirred in the colloquial Andalusian Spanish which was their native tongue. Nicholas listened with half an ear. The poison daily instilled by Boothroyd was beginning to do its work. There was real discontent at large now among these people. They did not accept the evacuation, they criticized the way it had been done, and now anxiety was growing because of what was likely to happen to their wives and children as a result of yesterday's action at Oran. Across at the other end of the shelter he saw one of Boothroyd's group, a charge hand in the Dockyard, talking excitedly to the half-dozen people in his immediate vicinity. These people were ripe.

He was jarred out of his thoughts by the vibration and the dust caused by the first bomb to fall from the air into the labyrinth of Gibraltar. If that had been aimed at the Dockyard the aim was not very good. There was a moment's pause and then an excited reaction in Spanish. The British sergeant and the two lance-corporals near to Nicholas looked across at the Gibraltarians and then at one another:

'Like a lot of flipping magpies,' the sergeant said scornfully, sucking his teeth, 'chatter, chatter, chatter, caw-caw-caw.'

About a quarter of a mile away Grace had just poured out two stiff brandies for David and herself when the sirens had sounded. This was the first dinner they had ever had alone together at the Line Wall House. Her father was over at San Roque for the evening and in another half-hour she must herself be gone before the frontier was closed for the night. To have got David to herself even for this brief time was almost miraculous and she heard the undulant wail of the air-raid warning with dismay and anger.

'I must get back to the ship,' David had said at once.

'I'll run you down,' she had replied with a chill at her heart. Curse the war and curse the immediate dismissal of herself, of the evening she had created for them, indeed of their whole significance for each other. She could have cried out in rage. One moment he was there in the drawing-room looking at her with those tender eyes, the next he was a crisp naval mechanism, ordering his thoughts, working out a plan, looking at his watch, thinking about his sacred ship, putting on his responsibilities with the uniform cap that lay in the hall. Well, there it was—you had to accept it, you had to endure. She shrugged her shoulders and a minute later they were out of the house walking quickly to where the car was parked.

She drove fast and they did not speak on the short journey to the pens. The barrage from Europa Point was just beginning as they reached the ship.

'What will you do?' he asked as he got out.

'Go to San Roque straight away.'

'Well . . .' he said, for a moment hesitating whether to try and make her go to a shelter and then suddenly he came out of it all for a single blinding instant.

'I love you, Grace,' he said looking at her intently, 'I love you very much.'

'I love you, David,' she answered, her heart ablaze. 'Take care of yourself.' Then as though jerked away by a string he was gone, quickly moving up the darkened gangway, lost among the tin-hatted sailors near the dimly seen guns. She turned the car abruptly and set off for the North Front. If only a bomb could fall on me now, she thought, now I could go through the fire itself. But no bomb fell on Grace that night.

5

Operation Catapult was not tidied up and put away into history until July 8th. On that date, at Dakar, on the western-most tip of Africa, H.M.S. *Firesprite* formed part of the anti-submarine patrol for H.M.S. *Hermes*, the carrier, while her aircraft torpedoed the new French battleship *Richelieu* and the ship's motor-boat crept in under the Frenchman's stern and dropped sufficient depth-charges to distort her propeller shafts and thus make any movement impossible for her. This was the final stroke in the sorry elimination of the French Navy from the Second World War.

Dakar is only fifteen degrees north of the Equator and some 2,000 miles from Gibraltar. It seemed to David that his day in Gibraltar and his dinner with Grace had become in a few short hours nothing but a moment's brilliant interlude in a long period of sea-time, enjoyable in itself but brooded over in the tropical heat by the grim purpose of their venture south. Yet the voyage itself was a rest. They averaged over thirty knots so that they were virtually in no danger from submarines. The weather was of the sort that people hope for on expensive pleasure cruises. The voyage took three days' steaming and the ship's company of *Firesprite* had by this time become adept at both resting themselves and at cleaning up the ship whenever the luck of the draw allowed them a breathing space.

David himself alternated between staring in a bemused fashion at the hard, sparkling Atlantic and lying on his bunk staring equally bemused at the deck-head of his cabin. In both positions the problem of Grace and of Pam chased itself round and round his mind. He was in a state of inner chaos, where nothing added up and where his feelings and his instincts warred against the knowledge, the upbringing and the puritanical streak which his passage through life so far had imposed upon him. He knew also that he must not for long allow his peace of mind to be disturbed: personal anxieties were of no help in the command of one of H.M. Ships: a solution of some kind would have to be found but what it was likely to be he had no idea at all. He could see no way out but merely to acquiesce in such a state of affairs was against his nature. His instinct—and it was usually sound—was to turn his attention on to something else: then, in some extraordinary way, time and what he had seen described as a 'creative pause' did its work and something new came about.

The key to it all was the search for meaning. Life in all its phases was essentially neutral—it could be good or bad depending on how you took it. Once you scented the meaning invisible behind any event, you could accept the greatest disasters and grow from the energy they contained. But how did that help him over Grace? He saw now that Pam, caught in the closed circle of her intensely feminine preoccupation with herself, no longer had what he wanted—if ever she really had.

Yet he had loved her once. Looking back on it now he thought he knew when the disillusionment had begun. There was a picture of her which had printed itself on his mind very early in their marriage. She had been squatting in front of the fire one night, wearing nothing but an old Hong Kong kimono her mother had given her, staring lost into the glow of the fire. He had slipped the thing off her shoulders and was stroking her neck, intensely aware of her small naked breasts and of how much he adored her. For a time there had been silence and then she had said, 'I don't see why we can't have the Sunbeam-Talbot. The Hillman's so shabby and after all John Cressiter's the same seniority as you and *they* have one and I know Margery hasn't any private means . . .' and she had gone on and on and on, as he had massaged her neck and loved her, and did not tell her he had given up smoking to help pay for their holiday in France. Even in those days she took what he had to offer for granted. She was eaten by an avarice for things or suffering nobly when she could not have them. She could not see that clothes and possessions only had meaning up to a certain point. 'Things' had dragged them both down: worming away at his love for her, disparaging his efforts to give her everything this side of bankruptcy, feeding on her with envy of others and the sour despair of always wanting more, of never rising above it, of never seeing that it was he and she alone which were important. With Pam it was always the look of the thing that mattered, and he had gradually come to realize that she was not the sort of wife which a young naval officer living on his pay could afford. She should have married a much wealthier man.

With Grace there was understanding. Even as he thought about her, remembered her smile and her dark troubled eyes,

[250]

his heart seemed to glow as though new life was being breathed on to a dying fire. But what was he to do? What could he do? Tell Pam he no longer wanted her and would she please kindly divorce him? It was never as simple as the books made out. Then there was Boofles spidering away in a prisoner-of-war camp. There was Grace's religion that would mean for her an enormous—perhaps an impossible sacrifice. Yet their hearts cried out to each other in the darkness and the loneliness of this terrible time when perhaps the new Flood that would one day re-engulf the world had begun, with the Rock of Gibraltar behind them both as a symbol—but a symbol of what? He lay on his back, staring at the deck-head. A deep sigh of helplessness at it all escaped from him. There was a knock at the cabin door.

'Captain, sir? The First Lieutenant said to tell you Cape Verde is in sight.'

'Very well,' said David getting wearily to his feet and going up once more to the bridge. The Dakar incident had begun.

XIII

THREE days after, when *Firesprite* returned to Gibraltar, a massive crisis was working itself up to a climax. Oran had begun it and now Dakar had finished off any feeling of kindliness the Moroccan French may have felt towards the women and children of Gibraltar. Without ceremony, without warning and without consideration of any kind, the evacuees were ordered pell-mell aboard any ship going to or past Gibraltar.

The collapse of France and the knowledge of what had so recently happened to their own evacuees in their own country now provoked the utmost callousness on the part of the French colonial officials concerned. The Gibraltarians must be shot out of Morocco and shot out quick whether they were old, infirm or dying, whether they were mothers in labour or with babes in arms, whether they had their few pathetic possessions or whether they were for all practical purposes destitute. There was a knock at the door, soldiers stood waiting and an order was given to leave instantly for a ship then at the jetty. The Gibraltarians found themselves at the receiving end of all the pent-up vindictiveness engendered by the fall of France and the destruction by the Royal Navy of the French Fleet.

In Gibraltar itself there was confusion, uncertainty and an outbreak of serious trouble. This was occasioned by one of Fortin's rare errors of judgment. The Colonial Office, on a Cabinet decision, had told the Governor that evacuees from Gibraltar must now be sent to England, to London in fact, where in one central block of buildings they could be properly cared for. In view of the threat of invasion under which England then stood, this was a somewhat surprising decision. It would result in greater physical danger to the women and children of Gibraltar than if they had stayed.

'The local point of view,' the Colonial Secretary observed to Fortin, 'is simple enough. People are saying their families might just as well have stayed on the Rock.'

'Are they now?' Fortin said curtly. 'Has no one any imagination? What do they fancy a siege would be like with their wives and children mixed up in the fighting? The Rock's a fortress.'

'I know, sir, but they're thinking of themselves.'

'Then they can damned well stop it.'

'Feelings are running pretty high in the town.'

'I can't help that,' Fortin retorted. 'We got rid of the dependents once. I won't have them coming back now and starting it all over again.'

He felt unusually disturbed and uncertain. It was not an easy decision to make. It would be no pleasure to any of them enforcing it.

'Then what's to happen when the ships arrive in the Bay?' the Colonial Secretary asked.

'The evacuees are to stay on board. We had enough trouble getting them away to Morocco. If we let them land and go back to their homes now there's only going to be more bad feeling and confusion when we uproot them again in a few days' time and shift them to England. I'm sorry but I must draw the line somewhere.'

'With respect, sir. . . .'

'No!' Fortin said imperatively, 'I don't want any argument. They're to stay on board their ships out in the Bay and that's final and definite.'

'Very good, sir.'

When the Colonial Secretary had left the room, Fortin stood up and for a few moments remained staring down at the patio mastering the deep anger he felt. He did not enjoy being hardhearted. He realized the Colonial Secretary thought he was badly misjudging the temper of the men of Gibraltar and the power this temper could project. He did not care. He was Governor and for once he determined to exercise his absolute authority and to stand no nonsense about it. None the less he was far from happy with the state of affairs as he saw it.

Elsewhere in Gibraltar, however, Boothroyd and Nicholas were making no such mistakes. To each in his separate thinking this was an opportunity which would not recur. It had to be seized and exploited for all it was worth.

[253]

Boothroyd knew his job all right. He had been sent to Gibraltar to collect round him a nucleus of saboteurs, to train them under discipline and to hold them ready for whatever purpose might be decreed. Hobart knew there must be a Boothroyd there, but still had not discovered his identity. This in itself, he had to admit, was an achievement on the part of the enemy. He kept a fairly close check upon Nicholas but this had not led him to Boothroyd who took good care to do his job in the Armament Supply Department of the Dockyard with loyalty and enthusiasm. In fact from many points of view Boothroyd was the last person to attract suspicion. He was competent, popular with other dockyard officials and a sidesman at the Cathedral where the Dean valued his earnest efforts and which provided him with the sort of alibi he needed.

By July 1940 Boothroyd had five good lieutenants with jobs in different parts of the Rock. There was also Nicholas, whom he no longer regarded as reliable and whom he would only use in real emergency. Nicholas had been told to cut down on his drinking but by now the habit encased him. He was also no longer amenable to the discipline—or not to the degree of discipline which Boothroyd saw fit to impose. Nicholas had become a problem but in the crisis which had overtaken Gibraltar where there were boatloads of women and children separated from their men by a few yards of water and the bans and obstructions of officialdom, then every available force must be brought to bear until the maximum chaos and discontent had been achieved and had possibly resulted in violent action. Nicholas could surely be relied upon to play a part in this.

Firesprite berthed shortly after ten in the morning and when David walked round to the Dockyard Tower, which he did for exercise after the cramped days at sea, he at once became aware that something was 'up' in Gibraltar. Even from the pens, the Dockyard sounded ominously silent, the streets were filled with clusters of men talking excitedly and indignantly. There was a wariness in the eye, a kind of bridling in the way people moved, a dangerous temper in the air. In Commercial Square, the real centre of Gibraltar that had now been renamed John Mackintosh Square, in front of the City Council offices, a crowd was collecting. It was a civilian crowd. Both Police and Military were conspicuously absent. For the moment it was a crowd without a leader but soon one would be spawned up, soon the occasion would produce its orator to give expression to the powerful feelings of injustice and resentment which had drawn them all there and which continued to empty offices, shops and dockyard establishments till the working population of Gibraltar had been gathered together into a vociferous mob.

Some of the shops in Main Street were putting up the shutters, so recently taken down for another day's trade; the Commissioner of Police was conferring with his principal officers; the Governor had been warned; members of the Evacuation Committee, slipping quietly into the City Council offices, peeped through the windows at the growing crowd; Boothroyd stood in one corner of the square in the shade of a cigarette kiosk, watching, spotting, judging the moment, relishing the knowledge that whatever the outcome of the day the forces he represented had been immensely strengthened by what was then taking place.

David's business at the Dockyard Tower did not take long. The Yard had been unusually quiet as he walked through it and now seemed more so as he went round to Grace's office. It was deserted. He had commented on the crowds in Gibraltar to the staff at the Tower but this had been airily brushed aside with the remark that 'there was a bit of bloody-mindedness about the evacuation—nothing to worry about.' David was not so sure. He had been a sub-lieutenant in the *Rodney* at the Invergordon Mutiny nine years ago. It had made him unusually alert to the temper of disaffection and mutiny. He was by no means convinced that what he had seen in John Mackintosh Square was 'nothing to worry about'. Thoughtfully he retraced his steps back into the town, noticing that only one policeman was on duty at the main gate of the Dockyard and that was an elderly sergeant.

'All by yourself, Sergeant?' he said as he returned the salute.

'Yes, sir. There's a protest going on about the evacuees. What I say is—you can't keep a man and his wife apart, sir, not when one's here and the other's just out there.'

'Where's your wife, Sergeant?'

'She's out there, too, sir, but I said I'd look out here while the others have a go at the City Council. Something ought to be done about it, sir, there's no doubt about that.'

He continued on into the town, through the South Port Gate, along the southern end of Main Street and past Government House. Uncle Giles had a little trouble on his plate. Making people do things they did not want to do was always unpalatable. The scenes at Oran and Dakar came back vividly into his mind. None of them had enjoyed doing that. Now Uncle Giles was forced to be equally ruthless with the people of the colony he had been sent to govern, people whose loyalty he needed, yet who were not under the same watertight discipline as the Services. It was a dirty, horrible time.

By this time the crowd had enormously swelled in John Mackintosh Square. David moved round the perimeter, tasting its temper, wondering how it would vent its anger. He felt a touch on his shoulder and turned. It was Grace.

'David! What are you doing here? I didn't even know you were back.'

'This morning. What's going on? And what are *you* doing here?'

'I've come to join the protest. It's red tape gone mad. You *cannot* keep a lot of women and children cooped up there till the right ships arrive to cart them elsewhere.'

'Have you told your father?'

'Of course I have. He says once they're ashore they'll never leave again. I told him they should treat us Gibraltarians as human beings not as "things" to be shuffled about as they like.'

'Suppose the crowd doesn't get what it wants?'

'There'll be a general strike.'

'I should think Uncle Giles has faced worse things in his time.'

'I dare say he has. The point is he needn't. He's only got to be reasonable: they'll do anything he wants if they can only see their wives and children again.'

'Why don't you tell him so?'

Grace looked at him incredulously.

'*Me?* It's nothing to do with me: anyway I'd never be able to put it over properly. It would be terrible cheek. I'd never get in. Why should he listen to me?'

'But you feel about it strongly.'

'Of course I do.'

'Well, Hobart or Seale would take you in. I think you ought to do something about it.'

One of the City Councillors, a leader of the Jewish community who had been against the evacuation, was standing on the roof of a taxi haranguing the crowd, telling them how he had opposed the decision but how helpless he had been. It was better to accept the Governor's decree. He spoke in Spanish which David did not understand, but Grace did and shook her head.

'That's no good. That's not what they want to hear.'

Then to her astonishment another man jumped up on the roof of the taxi, said something to the City Councillor who rather uncertainly yielded the stage to him, and then began to shout in Spanish in a much more authoritative way.

'Good heavens, it's Nicholas!'

It was indeed, and what Nicholas had to say was much more to the temper of the crowd.

'This is a lot of damned, flipping nonsense,' he began, 'and we all know it. That's why we're here. There's a war on. We may never see our wives and our children again: when they go from here they may be sunk at sea, they may be bombed, they may be blown to pieces, they may simply die—and that can happen to us as well here. This may be our last chance to see our nearest and dearest. What stands in our way? The petty, self-important laziness and pride of the British Colonial Civil Service headed by an unmarried Governor entirely blind and callous to our sufferings. . . .'

There was a wild outburst of cheering which drowned the next few sentences.

'He's coming out in his true colours at last,' said Grace, the anger in her now dividing between sympathy for the Gibraltarians Nicholas was inciting and disgust at the way he was doing it. This was her own brother-in-law. But there was to be a further surprise. Out of the main door of the City Council offices walked her father. He, too, looked severe and angry. He made his way to the old taxi on the roof of which Nicholas was standing. For a moment or so he looked at his son-in-law

[257]

with loathing and contempt. The crowd, which recognized him, fell away making a circle round them. Jaime did not try to emulate Nicholas by climbing on the roof of the car. He stood on the mudguard waiting for Nicholas to pause. Then he said:

'Pay no attention to this young man. You are being deceived. He is not one of us and he has not got your best interests at heart. He is inciting you to violence. . . .'

There was a roar of disapproval from the crowd. Most of the individuals forming the mob knew and respected Jaime but he represented at that moment everything their will was against. He was wealth, privilege, the established authority then being questioned, the autocracy which was removing the women and children from Gibraltar for purposes, among other things, of guarding its own power. There was an ugly murmuring undertone in the crowd. On an impulse Grace clutched at David's arm.

'Come with me,' she said, 'I *am* going to see the Governor.'

It took them about five minutes' hard walking along Main Street to reach the Old Convent. All the time people were still being sucked towards the Square as though by a whirlpool they could not resist.

They went along to Seale's room. Dicky stood up surprised to see them.

'We've just come from the Square,' David said. 'Grace wants to see H.E.'

'He's got the Colonial Secretary and the Commissioner in with him,' Dicky said, 'but I'll ask if he can see you. What do you want to sell him—vacuum cleaners?'

'There's a nice line in riots starting up outside the City Council offices.'

'Drama at last on the Rock?' Seale said with a touch of disbelief. 'I'll break in and see what the form is.'

By this time Grace was beginning to have second thoughts. The mob in the square was one thing: the cool detached grandeur of Government House another. She found herself shaking slightly. What was it to do with her? Or with David for that matter? She looked at him and drew a gust of strength from his calm, smiling eyes.

'Remember your aim,' he said quietly. 'You want to do something for them, don't you? Not just make a protest about a protest. There's nothing to be scared of. I've no right to be here either but I'm his nephew and it's your father—so—take a deep breath. . . .'

Seale came back into the room.

'His Nibs will see you both now,' he said, 'you lucky things.'

They went into the Governor's private office. The Colonial Secretary looked at them curiously but with sympathy: the Commissioner was clearly annoyed at the interruption. Fortin stood up looking at both intently.

'Well, David,' he said, 'what is it?'

David looked at Grace and nodded to her to speak.

'We've just come from John Mackintosh Square and there's a very ugly crowd . . .' she began.

'That's what we're discussing,' Fortin cut in.

'I've just seen Nicholas Pappadopoulos working them up and my father trying to calm them down. Instead Father got shouted down. There's going to be violence.'

Fortin glanced at the Commissioner who nodded and left the room.

'Is that how it struck you, David?'

'Yes, sir. They're very angry. They don't want any soft words.'

Grace took a deep breath.

'Why I've really come,' she said, 'is to beg you to let them come ashore—however difficult it is—for pity's sake—*please*.'

There was a long pause. The quiet in the room was almost tangible. A pattern of flies floated and criss-crossed up near the ceiling. The palm-trees in the patio stirred in a breeze. From the Bay the deep melancholy note of a ship's siren penetrated the room. Then very faintly came the sound of distant shouting, and at the same time Seale rushed into the room to say that fighting had broken out in the Square. The Commissioner of Police had gone to take charge personally. Seale was followed almost at once by Freddie Smallbones who announced that a mob was marching on Government House, led by Nicholas Pappadopoulos, in order to present a petition.

Then things began happening quickly: the Services were

alerted and a plan for coping with civil unrest put into operation. At that moment the news came that Jaime Barbarossa had been hurt. For Grace the abstract flashed instantly into the personal and particular. All thoughts of the welfare of evacuees vanished from her mind as, followed by David, she ran out of Government House.

They could hear a few outbursts of shouting but in general it seemed to be an ominously quiet mob. Perhaps the incident over Jaime Barbarossa had released some of the heat, perhaps once a victim of any kind had been found for the violence a mob generates then the purpose of that mob has been partially satisfied. These were the thoughts in David's mind as he strode along beside Grace, remembering that grey autumn day at Invergordon nine years ago.

When they reached the square, Jaime was in a very bad way. He was being lifted into the old taxi around which the incident had taken place. He was unconscious and bleeding profusely from a bad gash on the head. No one knew who had thrown the stone: no one had seen and no one had been arrested, though now there seemed to be no one left in the square except soldiers and police. At one moment Jaime had been on the running-board trying to talk down his son-in-law, at the next he had been struck on the forehead fairly and squarely by a jagged stone and then in falling had twisted and had cracked open the back of his head on the kerb of the gutter.

'Where's the driver of this taxi?' David called out, but as no one answered he decided to take charge himself.

'Hey! you there!' he said to one of the stunned by-standers, 'give this engine a swing.'

He jumped into the driver's seat and in a moment or so with a crash and a bang the ancient taxi sprang into life.

By this time Grace had torn off her jacket to try and staunch the flow of blood and with her father's head in her lap, she sat in the back of the rickety old cab trying to cushion the shocks of the crooked ill-surfaced road up to the Colonial Hospital. About half-way there, the enemy reconnaissance plane which now paid Gibraltar a morning visit was sighted and the air-raid sirens began to wail. Jaime continued to lose a great deal of blood and most of it seemed to be over Grace and the car.

Down at Government House, Fortin was accepting the verbal petition made by Nicholas and the two dissident City Councillors on behalf of the demonstration now packing Main Street at the Convent Place. Out in the Bay the ships from Morocco, filled with the women and children of Gibraltar, swung to the changing wind, waiting impatiently to be told their fate.

2

Throughout that day, together or apart, Grace and David drew nearer and nearer each other in themselves. Jaime remained unconscious and in a dangerous condition. Except to change her clothes, covered as they were with blood, except to telephone San Roque and break the news to Rosita, except to snatch a cup of tea and some biscuits at the house, Grace spent all her time at the hospital. David, perforce, had to return on board. He had work to do. As soon as Jaime was in the doctor's care and the taxi had been given back to its woebegone owner, he had returned to the ship and got on with the day's routine. There was a report to write on *Firesprite's* trip to Dakar, provisions, oil and water had to be taken on board, defects attended to. This was all automatic work which had to be done each time they came into harbour and there seemed to Jimmy Allendale to be more effort of this kind to be made in a destroyer than in any other type of ship as the men in proportion to the job were fewer. But then this was a natural thing for any first lieutenant to feel since it fell upon him to organize the ship and to see that it was kept in a fit state for the captain to command.

David told his First Lieutenant what had happened that morning in the town. Then they studied the situation together. *Firesprite* had been put at eight hours' notice for steam.

'Unless some real emergency crops up,' David remarked, 'we should have a night in at last. I'd like to help Grace as much as I can so I won't be on board much as long as we're at eight hours' notice. But you know where to get me. I'll either be at the hospital or at Line Wall Road. How does that affect you, Jimmy?'

'I'll be stopping aboard, sir, in any case,' Jimmy said, lying

[261]

loyally. He had had a monster run ashore planned with the Number One of *Forthright* but instead he would get his head down and write some letters on board. There was no reason at all why both he and the Captain should not be ashore at the same time. Nothing could happen to the ship at such long notice for steam. She was in a heavily protected harbour. They had just finished a hazardous operation and a round trip of 4,000 miles. They had to relax. Nevertheless Jimmy Allendale, who hoped soon to be getting a command of his own, was fully imbued with that remarkable sense of responsibility, never precisely defined but always present, which is the main characteristic of the sea-going naval officer. There was no official need for him to remain on board: he just thought he would stick around.

In this understanding he had an ally in the Chief. Lieutenant (E) Thomas McGregor, R.N., who had been promoted from the lower deck, respected his Captain in much the same intelligent way as the First Lieutenant. He did not phrase it like that to himself. In fact he did not think about it at all. The skipper was a good 'un and that was all there was to it. His Scottish reserve inhibited gush and adulation in any shape or form, but he appreciated his Captain. He understood something of the weight he bore and there were almost no limits to which the engine-room department of *Firesprite* could not be driven in support of the 'old man'.

By the time David was really free of the ship and had again gone ashore in the Dog Watches, a number of things had happened in Gibraltar. To begin with, no work had been done all day. It was true there had been no more rioting and indeed this would no longer have been possible. There were armed patrols all over the town. But whilst any further outbreak of violence would have been instantly suppressed, if men were to be forced to work at the point of a bayonet, a general paralysis would soon set in. Altogether it was a day of chaos and distress.

Fortin endured this painful state of affairs in the growing knowledge that he had made a mistake and that sooner or later he would have to put it right. By the late afternoon it became quite clear that what he had on his plate was an unofficial general strike.

'That being so,' he said to an emergency meeting of the Defence and Evacuation Committees, 'I have decided to bend to the wind. The wives and the children may come ashore but I want them warned to be ready to leave again at very short notice. This goes very much against my better instincts but we must face the facts as they are.'

As soon as he had given his decision he dismissed the conference. He did not wish their endorsement or approval. It had been difficult to walk back on his previous decision. He felt depressed and drained of energy. Somehow or other he had lost the way and it was this which upset him far more than the loss of face which this climbing down entailed in the eyes of Gibraltar.

The day's activities and the breakdown of 'God's plan' suited Boothroyd very well indeed. In fact it could not have been better except for that gormless, alcoholic idiot—Nicholas Pappadopoulos—now publicly branded as an agitator and thus useless for any more secret purpose. From now on he would always be suspect. Indeed Boothroyd had been told that the Governor was considering whether to proceed on charges of disturbing the peace which the Police wished to prefer against Nicholas and other ringleaders. The attack on Jaime Barbarossa was thus crucial. If he should die the Governor's attitude must inevitably harden.

As for Jaime, himself, he still lay balanced precariously between life and death. He had been given a blood transfusion: the primary shock was over but it was the secondary which could kill and that still lay ahead.

Fortin and Seale had been to the Colonial Hospital to take a look at Jaime and there had met Grace and David for the second time that day.

'I try to keep clear of private affairs,' Fortin said to her gravely, 'but so far as your father and his son-in-law are concerned, I don't see how I can any longer. Will you come and have a word with me about it as soon as you can?'

Grace looked at David and then at the Governor.

'Could we come now?'

'We?'

'Yes, sir,' David put in quickly to kill the embarrassment,

'I'd like to lend a hand if I can. Grace has a lot on her plate at present.'

'Yes, of course, David,' said His Excellency, giving them a sharp look. You could never hide things for long. Hobart and Seale had both dropped hints about the feeling there was between Grace Millingham and his nephew. He had even suspected it himself in the early days. Now, in the cold draught of a crisis, they had drawn closer together, inevitably showing their real feelings underneath.

'I understand you've taken to driving taxis about the Rock,' said Fortin, 'but if you like you can come back to the Convent with me now.'

3

Nicholas found that the morning's elation had very quickly disappeared, and that much as he hated his father-in-law he was becoming anxious about him. He had been up to inquire at the hospital but the news was not comforting. The sour taste had returned. For a short time, when impulse and the spirit of revolt had driven him to jump up and lead the angry crowd, he had experienced a wonderful feeling of liberation from himself. Indeed when the stone had been thrown, he knew nothing about it since he had already begun to lead the crowd towards Government House. Until afterwards he had had no idea how badly hurt Jaime had been and then only when an Inspector of Police had come to question him. He was not really sorry in the conventional sense: his brain told him that Jaime deserved everything that came his way. But he was disturbed about its effect on himself, on Rosita and on the general situation in Gibraltar. He realized that now he might very well be deported on some trumped-up excuse, and he also realized that he now wished to stay in Gibraltar more than ever.

In the afternoon he and Boothroyd had met by arrangement in the Tribuno Bar. By then the evacuees were landing and the attention of Gibraltar, and its security forces, lay elsewhere. The day had been won and Nicholas expected at least a word of praise. Instead Boothroyd had said aggressively in his thick Yorkshire voice:

'I suppose you're patting yourself on the back. I suppose you're pretty pleased about this morning.'

'In one sense—yes. I should hope you are too.'

'You realize you've put yourself out of the running from now on?'

'Out of what running?' Nicholas said angrily.

'We needn't go into that.'

'Needn't we? That's precisely what we ought to go into—you and I. You walk in here, you make a lot of assumptions, you order me about—who the hell do you think you are?'

'You drink too much,' Boothroyd said and with a surprising speed had paid for the round and slipped out of the bar. He would never risk any sort of public incident. He was a very wary gentleman indeed. Moreover he had put Nicholas at a disadvantage: he had got him steamed up and then had left him with the pressure unreleased. This would result in violence—in drink or a woman or both—that was the pattern of despair. But a woman, these days, meant crossing the frontier into La Línea: it meant formalities and tedious effort. Alcohol was very much better. Alcohol didn't cling to you and start crying, alcohol had no baby to taunt you with, no father-in-law to damage your peace of mind, no sense of utter, unbearable futility—at least not while its power was in you. 'God bless you, Alcohol!' Nicholas said to himself and ordered another double cognac. He deserved something to drink. Gibraltar should have clubbed together and bought him one. Gibraltar owed him a lot that day.

4

Over in San Roque, when Rosita first heard the news, she decided her mother must not be told. By now Edie was a bedridden, paralysed invalid whose world had narrowed down to the four walls of her room and who, strangely enough, accepted this state of affairs as though she had long ago ceased to be the well-known Mrs. Jaime Barbarossa but was now acclimatized to being a sort of inert domestic problem.

The baby had started crying as Grace had rung up and although she knew Conchita would be with it, she went straight up to the nursery to see that everything was all right. But this was a mechanical reaction. The baby was quite all right and Conchita was cosseting it as she loved to do.

She went out on to the veranda and sat down, looking at the Rock, trying to visualize the scene Grace had described and to get over the shock. Shock was an odd thing, she decided. It left you, so to speak, looking over your shoulder. Well, there it is, you said, but what next? Where would the next blow fall? She did not connect the accident which had befallen her father directly with Nicholas and yet she understood it as an inevitable outcome of the hidden war there had always been between them. Confused as she had been before, her loyalties were now confounded. What had the Barbarossas done to deserve such a messy state of affairs? Who was to blame? As always, the thought of her baby came into the forefront of her mind and with it a positive feeling in the heart, an ache that was none the less pleasant, which brought the tears to her eyes. To say that life went on all the same was a cliché, yet when you glimpsed the wonder it provoked, your breath was taken away. Father O'Reilly had put this thought in her mind one day when she was very low and she had fed on it ever since.

Nowadays Nicholas never came to the house. He had once suggested they meet in La Línea and had even made a date—but although she had waited an hour beyond the time, he had never shown up. This is my husband, she thought, the man who only a year ago used to burn me up with his touch, the man I did love—I *did* love him, she kept saying to herself as the tears came, I *did* love him, I did. But what was the use? He no longer needed her. Whenever she faced up to the truth, she saw now that he never had. Somehow or other by some ghastly irony she had got herself involved with a man impervious to ordinary human pressures, a man given a powerful magnetism who had thrown it all away for a hotch-potch of theories, a waywardness entirely beyond her control. She sat there, the tears pouring down her cheeks. Upstairs the baby began crying again and her mother, impatient for attention, rang the bell beside her bed.

She's a good-looking girl, Fortin thought, no wonder he's attracted. Well, it wasn't going to be easy for them. He sat listening to Grace's description of the tension between her father and Nicholas. Arrogance, he supposed, was behind it on both sides and arrogance had been paid for in two hopeless marriages and the possible wrecking of a third. He shifted his attention to his nephew and thought of Pam. What had made him marry that empty ninny? Perhaps he had changed. He must have, in fact. Now he was a grave responsible man. But the wife would not change: she would be left further and further behind. No wonder he saw in Grace some of the qualities he needed and would never find in the girl he had married. Grace, too, she must see in him the rain the desert cried out for: he remembered with difficulty the preening, self-loving young naval officer who was so ashamed, as Hobart had put it, of having been 'caught' by a native girl. How easy it was for a moment's folly to be dragged out into years and years of payment.

Then Fortin thought of his own womanless life. His time in the desert; the firm friends he had made; the longing he had always had—for what? The human companionship of a wife? A wife and a family—a neat tidy routine existence—that had never been his life and now that he looked at his nephew he saw that it was not there either. Perhaps that was what had taken him to sea? The sea and the desert had a great deal in common as testing grounds for the spirit.

'I've tried to help where I can,' Grace was saying. 'Since we've been at San Roque I've offered him lifts or to loan him the car but it doesn't seem to make much difference. He's lost interest. He works at night and the rest of the time he just seems to drink.'

'He certainly wasn't drunk this morning,' Fortin remarked.

'He probably will be by now.'

'His editor speaks very highly of him. He doesn't want to lose him. He says there's never been anyone of that quality on the paper before.'

'He could be a wonderful husband.'

'Then what is it?'

'I don't know,' Grace said, looking him straight in the eyes. 'I suppose when it comes to the point there's very little you can do about anyone else. People go up and people come down.'

'There's quite a lot *I* can do about him,' Fortin said briskly. 'I can have him out of the Rock for a start.' He knew what Grace meant and he agreed but this was no time for metaphysics.

'Yes, sir,' David said as though Uncle Giles had been talking to him. He knew there was a queue of people outside to see the Governor. Smallbones with a pile of papers, the Colonial Secretary waiting in Seale's cuddy, the Commissioner of Police. The telephone had rung five times since the interview had begun. The C.R.A. expected him up at Europa: the Admiral wanted him to look round at the Tower. Yet in the evening of what had been one of Gibraltar's most dramatic days, he sat quite still, apparently relaxed yet very much there—very much the diamond point of power in the Fortress and Colony of Gibraltar, with everything revolving around him at different speeds, just as it did with David in his ship, the very centre of intense movement, yet himself poised and calm and tranquil.

'Well,' said Fortin bringing the interview to a close, 'we'll see what happens about your father. I'll think it over a little longer. But I think he'll probably have to go. However . . . thank you for coming along.'

A few moments later they were out in the hot, dusty garishness of Main Street where the Indian stores and the noisy cafés were once more open for business.

6

They went up to the hospital but there was no change in her father's condition, and as he was still unconscious, nothing they could possibly do. They returned to the house.

'I don't know what there is to eat,' Grace said, 'but we'll find something to cook up.' The servants, subject as everyone else was to the curfew and the closing of the frontier, had already gone and they were alone in the house.

'Does your father normally stay here by himself every

[268]

night?' David asked. The house was in itself so secluded that even with Gibraltar teeming around outside, there was a slight eeriness in the silence and certainly a mystery in the shadows of the patio and the long tiled corridors with the iron grille doors at the end.

'But the house is all right both to Father and me,' Grace explained, 'it leaves us alone. Mother always hated it—always wanted to hear other people moving about, making a noise. To me it's alive. We like each other, the house and I.'

'We like each other too, don't we?' David said gently and took her in his arms. What was the scent in her hair? Jasmine, freesia, or was it no flower but simply a ravishing, subtle, infinitely complicated scent? He buried his face in her hair and drew in a breath and with it, so it seemed, a little of the essence of the woman whose arms were tight about him yet whose supple body lay against his, relaxed and yielding. Even before he kissed her, he knew then that this was the moment when she had given herself to him, that it was always intended this way and that this, at this instant moment, was pure and real, far beyond sensual passion yet riding on top of it precariously. It was the breathing which keyed it, the slow conscious depth as the air and the scent entered your body, the strange quietness of this kind of breathing—not holding your breath, yet no longer subject to that quick, noisy asthmatic pump which drove you every day through life. It was like tiptoeing into a darkening cathedral on a winter's night as the light died outside and the mystery within beckoned you on and on, and you felt a little afraid and yet certain, a child holding an invisible hand, with tears in the eyes and yet happy, being silently led on step by step through each invisible stage of this, the prime mystery of life, where the word sex with its muddy associations seemed wholly out of place, where gentle fingers and soft, lingering lips seemed to draw up your being to a pinnacle of experience, to that point where two bodies in racing, feverish motion with the strange animal cries that come in the depth of the night, create in conjunction the tearing inexpressibility of that deep, deep climax, the sudden wild release and the flowing velvet peace which enfolds as the movement and the moment steal quietly away.

In the middle of the night Grace said, 'You know, I shouldn't be in Gibraltar at all,' but David stopped her with a long, slow kiss. Then later, 'And I never gave you anything to eat. You must be starving.'

'Food is so very important,' he murmured, 'so very, very important.' He kissed the small, firm nipples and stroked her rich, wonderful body and knew that the morning and the sea and the war and the whole grinding apparatus of life must be only an hour or two away but that in the meantime this and this alone was real and real to a degree he had never experienced before.

Presently she began to cry. She made no movement and it was only when a tear fell on his chest that he realized her state. She did not speak and he knew there were no words which could touch or relieve. This was not to be analysed or thought about, not to be dragged down to the level of logic, morals and the coming day—this was simply to be borne and understood, rare and invisible yet to both of them it was something of a deeper quality than either had ever known before.

'If only we could be finished with it now,' she whispered in the end, 'die in our sleep and never wake again. I do love you so terribly, David, I can't bear you to go away—I can't bear it— I can't. . . .' Then the tears came, this time in wild, heaving gasps and she clung to him.

'I hate life,' she cried, 'I hate it. I'd like to die now.'

He calmed her down and then for a time they lay there wide-eyed in the darkness as the fronds of the palm-trees rustled slightly in the breeze, as the coming day advanced upon them like a wary, bad-tempered dragon in search of prey.

At about four-thirty in the morning the telephone rang. They were asleep in each other's arms and both awoke with a start not knowing where they were, as though the bell had jangled right through their bodies. The phone was in her father's room and for a second or two she let it ring, then throwing off the thin sheet which covered them she went along to answer it, a horrible foreboding in her heart. David lay still in bed watching her go. There was now that trace of light in the sky which precedes the dawn. She had walked out naked and the light had given her body a kind of magnificent glow.

Until then the Catholic modesty into which her personality had been submerged would have made her ashamed. Tonight, though, she had come alive to many things in herself. Now, whatever the payment to be exacted, however much she had sinned in the conventional religious sense, she was awake and aware in herself. The tears she had shed and the strength she had drawn from David, had both combined to cut in one firm sweep the main strand of that clinging, suffocating ivy of false personality which had been her outer skin and which had reached its maximum growth in her marriage to Lance. Now once more she was whole and fulfilled, and as she felt the night air on her naked body and the cool tiles under her feet, she knew that this little action of walking along to her father's deserted room perhaps to hear evil news was symbolic of the real person in herself which she had rediscovered that night. In David she had found herself at last. She was whole. From now on she would never really care what anyone thought about her.

But it was not the hospital, it was Jimmy Allendale's anxious, apologetic voice. *Firesprite* had been brought to 'Immediate' notice for steam and they were to report the soonest they could be ready in all respects for sea.

7

Jaime Barbarossa did not die and Nicholas Pappadopoulos was not banished from the Rock. As the long summer of 1940 wore on, Jaime gradually recovered. He left hospital after ten days and then went to Madrid to stay with his brother. Largely on the insistence of Hobart and backed by Fortin, the Commissioner of Police dropped the charges the authorities had wanted to bring against Nicholas.

Hobart had found out quite a number of things from that violent day. He still had not been able to pinpoint Boothroyd, but he now knew three of his five lieutenants and the field was narrowing down. In the meantime the steady corrosion going on in Nicholas was watched clinically by the Security Forces. Sooner or later the crack would come or there would be another explosion as there had been over the evacuees.

[271 [

The evacuees themselves had been given scant opportunity of settling back into Gibraltar. Throughout July and August ship-load after ship-load left for the United Kingdom, and by the time the Battle of Britain began the Royal Palace Hotel in Kensington had become a Gibraltarian colony. The 3,000 male civilians and the 26,000 men of the Services who remained in Gibraltar now settled down to what for all practical purposes was a non-belligerent siege.

During August the Falange began to intensify their campaign for the return of Gibraltar into Spanish hands. Courtesies between the Governor of Algeciras and the Governor of Gibraltar continued to be exchanged but there was a growing feeling of insincerity from the Spanish side and it became noticeable that the eagerness to call was at its height immediately after an air-raid. Sporadic bombing from French aircraft based on Morocco and Italian aircraft from Sardinia continued. Submarine attacks in the Straits of Gibraltar, the worsening position of Malta, the coming and going of the great ships of Force H, the closing down of the bars at 9.30 p.m., the curfew and the deadly monotony of work, sport, drink and the cinema or an E.N.S.A. concert party to round off the day, the habit of always catching the six and the nine o'clock B.B.C. news, the utter private dependence upon the mail and the miseries of not receiving any, the opening of Gibraltar's own Spitfire Fund—such were some of the different facets of the Gibraltar scene during the summer and autumn of 1940. Meanwhile, David in H.M.S. *Firesprite* became used to a kind of syncopated routine of patrolling in the Atlantic and western Mediterranean and of escorting convoys to the relief of Malta, returning grateful and exhausted to the haven of the Rock and the deepening love which Grace bore him and which seemed to encounter more and more difficulties in its expression, the deeper it went.

PART THREE

XIV

MIDWAY through November of 1940, Jimmy Allendale got a command of his own and was appointed away from H.M.S. *Firesprite*. He was relieved by an R.N.V.R. Lieutenant called Roger Soakes, a name hilariously received on the lower-deck, the more so since, having been a cattle-rancher in the Argentine, he had a way of living up to his name. David saw the change take place with private regret. He and Jimmy had become very fond of each other through the fifteen months of peace and war they had been together.

Soakes was altogether a tougher specimen than the out-going First Lieutenant. He came from one of the 'Tribal' class destroyers with an excellent reputation. Now, of the original complement of officers, only the Chief remained. The Captain, the Engineer Officer, the Coxswain and Leading Signalman Jones—now well up on the roster for Yeoman of Signals —comprised the core of experience in *Firesprite* upon which the others drew. Together they had all been through that first dark northern winter of the war, the Norwegian campaign and the evacuation from Dunkirk. Now they and the new-comers had also been blooded in what came to be known as 'Force H Club Runs' to the east.

These were the escorting of convoys to Malta through the 'triangle of fire' roughly drawn from Cape Spartivento in Sardinia to Cape Bon in Tunisia and across to Sicily. Within these Sicilian narrows the Italians could and did bring overwhelming attacks from the air to bear upon any shipping unwise enough to try and break through. But of the Italian Navy, except for the lurking submarine, almost nothing was ever seen.

On the first patrol they did since the change of first lieutenants the weather became worse than anything they had yet experienced. Their patrol line was across the Mediterranean from Cartagena in Spain to Oran and the gale caught them half-way towards the Moroccan coast.

'Here comes a flipping good soaking,' the mess-deck said.

'The new Number One's brought his own weather with him.'

This proved to be only too true. Leaking ventilator cowls flooded the mess-deck, the ship would leap through the sea with a shuddering jar almost bad enough to shake out her rivets, life-lines had to be rigged along the deck, the splinter plating on the fo'c'sle carried away and it became almost impossible to man B Gun for the crashing sweep of the sea up to and at times over the bridge. Mediterranean weather blows up quickly and usually does not hold for long but this gale lasted nearly four days. It gave Soakes a kind of compressed experience of the ship and the opportunity to show David what he could do when they were at last forced to heave to in order to try and make good the damage inflicted by the storm.

He worked quickly and with confidence: despite the wavy stripes on his arm he made it clear from the start that he knew quite as much about destroyers as Jimmy Allendale and that he intended to get on with the job whatever the opposition from sea, storm or human nature. He was not as young, he had neither the charm nor the likeableness of Jimmy Allendale but as David sat wedged on his high seat, dodging the spray from behind the glass screens of the bridge, he knew that he had, if anything, got a man of more determination than his previous First Lieutenant. Perhaps he would be feared and respected rather than liked but, as David stared out at the turbulent, bucking sea, he knew there was no harm in that.

A storm makes extra demands on the attention yet, paradoxically, gives a kind of inner detachment. Thus while the elements threw all they had against the sturdy little ship, David found himself going back over the last few months, taking stock and reflecting on all that had happened.

The relationship with Grace had deepened, apparently thriving on the difficulties which crowded in almost at once on their first experience of each other. Each time he returned from patrol he would go across to the house in the Line Wall Road as soon as he could get free of the ship. Almost always she had known ahead of his arrival, had made preparations and had managed to be there waiting for him—or if not she would soon arrive eager and excited from the Dockyard.

But in the daytime there were servants about and later on when her father had recovered, he too would often be there for his afternoon siesta. She was not allowed to stay in Gibraltar overnight—and though occasionally he would sleep ashore, at the house, for a short break from the ship, it was part of the Gib frustration that they could never spend the night together as both of them ached to do. Thus their love-making became a snatched, hole-in-the-corner, restless affair—unsatisfactory to both, seeming only to add to the yearning from which neither was ever wholly free nor, in honesty, did either ever wish to be free. Yet as time went by they steadily grew into each other. More and more it was as if each were a part of the other. Both had long since given up questioning this state of affairs, or even justifying it to their consciences. Less and less could their outer circumstances be controlled in any way. Life saw to that. You simply shrugged your shoulders and took every moment that was given.

Sometimes they would do things together—parties, E.N.S.A. shows, tennis and swimming—as though they were a long-married couple. Sometimes when *Firesprite* was docked for a bottom-scrape and a boiler-clean, David got permission to put on plain-clothes and cross into Spain to stay at the San Roque house. Jaime saw what was happening between them but he would no longer interfere—indeed since the day of the riot he had been very much changed in himself. He was quieter, he observed more, and reacted less. It was a great secret not to react.

Father O'Reilly was more restive. He too saw what was happening and he had once tried to remind Grace of her duties but she sent him off with a polite but definite, 'This is my business and I must be allowed to think it out for myself.' She went regularly to Mass but not to communion and though this troubled her deeply, she had turned deliberately away, aware of the price to be paid and, for David's sake, eager to pay it.

Meanwhile Pam and David drew further and further apart. She had got a transfer to Portsmouth where, despite the more intensive air-raids, life was gayer and London only an hour and a half away. She talked vaguely of applying to be sent to Gibraltar but from the way she now wrote, David very much doubted that she would. A certain Paymaster-Lieutenant Basil Foster on the C.-in-C.'s staff at Portsmouth had begun to appear and reappear in her letters and she was patently not as miserable as she had been at Scapa and Rosyth that first winter of the war.

His reflective mood seemed to feed on the storm and he thought about the other people in his life such as his brother in the Army who had been sent to Malta, an assignment brushed off casually enough as 'tricky'. It was certainly that. *Firesprite* had put into Malta once at the end of a club run but their arrival had coincided with a particularly vicious raid and there had not been time to establish contact with his brother. However, Jaime's sister who had married the Maltese Count had had him out to the house near Cittavechia and an occasional letter completed the circuit.

As the storm continued to rage and a signal was received telling them to return to Gibraltar, David thought about his brother and the ordeal Malta was beginning to endure. It was not a pretty picture. However vulnerable the Rock might prove to be in the end, its apparent solidity was both impressive and heartening. Malta was a big flat island with the enemy only a few minutes' flight away. But the Rock, with neutral Spain as its hinterland, offered a home-coming to club-runners from the east which at least in the mind appeared secure and invincible.

Even now, as it loomed up through the racing storm clouds with the mountains of Andalusia occasionally in sight behind, the simple fact that Gibraltar was still there sufficed in some miraculous way to restore a depleted courage. Endurance would in the end reward them all with victory. Malta gave him the odd feeling that one day it might suddenly disappear, sinking quite unnoticed under the surface of the sea, leaving not a trace. The Rock was the Rock.

An hour or two later *Firesprite*, *Forthright* and the rest of the flotilla passed through the boom, berthed as usual in the pens and let the dockyard get to work on their sores. Up at the Line Wall Road, Grace welcomed back the man she now put at the centre of her life. Then a few hours later she returned mutinously over the frontier into Spain and David repaired upstairs for a good but lonely night's sleep in a bed that did not pitch or roll twenty times in a minute.

2

They did not have long in port. There was a convoy for Malta and Alexandria assembling in the Bay and there were also 700 R.A.F. reinforcements for Egypt taking passage in the cruisers *Manchester* and *Southampton*, which themselves would be joining the Eastern Mediterranean Fleet.

'I knew we were about due for another club run,' the Chief groused as he read the order to raise steam. 'I can tell the moment the A-bracket starts to play up. The old lady's getting in a tizzy about something important.'

'Without disparaging Dr. Goebbels' favourite ship,' the First Lieutenant remarked, looking out of the scuttle and across at the mighty *Ark Royal*, 'I wish we had that dirty big *Illustrious* around with her fruit machine or whatever it is.'

The arrival of the new aircraft-carrier *Illustrious* in the autumn with the first primitive radar on board had given the Italians a big surprise. For the first time shadowing aircraft were shot down before sighting the fleet and enemy bombers had been scattered and attacked long before they were ready to drop their bombs. The British were a jump ahead and it was disconcerting. No one quite knew what it was but it got the convoy through in a highly efficient fashion. *Ark Royal* was a splendid ship but she did not have this magic device which would soon revolutionize the war. However, *Illustrious* was the other side of Malta and part of the Eastern Mediterranean Fleet. About two weeks before, she had made a daring raid upon Taranto when her torpedo aircraft sank the battleship *Littorio* and hit two 'Cavour' class battleships. The Eastern Mediterranean Fleet was based on Alexandria as Force H was on Gibraltar. When a through-convoy was passed the two forces would meet in the centre near Malta. This was what the Chief called a 'run of standard specification', and the convoy they were about to take on looked as though it would fit this description exactly.

The weather was now clear and calm, the violence of the

[279]

storm they had so recently endured being almost impossible to imagine the night they sailed. There was no moon but the visibility was, alas, exceptionally good. The Admiral, leaving no possibility unexplored, had issued a signal saying: 'The Chaplains of the Fleet will pray for fog.' The result of such intercessionary efforts as were made was a clear visibility of about a hundred miles. So on Monday 25th November the *Ark*, the *Renown*, three cruisers and eight destroyers slipped out of Gibraltar with the convoy and headed east.

The next day and night were tranquil enough. With the Atlas Mountains and the North African coast to starboard, with an occasional reconnaissance sortie flown off from the stately *Ark Royal*, with two possible submarine contacts depth-charged without apparent result, with the great bulk of the battle-cruiser *Renown* as comforting to be with as if the Rock of Gibraltar itself had put to sea, they reached the longitude of Sardinia without incident. Then a signal was received which completely altered the picture. An Italian Fleet comprising at least two modern battleships and six cruisers was at large in the Tyrrhenian Sea.

As it happened the timing could not have been better from the British point of view. The two cruisers which were going through to Alexandria were being replaced for the return journey by two others, the *Newcastle* and the *Berwick*. These had already penetrated the Sicilian narrows and were to hand, together with the battleship *Ramillies*. For the battle of Cape Spartivento, therefore, Admiral Somerville had a formidable force with which to smite the enemy. And late in the morning of the 27th the Italians were sighted away to the north.

The convoy was diverted to the south, with its close escort and Force H, with *Firesprite*, *Forthright*, and the rest of the destroyer screen racing ahead, tore off north to give battle.

'Do you think the bastards will stay *this* time? Or are we going to have to chase them into their own back-yard?' the Chief asked David, on reporting that steam for full speed was available. It was nowadays the first thought which occurred whenever contact with the Italian Navy was established. Speed was the great asset of Italian warships but to date it had always been used for escape. Perhaps this time they would fight it out.

Already *Renown* and the cruisers were firing at the enemy and the high-speed action had begun.

This was one of the very few moments when David wished he had command of a bigger ship. He looked down at the guns' crews, hooded in anti-flash asbestos and tin-hatted against splinters. He thought about the rest of the ship at its 'Action Stations' ready at winch and ammunition hoist, at torpedo tube and depth-charge rail to make *Firesprite* of maximum flexible use. He thought of the Chief with his three 'kettles' brewing up nicely and the 36,000 horse-power turbines thrusting the ship north at its maximum speed—but in a Fleet action such as this the little destroyer's four 4.7-inch guns could never be effective, would not in fact be used, with salvoes of fifteen- and eight-inch shells already flying over their heads. The torpedo was their main offensive weapon but to fire torpedoes meant to get in close.

'I knew it,' he muttered to himself, 'I knew it.'

The Italians had already turned away and were speeding off to the north. The British had scored no hits. Why this slowness off the mark? Why? Speeding along at over thirty knots he had a feeling of irritation. Already the Italians, on the run, had hit and partially disabled the *Berwick*. It looked as though they were getting away scot-free.

In one sense they did. No Italian ship was sunk or severely damaged. But in other ways a bigger victory was won. The Italian Fleet was chased to within thirty miles of its own coast-line, the convoy was passed through the narrows unscathed, Malta and Alexandria both being successfully reinforced, and for the next two months the moral effect of the Battle off Sardinia was to re-establish the Royal Navy in a dominant position over the whole of the Mediterranean Sea.

The action was broken off at twenty past one in the afternoon, *Ark Royal's* ancient Swordfish aircraft having failed to delay the Italians with torpedo attacks, and although both the British Fleet and the convoy suffered a half-hearted air attack later in the day, when Force H returned to Gibraltar there was good reason for the flood of congratulation which descended upon them. They had not sunk the Italian Fleet. That would certainly have been final but they had scared the pants off them again and that in many ways was to have a far deeper effect on the Italian Navy's morale. They would have to dare considerably more than they had up to now before Mussolini's *mare nostrum* was really what he claimed it to be.

3

The second Christmas of the war came and went. At least *Firesprite* started it in harbour and not, as they had done the previous year, rolling about a sub-arctic sea. This year Grace's job in the Dockyard Welfare Organization was of direct help and the four original ships of Gibraltar's Very Own Flotilla were liberally decorated with tinsel and streamers on a peacetime scale.

The weather was again squally and they were glad to be in harbour. David and the First Lieutenant, who had already been subjected to some 'Pampas-style' hospitality on the messdeck, attended morning service in the Cathedral. In the middle of this a lieutenant walked up the aisle, whispered something to the Admiral who then got up and left. This was a bad omen. Soakes nudged David and raised his eyes blearily to heaven. There was trouble brewing and the Admiral had gone to stir up the pot. Almost invariably that meant that the 28th Destroyer Flotilla would proceed shortly afterwards to sea.

This proved to be so. A United Kingdom–Gibraltar convoy was due in from the west the next day. This convoy, ultimately headed for Greece, had been savaged in vicious weather by a 'Hipper' class cruiser. Force H would kindly oblige a day earlier than intended and proceed forthwith to sea. This news, however, was not broken to the 28th Flotilla until Christmas Day had got fairly and squarely under way.

The buzz, though, had preceded it and the ship's company of *Firesprite*, guessing only too well what lay ahead, had shrewdly compressed their day into a hard forenoon's drinking. Every drop of illicitly stored rum came out. Bottles of beer from the wardroom went forward to the mess-decks and a bucket of whisky acquired by the prompt action of Stoker Blackburn when a case *en route* to the destroyer alongside had been accidentally dropped—all combined to make the mess-decks of

Firesprite a noisy kind of alcoholic hell. Christmas Day is no time for the Naval Discipline Act, and David, in a sense, felt well on the side of his ship's company. They had been worked off their feet these last three months: they deserved a break: provided they could do their jobs, and he had no qualms about that when it was necessary, he was not going to ask awkward questions. The Coxswain was a man of understanding: there might be a terrible noise and a number of the younger Hostilities-Only ratings were going to be very sick but nothing on the lower-deck would get badly out of hand. They would eat, drink and be as merry as they knew how and then they would go to sea.

They were ordered to sail about 1.30 p.m. and in the meantime Hobart, Seale and the Barbarossas had all come aboard for a running Christmas party held in the wardroom. Beyond the breakwater it was gusty and there was a lop on the water, even in the Bay itself. Outside in the Atlantic a full gale was blowing and that was where they would be going in so short a time. I did not bear thinking about and so none of them did.

Seale and Jaime had an official function to go on to and only stayed a moment or so. Before leaving Seale drew David to one side and said:

'Rosita came in this morning with Grace.'

'Then why isn't she here?'

'She's with Nicholas.'

'By invitation?'

'No. He treats Christmas Day as every other day in the year. He doesn't believe in the thing. And he hasn't been near Rosey and the child for months—as you know. Apparently Rosita felt so awful about it she took her courage in one hand and stuffed away her pride with the other and just came in to see him. It must be a grim little morning for both of them.'

After the two A.D.C.s had gone back to Government House, David said firmly to Grace:

'You've got your car, haven't you?'

'Yes, why?'

'Come on. We're going to fetch Rosita and that ullage of a husband of hers. It's Christmas Day and we've got a lot of brandy aboard. He likes brandy, doesn't he?'

'He'd never come.'

'You never know till you ask. Come on.'

Against her logical thinking, she allowed herself to be pulled into the plan and a few minutes later they were hammering at the door of Nicholas's room. Rosita opened the door and gasped in surprise.

'Can we come in?' David asked. 'We want you and Nicholas to come and have drinks on board *Firesprite*.'

'Well . . .' Rosita was taken aback. Nicholas was still in bed and she had her sleeves rolled up and a damp cloth in her hand. It was some Christmas morning for her. David summed up the position in a moment and decided to press on. To hesitate now was to leave things worse than before. Gently but firmly he pushed her to one side and went into the room, Grace remaining at the door with Rosita.

'Five minutes to get dressed, shaved and come back with us on board for whatever we've got left of our Christmas Day,' he said briskly and looked into a face expressing its habitual and disdainful scowl.

'I don't think so, thank you very much,' Nicholas said and then stared up at the ceiling as he had done hundreds of thousands of times, 'I'm very comfortable in bed.'

'Don't be such a bastard. Do something for someone else for a change—even if it's only that. It won't be for long. We're going to sea and it *is* Christmas Day, however much of an atheist you are.'

Nicholas removed his gaze from the ceiling and fixed it once more on David. He was neither angry nor flattered. He was simply curious that this 'lover of Grace's', as he thought of him, should take so much trouble and should now be trying to browbeat him to do something he had no intention of doing.

'Come on,' David said, as a doctor might talk to a difficult patient, 'you can do it if you try.'

Then one of those unseen, un-understood processes which can take place in a human being when his attention is elsewhere, suddenly bore fruit and Nicholas found himself touched against his will at the gesture being made. His mind still rejected the thing out of hand and his heart had been for so long numb that it automatically followed suit. Now, though, it had

[284]

unexpectedly stirred on its own. Why not? something in him began suggesting, why not?

'Well, all right,' he heard his voice saying in astonishment, 'I'll do as the Captain says.'

Over the next three days as they forged out into the Atlantic, rendezvoused with the badly mauled convoy and began bringing it safely to Gibraltar, David tried to fathom the complicated paradox of someone like Nicholas. What was it that made him, in David's view, such a rat when underneath he strongly suspected him of being a likeable human being? Was it vanity or inverted arrogance or what?

The Greeks, and David regarded Nicholas as no different from the other Greeks he had met except for his English schooling, behaved like spoilt children whenever they ran into something bigger than themselves. They were brave enough; Metaxas' firm 'No' to the Italians and the subsequent disaster they had inflicted on Mussolini's ill-conceived invasion of their country had proved that. But this was more bravado rather than a calculated courage. No wonder they never had been and never would be a match for the Turks. There was a waywardness, an evasiveness in the Greek character which was appealing in children but rather tediously dishonest in adults.

As the filthy Atlantic crashed and battered his ship and the latest victims of the war struggled to keep afloat long enough to reach Gibraltar, David found himself wondering if Nicholas Pappadopoulos had ever honestly faced up to the realities of the world he had been born into. Whose side was he on? David could see no difference whatever in the régimes running Germany, Italy, Russia or Spain. They were all equally sordid, equally evil. But perhaps he ought to do more about it himself. What was the use of tearing about the sea—when someone like friend Pappadopoulos was waiting at home to stick a knife in your back? Or was he? What was he really up to in himself?

4

What, in fact, Nicholas was up to was the long, long process of disenchantment which takes place before a man can turn

[285]

in another direction. During that second winter of the war while the scene darkened, the storms raged, and the Germans consolidated their hold on all they had gained; while the Western Desert became the heart of the war itself and Malta was being steadily reduced to ruin and starvation, the pointlessness of life, of what was going on in the war and of his share in it increasingly beset him. He had lost his way. Experience did not confirm or sanctify the theories he had so far held. And there was one quality he possessed which, in the end, was to form the pivot to his change of direction. He was intellectually honest and unafraid.

In life it is the small, half-noticed gestures, the apparently unimportant events which can really change a person's direction —the drip of the water-tap rather than the lightning flash. Drinking, in the way Nicholas took it, was a lonely business and threw him a great deal back upon himself. He continued to come into contact with mutinous and disaffected other ranks in the Services. He continued to push out at them the socialist ideas which at the end of the war were to enjoy an overwhelming triumph. He continued to absorb and digest the news and to run his newspaper efficiently, but in himself he had become much more of a hermit and he had stopped believing in what he was doing.

The day of the protest march, now over six months ago, had acted as a delayed shock to his system. He had come to understand, instead of simply imagining, that once a force is released you cannot control it. It controls you. He had been lucky. His father-in-law had been the only casualty and he had recovered. It might have got right out of hand, which would have meant bloodshed on a much greater scale. He saw how easy it was to pull the lever and destroy the dam. He was beginning to see a little more deeply into the meaning of events.

But there were still plenty of buffers between him and the truth. He had put Rosita and the child out of his mind. It was better to be quite separate. She had never really escaped, he told himself, from the Barbarossa family and now she was back in that particular prison again, well—there it was. . . . This was his blind side and he made no attempt to light up the

[286]

shadowy landscape. To begin with he had sent her money at odd intervals but during the autumn that had lapsed and he put it into cognac instead. The Barbarossas were rich. Let them look after their own.

However Rosita's sudden arrival on Christmas Day had shaken him out of his torpor. It was a tiny attempt to reach him again and she was still his wife. The gesture of disinterested friendliness made by that lover of Grace's, despite the bluntness of the way it was put, had also had an effect. Before he would have dismissed both these moves with a feeling of contempt. Now, for the first time in years, he recognized them for what they were—a kindliness towards another human being, a hand stretched out to help. Without mawkishness or sentimentality, he felt a slight stirring in his heart.

It was Hobart who tapped the next little wedge into the splitting wood. One night late in January, leaving the *Gazette* office about one-thirty in the morning, he found Hobart waiting in the shadows outside. He was alone and he had a car.

'I wanted to talk to you,' Hobart said, 'and this seemed as good a moment as any. Can you spare me a few minutes?'

'It's not a very good time for me: I've just had seven hours straight on.'

'Well, you could do with a drink, couldn't you? I know I could.'

'Very well.'

He got into the car, his senses alert. He felt towards Hobart much as he did to Father O'Reilly. He disliked yet respected them both. Their motives gave them away: yet both were sincere. The common ground between all three was a curious one, not at once discernible. It was simply that each had had experience of serving something bigger than himself. In each case that something was different and the things that Father O'Reilly and Hobart respectively served did not commend themselves to Nicholas.

Gibraltar was totally deserted at this time of night. The curfew was rigorous and a sharp wind from the north was blowing pieces of paper along the twisted streets.

'I live where I work these days,' Hobart said. 'I hope you don't mind coming to the office.'

[287]

'Why should I?' Nicholas said with a shrug. 'You're the one with the questions.'

The office in the Bomb House Lane was in fact ideal for its purpose, being on a curved corner with two separate entrances, each out of sight of the other. In Hobart's room there was a coal fire burning which he poked up into life. They did themselves well, these Security boys, he thought, and wondered what Hobart was going to ask and how he would put it.

'Well,' said Hobart, pouring out two stiff brandies, 'I'm going to exceed my terms of reference a good long way. I'm going to put myself in your hands, I'm going to tell you things you may be very surprised to hear—I'm doing this because I want your help and I want it badly. When you want something badly, there's always a risk to be taken.'

'I don't think I would,' Nicholas said. 'You know what the Press is once it gets hold of a story.' The fact that he worked on a newspaper was a good way of keeping off the real point of the meeting.

'You won't be printing any of this,' Hobart said, 'in fact you won't be breathing a word of what I'm going to say to anyone at all once you leave this room.'

'How do you know?'

'Because the Official Secrets Act applies to you just as much as it does to me. Because if you do, you'll be destroying me but, on the other hand, I shan't let that happen without seeing that you are fully disposed of—and that, I can assure you, is more than a possibility.'

'So now this is some sort of blackmail, a threat?'

'Only about the future,' Hobart said looking at him intently. 'The past is the past.'

'Well. . . .'

'Let me tell you what has happened so far,' Hobart pressed on quickly, 'and you'll see what I mean. Yourself first to begin with. When you were working in the film business in England you were a member of Klaus Zimmerman's study group and you then volunteered to fight on the Republican side in the Spanish Civil War. In Malaga you worked with Ortoña, in Madrid with Sankiewicz and in Barcelona with Stein and Deneshkino. But you were never a properly acceptable Communist. You were too independent: you wouldn't take the discipline: when you came to Gibraltar, which needed courage to do it the way you did, Myra Heisenberg did her best to bring you back into line, back into the fold—any way you care to put it—but she got nowhere with you in that sense any more than the others did.'

Nicholas sat boot-faced and still, ostensibly looking at the fire but in fact acutely aware of Hobart out of the corner of his eye. He had supposed his activities must have been noted in passing: he was appalled at the detailed facts which seemed to have been recorded about his life. He had not thought about Stein and Deneshkino for years—he had worked with them in another country and for another cause—yet here they were being paraded in front of him by this British Security Officer. His file must make interesting reading. As Hobart went on with the story, however, the shock passed and a perspective returned. After all, the past *could* be found out. If this was all it was about, the brave Colonel was not going to be able to bluff very far. The past was the past, as he had himself observed. It was the present and the future which mattered. Mentally he shrugged his shoulders and sat back. The British Security Service must do better than that.

'Then just before war broke out,' Hobart went on, casually looking at his glass, 'a man called Herbert Boothroyd was sent to Gibraltar to set up an enemy organization. This he has done with remarkable secrecy and success both in the acts of sabotage he has so far engineered and in the people he has persuaded into helping him in his work. I'm afraid, though, in his glib talk of Zimmerman that he has you fooled. He may talk about Karl Marx. He is, however, paid by the Nazis.'

Nicholas sat absolutely still. This was the body blow which winded him. He did not look at Hobart but stared, no more numb he hoped than before, into the fire. But all the time he knew that Hobart had him on the slide, under the light of the microscope like a particular microbe he had managed at last to isolate and now wished to study at his leisure. He had certainly taken a risk.

'Now, quite obviously at this point,' Hobart went on as if speaking to himself, 'I have to proceed with the greatest care.

[289]

I know that if I bluntly ask for your help I won't get it. I don't wish to do violence to your principles. On the other hand I have a feeling you've been changing your point of view. We all see things differently as time goes on and since I desperately need your help, I thought I would expose myself in this way, without quite knowing whether you'll understand me or whether you'll simply think this is some sort of trap and then turn it back on myself.' Hobart looked at him for a thoughtful moment before going on. 'In all these things there's a point of no return.'

'I don't see how I can help you,' Nicholas said, 'if you don't know what you want.'

'I know what I want all right and I think you do, too. I'm not sure I know how to ask you without making you feel that you're throwing away everything you've worked towards all your life.'

'But that's exactly what I would be doing, wouldn't I?' Nicholas said softly.

'You might see other ways of achieving the same end: you might modify the structure instead of knocking it all to pieces. It is being modified all the time. Besides we all have to survive.'

'What is being modified?'

'The British Empire you hate so much, our administration, our way of life, our outlook, behaviour, civilization. You used to think it oppressive from top to bottom, isn't that so? But perhaps you don't any more: perhaps you see some of its great qualities too and then perhaps you can see where to apply pressure so that a change *can* be made.'

'This is too theoretical for me,' Nicholas said dryly. 'You got me here for a particular purpose. What is it you want?'

Again Hobart did not answer directly.

'I suppose you can say to yourself—"why doesn't he ask Sergeant Elling of the Army Education Corps or Sub-Inspector Lopez of the Dockyard Police or Jack Robertson in the Electrical Department? They know far more of the set-up than I do." And you'd be quite right: they do. On the other hand, they are all fully committed. You're not. They've no choice—certainly not at this moment in time: you have. And when I

[290]

say choice, I mean a moral choice, an inner choice arrived at freely by yourself on your own.'

So Boothroyd's whole organization was known. He looked at Hobart with a new respect. It was clever to let it come out in this way, almost casually, in passing. So he knew it all: but also it was, or it could be, very dangerous for Hobart. As he had pointed out, Nicholas was not committed to the same extent. He could still warn the others before it was too late for them. He looked hard at Hobart: he had misjudged this rather easy-going temporary Colonel—he was certainly prepared to risk a lot for what he was after. He must be very confident indeed. This was the moment to go. He had some thinking to do. He stood up wondering if Hobart would try and hold him there until he had a satisfactory answer.

'I must be going,' Nicholas said. 'Thank you for the drink.'

'I'll run you home in the car.'

'Don't worry; it isn't far.'

'It's no trouble,' said Hobart; 'I can always do with a breath of air.'

5

The winter wore on and with it a growing certainty in David's mind that he wanted to marry Grace. This decision crystallized against a background of anti-submarine patrols, of occasional convoys to and from Malta—each one, it seemed, more hazardous than the last—and of dramatic 'mystery tours' as the lower-deck called them, in the company of Force H, for some purpose such as the bombarding of Genoa.

This latter event took place on Sunday, 9th February 1941. *Firesprite* and Force H left Gibraltar late on the preceding Friday, turning to the west with a U.K.-bound convoy for the benefit of the German spy organization in Algeciras. Then when night fell they doubled back quickly through the Straits of Gibraltar and the next day were at large in the Mediterranean, heading north-east past the Balearics through a deserted sea. The previous week they had come to very nearly the same place when Swordfish aircraft from *Ark Royal* had bombed the hydro-electric dam at Tirso in the north of Sardinia. But this had only been a partial success. The buzz was that they had come back to finish off the job.

But they travelled on through another night and at dawn made landfall on the Italian coast near to Rapallo. Force H then turned west and steamed in moderate visibility parallel with the land while the Fleet Air Arm bombed Spezzia, Pisa and Leghorn to the south. The destroyers were inshore of the capital ships and as they steamed past Santa Margherita, Portofino and the little sea-ports of the Italian Riviera on this calm Sunday morning, David became possessed of a great sadness at the bombardment which was now only a few minutes away.

The port of Genoa was about to be wrecked. No doubt the Italians would retort. In a few minutes blood on both sides would be spilt and the aggregate hate then swirling about the world would be increased. It made it worse to have known the places that were going to be bombarded as he did. He visualized it in his mind's eye. Ashore, black-shawled women would be bundling along to Mass: *bambini* would be in their Sunday best. He and Pam had gone to Menton for their honeymoon and had made a number of trips into Italy and along the Ligurian coast. True, the British bombardment would be confined to the docks of Genoa, no great beauty spots in themselves, but the necessity for it all—the way both sides in a war are trapped and must deny their humanity—suddenly struck David with inconsequential poignancy as the great guns of the battle-cruiser *Renown* and of the cruiser *Sheffield* began the twenty-six-minute bombardment of Mussolini's principal port.

It was certainly a daring stroke. Genoa is a clear 850 miles from Gibraltar. Force H provided a sitting target to the Italian Air Force a few minutes from their home airfields. Yet it was fifteen minutes before the Italian guns opened up in reply and by the time the British squadron withdrew, three hundred tons of accurately aimed naval shells had made a shambles of the port.

Once again the destroyers were virtually spectators. They were there to provide anti-submarine protection for the heavy ships but there were no answering 'pings' on their Asdics and so they went as they came, sweeping ahead of the Force but not otherwise involved. A few Italian shells had pitched near the ship, there had been a feeble attack from the air, but the enemy had clearly been caught off balance and this bold penetration was like stabbing a man having a siesta. It had been so easy, it was almost disconcerting.

Thus David again had time to reflect as the thin bows of *Firesprite* cut through the Mediterranean and each passing hour brought them nearer home to the Rock. What was it he had to learn?

It seemed that in life there was still a tiny element of choice. There was no escape from the great cosmic events. The war stirred up humanity in its huge cooking pot, rendering down a country like France on one scale and, perhaps, a man like himself on another. It was *how* you took things that mattered—there that a tiny choice existed. It was *how* you died that mattered. It was *how* you met a situation such as he was in with Pam and Grace that mattered. He began to feel he had drifted enough. The wind blew and the tide ebbed and flowed. You could go to sleep in the bottom of the boat, letting the elements take you wherever they would—or you could sit up and learn to sail into the wind and against the thrust of the tide.

No doubt life would soon separate him and Grace as it had split him away from Pam: but there was something talking to him now, something trying to tell him that to continue dodging behind life was of no use whatever. The problem would return and perhaps in more difficult terms. There was an inner compulsion to do something about the situation before life forced his hand. He doubted whether Grace could so deny her Catholicism as to divorce her husband and marry him, but he himself was not a Catholic. He no longer loved his wife nor, he suspected, did she love him. He had the option of divorce. It was time he faced up to such realities as he could see. He decided to write to Pam and ask for his freedom. At the same time he determined to say nothing whatever about it to Grace until the dirty work, as he put it to himself, was done and out of the way.

The sea-gulls mewed and swooped round the ship and far away to the west the top of the Rock of Gibraltar came into sight.

XV

DURING the late spring of 1941 Jaime Barbarossa got leave of absence and went to stay with his brother in Madrid. It was not a good time for Spain. Perpetually wretched, the country was now nearly starving. Oddly enough, however, this worked as much in favour of Gibraltar as against it. Franco had made it clear to Hitler that were the Germans to come, they would have to feed twenty-six million Spaniards at present kept going on shipments of grain from America. This impression was confirmed by the Fuehrer's own Intelligence organization. So the threat to the Rock, though in reality mounting silently like water behind a dam, was for the moment held back behind the Pyrenees, while calculations about wheat and the decrepit Spanish communication system were made and unmade and remade again.

But there was a point of desperation, his brother observed, where nothing mattered. Both sides knew that. And, although with a million dead in the Civil War, the last thing Spain wanted was more fighting on her soil—if there was no food then let the Germans come. Perhaps Portugal with her ancient treaty of friendship with England would throw open her ports to the Allies: perhaps the Iberian peninsula would once again become the battle-ground it had been in Napoleonic times—but, said the Spanish, if they were going to starve to death anyway, then what did it matter?

Jaime enjoyed getting away from Gibraltar. Another point of view, a different perspective, a breath of sharp Castilian air to freshen up the somewhat parochial values which a close confinement to the Rock induced—all these acted as a leaven through Jaime when afterwards he returned to Gibraltar. The deliberations of the Defence Committee and the other policy-making functions of the Government of Gibraltar were brightened up by comment from 'the gentleman recently returned from Madrid', as Fortin called him. Hobart, too, had been up to stay with his opposite number in the British Embassy, so that at this bad time Fortin felt that at least he had two separately focused eyes upon the Spanish scene, eyes and intelligences, moreover, which were up to date.

They had already had two serious scares. The previous October Himmler had visited Madrid and shortly afterwards there had been a meeting between Hitler and Franco on the Spanish frontier. The intelligence Hobart received about this meeting all pointed to a deal having been made and an attack upon the Rock being imminent. So for three weeks they had waited with anticlimax turning the tension sour. Then it began to be clear either that Franco had been cleverer than anyone imagined or that the German effort was being conserved for another direction. Now in the early summer of 1941 the situation was tending to repeat itself. There had been another meeting of the Dictators and another leak of intelligence about it. The temperature was rising again and in Gibraltar the omens, for the superstitious, were even blacker than before. The Rock apes were dying off.

The apes, symbolic as they were, were loved and hated in Gibraltar in about equal measure. They were all very well on the upper rock where they belonged, they were a great nuisance when they marauded down into the town. During a recent performance of *Thark* by the Royal Engineers' Concert Party at the Theatre Royal, two of them had been discovered up to no good in the gallery. They stole remorselessly and destroyed without meaning anything they could get hold of. However their special significance for Gibraltar was undeniable and when it became known that the last male ape had died after killing his offspring, Fortin decided to make this fact known in London.

The reaction was immediate. A cypher was received in the middle of the night saying that the Prime Minister himself was personally interested, that a fresh supply of Barbary apes was to be obtained 'forthwith' and a report made when the ape population of the Rock was once more in a healthy condition. So Ferris, Hobart's most reliable assistant, was despatched to Tangier, a number of cases of whisky were subsequently shipped over to Ceuta for various high-ranking Spanish officers and in return a consignment of crated apes arrived in Gibraltar. This was all a highly secret exchange operation and when at the end of the war the auditor inquired why the Government of Gibraltar had bought so many cases of whisky in 1941, it was difficult to prove with documents that the rate of exchange at the time had worked out at approximately a crate of whisky an ape.

But in the spring of 1941 when everything was going steadily downhill for the British, it seemed ironic and, at the same time, 'typical' to Jaime that Gibraltar should be worrying about its apes. The outlook—or what could be seen of it—was obscure. *Illustrious* had been severely damaged by bombs in January, and the withdrawal from active operations of this 'wonder ship' resulted in the virtual closing of the Mediterranean to Allied shipping. On the 6th April the Germans had invaded Yugoslavia and Greece, and what subsequently happened in Greece became a repetition in miniature of the previous year's Norwegian campaign.

Though Gibraltar was but a staging point for convoys to the east, these were now sparser and more savagely attacked. Jaime watched the British pouring into Greece the troops and material so badly needed in the Western Desert and then a few weeks later taking them out again. First the mainland of Greece and then the island of Crete were bloodily evacuated. The German Afrika Korps and the Italians sat astride the Egyptian border. Supplies for the somewhat demoralized Eighth Army had all to be sent round the Cape. Meanwhile his sister in Malta had taken up a life in the catacombs. Whenever he got really depressed, he thought about Malta where conditions would soon be desperate and an edible potato would become as rare as it was in Ireland during the famines of a century ago.

The little local routine went on. Edie fussed and grumbled at her nurse, Rosita devoted herself to her baby as though there had never been another in the world and Grace, with a sadness in the eyes he tried to avoid seeing, continued to go each day to her office in the Dockyard. He knew what was wrong but he was powerless to help. She wanted something she could not have and she chose to keep this entirely to herself. An occasional nondescript postcard from the Oflag in Germany arrived; David Evers in his destroyer came and went and the boredom and frustration of the invisible siege continued. The great British quality of endurance was having to manifest in Gibraltar without the relief of physical action. The routine simply went on, ships arrived and later on sailed, the Germans were winning the war and on the Rock very little happened at all.

2

Yet this was only the outer scene—the current film so to speak being shown on the screen. There were other films awaiting projection, and one of these was in very active preparation by Herbert Boothroyd. There was some urgency in this since his tour of duty in the Naval Armament Supply Organization was scheduled to end in September and he had been called upon for results.

Very naturally he kept this fact entirely to himself. Boothroyd's skill lay in making other people work, his power in being the only person in Gibraltar who knew what the plan was to be. Yet a sixth sense told Nicholas that something must happen soon, if it was to happen at all. Hobart, while he knew the connections and the people concerned, could not keep them under direct observation all day and every day but had to rely on significant information coming in from Police Sub-Inspector Lopez, the member of Boothroyd's inner group who had turned King's Evidence without Boothroyd knowing.

Since his meeting with Hobart, Nicholas had forced himself to think out his attitude all over again. He had had a certain experience in England, France and Spain of the submerged nine-tenths of an enemy fifth column. He knew a little of the world of spies, agents and saboteurs, and generally speaking he classified them as idealists or professionals. The idealists were always expendable. They were difficult to control but usually fearless. The professionals on the other hand would sometimes lose sight of their objective in the meticulous care with which they set about the job. He had made a mistake over Boothroyd. The mention of Zimmerman had led Nicholas to think he was a Communist but this was not so. He was simply a paid organizer of sabotage who would have sold his services in slightly

[297]

different circumstances to the British Government had the money on offer been great enough.

To achieve the socialist revolution, so the teaching ran, any means justified the end. Nicholas knew he would never abandon the left-wing principles he had so fervently embraced, but his experience in Spain of the way they were being pursued had sickened him and now Boothroyd completed the process. Boothroyd was mainly interested in money. In this sense he was highly professional. Nicholas knew something of the scale of expenses but the amount Boothroyd was to be paid disgusted him. This fact, which had been independently gleaned and was deliberately passed on to Nicholas by Hobart, was the final straw on the camel's back. The money Boothroyd was to get was nominally Spanish: its origin was German: it's object was the destruction of Gibraltar on behalf of Hitler. It struck Nicholas that there was very little idealism in this distortion of something which to him had been deep and genuine into a means of lining Mr. Boothroyd's pocket. Thus it lit up in him a slow, burning anger and brought into play the Cypriot craftiness which was in his blood. From that time on the seesaw tipped and Nicholas decided to allow Hobart the help he wanted.

Nicholas gave Boothroyd no inkling of this change of heart. He continued to be what outwardly he had always seemed— the sour, competent, hard-drinking, minor journalist, doing a routine job in a colony. They saw each other very little. The breach caused by Nicholas when he led the mob to Government House had never been healed but both knew that action of some sort was in the offing and that if it was to be action on any scale the whole organization would no doubt be needed. Moreover, because of his experiences in Spain, Nicholas was liked and respected by the other members of Boothroyd's inner clique.

3

In the meanwhile David had taken part in another event which once more altered the balance of naval power in favour of the British. At 2 a.m. on Saturday, 24th May, a 'Most Immediate' signal was received ordering Force H to sea. The 45,000-ton German battleship *Bismarck*, brand-new and so heavily armoured as to be almost unsinkable, had been sighted at sea through cloud and rain. This was on the previous evening and she had been seen east of Iceland in the Denmark Strait, together with her attendant cruiser, the *Prinz Eugen*, skirting the ice and heading south for the Atlantic convoy routes.

This was a situation of the utmost peril. Eleven convoys were then at sea in the Atlantic including an irreplaceable troop convoy of 20,000 men headed for the Western Desert. In the Mediterranean the effect on the Italian Navy of the Battle of Cape Matapan was wearing off. Greece had fallen and Crete had just been evacuated. Our Eastern Mediterranean Fleet had been reduced to two battleships, three cruisers and a handful of destroyers, and this was clearly a moment, with more than half the British Fleet sunk or under repair, when the Italians could easily seize control of the central and eastern Mediterranean.

Such then was the position behind their backs, so to speak, as Force H put to sea and headed west into the Atlantic at high speed. They were to form the lower jaw of a pair of pincers, the upper part of which comprised the Home Fleet—the two new battleships *Prince of Wales* and *King George V*, the *Hood*, the new aircraft-carrier *Victorious*, the cruisers *Norfolk*, *Suffolk*, *Manchester* and *Birmingham* and attendant destroyers. Numerically the odds were badly against the Germans: but in design, size and power no British ship could touch the *Bismarck*. The *Hood*, for so long the world's largest warship was now outclassed and had in fact been inadequately armoured. Four hours after Force H left Gibraltar for the north-west, dawn broke after a night of rain and snow and revealed the *Bismarck* only twelve miles from their shadowing cruisers, the *Norfolk* and *Suffolk* with the *Hood* and *Prince of Wales* seventeen miles to the north-west and just in sight.

The brief action which followed was disastrous to the British. First *Norfolk* was hit and on fire forward. The new battleship *Prince of Wales* suffered four hits, had her bridge destroyed and was holed underwater aft. Finally the *Hood* at 25,000 yards was hit by *Bismarck's* fifth salvo and in eight minutes blew up, the whole of her ship's company bar three being lost. The *Prince of Wales* withdrew from the action. The *Bismarck*, herself damaged and leaking oil, continued to the south-west, shadowed by the *Norfolk* and the *Suffolk*.

There was then a pause in the chase. All available naval resources were directed by the Admiralty to converge on the Germans. Shadowing was maintained by the two cruisers throughout the day and by *Suffolk's* primitive radar at night. From the far west the old battleship *Ramillies* was ordered to leave her convoy and place herself to westward of the enemy. Five hundred miles to the south-west the *Rodney*, another battleship, was ordered to close. Force H with *Firesprite* as part of the screen ahead of it, raced up and away from the Spanish coast. It was as though the *Bismarck* were inside a loose string bag which was gradually and invisibly being drawn tight around them.

But the sinking of the great German ship was far from being a foregone conclusion nor did it proceed, as the River Plate action had developed, in one continuous movement. After a day of high-speed shadowing in which both sides became preoccupied with their oil fuel supplies, the *Bismarck* turned on her pursuers in the evening. This brief action at dusk allowed the *Prinz Eugen* to escape at high speed to the south, to rendezvous with her tanker and then to return unobserved to Brest some ten days later. The fact that that was possible with so many hunters at sea was a reminder of the vast emptiness of the Atlantic and of the limitations of the early radar then available.

Back in Gibraltar Fortin and the Admiral watched the progress of the chase with most of the dispositions known. David's purview, however, extended only as far as the eye could see. They were told nothing by radio and very little by visual signalling. Yet it was the compact, businesslike Force H that was to seal the *Bismarck's* fate.

That the mesh of the net was still fairly large became apparent when *Suffolk*, the cruiser which had brilliantly and successfully shadowed the prey for two days, suddenly lost contact. This took place in foul weather at 3 a.m. and was occasioned because the British ships were in among known infestations of U-boats and, to protect themselves, zig-zagged. *Suffolk* had become used to losing the German battleship off her radar screen at the outer leg of the zig-zag and then finding her again on the next inward turn. But the *Bismarck*, too, had a radar system and the two ships were therefore invisibly conscious of each other. When *Suffolk* slipped off the *Bismarck's* screen, the German quickly doubled back on her tracks and was away into the night.

The situation had now taken a bad turn for the worse from the British point of view. They had let slip the *Prinz Eugen*, were they also to lose the *Bismarck* with the sinking of the *Hood* unavenged and the potentiality of her threat as high as ever? Moreover the oil fuel situation would soon be critical. It is no great matter to refuel destroyers at sea and *Renown* duly supplied her escorting force. But the heavy ships of the Home Fleet to the north, with three days of high-speed steaming behind them, were dangerously near the point where they must either reduce speed, refuel or be towed home, a splendid series of targets for the U-boat packs.

The whole of the next day was spent fruitlessly searching and it was not until 10.30 a.m. on the 26th May that two Swordfish from the *Ark Royal* spotted the German battleship. It then became clear that she was making for Brest and not the North Sea as the C.-in-C. of the Home Fleet had surmised.

Now a number of events happened in quick succession. Captain Vian in the *Cossack*, having intercepted a signal from an aircraft giving the *Bismarck's* position, left his convoy and without further orders made for the quarry. At the same time Admiral Somerville detached the cruiser *Sheffield* and sent her ahead with *Firesprite* and *Forthright* to close and shadow the enemy.

This was not, unfortunately, made known to *Ark Royal*. Hot on the chase, her aircraft 'found' with their newly installed radar system, and homed on to the *Sheffield* which they favoured with an aerial torpedo attack.

'Christ!' said Robert Soakes who was on the bridge with David at the time, 'Look at that!'

The weather was rough and the visibility poor. *Sheffield* had suddenly swung hard astarboard as a clot of some fifteen aircraft bore down on the ship. The miraculous old Swordfish aircraft, which had the reputation of being so slow they could not fly out of the fumes of their own exhausts, were easily recognizable and were almost sitting targets but *Sheffield* did not open fire. Her Captain luckily realized in the nick of time what had happened and told them in very plain language to go back to the *Ark* and think again.

'Force H at its brightest and best,' David observed, 'flat out into the Atlantic for a thousand miles in order to get sunk by our own aircraft.'

'What a shambles!'

This was a favourite remark of Roger Soakes and there seemed of late to be more and more occasion to use it. It symbolized the rather restful, tooth-sucking attitude Soakes had always brought to bear on his life. He had proved himself much more efficient in practical matters than Jimmy Allendale but David enjoyed his company far less. There had been a slight father-and-son relationship between him and Jimmy which stemmed from the same basic background, their respective ages and his own greater experience. But Roger Soakes was a year older than David himself and life on an Argentine *estancia* had given him a tough, almost sarcastic personality. They did not find the same things funny and somehow the running of the ship had become much more of a cold, calculated business. There was less nonsense, and on balance things were more smartly done, but there was also less humanity and the ship's company did not love him as they had Jimmy with his many foibles and faults. David realized this without being able to do anything about it nor indeed especially wanting to.

But it made for greater loneliness during these unending repetitive hours on the bridge. David was getting stale. There had been times of late when he felt almost totally unconscious—simply a naval machine that could listen, calculate and give orders, but without any inner life. He needed a long spell of leave and he needed Grace, neither of which he was likely to get. In the meantime the job continued to eat up his waking attention.

He had not written to Pam about a separation or a divorce. It seemed so unworkable. If he could have married Grace the next day then it would have been easier. But Grace's life was as confined as his own with the added pressure of the Roman Catholic religion behind it from which she would never be free. So the weeks and the months went by: the emotional ferment continued to bubble but there was no practical resolution for any of them. They were effectively separated by the war and, so far as Pam was concerned, he had the impression from her letters that the Paymaster-Lieutenant at Portsmouth was proving to be more and more the solace which she needed. She had never written with clarity and now the letters which he received were short masterpieces of confusion.

But this 'private thinking' as he called his own brand of daydreaming, was only allowed back into his consciousness during a lull in the job. The current pause was now over. A couple of hours after *Sheffield* had been attacked by the *Ark's* aircraft, the cruiser established contact with the *Bismarck*, forty miles to the north, and, using *Sheffield* as a beacon this time instead of a target, fifteen aircraft again flew off from the *Ark* in bad weather and pressed home with immense determination, a torpedo attack on the enemy which with two certain and a possible third hit, was the decisive strike upon which the action turned. A shadowing aircraft reported that after the attack *Bismarck* made two complete circles out of control and what in fact had happened was that her starboard rudder became jammed hard over and it proved impossible to free it. Thus the German ship became unmanœuvrable and could only proceed at slow speed. This was to be her last night.

By now the net was drawn tight and though none of the British battleships had yet reached a killing position, it was now only a matter of hours. During the night *Firesprite* and *Forthright* joined forces with *Cossack* and three other destroyers, one of them Polish, and carried out a torpedo attack on the *Bismarck*. The weather had steadily worsened and by morning a full westerly gale was blowing. Indeed, to attack with torpedoes at close range and high speed from three separate directions at night would have been difficult enough in good weather conditions—in the big sea then running with the wind behind it, daring verged upon foolhardiness.

But the attack was made. As they pounded in, the Sub on the torpedo sights remarked that it would have been difficult

[303]

enough to hold the Rock of Gibraltar on a steady bearing in such conditions and at one stage the dark bulk of the *Bismarck*, intermittently looming up in the night, bore a passing resemblance to the Rock. Then the searchlights opened up and the attack was pressed home against answering gunfire from the *Bismarck's* secondary armament. Neither torpedoes nor gunfire found their target and in ten minutes it was all over. *Firesprite* and *Forthright* returned to the vicinity of the *Sheffield* and the night wore on while the Commander-in-Chief, Home Fleet, in the battleship *King George V* from the north, and the *Rodney* from the south drew nearer for the final attack in the morning.

The end was macabre and even to David's hardened eyes grim and filthy. The *Hood* disaster had at least been quick. A hit in a vulnerable spot, a rage of fire then the one total explosion. With the *Bismarck* he felt the same disgust as at a botched bullfight where the bull has not been properly killed and the memory of the mauled horses returns to sour the taste. *Bismarck* had been on the run for four tortured days. Since the previous night she had been virtually out of control as a ship and at dawn was found to be steaming in the wrong direction. Indeed at midnight her Captain had signalled the German Admiralty: 'Ship unmanœuvrable. We shall fight to the last shell. Long live the Fuehrer.' There was to be no repetition of the *Graf Spee* events. Her armament was intact though the guns' crews were exhausted and in many cases were asleep at their posts.

Shortly before 9 a.m. on the 27th, the sixteen-inch guns of the *Rodney* opened up, followed almost at once by salvoes from *King George V*. *Bismarck* was hit straight away but her own gunfire was still accurate and her third salvo straddled the *Rodney* without, as it happened, causing much damage. But the British ships could move and she could not. Thus time and the weight of attack was against her. Her turrets slowed down in their rate of fire and then one by one fell silent. In half an hour a huge fire was blazing amidships, roasting the crew alive. Listing heavily to port only an occasional, inaccurate shot now left her guns and at this juncture H.M.S. *Rodney* closed to a mere 4,000 yards and poured salvo after salvo on to the stricken ship.

[304]

Even then she would not sink. Surging helplessly in the high sea then running she seemed to David to be no more than a ghastly metal hulk bursting her ribs with a volcano of fire. Nevertheless it did not reach her magazines nor did it blow the ship apart as it had done the *Hood*. She would not sink, and it became obvious that gunnery would not despatch her. The cruiser *Dorsetshire* was then ordered to close and it was her torpedoes which eventually blew the bottom out of the ship, so that two hours after the first salvo had been fired, *Bismarck* at last turned over and slowly sank.

One hundred and fifteen German sailors survived alive out of a crew of nearly two thousand, and the rescue of these from a turbulent quagmire of floating bodies was delayed when *Firesprite's* Asdic reported a U-boat on the scene. It was from beginning to end the most terrible naval calamity David had ever witnessed. What he had now seen with his own eyes far surpassed the very worst ghastliness he had imagined possible since his first days as a small cadet when the glamour of victory and the exercise of power at sea had been offset by his naval instructors with some cold professional facts about what happens at the receiving end of a bombardment. Now he had seen the worst—the very pit of war.

4

Hobart now had two people working for him inside Boothroyd's organization. It was true that the amount of help from Nicholas had not been great. He did not expect it at that time. He did not press him. He had taken a very real risk in approaching Nicholas at all. He was content that the idea had been accepted and with it the implications. The opportunity to use him would present itself later. In the meantime there were other worries.

The security situation in Gibraltar was bedevilled by a number of unknown factors which kept Hobart on the hop. For a time he had thought Boothroyd the core of it all but now he was not so sure. There had been three underwater explosions in the harbour, one of them slightly damaging *Renown*. They might have been delayed-action aircraft mines—though no one had seen them drop—they might have been laid by midget submarines or by what later came to be known as frogmen, or they might be the result of sabotage. The disturbing fact to Hobart was that Boothroyd appeared to be as much in the dark as himself. It looked as though there might well be two separate organizations working in Gibraltar, each independent, each unknown to the other.

It always seemed odd to Hobart, as he smoked his pipe and brooded in the little office in the Bomb House Lane, that he of all people should find himself so heavily involved in intrigue. He had always thought of himself as an open-hearted, rather simple man, absorbed in his wife and children. Until the war he had looked upon his job as part of a fairly well-defined game of chess in which the enemy made all the first moves and in which you were always on the defensive, always countering an attack. The prize consisted of facts and figures, information, intelligence. Now, however, the chess simile was not really adequate. It had become much more of a big business. It was no longer merely figures and dispositions that both sides were after. Effective military strength was what mattered and this brought sabotage to the fore. In fact, while it was still vital to the enemy to know what was going on, in and through Gibraltar, the destruction of the Rock and its facilities was obviously a much bigger prize. So sabotage now ranked as the major risk.

It was Fortin's idea to get Boothroyd away from the Rock ahead of his time. To him this was a piece of elementary tactics. If the enemy expected a dawn attack, the smart thing to do was to surprise him at midnight. So when Hobart had told the Governor all that he knew and most of what he suspected about Boothroyd, steps were taken by the Admiralty, without questions being asked, for Boothroyd to depart in July instead of September.

When this news was broken to Boothroyd, he at once protested to the Admiral-Superintendent, invoking every Dockyard regulation he could lay his hands on. He was a civilian under contract, not someone in uniform to be ordered about at a moment's notice. His appointment was not due to end till September. He did not wish to be difficult but was it quite fair? Moreover the Dean of Gibraltar had found him very useful and was now only too eager to ask for his deferment. He did not make the mistake of being indignant, he simply stated the regulations and left it to higher authority to treat him properly. The Admiral went into the case and took it up on his behalf. His Department at the Admiralty, however, prompted by the Security Service, replied by merely sending out his relief. It was this sudden numbering of the days which provoked the crisis.

The evidence which was later produced at Boothroyd's trial made it seem a comparatively simple matter to bring in a bomb and blow up the Rock. But the almost complete secrecy with which this was done, virtually under Hobart's eyes, was in itself an appreciable feat. The placing of the bomb was a triumph. It required a set of duplicate keys to the magazines which one by one had been copied and cut by Boothroyd over the months. It required an exact knowledge of when each sentry was on and when his attention could best be distracted without causing suspicion. It meant that the pieces of the bomb mechanism which had been separately collected in Tangier had each to be brought into the Dockyard, hidden and then quickly and expertly assembled. Finally, the time it was to explode had to be judged, the mechanism set and started, and then avoiding action taken by those in the know. All this process had to be put through a good two months before Boothroyd had intended it and it was this pressure, in the main, which caused the plan to misfire.

At this time there was still a weekly Bland Line boat to Tangier. It ran at week-ends when Gibraltarians whose families were in Tangier seized the chance of seeing them again. Boothroyd, as a civilian, had the right of visiting Spain and Tangier whenever he wished, and he frequently went across to Tangier where the Dean of Gibraltar had given him contacts. His voluntary efforts as a sidesman at the Cathedral, in fact, stood him in very good stead.

He did not only see the Dean's contacts but they provided an admirable cover for the 'chance encounters' in the Suk whilst ostensibly shopping. In this way, in meetings which rarely lasted over ten minutes, the main tide of espionage into and out of Gibraltar had ebbed and flowed in complete secrecy over the past year. These meetings had had their counterparts both in Algeciras and La Línea and comparatively few of these ramifications were known to Hobart.

The climax came in mid-June 1941. German pressure on Spain reached a new peak and though, a week later, this was seen to be a feint, both the German and British nerve systems in so far as they covered Spain were taut. It was easy to say that there was now, after two years of war, nothing new in this. There was no comfort in it either. Each time it recurred the threat was real. The Germans *could* enter Spain when they chose: they *were* there in force poised behind the Pyrenees. Greece and Crete *had* just been cleaned up and they were in a new position of power in the eastern Mediterranean. The Rock *could* be reduced to a shambles by the Algeciras guns. A desperate, broken-backed siege in the rubble *could* very easily take place. These were the realities Fortin and Hobart woke up to every single dusty day of the summer. They read, sifted and judged the Intelligence reports coming in, but in the final analysis it was their instinct they relied on and both Fortin and Hobart's intuition began insisting like the throb of a heartbeat that an attack was upon them.

This, then, was the invisible background in Gibraltar on Friday, 20th June, when Boothroyd committed himself and put his bomb plan into high gear. On Saturday the bomb was in position in one of the inner magazines from which a train of explosions might best be started, the time mechanism was put into motion set for eight o'clock that night. Boothroyd with his usual overnight handbag caught the midday boat for Tangier, having destroyed in his accommodation all trace of his hidden activities. The Spaniards who had done the final work on the bomb had both crossed the frontier into Spain and Juan Menendez, of the Naval Store Department, the only one of Boothroyd's inner group who had also been concerned in the placing of the bomb, was going to warn the others during the afternoon to take a trip to Spain and suffer a minor accident or illness which would legitimately keep them out of Gibraltar that evening.

At least this was what Boothroyd intended, but it was at this

[308]

point that the incalculable entered in. He had never wished to use Menendez and with a little longer time in hand he would have had a new agent completely trained about whom the others would have known nothing at all. But time pressed and on balance he had decided that Menendez, with his job in the Naval Store Department, was preferable to a man whom he had not yet properly studied to the full. So Menendez and the Spaniards did the actual placing of the bomb, and Menendez alone in Gibraltar knew what had happened. The others—Sub-Inspector Lopez, Sergeant Elling and Nicholas—were completely in the dark.

It had been Menendez' intention to warn Lopez who had been on duty at the North Gate that morning and Elling who would be at the Garrison Library with Nicholas, as soon as he left the Dockyard himself. Menendez worked in a shed near the smallest of the dry-docks in which, as it happened, H.M.S. *Firesprite* was then having her bottom scraped. The bomb had been placed shortly before the noon hooter went, the magazine had been locked and Boothroyd, satisfied that all was going according to plan, had then slipped away to catch the Tangier boat. Menendez returned to his office to tidy up and be seen for alibi purposes but his mind was completely preoccupied with the fatal step that had just been taken. As he walked along the edge of the dry-dock, therefore, wondering in passing how much of that destroyer would be there the next day, he did not observe that a crane was still traversing and the next thing he knew was a blow from the jib on the back of his left shoulder as though someone had given him a slap. It was not much more than a nudge but it was enough to make him lose his balance. His foot caught in a wire and then with a yell of pure panic and after a giddy few seconds' fall, he fetched up at the bottom of the dry-dock with a broken leg and a cracked skull.

Both Roger Soakes and David were on board at the time and Soakes was standing on the quarter-deck examining a bit of welding. He heard the yell and rushed to the side. There was no water in the dock and Menendez must have fallen about thirty feet on to the stone tiering which curved in under the bottom of the destroyer.

'Christ!' said Soakes, 'what a shambles!' Then at once taking charge of the situation, he shouted to the Quartermaster to get the Neil Robertson stretcher and the first-aid box out of the wardroom flat, grabbed the two nearest hands and ran off the ship, down the dock steps to the stricken man. Menendez was alive but unconscious. He was bleeding badly from the head and to begin with Soakes was not sure whether he ought to be moved. *Firesprite's* doctor was already ashore.

'He would be!' Soakes cursed as he looked at the casualty. 'This is a fine evolution for a Saturday forenoon! Cor!'

'Is he alive, Number One?' David called down from the deck above.

'I think so, sir. His head isn't too good. I'm not sure about moving him.'

'I've sent for the ambulance. Better get him up on the stretcher if you can.'

Up on the dockside, while they were waiting for the ambulance, Menendez half came back into consciousness and began muttering in Spanish. By this time a crowd of 'mateys' had collected and David asked them what he was saying. But they were from Spain and spoke no English. A moment or two later Menendez' Gibraltarian assistant from the store where he worked arrived on the scene and after listening to the muttering for a moment or so looked up at David and the *Firesprite* officers.

'Was there an explosion?' he asked. 'He keeps saying the explosion was not his fault.'

'The poor sod must think a bomb fell on him,' Soakes said. 'No—there was no explosion: the clot simply walked into a crane and lost his balance.'

Sub-Inspector Lopez was just going off duty when the ambulance call had come through. No name was given and there was nothing to indicate that this was any different from any other dockyard accident. Carelessness and its resulting casualties were always taking place in ships in dry-dock. Thus his suspicions were not aroused and as the ambulance took Juan Menendez to the Colonial Hospital, it passed Sub-Inspector Lopez on his way back to the barracks. Thus the chance of alerting Gibraltar to what was then in process of happening was missed by inches and the Saturday afternoon began much as any other.

David had arranged to play tennis with Grace, Hobart and a Wren from the Old Naval Hospital. After the game and while they were having tea at the Naval Officers' Pavilion, David recounted what had happened that morning, mentioning the illusion the chap had had that he had been struck by a bomb.

'I suppose everyone's so air-raid minded nowadays,' he commented, 'that if you lose consciousness through a sudden shock of any kind, the first thing you think of is that a bomb must have fallen.'

'Oh! I don't know,' Hobart said, 'that's a bit far-fetched. He probably had some sort of phobia of bombs, that's all.'

'I'd like to meet someone who hasn't.'

'I mean—a lot of the Spaniards are windy.'

'He wasn't a Spaniard, he was a Gibraltarian.'

'Was there a big clang of any kind when it happened?'

'I don't think so. Just the usual peaceful noises of riveting and air-compressors.'

'What was his name?'

'I don't know. His mate said it was Juan Fernandez or something like it.'

'That's an island in the Pacific,' Grace said. 'You're thinking of Robinson Crusoe.'

They all laughed and Hobart thought no more of it. Thus the second chance of realizing what had really happened came and went.

'Dicky Seale wants us to rally round tonight,' Hobart said, 'while his sacred Royal Marines Beat Retreat.'

'*His* Marines?'

'Well, you know what I mean: they're actually from *Renown* but Dicky has a proprietary feeling for any Bullock on the Rock. He's as proud of them as *we* all are of our Very Own Destroyer Flotilla,' Hobart said with a dig at David. 'Bless his heart—as bait he's offering Pimms Number One in the cuddy afterwards.'

'I was going to invite you all back on board,' David said, 'for hot, dusty drinks in the dry-dock. I suppose a chance to

[311]

watch the leather-necks stamping about making an exhibition of themselves ranks above that. What do you say, Grace?'

'I'm for the Marines. Let's go back and change and then meet—where?'

'Why not the Bristol?' David suggested. 'We can get up a good head of steam there to fortify us for the ceremony.'

Meanwhile, in the deepest magazine under the Rock, the time mechanism on Boothroyd's bomb quietly moved. Boothroyd himself was just landing in Tangier from the S.S. *Rescue* and up in the Colonial Hospital Juan Menendez was beginning to grope his way back into consciousness and to remember what had been done immediately before his accident.

XVI

D URING the afternoon Nicholas had expected Boothroyd
to look in at the Tribuno Bar and when by four-thirty
there was still no sign of him, a warning-bell began to
sound somewhere in his consciousness. Although the intelligence which flows into a newspaper office is less specialized
than the facts and figures Hobart laid in front of the Governor,
Nicholas was equally sure that the Germans were on the point
of striking through Spain.

He assumed that this would link up with action on Boothroyd's part and he had, therefore, been doubly wary over the
past week. Before he would not have thought it odd that
Boothroyd had not shown up: now he began to be very suspicious. Abruptly he stopped drinking, left the Tribuno Bar
and went back to his apartment. He took a shower and sobered
up. The feeling of being ill-at-ease steadily grew.

He decided to seek out one of the other members of Boothroyd's clique and see if he could glean any news that way. Just
as he was leaving, there was a knock at the door. It was Father
O'Reilly. This was the last person he wanted to see.

'Is this a social call? Because if so I'm afraid. . . .'

'It is not,' Father O'Reilly cut in. 'You ought to know me
better than that by now. . . .'

'Well, come in,' Nicholas said reluctantly. 'I can only offer
you brandy, I'm afraid.'

'No, thank you.' Father O'Reilly brushed aside the offer
and did not come through the door. 'I called in only because
it's on my way anyway and because you may be able to help
them up at the hospital. Do you know anyone called Juan
Menendez, who works in the Dockyard?'

'No,' said Nicholas instinctively lying. 'Why? Am I supposed to?'

'He had an accident this morning. He fell into a dry-dock
and broke open his skull. I happened to be visiting the man in
the next bed. The doctors say he has hallucinations that a

bomb fell on the Rock and blew him up and that you were to be told. No one can make head nor tail of it up there—so I thought I'd look in and tell you. If you don't know the man, then it doesn't matter. He may have picked up your name anywhere. It's the sort of name you don't forget.'

'Is he a tall man with spectacles?' Nicholas asked, drawing a precautionary red herring across the trail.

'No, he's a small man with a pock-marked face and rather prominent teeth. Oh! well, if you don't know him, that's that. He seems to have no relatives in Gibraltar and that's odd in itself. His wife was evacuated with the others but as you know most people have family connections of some sort or other. This man has no one at all. Well—I'll be on my way: don't let it worry you.'

'Thank you,' said Nicholas blandly, 'it won't. I suppose there might be a story for the *Gazette* in it. Who pushed him into the dry-dock?'

'No one did. A crane swung round and knocked him off his feet.'

'An act of God?'

'Or one of the King's enemies,' Father O'Reilly said as he went down the stairs, wondering once again why he bothered with the Cypriot gentleman when his every instinct as a man was to give him a first-rate hiding. Poor little Rosita, he thought, she had picked a bad one. He went off down the street waving at people he knew, blithely unaware of the part he had played in the Boothroyd plot or that in a few hours' time the Rock was likely to blow up under his feet.

Nicholas could scarcely wait until the priest was out of sight before setting off straight away for Boothroyd's lodgings. If it was the Juan Menendez he thought it was, then what could possibly have gone wrong? What could be brewing and what was behind this feeling of burning anxiety which now beset him? One of Boothroyd's strictest instructions was that members of his group were never to visit each other in their lodgings or apartments and only an acute sense of emergency took Nicholas along now. Bothroyd's apartment was shut and a neighbour said he thought he had gone over to Tangier for the week-end. That clinched it. Nicholas still could not pin it down

[314]

exactly but he now felt as though he ought to be running. He grabbed a taxi and made for the Colonial Hospital through crowds that were beginning to gather for the ceremony of Beating Retreat.

At the hospital they let him see Menendez but although it established his identity he had lost consciousness again and to make matters worse was now under morphia. The nurse repeated the story about the bomb falling and the need for Nicholas Pappadopoulos to be told, substantially as Father O'Reilly had got it, but by now he could scarcely wait to hear it. Now he knew something must be in train, something of very great danger to them all. He had kept the taxi waiting and, running out of the hospital he told the driver to go at full speed to Hobart's office in the Bomb House Lane. But Hobart was not there. The Duty Clerk said he would be at the ceremony outside Government House but beforehand had gone to the Bristol.

He ran to the Bristol but Hobart was not there. By now a sizeable crowd had collected in Convent Place. To force his way through this crowd was in itself a feat, to find Hobart in it virtually impossible. The ceremony would last about half an hour—was he to wait that long? Or what could he do? As the Royal Marine contingent came marching smartly down Main Street led proudly by the Drum Major of Force H, a feeling of frustration and despair overcame him. At that point he all but gave up. Then suddenly across the street he caught sight of Grace and beside her Hobart. He started to force his way across and was, without thinking, going to dart in front of the advancing Royal Marines. But two large able-bodied seamen from H.M.S. *Renown* gripped him firmly by either arm and hissed at him:

'Don't you show no disrespect to our Royal Marines. You stop where you are.'

At this Nicholas lost his temper. He swore and he cursed but the more he struggled the more tightly they held him.

'I tell you,' he managed to get out, 'we may all be blown up any minute.'

'Now fancy that!' said one Able-Seaman to the other. 'Pity Charlie Knowall can't come to sea with us for a trip, isn't it? Then he could find out all about it, couldn't he? But you're not at sea, chum,' he ended with solid lower-deck wisdom. 'You're safe and sound on the Rock of Gibraltar—and that's the safest place in the world, didn't you know?'

'Hobart!' Nicholas yelled in a lull in the music, 'Colonel Hobart!'

By good luck Hobart just heard, saw what was happening, darted across the street and to the sailors' astonishment ordered them curtly to let Nicholas go. Then a way opened before them and without further ado they slipped through the crowd to the back.

'Well?' said Hobart when they were at last free of the crowd, 'what was all that about?'

'I don't know,' Nicholas said helplessly, straightening himself as best he could, 'I think something terrible is going to happen but I don't know what.'

'Something terrible nearly did happen. You nearly got lynched. You ought to know you can't cock a snoot at the Royal Marines in Gibraltar.'

'To hell with the Royal Marines,' Nicholas said sourly and then with the ceremony and the crowds still as a background he began telling Hobart about Menendez, the accident, the hallucinations about the bomb and Boothroyd's absence in Tangier.

'And now Menendez is under morphia,' he said, 'and perhaps it's a phoney scare after all.'

'No,' Hobart said, 'this doesn't strike me as a phoney. This is the sort of timing the enemy want. The big explosion and then the big push. Come along to the office. We've got some quick finding-out to do.'

So while Nicholas sat brooding in the old leather armchair, Hobart put the Security Services into a state of top emergency. Sergeant Elling was whipped out of the Library and brought down, to his astonishment, for interrogation. Inspector Lopez was pulled in. The Senior Medical Officer at the Hospital was asked to do anything he could to bring Menendez out of his trance. The Duty Staff Officers in the Dockyard and Fortress were alerted and so, brought up by an infuriated Seale from the most interesting part of the ceremony, was the Governor.

Elling, though badly scared and shocked at seeing Nicholas in Hobart's office—and a little later Inspector Lopez—refused to admit to any knowledge of any kind and Hobart formed the impression that he really did not know anything of material help. It was seven o'clock. He was held in the guardroom, a shattered man.

'I'm going up to see Menendez,' Hobart remarked to Nicholas, 'you'd better come too.'

'This may still be a wild goose chase,' Nicholas said almost apologetically as Hobart drove up to the hospital at a furious pace.

'I only hope it is.'

'Of all the people, in fact, Menendez is the least likely to have been given anything practical to do. As you can see—he couldn't even walk along the side of a dry-dock without falling in.'

'Hm!'

Like Nicholas, Hobart's rational mind refused to accept such flimsy evidence for a panic. Were he writing this up into a report, it would scarcely stretch to a paragraph. But it was not the rational mind which drove him now to pound along to the ward, to glare down at the unconscious Menendez and to fume at the doctors for not being able to wake him up. In the meantime all over Gibraltar—except in the magazine where the bomb itself had been placed—Security forces were carrying out special checks on oil-tanks, ammunition lighters, mine and torpedo depots and other vulnerable points. Nothing in the slightest degree suspicious was found. Over in Tangier Boothroyd was taking coffee with some of the Dean of Gibraltar's friends. Down in Convent Place, the Royal Marines, having symbolically beaten retreat from the fields and summoned the peasantry to take shelter within the castle walls were now in actuality stamping back to H.M.S. *Renown* with more than half a thirsty eye on the Ince's Hall N.A.A.F.I. Canteen which they passed *en route*. The clock moved steadily nearer to 8 p.m.

After the ceremony David and Grace had gone up with Seale for the Pimms which was to be their reward for 'jollying on the Jollies' as David put it. There was no sign of Hobart and Seale himself seemed to have lost his usual calm cheerfulness.

'There's a flap on,' he said briefly, waving them to help themselves and disappearing for the third time to answer a summons from Fortin. 'There've been demonstrations outside the British Embassy in Madrid.'

'That's one thing about being in dry-dock,' David remarked, 'if the Rock gets totally out of control, there's absolutely nothing you can do about it. It's a wonderful feeling of irresponsibility. The Rock can blow up all round you but there's nothing to be done except wait for the dust to settle and then shove off to sea.'

'If you can get out of the dry-dock,' Grace said, 'and I hope you don't. A long spell of local leave is my prescription.'

'With the square-heads bashing away at the gates? Some leave that would be!'

'They won't do that.'

'Isn't that what all the panic's about? I expect Dicky to come striding back in a moment like someone in a George Arliss film and say, "Gentlemen, the enemy are without. Let us take cover, draw our swords and fight to the last dying breath!"'

But Seale was a long time in coming back and when he did so it was with Hobart.

'I'm afraid I can't make it tonight,' Hobart said, 'you'll have to go on without me.'

'I can't be let out either,' Seale said. 'Isn't it a bore? Anyway, let's finish up the Pimms.'

Then Jaime arrived. He had spent the afternoon at San Roque and on coming back the Spanish Frontier guards had again been changed and were again making things tough.

'There's something in the air,' he said, 'I don't like the feeling at all. I think it would be a good idea, Grace, if you went home now.'

'Why?'

Jaime shrugged his shoulders.

'It's just a feeling.'

'If there's going to be a crisis I'd much rather have it in Gibraltar—thank you very much.'

'And your mother?'

'You know it won't make the slightest difference to her. She'll only notice I'm not there two days later.'

'Well . . .' said Jaime and then an orderly asked him to speak to the Governor.

'I think this is my cue to remove you to dinner at the Rock,' David remarked, 'leaving the experts to get on with their splendid crisis. If the Germans are really coming, then we'd better have one good meal before they arrive.'

It was ten minutes to eight.

3

No one in Gibraltar except Menendez knew that a bomb had been set to explode at 8 p.m. and Menendez did not recover consciousness till nearly twenty past eight. By this time Nicholas had completely lost his previous feeling of urgency and pressure. He decided he must have misinterpreted Boothroyd's absence and Menendez' hallucinations. Life was going on as before. He knew that he had infected Hobart but it was an instinct which had come and gone. He left Hobart to get on with it and went to the *Gazette* office to start the evening's work. He felt deflated and depressed.

Reuter carried reports of anti-British demonstrations in Spain and a rumour from New York that Hitler, having occupied Greece, would attack Gibraltar to secure the western end of the Mediterranean. Well—he'd read those rumours before. He started his work: but his mind was elsewhere. The restlessness remained. On an impulse he called his assistant across and turned over the paper to him. This was something he had never done before. No matter how soaked in brandy he had been, he had always somehow or other done the job, been there, worked, fulfilled his responsibilities. Tonight that was no longer important. Tonight there was something else to be done. He decided he needed a long, long walk.

As he left the office, the sergeant who now collated the agency reports came running after him with a message. The German attack on Russia had begun. He remained with the tape in his hand staring out at the last of the evening light fading behind the Algeciras hills. So—that was the way it was. An attack on Russia. He placed it in his mind like a new piece of furniture and then walked round it looking at it from different angles. An attack to the east meant that a drive south through Spain was much less likely—unless the Rock was to be had for the picking, unless a diversion had been arranged to keep the Allies busy in the west. A diversion centred on Gibraltar! Suddenly the panic returned, suddenly it was as though some-one had turned on a stream of burning hot air again. Walking as fast as his legs would take him, he reached the Colonial Hospital just as Menendez was coming back to consciousness.

In the early stages Menendez was still under the impression that the bomb had gone off and that somehow it was that which had blown him up. He started to whimper. He tried to explain. The doctors let Hobart and Lopez into the room and, after a short argument, Nicholas as well, but none were to be visible to the injured man since another shock might be fatal. In consequence all three stood slightly behind the bed-head out of range of Menendez' eye-line. The little Gibraltarian with the pock-marked face was in a pretty bad way. A strong feeling of guilt pressed down on him. He mumbled and explained in Spanish, perhaps to the doctor perhaps to himself that his Republican sympathies in Spain had made him do it. England had let them down. He had not been paid. No—he had not taken a penny and he could prove it. Later—all that must be settled later. Payment by results. Gibraltar belonged to Spain, that was the point. Then, as a momentary gap came in the mist —was *el greco* all right? Nicko the Greek, the only person who understood. Had he been killed too? He had meant to warn him—then again he lost consciousness as the doctor and nurse examined him anxiously. It was nearly half past eight. The explosion was overdue by almost half an hour.

Ten minutes later he suddenly burst back into consciousness, a look of unearthly terror on his face. He began calling for Nicko and at a nod from the doctor Nicholas stepped into the line of his vision and identified himself. There was then a pause as Menendez studied his face trying to focus his eyes and steady his consciousness. Then it all came in a rush. It was clear the little man knew he was dying and desperately wished to atone. He described the placing of the bomb and its setting: he gave the angle at which the firing device must be held if it was not to detonate by vibration: he told everything it was necessary to know. Then consciousness and speech again departed, this time for good. Half an hour later he was dead.

As soon as the material facts had been revealed Hobart, Lopez and Nicholas slipped from the room, ran out of the hospital, jumped into Hobart's car and drove at full speed to Government House. It so happened that both the Admiral and the Deputy Fortress Commander were in with the Governor and Hobart, dragging Nicholas after him, burst in on them without ceremony and abruptly told what had happened. Fortin listened in icy silence, aware as the facts came out that he stood once more in the presence of Fate, as so long ago he had similarly stood when advancing alone and unarmed on to that fort in Waziristan. When Hobart had finished there was a moment's silence. Everyone looked at Fortin and Fortin looked back, first at each one in turn then at the wall above their heads.

'So,' he said at last, 'either the detonator has been wrongly set or it has jammed. Menendez says if it is moved it may go off there and then, and we must presume he knows what he's talking about. Where exactly is Magazine D.Seven?'

'Plumb in the centre,' the Admiral said, 'almost directly underneath the Ince's Hall canteen. About two hundred yards from here.'

'Then we must clear the town. Now. Get the people this side of the Ince's Hall to the North Front and the other up to Europa. Clear everyone in the Dockyard away to the south. Ships alongside must get out of the harbour as soon as they have steam to move. Meanwhile the Naval Bomb Disposal Officer had better get himself organized but he's not to enter the magazine till the town and Dockyard are cleared.'

'I would like to volunteer to get it out,' Nicholas said quietly. Another momentary silence fell. Fortin looked at him coolly.

TR—L*

To Nicholas it was as though he were pressing into his soul.

'Do you know anything about bombs and detonators?'

'A certain amount.'

'This is a job for experts.'

'Can I help? Be an assistant?'

Fortin glanced at the Admiral and then back at Nicholas.

'If the Admiral agrees and the Bomb Disposal Officer will have you.'

'Thank you, sir.'

So it began. At ten to nine, fifty minutes after the Rock was scheduled to blow up, the Fortress was alerted to an emergency state and the great evacuation began. Patrols, police, the fire brigade and the one public address van in Gibraltar were all pressed into service and the great trek north and south in truck, bus and on foot began. The news spread fast. Soldiers, sailors and airmen poured out of the cafés and bars: shopkeepers hastily pulled down the shutters: musicians laid down their instruments and cabaret artistes stopped dancing: the Bristol Hotel was cleared to the north and the Rock Hotel to the south. The frontier was closed to anyone entering Gibraltar. In half an hour two main streams of several thousand people were heading for the North Front in one direction where the 1,400-foot cliff-face might shelter them, or perhaps crumble and fall on them, and for Europa Flats in the other which was as far south and away from Magazine D.7 as it was possible to get. In the harbour the *Renown* and *Ark Royal* which had steam enough to manœuvre were putting to sea. In the Dockyard all-night work stopped and the machinery shut down. This had all been thought out and prepared for had the Rock come under attack from Spain and had it been necessary to put Plan P into operation.

At ten past nine just after Father O'Reilly had administered the last sacrament to Juan Menendez, as all around patients were being moved by stretcher and ambulance out of the hospital and away, the air-raid sirens sounded and a mixed posse of Vichy French aircraft from Morocco attacked the Rock in a half-hearted fashion. That night Gibraltar gave the visitors all it had, a single unlucky bomb at this juncture being capable of producing results undreamed of by the Vichy French.

[322]

For the next twenty minutes therefore, as the exodus continued and the population of Gibraltar was concentrating at the north and south ends of the Rock, the blackout and the threat from the sky was added to the load of anxiety borne by those in the know.

Down in the Dockyard the Bomb Disposal Officer was with the Admiral, Hobart and Nicholas. A casual-looking R.N.V.R. lieutenant with freckles and a mop of red hair, you wondered what had taken him into this dangerous and intricate job, but when you observed his movements and especially his hands, the impression of casualness went. He came from a long line of manufacturing jewellers and his hobby in peacetime had been racing motor cars. He had taken one look at Nicholas and politely refused his offer of help.

'If you haven't been trained for the job, it really makes it far more dangerous for everyone else,' he said, 'unless you know this particular bomb, that is.'

Then Nicholas decided for a reason he was never to understand that he must tell a lie. Perhaps, behind it, was a wish to expiate, to pay in some measure for his share in the way things had gone. Perhaps, as Fortin would have phrased it, it was simply a sense of his fate.

'I know that mechanism,' he said, 'I helped assemble it.'

He was aware of the cold stares of the Admiral, Hobart and the Bomb Disposal Officer. Now the die was cast. The lie was spoken and now, even if he wished to retract, he could not clear himself from suspicion. It struck him in the short silence which followed that the penetrating attention of the Senior Naval Officer, of the young R.N.V.R. and of Hobart was the hardest inquisition he had ever had to bear in his life.

'All right,' said the B.D.O., 'if the Admiral concurs, you can come along.'

They looked at the Admiral who nodded briefly. The final, unlooked-for trial had begun.

4

Grace and David in the company of everyone else dining and dancing at the Rock Hotel that Saturday night found themselves brusquely ordered out and told to start walking up the Mount Road towards Europa. The effectiveness with which a Royal Marine patrol emptied the hotel was remarkable. The band was stopped. The Royal Marine lieutenant in charge abruptly informed them of the Governor's orders. The hotel was to be cleared forthwith and no delay of any kind could be accepted. The lieutenant asked for their co-operation, quickly spotted a colonel in one corner whom he asked to take charge, then went and cleared the bar, the kitchens and all the rooms. In under a quarter of an hour the Rock Hotel was deserted and a long snake of people, joking or griping had begun trudging up the road as the air-raid sirens brayed and the A.A. barrage began.

David's first reaction was that he must at once return to his ship, no matter what the Governor might say. When they left the hotel, therefore, Grace said quickly that she could look after herself and David turned to go down towards the Dockyard against the tide. But he had not gone ten yards when he was halted by a voice calling out to him:

'Where do you think you're off to, Evers?'

He recognized his Captain (D), speaking from a car pulled into the side of the road and packed with officers from the Tower.

'Back to the ship, sir.'

'Didn't you hear the Governor's orders? The entire Dockyard's been evacuated.'

'What about the ships?'

'Those that can't put to sea have been cleared—completely. There's not a soul left in the danger zone.'

'But surely . . .' David began. This was against his deepest naval instincts. He *must* go back on board.

'Come along, Evers. Get on out to Europa as soon as you can. There's not a human being left in the Dockyard.'

The car drove off leaving David stopped in his tracks. He felt bewildered and astonished. All his training urged him to go back to his ship but this direct order he had received cut across feelings and instincts. It was an extraordinary state of affairs. Yet he had no option but to obey. So he turned in the other direction and in a few moments had caught up with Grace trudging along the road.

'Perhaps the Rock *is* going to blow up with us all,' he muttered. 'Are you all right, Grace?'

'Yes, thanks, I'm fine.'

As they walked on, lorries overtook them filled with people from down in the town. To begin with the lorries headed in one direction—south to Europa—but after about ten minutes they started to return empty for further loads and then, on the narrow, twisting road, chaos began. Since an air-raid was in progress there was also a blackout. In addition the road became choked with people walking and with cars and more lorries leaving the tow. Soon there was a dark mass of vehicles and people completely filling the road on which the only movement was to those on foot.

'Now I know what France must have been like,' Grace said, 'when the Germans poured in—only very much worse.'

'It's altogether safer at sea,' David remarked as a truck shaved past him in the dark. 'This'll teach *Firesprite* to have her bottom scraped.'

A little later on Grace commented:

'Do you suppose Nicholas had anything to do with this? It was pretty odd of him seeking out Hobart like that in the crowd.'

'I should think it's entirely his doing,' David said sourly.

'Single file, keep well in to the left,' a motor-cycle despatch-rider shouted as a way began to be cleared for another convoy of lorries.

'Perhaps your father was right,' David said presently, 'and you should have got back to San Roque while the going was good.'

She slipped her arm into his in the darkness and squeezed it.

'Did you want to be rid of me?'

'Yes, of course. We see so much of each other, don't we? It's just that perhaps it might have been better.'

'Whatever's going to happen I'd rather be here with you than safe in San Roque.'

'Would you, Grace?'

'Always.'

She knew he wanted to say something but was hesitating. They trudged on in silence for a while, Grace walking ahead

[325]

whenever a passing lorry forced them into the ditch. After a time he said:

'I think this has gone on long enough. If the Rock Hotel is due to blow up we're far enough away now for it not to matter.'

An idea struck her and she took hold of his hand.

'Follow me,' she whispered as a new burst of A.A. firing began. A little way down to the right she remembered the ruined chapel of Santa Teresa of the Doves. As children she and Rosita had come up to play with friends who had the next-door house and there was a break in the wall over which it was possible to scramble and by which a tiny ruined patio could be gained, covered now with creeper and dead leaves. Unnoticed in the dark they slipped out of the cavalcade and in a moment or so were stumbling down a forgotten path to a dimly seen wall at the bottom. Grace searched her memory for the way and to her delight soon found the gap in the crumbling wall.

'Lift me up,' she said, and then in a second she was on top of the wall and could see the little flagged yard with the outline of the ruined church, black against the night sky and the Bay below.

'This is it,' she whispered, and leaning down helped David to jump up beside her. 'We used to come here as children. It was once the private chapel of the Giberti family but they sold the house and the chapel fell down from neglect. We'll be quite safe here till it's over—whatever "it" is.'

They jumped down the far side. The guns still thundered, but the raid was nearing its end. During the lulls in the firing they could hear the voices of the procession they had left still tramping on above them and about thirty yards away.

'There used to be an old stone bench . . .' Grace said. 'Ah! here it is!'

He put his arm round her and drew her close in the darkness. The crickets, disturbed into silence by their unexpected arrival, began once more to chirrup. Somewhere near, a branch of honeysuckle filled the still air with its heady scent. Had they then known that a small party of men among whom was Nicholas was at that moment at the mouth of the underground corridor leading towards Magazine D.7 where a detonating mechanism lay upon which was then centred the fate of the Rock, they would have been politely interested but no more. The Rock might well have blown up—as it was so close to doing—but this would not at that moment have mattered to David and Grace as they sat there in the shadowy, deserted and forgotten patio, locked in each other's arms.

'Will you marry me?' he whispered, 'now—the real you— the real person I need? Grace?'

'Yes, David,' she whispered into his chest, 'I will. I will. I don't know how but I will.'

'I love you,' he said after what seemed like an age.

'I love you too,' she answered. 'Nothing else matters at all. Nothing at all.'

'Whatever the complications, the snags or the difficulties? Remembering Lance in Germany and Pam in England?'

'Yes, David,' she whispered and began to cry, 'I will—I will.'

5

The Town of Gibraltar was now as dark and deserted as a ruin, except for a very occasional cat and the rats. Indeed the rats with their human instinct for danger were out and about the streets in droves, suddenly visible as they crept in short bursts of movement along the gutters or in darts across the cobblestones, ostensibly in search of food, in reality alert and wary at the extraordinary silence and absence of human beings. Fortin had noticed them as he and Seale, the last two to leave Government House, drove along Main Street past the Casemates and out to the North Front where now a mass of humanity stood or sat in unorganized groups, waiting for the big bang to come.

Meanwhile, well into the Rock, Nicholas and the B.D.O. had reached Magazine D.7. It seemed to Nicholas that by now he had lived his life many many times over. To begin with he had been quaking with fear and this reached down deeper and deeper inside him the more they penetrated under the Rock itself towards their objective.

His companion seemed casually unconcerned. As they

walked along the corridors past the eerie-looking bins, the racks and the caves full of shells, bombs and cordite, Nicholas studied the other man surreptitiously and with something like awe. He was younger and he exhibited no visible trace at all of the fear Nicholas felt. He wondered if this was because of the sort of person he was or whether it was the result of training and discipline. Nicholas had never been so desperately close to danger before. In the Spanish Civil War he had frequently found himself in a number of tough spots but the danger was usually visible, and at the least calculable. Here it was invisible and absolute. Either they would extricate the bomb and neutralize it or there would be a flash and then nothing. Upon the two of them at that time the fate of the Rock depended and on what happened to the Rock quite possibly the outcome of the war. He wondered if the B.D.O. realized any of this. The cool detachment of the other young man continued to make an enormous impression. From it he derived a certain strength himself. It also admitted him once again to humility.

He thought, too, about himself, looking back on his strange twisted life. All his values were now in the melting pot. At this moment Panzer divisions were rolling east into Russia. He held that picture in his mind for a time but it no longer mattered and now he was surprised it ever had. He thought of Rosita and the way he had treated her and this made him deeply ashamed. Too late, a voice said in him now, too late. But his heart formed her name, his heart offered up a penitence and asked mutely to be forgiven. And it was this greater emotion of real humility and love which overcame his fear as the Bomb Disposal Officer carefully opened the grille of Magazine D.7 and softly they stepped inside.

It was not a large vault and it contained naval six-inch shells. Next door came the first of the magazines containing fifteen- and sixteen-inch shells, each of which weighed approximately a ton. Boothroyd had calculated that an explosion in the smaller vault would act as a primer and would cause a chain effect of detonations which, once started, could have blown the Dockyard and the town to pieces.

Menendez had told Nicholas that the bomb had been concealed inside an ordinary six-inch shell case and that it was well down to the right. At first glance, therefore, the magazine revealed nothing out of order, nothing out of place. In what seemed to Nicholas an absolute silence they listened for any sound from the mechanism which would give away its position. But nothing whatever disturbed the stillness.

'Wherever it is it must have jammed,' the B.D.O. whispered. 'You say there's no booby trap?'

'No,' said Nicholas. Why was he lying? He had never seen the thing before. Why was he here? He felt more strongly than ever before that he was playing a part—and a part only accidentally his. But why? Why did he have this obsession in his mind about 'payment'? What was it all about?

The shells had all been methodically stacked but there was one in the second row from the bottom which was very slightly out of place.

'My bet is it's that one,' the B.D.O. said, 'and that means moving all this lot on top.'

In a way it was a relief to have something to do with one's hands and body. Methodically and quickly they began to clear away the shells on top, carrying each one between them out into the passage. With each shell moved away from the immediate vicinity of the bomb, the danger of an explosion which would endanger the whole Rock was lessened, but a single detonation in that enclosed space could still have unpredictable results.

It took them fifteen minutes before they had isolated the suspect shell. All this time Nicholas could not keep his eyes from returning in a hypnotized fashion to Boothroyd's bag of tricks, as the B.D.O. so casually called it.

'Now—a minute's breather in the corridor, then we'll have a bash at it,' said the B.D.O. adding conversationally. 'This is the moment I always feel I could do with a 'bine.'

The thought of lighting up a cigarette at such a time was the last thing to enter Nicholas's mind. However he shrugged his shoulders and agreed.

'How many times have you been through this performance?' he could not help asking.

'This is only my eighth,' said the other and then to stop further discussion: 'Right—here we go.'

[329]

Nicholas was just ahead of the Bomb Disposal Officer as they entered the magazine and it happened. Whether vibration had restarted the mechanism or whether it had been wrongly set could now never be known. As Nicholas and the B.D.O. stepped inside the magazine there was an unearthly violet flash and the bomb went off. It killed Nicholas instantly, blowing his body into fragments but his position at the time of the explosion slightly deflected the pressure wave from the Bomb Disposal Officer who was thrown out into the tunnel and knocked unconscious against a stack of shells. But the force was spent. The tunnel became filled with dust and fumes but there was no subsequent explosion. Part of the ceiling of the vault broke away and a rubble of limestone in which fragments of Nicholas's dead body were disgustingly interred was all that remained of Magazine D.7. But the rest of the tunnel stood firm. The vast content of high explosive which had come so near to blowing the Rock apart remained untouched. The incident of Boothroyd's bomb had come and gone, claiming two lives as the immediate price of its failure and later, when Boothroyd was caught and hanged, a third.

XVII

As 1941 wore on Fortin came to see the bomb incident as a milestone along the road of his Governorship. The declaration of war, the bomb plot and the arrival of the Americans—each represented the ending of an era. Throughout the rest of the war, of course, minor sabotage continued. The disturbing activities of frogmen operating from a disabled and apparently innocent Italian ship interned in Algeciras surprised and bedevilled Hobart and the Security Services but after Boothroyd was executed no major enemy organization functioned within the Fortress of Gibraltar.

Boothroyd was caught because he returned to Gibraltar under the impression that the bomb had failed to explode. Since he was confident that there was nothing to connect him with what had happened, he decided to return as if he had simply been over to Tangier for the week-end. He was allowed to land unmolested. Hobart calculated that he would try and contact Menendez as soon as he could and this proved to be so. As soon as he had dumped his bag at his own lodgings, which were undisturbed and thus aroused in him no suspicion, he went straight along to the tenement block on Grapeshot Hill, knocked at the door of Menendez' flat and was surprised to find it opened at once.

'Come in, Mr. Boothroyd,' said Hobart, 'we're all so glad you came back.'

The room seemed full of Security Police and Boothroyd's first instinct was to cut and run. Then he decided to bluff it out.

'There must be a mistake,' he said, turning to go.

'No, don't go,' Hobart said calmly, the reward for all his work in this one conclusive sentence. 'I have a warrant for your arrest as a traitor.'

The two Spaniards concerned with Menendez in the placing of the bomb were never seen in Gibraltar again. The Bomb Disposal Officer was awarded the George Cross. What remained of Nicholas was buried at the North Front cemetery. The great wheel of the war continued to turn and soon the memory of the Cypriot misfit, the refugee from the Spanish war, the hater of the British Empire, the defender of local civil liberties, the unwilling husband and the desperately unhappy man began to fade from people's minds. Only Rosita and the baby remained, as it were, with the pattern of their lives fused for ever into a different shape.

It became clear to Fortin as the autumn came and went that Jaime was ageing fast. Neither man encouraged an intimate approach. When his Gibraltarian A.D.C. had had his head broken open, thanks largely to his son-in-law and when, in turn, that son-in-law had been blown up by a bomb which he had in a sense helped to place, the effect on both was to inhibit further the relationship. Fortin had made a gesture of sympathy and understanding but Jaime seemed unable to accept it. He preferred the shield of formality. It occurred to Fortin that this attitude disguised a deeper and deeper retreat. Each shock —first of his wife's illness, then of Rosita's enforced marriage, then of the violence done him by the mob and now the death of his son-in-law appeared to drive him further and further into himself. If life was a cave, as Plato's myth described it, then the siege on Jaime was forcing him further and further underground and away from the light. He fulfilled the requirements demanded of him by Government House and his business with mechanical efficiency. His heart, though, seemed turned to stone.

2

A week after the bomb incident the Naval Half-Yearly Promotions fell due on the 30th June and David found himself a Commander. This event coincided with the decision arrived at while in dock at Gibraltar that the engines of H.M.S. *Firesprite* needed a far more extensive overhaul than had appeared at first sight.

This meant a long refit in England. It meant leave and quite possibly for David another appointment. Both the leave and the refit were overdue but David put in a special plea to remain with the ship he had come to know so well and this request was powerfully backed up by his Captain (D). Since the various 'private navies' within the Navy, such as the destroyer and submarine commands, are largely autonomous in the way their officers are appointed and their ships are manned, David was virtually assured before leaving Gibraltar that he would return in *Firesprite* when the refit was completed and would then take over again the half division of 'F' class destroyers which was all that now remained of the original 28th Flotilla.

So, towards the end of August, after a few more local patrols, *Firesprite* was ordered to Portsmouth. Grace knew what was in the wind. She feared and she hated this break. As it drew nearer she could no longer contain herself. Each time she now spent with David ended in a flood of tears. She would cling to him fiercely as though by hanging on to him physically she could somehow or other arrest the course of events.

'Don't take it so personally,' he pleaded, 'you make it worse for both of us.'

'I can't help it, I can't help it,' she cried wretchedly. 'It's no good telling me to be detached and calm and cold. I love you and it's desperate. You're going away. Perhaps I'll never see you again.'

'I think you will.'

'You don't know. Nobody knows. All that is absolutely horribly certain is that you won't be here. You'll be thousands of miles away, out of reach and—I can't bear it—not now.'

On another occasion he said suddenly:

'I believe you're jealous of Pam. You aren't, Grace, are you?'

'Of course I am,' she said with a flash of anger. 'She's your wife and I'm not. Of course I'm jealous of her and envious too.'

'You've no need to be.'

'My dear David,' she said scornfully, 'I'm a woman. I know what she can do if she chooses not to let go.'

'She has none of the things I love in you. She's terribly selfish: she doesn't know how to give. You have a capacity for happiness she won't ever know.'

'She has you.'

'Only in name. You're the one I really love.'

[333]

'I can't help it, David,' she cried miserably, 'she's still your wife and I have a husband in a prison camp.'

'But you *will* marry me, Grace, won't you, as soon as we can both get free? Religion or no religion—whatever the snags and the difficulties?'

That strange look of compassion came into her eyes as though she was experiencing far more than she could possibly express. Instinctively her hand went out to touch his cheek. 'Yes, my darling, as soon as we both get free.'

But then she began crying in a hopeless way as though no one could reach her, as though she had been utterly abandoned, as though nothing was ever going to go right again in her life, as though they had been exchanging words with a surface meaning, both of them knowing in fact that they would never ever really be free.

Then one day *Firesprite* was gone from the pens and Grace knew it would not be a matter of a week or ten days before the rakish little ship would be slipping back into her familiar berth, it would be at least two months and it might be never. Then the loneliness really gripped her and twisted her heart. Both Hobart, who understood in a protective, masculine, bearish way, and Rosita who had explored some of the other backwaters of solitude and despair, came to her aid, making her do things, see things, put out effort into other directions. It helped and she was grateful: but the pain of wanting him returned like a persistent headache only for a time diminished by aspirin. David—David—David—her heart said with its relentless, aching rhythm. She *needed* him and though in one way she knew she had him, in another it was the essential unpossessability of the human heart which grieved, the sensitive coming-to-know that there could be no permanent giving and taking in marriage on the high level, the 'heaven' to which for brief moments their love had given them access.

It was then that she decided she must have a child and a child of his. Perhaps this decision, arrived at so to speak in her marrow, became crystallized through watching Rosita out of the corner of her eye. Rosita, it struck her, had grown far beyond the actual experiences she had had. Grace could scarcely recall even how she had looked in that last frivolous summer of the

[334]

peace, so long ago now, when the trivial round of parties and social life was all that mattered, when the impact of Heart Throb Number One had been a joke, not to be taken seriously when set against the importance of a match with young Juan Giberti or Carlos Emerson-Lopez or even 'the new A.D.C.' their mother was always expecting. How changed it all was! The initial plunging mistake following upon the rocket trail of passion, the hopeless straining to make Nicholas something he could never be, the long humiliating self-abasement of living in San Roque with an uncaring husband only a few miles away, a husband who never troubled to see her and who had no real use for her at all.

As Grace thought back on it all, her respect for Rosita grew. She could have taken it—and their mother's febrile, bed-bound taunts—so very differently. Rosita never complained, never thought herself maltreated by Fate. She had done something by worldly standards stupid, by her own essence real and necessary: she had seen the price to pay and she had paid it and now, Grace was just beginning to see, she had got something out of it very rich and rare. Now, when the events leading up to Nicholas's death had been broken to her, the grief her heart felt was of a different, rarer quality. The grief was genuine but it seemed actually to feed her. Watching her and reflecting on this, Grace found herself astonished and full of love for her sister which also was of a different, rarer quality. And the little child, now just beginning to walk, was the burning spot upon which these rays of love were focused. It was the child that mattered.

3

Meanwhile, back in Portsmouth, David had not faltered in his resolve as Grace had more than half-expected him to do. He had not run away and he had not deferred the painful business which he knew must be put into train. Pam had been waiting for him with a hyper-anxiety, a brittle, nervous gaiety which deceived neither of them. She lived in the Wren's Quarters. For a married woman this was a chilling experience and when he collected her the first evening he had had to fight back his pity. He had asked her to dinner at the Queens where he had taken a room and there during the meal had managed to make her relax and admit into their conversation what both of them knew to be true, that they no longer had anything to say to each other, that their marriage to each other had in reality long been dead and that now to have gone through the conventional motions of making love to one another simply because they were married and had not seen each other for some time would be a travesty and in a way a form of adultery.

So well did they comprehend these things about each other that it astonished both of them and in their joint understanding the whole project was nearly wrecked. But as the evening wore on David talked to her of his feelings for Grace and she of her own for the Paymaster-Lieutenant. Then they were invaded by a sadness at the things the war had done to them both and to their marriage and Pam cried a little over the coffee and the brandy which followed. But they were different tears from the ones she had shed all that time ago at Scapa. Both of them had grown and she cried now not because of frustration but at the sadness of their not having grown together.

'I did love you, darling,' she said, 'simply enormously. I thought you were dreamy but you know, all the time, I knew it would never work. You were always the serious responsible naval officer—in a way you symbolized all the sort of thing I've been trying to get away from all my life.'

'But surely your . . .' He hesitated, not knowing quite how to describe the Paymaster-Lieutenant. 'I mean, he's in the Navy too, isn't he? I mean the R.N. It's his career.'

'Yes, darling, but he won't be for long. He hates it. He's going to be an actor after the war. He's creative.' She paused and lit a cigarette. 'Really, you know, that sort of life is far more "me" than this,' she waved vaguely at the dark panelling of the grill-room, presumably indicating the dockyard port which lay outside.

'Oh! I see,' said David. 'Does he want to marry you?'

'Yes, of course,' she said but there was a tiny hesitancy in her voice. 'I don't know that I ought to, though. I don't want to hold him back in any way at the start of a new career.'

'For heaven's sake,' David expostulated, 'the war is nowhere near over yet: he's going to have to wait some time to start that career.'

'Yes I know. It's a big sacrifice for him.'

'Hm!' said David, thinking privately that a bigger sacrifice for the Paymaster-Lieutenant would be a sea-going appointment and some of the gruelling experiences the *Firesprite* had undergone.

'Do you want to marry him?' he went on after a pause.

'Yes,' she said firmly, 'yes, I do.'

'Well then, will you divorce me if I give you the evidence.'

It was logical and he said it as gently as he could but the tears burst out of her eyes. She wiped them away with her handkerchief and sat looking at the remains of the meal, a forlorn little figure in her trim Wren officer's uniform with its short skirt and tight waist, with her hair as long as she dared stretch the regulations, with the bright red finger-nails forbidden by the Superintendent of the Women's Royal Naval Service—and, hidden behind this outer costume, the frail, pretty, empty-headed girl he had once loved so much.

'God!' he muttered, 'the things life does to you. . . .' The *Bismarck* episode was nothing compared with this.

'I hate it too,' she murmured, managing to beat back her tears. 'I hate it. I wish so often I could die in the air-raids—poum! like that: but it never happens that way, does it?' Then she looked him straight in the eyes through the sparkle of her tears.

'She'd be very good for you, darling,' she said, 'and if she's willing to divorce that pin-up boy and marry you—in spite of being a Catholic, she must really love you.'

'I think she does,' David said. 'I think we both of us do.'

'Well, then . . .' She clutched and unclutched her little handkerchief, in reality relieved and yet hating the emotional drag of it all.

'But I don't think I'd ask you,' David said, 'if I really felt this chap wasn't going to stand up properly for you—I mean, if he's only thinking of himself he's bound to let you down. Perhaps he only wants to go to bed with you.'

'No,' said Pam, 'we needn't go into that side of things. Basil's not sure of himself—not in the way you are, darling, over the sacred Navy. Of course after a time he'll want to be free of me but in a funny way underneath he won't. He needs me: he really does, far more than you do or ever did—and I think I'm the person to give him what he needs in the way he needs it. Isn't it queer to be talking like this, David? I know I'm going to hate it when you take me back to the Wren's Quarters instead of going upstairs to bed in the old, familiar way. But at the same time I know it's right—and I still love you, David: I always shall—only now it's different.'

'Yes,' said David, 'it's different all right.' At that moment he did not feel far off tears himself.

'Well, let's get it over with,' she said a little later, 'I loathe and detest things dragged out. You know that. I'll do what you asked me a little while back. I . . . I shan't like it and I shan't stop loving you but it's better it should be tidy. Now let's get a taxi very very quickly and you can take me home—if you can call the Wren's Quarters home.'

Then with a resoluteness in which David suddenly saw the generations of naval forebears which had gone into her make-up, that Navy she was so anxious to escape from and yet which bound her in so many obvious and subtle ways, she walked out of the room her head high and her body erect.

4

During the three months when *Firesprite*'s basic refit was in progress, the view from Gibraltar was somewhat more tranquil. A thousand miles to the east, Malta was being successfully maintained and even a small cruiser force, Force K, had now been based upon it, to harry the Axis supply-line to North Africa. The Eighth Army had begun to advance. Tobruk was soon to be relieved and, by the end of the year, Benghazi would have been retaken. The United States, though still technically neutral, was hovering on the brink of war. The Atlantic Charter had been drafted and construction of the first 312 Liberty ships put in hand.

From Gibraltar itself Force H, though the famous *Ark Royal* was at last sunk in November, was still guarding the western end of the Mediterranean and keeping an eye on a possible break-out of the German battle-cruisers from Brest. Though supplies were now sent all the way round the Cape of Good Hope, the build-up of our Middle East forces continued. Back at home agitation for a second front in Europe had begun. The key to it all, in fact, was Russia.

In the Mediterranean, as Fortin had correctly concluded, this apparent lull could be attributed to the withdrawal of the Luftwaffe and the losses being sustained by the Germans in Russia. Air power, and to be practical, only German air power, was what mattered. The Italian Air Force could be bluffed or frightened away as their Navy had been: the Germans never.

In Gibraltar the Royal Air Force was more and more in evidence. By now the North Front had been completely transformed. All trace of the race-course with the trees and verdure of the Victoria Gardens beyond had now been obliterated. Indeed, it required a strong imagination to recall that a bare eighteen months ago the last horse-race had been run. At first the airstrip had reached only to the road leading across the neutral territory to Spain: but heavier aircraft made its extension inevitable. By now it was well out into the Bay. The rugger field lying athwart the runway had continued to be used when aircraft were not actually landing or taking off but now it, too, received its death sentence and to make the occasion the goalposts were piped back into the Garrison to the strains of the 'Dead March' played by a lone piper of the Garrison Independent Company. This new and inexplicable British ceremony caused German observers in Spain a great deal of puzzlement. Was it, they queried, designed to camouflage some other and perhaps more significant event? The British with their regimental mascots had a well-known sentimentality towards goats, domestic animals, their stupid apes, etc. That was understood. But goalposts? What was the significance of that?

The autumn saw Boothroyd tried and sentenced to death, Mr. Pierrepoint being flown out from England for the hanging. The removal of this abscess from the invisible body of the Rock had an all-round effect on morale. The nadir had been reached in the summer but by late November 1941 the pendulum had already begun its swing in the other direction. Boredom and inaction continued their sapping effect but despite that morale in Gibraltar continued to improve. In addition, the Russian campaign, by drawing away from the west the main German effort, lessened the pressure on Spain and thus also the threat to Gibraltar.

Through it all Fortin sat in his spartan room at Government House, watching and assessing the turn of events, taking in, digesting and transmitting the reports made to him from the fortress and base he commanded, fitting the changing condition of Gibraltar into its immediate surroundings and then in deeper perspective into the general scene, entertaining visitors from the United Kingdom on their way out and other returning personalities headed for London from the east. Cabinet ministers, journalists, star entertainers, together with Admirals, Generals and Air-Marshals, all came and went as they do in most Government Houses all over the world. Freddy Small-bones cleared, refilled and cleared away again the 'In' and 'Out' trays on his desk: Dicky Seale and Jaime knocked at the door, introduced and later removed the human traffic passing through a Governor's purview. Spitfire Funds were opened and closed: E.N.S.A. parties came and went: the Military Governor of Algeciras continued his formal calls which Fortin reciprocated: in the Dockyard the incessant noise of air-compressors and the resultant tunnelling out of the Rock proceeded: a bad landslide took place at the north-east corner of the Rock, cutting off Catalan Bay and necessitating the making of an emergency tunnel: out in the Bay the sleek Catalinas took off, patrolled west into the Atlantic and east into the Mediterranean and then like slow silver birds landed again: the Bay itself drained and then filled up with shipping in a regular rhythm and every day, as usual, rain or shine, over ten thousand Spaniards entered the fortress in the morning and left again at night.

It was now nearly eight months since Fortin had suffered a malarial attack. His health was indeed better than when he arrived and in a series of private notes from the War Cabinet offices he was again being sounded out for an appointment in the Middle East. The idea of returning to the Arab world and to the desert which had been so great a part of his life became more and more attractive yet still, inside himself, something held him back. He did not know what it was but he sensed that there was still some further duty to fulfil in Gibraltar. He knew it was there but on Sunday, 7th December 1941, the day Japan put Pearl Harbour into the history books he could not possibly guess that it would be to pass through Gibraltar the greatest amphibious operation which to date the world had ever known. For Operation Torch still lay eleven months ahead.

5

Pearl Harbour was an event on the scale of the world itself. At this point in time the story of humanity veered in a slightly new direction, in another sense it was at this milestone that the outcome of the war was no longer in doubt. From the moment the United States entered the war, the question was no longer 'whether', but simply 'how' and 'when'.

The news of the Japanese attack did not reach Europe till the evening of that fateful Sunday. In Gibraltar the week-end showed no outward sign of being unusual. Things were quiet at the Convent and Jaime had invited Fortin and Seale for Sunday luncheon at San Roque. Hobart was away in Madrid till the evening: no V.I.P.s were expected, and except for a Malta convoy assembling in the bay nothing of importance was on the Short List.

Grace had come into Gibraltar with her father on the Sunday morning. They had both gone to Mass and then he had had something to do at Government House, she had looked round at the office in the Dockyard where a special consignment of comforts had to be ready for the convoy that evening. There by luck she found a letter awaiting her from David. She did not stop to consume it then, since she was in a hurry, but put it away in her handbag intending to read it when she could be quite alone later in the day. There had been a long gap since the last letter from David had arrived and she had begun to wonder what had happened. She knew the refit was over and the future still unknown. This new letter might contain a clue.

The power of such a letter was extraordinary. She almost purred with pleasure as she picked up her father and drove back with him to San Roque slightly ahead of the Governor. She had had a letter from David. A letter from someone you loved acted like a diamond into which you imagined an infinity of light had been compressed. Bring it out into the light of your consciousness and it could blaze at you like a tiny sun, your love creating and recreating itself in a seemingly endless sparkle.

The good state engendered by this unopened letter yet to be enjoyed radiated from her and affected Jaime, as she sat beside him in the car. Normally they talked very little to each other, each being reserved, each a little wary of the other's insight. Today, however, Jaime was in a talkative mood. He had long been mulling over a plan for getting Edie away to his brother's in Madrid and now that the tide of anti-British feeling in Spain was ebbing, he thought it a good time for putting it into effect.

'It would give you and Rosey a break too,' he said with a sideways glance at her, 'I think we're all a bit stale.'

'I'm all right,' Grace answered cheerfully, 'considering the war and all that.'

Jaime drove on for a while in silence, then suddenly said:

'How's David getting along? Have you heard from him recently?'

'He's fine,' Grace replied and then on impulse, 'he's getting divorced.'

'Oh!' said Jaime imperceptibly stiffening, 'I see.'

'Do you, Father? I wonder. Suppose I told you I wanted to as well? What would you say to that?'

'You know that's impossible for us,' Jaime said gravely and wondered what would come next. He did not have long to wait.

'No, Father, it's not at all impossible. In fact that's what I intend to do as soon as the war's over and Lance is released from prison.'

There was another long pause.

'Is that all your religion means to you?' he said in the end.

'No, Father,' Grace said with an emotional calm which even a few months ago would not have been possible. 'It means

[342]

simply that I'm growing up. You know as well as I do that I can probably get an annulment. I think I could prove I was forced into marriage with Lance by Mother against my will. It would cost money, Father,' she went on with a slightly cynical smile, 'but the Barbarossa family resources can no doubt manage a suitable contribution to the Papal Exchequer—and that is what I should ask you to do if I wished to go on being a hypocrite. And possibly you'd do it, Father, for me—especially if Mother is no longer there to resist it. However I don't wish to go on being a hypocrite. I married Lance and the marriage was properly consummated by all normal standards. But through no fault of mine—and possibly not of his either—it hasn't worked out. Our marriage is as dead as a corpse and was so from the very first days. God didn't make that marriage, Mother did. When I was a girl, educated as I was, how could I possibly know what was right when my heart said one thing and the Church another? Now I'm a woman and I know.' She looked at his troubled face and then gently touched his hand. 'I shan't ask you to go through the farce and expense of procuring an annulment: I shall simply get divorced, Father, and if David still wants me I shall marry him just as soon as I can.'

'Then you put yourself above God and His Church. I've never been a very religious man, Grace, but I wouldn't dare to do that.'

'It isn't that,' she said very quietly and gently, 'but sometimes you're told things in your heart. Sometimes you can really *know* . . . and when something direct like that happens, there isn't any conflict any more, you simply know. . . .'

She knew he would never understand. He expected to be argued with, pleaded with, apologized to: he could not comprehend that there are inner experiences which melt away all the anxieties of a lower and more outward level.

'You see, Father,' she finished off simply, 'when girls are brought up as Rosey and I were, your birthright is stolen from you before you're awake. The Church tells you and the Church knows best. But suppose you suddenly wake up? Suppose you suddenly realized you're in prison and that the Church is one of the ways of keeping you there, docile, subservient, afraid? Suppose you realize that sometimes the Church

[343]

doesn't know best? Suppose you realize that God is here in your heart and that you can hear Him if you listen and that it's nothing whatever to do with going to Mass, nothing to do with anyone outside yourself, least of all your familiar comforting or frightening priest—but that it's to do with you and you alone? Well, then, Father, what happens then?'

'I don't know,' Jaime said severely. 'Such an experience has never happened to me. But then I would never put myself above the Church.'

There was a long silence and it was not until they had turned into the drive of the San Roque house that Grace spoke again.

'You see, Father, I'm no longer afraid. It isn't defiance, as it would have been only a few months ago, as I'm sure the Church will say it is now. There's no inner struggle in me about this at all. I just *know* about something and I'm no longer afraid. You understand that, Father? I've found myself and I'm no longer afraid.'

As they got out of the car Rosita came along the terrace to meet them. From the way she walked Grace could tell there was something wrong.

'Mother's had another attack,' she said, 'about twenty minutes ago. I've sent for Doctor Gonzalez but she looks pretty bad.'

They ran upstairs. Although this event had long been anticipated, it was still a frightening thing when it happened. As soon as she entered the room she knew her mother was dying and when the doctor arrived shortly afterwards he confirmed it.

'I'd better go and fetch Father Drayton,' Grace said. This meant another trip to Gibraltar but old Father Drayton was undoubtedly the priest her mother would have wanted had she been able to speak.

So, glad to escape from the heavy atmosphere and the explanations to Fortin which would soon be necessary, she set off back to Gibraltar. Retracing the journey physically, at the same time she went over what she had said to her father, remembering her feelings, her tone of voice and her father's reactions and wondering whether there had been any profit at all in speaking as she had. Perhaps she had simply given offence.

[344]

Certainly nothing was definite: nothing was settled. She was still married and so was David.

And yet in a way by not dodging the issue any more, by taking responsibility for a conclusion she had arrived at inside herself after much searching of the heart, she had been rewarded with a feeling of freedom and lightness. It was a visible step on the ladder to becoming herself. How long she could remain on that step and what the eventual outcome would be she did not know. But not to be afraid of speaking out to her father, had been like diving for the first time from a greater height than she had so far dared, and doing it with success. What would now be the state of affairs when her mother died? Were she and Rosita to stay on in the San Roque house? She felt certain her father would want to close it down and send his two daughters away to Madrid. In turn she was equally determined not to go.

When she reached Father Drayton's lodgings she found him waiting outside with instructions that she was to go round by the Cathedral as the Bishop himself would come. A few minutes later she was again driving back to San Roque with the revered and beloved head of the Roman Catholic Church in Gibraltar seated with old Father Drayton in the back of the car. Following hard on the heels of the conversation she had had with her father it struck her as ironic that almost instantly events should bring her face to face with this man of spiritual authority, this old friend of the family, possessed of an experience and a depth she could never hope to achieve, who was coming out of his own volition to administer the last rites to her mother—that mother who, in a sense, had been the worst enemy her children could have had. Before she would have felt guilty and ashamed but now she was astounded to find that the new strength she had been given preserved her—neither defiant nor afraid but simply calm and watchful.

6

Edie died that same evening. She never regained consciousness and so was unaware of the honour done her by the Bishop, an honour she would so much have relished in life. The local

[345]

priest was summoned and indeed at one stage the house seemed filled with priests, Father O'Reilly, too, having come of his own accord from Gibraltar. She would be buried in the family mausoleum started by Jaime's father in San Roque.

As the daylight faded bad weather set in and when, in the upper room overlooking the Bay, the death rattle came, a fierce storm had begun to beat upon the window-panes. The uncertain Spanish electricity supply failed as it so often did under the slightest stress and the house reverted to oil-lamps and candles. Fuel was as rare and costly in Spain as food these days and very often the drawing-room fire was not lit for economy's sake. Tonight, however, some instinct of defiance against the physical death then present in the house made Grace have a big fire blazing in the drawing-room, a fire reminiscent of the days when Grace and Rosita had been children and a king still sat on the throne of Spain.

There was much coming and going in the house that night and in view of what happened this was just as well. The corpse was laid out and measured, her things set in order. News of a death spreads quickly in a village the size of San Roque and a stream of callers began to come and go. The storm and the wind grew worse.

Though their mother's death had long been expected, they were all of them stunned in different ways. The most ordinary household activity now took place against the realization that upstairs *la señora* lay dead. Jaime fell to a silent brooding in front of the fire: Rosita, again privately glad to have the child to attend to as she had so recently when news of Nicholas's death had struck her, began to let her thoughts play on the future. Upon Grace, now the lady of the house in fact, as she had for so long been behind the scenes, a sense of reaching ahead into time visited her so that what followed, though a tremendous shock, was in some extraordinary way already there and known to her.

Between eight and nine that evening Hobart took advantage of his standing invitation and dropped in unexpectedly on his way back by road from Madrid. On hearing what had happened he said he would go on to Gibraltar straight away. But Grace, with an affirmative nod from Jaime, asked him to stay

[346]

for dinner and he was thus very much to hand when Maria, one of the servants came running in great agitation to summon Grace to the kitchen. The storm was now at its height and since the servant appeared to be inarticulate, Grace went along anticipating in her mind the disasters which could have happened.

The first thing she saw in the kitchen was a *guardia civil* whom she knew to be the maid's fiancé, the second, dressed in nondescript peasant clothes, his skin tanned like a gipsy's and his hair dyed black was Lance.

7

After a moment's paralysis her brain raced as it never had before. Was the *guardia civil* here officially? Was there immediate danger? Whose side was he on? Lance had his back against the kitchen wall between window and door, instinctively taking the safest position in the room should anyone burst in from the outside. He was soaked to the skin and the first impression she had was of fear. He stood tensely still like an animal aware of being stalked. His eyes, though, were granite-hard and he made no sign of recognition. The *guardia civil* was the first to speak. He did not smile either but he was evidently disposed to do business.

'This man says you can vouch for him, señora. I intercepted him on the road. I should take him to headquarters, you understand, but I have left my companion to guard the bridge and I have brought him here because he says he knows the señora's family. Now I must return on duty. You will realize, señora, that these are dangerous times. It will be very unwise if anyone in this house should speak about tonight. We are all in each other's hands.' The strong, natural dignity of the Spanish peasant sounded strangely in keeping with this extraordinary situation, with the storm raging outside, with the two candles guttering on the kitchen table, with her mother lying dead upstairs.

'You are Pepe Antonio, isn't that so? and you are from Logroño,' Grace asked. The *guardia civil* nodded gravely. He would need to be very well paid, but to offer him money at this point would be fatal. He must not be humiliated in any way in front of Maria.

'I understand that the señora's mother has just died,' he went on and crossed himself. 'God rest her soul. It is a bad time for all of us, señora. Permit me to offer my humblest sympathy. Now I must return to my duty.'

'It is a terrible night for guarding a bridge,' Grace said. 'Will you not have a glass of cognac before you go ? Or perhaps you will take the bottle so that your companion, too, may warm himself?'

The cat-and-mouse game continued but Grace knew there would be no additional danger manufactured by Pepe Antonio.

'Thank you,' he said, 'the señora is very thoughtful. Then later I will bring back the glasses.' He gave the flicker of a glance towards Lance by which Grace understood that there was very little time. Lance must be gone by the time the *guardia civil* paid his next visit. The stroke of luck of Hobart being present at this moment with a British Government car was extraordinary.

All this time Lance had not spoken or moved. Pepe Antonio bowed and began to walk to the door. Grace told Maria to see to the brandy, again thanked the *guardia civil* and then when the door had closed behind them flew over to Lance.

'Are you all right? You're drenched. You're not hurt?'

She hugged him tight but there was no answering gesture. He kissed her formally on the cheek as though they were acquaintances meeting again after a few weeks' absence.

'I'm all right but I haven't much time. I have to get to a certain house in La Línea by nine-thirty.'

'Hobart is here,' Grace said. 'There's a fire in the drawing-room. Father will lend you some clothes.'

She led the way along to the drawing-room, her thoughts reeling. David at once came into her mind. With Lance free, what was to happen about David? David—Lance: Lance—David, her brain helplessly repeated the names as they went along the dark corridor to the low, white drawing-room. Then as she opened the door and went inside the immediate aim reasserted itself. Lance had to reach Gibraltar. Nothing else mattered for the moment but that.

[348]

'We have a visitor, Father,' she said, 'a very unexpected visitor.'

Her father stood up with his back to the fire peering at the door. Lance had instinctively kept back within cover of the shadow from the hall outside till he had seen the room for himself. He had evidently learnt a lot on his long journey back from Germany. At the same time Hobart had made himself all but invisible in the shadow of a tallboy. Grace noted these little actions in passing. They added to the tension in the room. The fear Lance had exuded in the kitchen now caught her up as she saw Hobart's hand go inside his tunic. She had never realized before that Hobart—dear, quiet, kindly Hobart—always carried a gun. How odd! And there they stood, Lance lurking at the door and Hobart perfectly still and watching by the window.

'Who is it?' said Jaime. 'Come on in whoever you are.'

'It's Lance,' she said, taking him by the arm and drawing him into the room. 'He needs some dry clothes.'

'Good heavens above!' said Hobart, relaxing and coming to the fire, 'that's an achievement!'

'I must get on as soon as I can,' Lance muttered. He seemed to talk without moving his lips. He still looked furtive and afraid.

'You'll be safe here,' said Jaime, 'certainly for the present. Have you any papers?'

'A Spanish identity card and worker's permit. I got them in the north.'

'Well, then. . . ?'

'There are two others. They'll be expecting me in Calle de la Virgen, La Línea.'

'English?'

'One English, one Dutchman—if he's still with us, that is.'

'Oh!' said Hobart, watching him acutely, 'where did you pick him up?'

'In France. He seems to know the ropes very well. A little too well.'

'But this is the end of the run. If he's come as far as this, then surely. . . .'

'Exactly,' Lance interrupted, 'the frontier at La Línea is the end of the run, isn't it? Once he knows how escaped prisoners of war cross that frontier, he'll know it all, won't he? And if he should happen to be working for the other side. . . .'

'Father,' Grace cut in, 'he must have some dry clothes.' She poured out a stiff brandy and gave it to Lance but he waved it away.

'I'll wait for all that till I'm safe in Gibraltar again.'

'Well, then, some food?'

'No, I'm all right, thanks.' He might have been a complete stranger and a rather hostile one. There was no trace of that once famous charm of his. The four of them looked at each other, each guarded in a different way. 'And don't worry about the clothes. I'm hardened to this'—he went on, indicating his water-logged suit—'if I was going to catch my death of cold, I'd have died long ago.'

'Then I think we'll go now,' Hobart said firmly, and without further ado they went to the door, got into the car and drove off. The gale still blew in gustily from the Bay.

Number 17 Calle de la Virgen was of course known to Hobart. Virgin Street backed on to Gibraltar Street and together they formed the spine of La Línea's red-light district. Most of the brothels, which were under direct Spanish police supervision, were anti-British listening posts but Number 17 was owned and run by a woman well paid by the British Security Service. It had been of secret use in the Spanish Civil War. Now it was one of the terminal collecting points for the escape route through France and Spain.

The short drive into La Línea was eerie because in addition to the danger which threatened, the electricity supply was still not working and only an occasional window had a pale candle or oil-lamp burning inside. Hobart stopped the car at one corner of a small derelict park, told Lance how to reach Number 17 Calle de la Virgen and said he would await them. The rain beat slantwise across the street and La Línea was deserted. As Lance got out of the car, Hobart slipped the gun into his hand.

'Careful,' he said. 'You may need it for your Dutchman—if he's still there.'

'Thanks,' said Lance and disappeared into the rain and the

night. Hobart lit a cigarette and sat waiting. He had had a frustrating time in Madrid and had privately counted on an evening's relaxation in San Roque. Now there was this unexpected situation. He thought with surprise of Lance's escape and with admiration of his long, dangerous journey from Germany to Gibraltar. A series of minor miracles must have conspired to produce this extraordinary result—and how different a person this was, this toughened young man to whom he had just lent his revolver, from the effete, effeminate Flag-Lieutenant, the Boofles of Fat Barclay's time. Yet what was it about Lance he did not trust? He shrugged his shoulders and put it once again at the back of his mind. All the world was a stage, he reminded himself, though some of the odd parts one was called on to play in a lifetime would have astonished the Bard himself. He thought of Cornelia and the children in that quiet New England house and here he was waiting in a dark street in a foreign country to help smuggle across the frontier some escaping prisoners of war amongst whom was a possible spy. It was the sort of adventure you read about in a boy's magazine yet here he was, a sedate father of three, daily involved to a greater or lesser degree with skulduggery of one sort or another in situations where the ready use of a revolver was taken for granted and where a decision to destroy a human life was either instantaneous or else too fatally late. Afterwards looking back on that night, it seemed as though the thought presaged the event for this was to be the first time he had ever killed another man.

His meditation was interrupted by the arrival of Lance and the other two. Lance got in the front with Hobart, laying the revolver between them.

'I was evidently wrong,' he said with a slight jerk of his head at the Dutchman, 'everything in the garden's lovely.'

Hobart turned and took a quick glance at the other two in the back. The Dutchman was in a highly agitated state. All were soaking wet and gusts of rain continued to beat down on the car.

'Now,' said Hobart, starting the engine, 'when we get to the frontier this is what will happen. The Spanish know this car and they know me—but they have to have time to recognize me. So I shall slow down, lean out of the window to identify myself and then as they walk over to me drive on. They're quite used to that and as this is a government car they won't take any action. There's a rug in the back—you two get under it and as far down on the floor as possible. You keep out of sight here in the front, Lance. Right, get yourselves set now.'

It was a roomy left-hand drive Humber and they were soon hidden on the floor as directed. Hobart pulled his two suitcases on top of them and then drove off. At the frontier the weather was keeping the guards inside and the gate was shut. Hobart turned the headlights full on and a sour-looking soldier came out of the guard-room towards the car. Hobart quickly got out, revealing himself in the headlights and making a remark about the weather in the hope of deflecting away the soldier's attention but the soldier came on nonetheless and was just about to open the nearside rear door when a voice from the guard-room told him not to worry '*el señor coronel*' but to open the gate and let the car through. Hobart recognized the voice, called out his thanks, hoping that the enormous relief he felt was not too obvious, and then as the gates were opened he got back into the car and drove through. The lights in Gibraltar had not failed in the storm and since there was no air-raid and therefore no blackout they seemed to twinkle with an especial brightness as they began driving across the neutral ground away from darkened Spain.

'All right,' said Hobart, 'you can sit up. We're nearly there.'

Then it happened. The Dutchman sat up with a jerk forcing the suitcase which had been on top of him against his companion in the back, snatched open the door and jumped out, giving Lance a good whack on the back of the neck as he went.

'Christ! You dirty double-crosser,' said Lance and grabbed towards the gun. But Hobart already had it in his right hand, jammed the brakes on hard and then whipped out of the car after him. The man was running back towards Spain.

'Stop!' yelled Hobart. 'Stop where you are!'

But the man paid no attention and continued to run. Then in a split second came the dreaded decision he knew he must take. Hobart raised his revolver, took careful aim and fired three times. The man stumbled briefly and then fell to the

[352]

ground. By this time Lance and the other Englishman were out of the car beside Hobart.

'Get him,' shouted Hobart. 'I'll back the car.'

This had taken place about halfway across the neutral territory and, in the wind and the rain, it was unlikely that the shots had been heard, but time was of the essence. Hobart backed the car, by now shaking wildly himself. When he got the car back to where the man had fallen, he found Lance and the other standing over a corpse.

'Get him into the back,' Hobart said, 'quick as you can. I don't want the Spaniards in on this.'

A few minutes later they were across and safely home within the boundaries of the Rock. No one spoke. The awful thing that had happened held them in a paralysed silence until the rough, good-natured British frontier guards began the restorative process.

'There's a cup of tea in the guard-room, sir,' said the officer-in-charge to Hobart and the other two. 'If you'd like to go inside while we clear up this lot in the back of the car. Have you heard the news? The Japs have attacked the American Fleet at Pearl Harbour. The United States has declared war. The Yanks are in it at last.'

TR—M*

XVIII

THAT night as the storm blew itself out a number of people both in San Roque and Gibraltar tried to digest the events of that extraordinary day. In Gibraltar, in his little room in the Bomb House Lane, Hobart fortified himself with Scotch, attempting to rationalize to himself the first human life he had ever taken. He stared into the fire and ached for the presence of Cornelia who alone would have understood, alone could have helped to comfort him through this intense loneliness in which he found himself. But Cornelia was thousands of miles away in a country itself at that moment reeling from an outrage.

The firelight flickered and the whisky tasted sour in the throat. Tomorrow he would make his examinations and prepare his report. Thank God he had someone of the calibre of Fortin to go to, a man who had himself been through this particular testing himself, a man with the power to absolve. He got up suddenly, went through into his bathroom and was violently sick.

Elsewhere in Gibraltar Lance lay in bed safe and unafraid for the first time for six weeks. He too was almost at breaking-point but the reasons were entirely different. This should have been a night of deliverance, a night when the long anxiety was ended, but the dead Dutchman, though now proved by his actions to have been what they had suspected, lay heavy on his conscience. It was Lance who had allowed the Dutchman to attach himself to their party, Lance who had let him in. What worried him most of all, however, was the meeting with Grace and this because in fact it had meant absolutely nothing at all. She had made a gesture of warmth and of welcome but he could not respond. In a way it was a relief. In another it was more disturbing than he cared to admit. His restless mind went over the vivid and separate incidents of his escape from the Oflag and those of his long journey south. It was like an endlessly repeating gramophone record culminating in the emotional blankness of the meeting with Grace and then in that frightened-looking, twisted face—that face that had so recently meant so much to him—lying in its pool of blood on the neutral ground as the storm raged and Hobart had backed the car to where the body had fallen. Now it was over and he was free once more on British soil. Yet he could not relax. The dead man had a greater hold over him than his live wife, traitor though he knew him to be, the dead man with the soft, hurt eyes and the athlete's body. He did not want to take the sleeping-pills the doctor had given him. But the dead man had left him his legacy of guilt and from that there was no escape. He could not relax. So, after fighting it for a time, he took the pills and soon the drowsiness came. There was a merciful limit to what one's conscience could accept.

Over in San Roque there were no sleeping-pills for either Jaime or Grace. With Edie's death Jaime had a kind of prescience that he, too, would soon be finished with it all. That was now a comfort. He felt old and tired, dogged by a feeling that the world was out of joint and that both he and Edie had failed in their allotted tasks. He thought of the conversation he had had with Grace in the car and then of the miraculous appearance of Lance out of the heart of the storm. Well, that was her life—her problem. But then there was Rosita, too—his pretty child with all that disintegrating story of Nicholas behind her. He and Edie had failed with their children: they had failed both to give them what they needed and to make them what they had intended them to be.

Now Edie was gone and soon, pray God, he would be allowed to lay down his burden as well. The Bishop had understood. He had turned to Jaime just before getting back into his car. 'We do what we can,' he had said, 'by our lights and to the best of our ability and God in His Mercy judges us by the sincerity of our efforts. No one man can put the world or his family to rights. Do not distress yourself too much,' he had said and Jaime had felt a moment's peace in the smile the old Bishop had given him as he had got into the car and had been driven away into the stormy evening, back to the Rock, back to the war and the world as it lay around them in its dire and terrible condition. God in His Mercy would wipe away all tears from the eyes, but as Jaime lay in the familiar darkness staring out at the dimly seen trees, he prayed in his heart that his own time would not be too long in coming.

Grace, too, lay sleepless and disturbed. She thought of her mother, quiet and still, with the candles burning through the night beside her yellowing face. She felt a great remorse in her heart, a penitence and a guilt. What was it she had to learn? Should she have been the docile, obedient cypher her mother had wanted her to be? Was it totally wrong to revolt, to struggle against her fate as she had done? Was she to give up David and try again with Lance? Nothing in her meeting with him so unexpectedly that night could give her the sign she was awaiting. Yet *was* she defying God's Holy Law? She seized up David's letter—so long out of date—and held it crushed in her hand—but no answer came. Tomorrow she must go into Gibraltar and face up to Lance, face up to whatever it was that Fate intended her to do. She did not know that at that very minute the gate in the boom defences of Gibraltar had been opened to admit into the harbour the battered little destroyer fresh from another Atlantic gale with its severe-looking Captain so intimately there at the very centre of her heart. H.M.S. *Firesprite* had returned to the Rock to become once again an active member of the famous Force H.

2

The next day, while Jaime and Rosita occupied themselves at San Roque with the funeral arrangements, Grace hurried into Gibraltar on a crisp, windy December morning, as disturbed in her mind as she had been the evening before.

First of all she went to her office in the Dockyard to explain that she would be away for a while. Her absence would not upset things unduly. A mother's death and a husband's arrival in Gibraltar as an escaped prisoner of war put into perspective the packing up of 'comforts'. She tidied her desk and then just as she was leaving for the Line Wall Road house, David walked into the office. For a moment the shock stunned her. Then throwing discretion to the winds they flew into each other's arms.

For what seemed an age they remained locked together, saying nothing but rocking gently, hugging and stroking each other. Grace's 'slave', the old dockyard pensioner who bumbled about with cups of tea surprised them in this position but they paid no attention.

'Mother died yesterday and Lance has escaped and is here in Gibraltar,' Grace said. 'But . . . *you're* here, my darling, you're here.'

But that sparkling initial moment of clinging when the world was created anew could not be held beyond its time. The Gibraltar day forced them apart. Both had their different duties to fulfil as elsewhere Hobart was attending the inquest and making his report on the shooting of the Dutchman, as Lance was equipping himself with new uniform at Gieves, as Fortin was studying the reports of Pearl Harbour which had come through in the night, as the Heads of the three Services were assessing the American Declaration of War in terms of Gibraltar and the Mediterranean.

As the day wore on and mechanically she fulfilled the various functions expected of her, making arrangements for Lance to stay at the Line Wall Road house and helping with the Gibraltar end of her mother's funeral arrangements, she knew that a show-down was in the offing. She and Lance and David must have it out. Since Lance had appeared at San Roque and all through the long night she had been wondering if he could stand the shock but when she saw him briefly in the morning she realized that it would not even be a shock. He did not care. He had always been distant: now he was glacial. Mastery of the fear he had experienced escaping and surviving had given him a rock-like exterior through which it was impossible to detect any emotion at all. She sat spellbound and full of admiration at the story of his escape. It seemed extraordinary that he should once have been nicknamed 'Boofles'.

But it was not going to be easy. He had hardened all round. She might try to make him welcome, to show her astonishment at his exploits, to offer him affection but he remained cold and inert. The pretty-boy-mother's-darling was gone for ever and Grace now found herself facing someone as grave as David but with a frigid contempt and sarcasm which before

[357]

had been trivial but now was at the core of the man. A sudden glint in his face reminded her of Nicholas. Perhaps it was that which Rosita had once found attractive for a very short time—that glowering scorn with which he looked out on the world.

'Now that your mother's dead,' he said, 'there's no reason why you shouldn't come home to England, is there?'

'Except that I don't want to.'

'You'll soon be Lady Pulborough. It might be a good idea if you learned how to cope.'

There it was—on her before she was ready, the situation fully formed and active about her, before she had worked out what she was going to say. They were sitting in the drawing-room of the Line Wall Road house at about six o'clock in the evening. Normally, with *Firesprite* in harbour, David would have been in the seat now occupied by Lance, her father just back from Government House would have been helping himself to a whisky and soda and Grace herself would have been mastering her resentment at having to go back into Spain overnight. Now she was impatient for escape and grateful that the regulations would force her not to be with Lance more than another couple of hours.

'Is that what you want me to do?'

'My dear Grace, you know my father hasn't much longer to live. Nothing can stop you becoming Lady Pulborough. You might as well know what that entails and learn to do it properly.'

She looked at him steadily.

'All that time in prison, Lance, did you miss me very much?'

'I thought about you a lot.'

'That's not the same thing.'

He gave her the basilisk glance.

'Let me ask you a question,' he said, 'what do you imagine it's like in a P.O.W. Camp?'

'It must be hell.'

'Certainly, but what does that mean? What do people think about, what do they feel?'

'I suppose they dream a lot. As we all do anywhere.'

'You live in the future. You correct the past in your mind, you brood about what you're going to do when you're free.

The more you brood the deeper goes the idea and the determination to realize it.'

'You've changed a great deal, Lance. You're not the man you were.'

'And do you care?'

'Oh! Lance, how unkind! Of course I care.'

Should she tell him? Now? And if so, how could she put it?

'That's because you always had a soft heart and because you thought you were hardly done by in your early life. You don't really care about me and I don't think you ever have.'

'That's simply not true,' Grace said hotly. 'You know perfectly well how it used to be. I adored you to begin with but you were such a snob, you looked down your nose at the Scorps, you felt ashamed to be married to one, you explained it away because my father had money and your family hadn't, you traipsed about as a Flag-Lieutenant but you never let us—you and me, Lance—you never let us grow into anything at all.'

'And now?'

It was on the tip of her tongue to say it, then again she paused.

'Look—you haven't been free twenty-four hours: wouldn't it be better to let this sort of discussion find its own time?'

'Grace, one of the things I decided upon in the P.O.W. Camp was a family and especially a son. What do you feel about that?'

'Oh! Lance, really. . . .'

'Oh! Lance, really,' he mimicked. 'There's the good old bourgeois reaction again—just because your mother's just died, it isn't "nice" to talk like that. . . .'

She stared at him completely calm.

'You *have* got me wrong,' she said, 'I'd go to bed with you now if I felt like it. I simply want to be treated as a woman, that's all. I'm not just a device for producing the son and heir you suddenly think you require.'

'In another few moments you're going to drive back to San Roque, aren't you?'

'Yes. I'm not allowed to stay overnight in Gibraltar.'

'You are tonight.'

'How? What do you mean?'

'I asked the Admiral and the Admiral asked the Governor. You have a special dispensation, Grace. Your dearly beloved husband has been behind barbed wire for the last eighteen months. It's quite natural he should want to sleep with his wife.'

So there she was, trapped. With David in Gibraltar, with an impeccable excuse in the death of her mother, quite apart from the curfew regulations, she was nonetheless brought face to face with what the world and the Church would have defined as her duty—and a duty in this instance with a further aim in view. This was the complete travesty of her heart. Over the last few months she had felt that deep, formless longing to have a child—but by the man she loved, not by this . . . this . . . she looked at him and then, on a sudden irresistible impulse, said the one unforgiveable thing, the one thing which she had known all along would split them asunder for ever.

'It may be quite natural, Lance, but I shouldn't have thought it would interest you.'

'What do you mean by that?' he said in a dangerously quiet voice.

'Since when have you been naturally interested in women?' she said. 'Why don't you face up to the truth about yourself? Or have you in these eighteen months in prison?'

For a moment she thought he would kill her: for a moment she was aware of bottomless, abysmal fear in herself: but he did not move. He sat immobile, frozen, completely still, his snake-like eyes boring into her soul.

After what seemed like an age she took a deep, shaky breath and looked down at the carpet.

'I'm sorry, Lance, I said it without thinking—I'm sorry.'

He sat on, still without moving, a sharp, stinging hatred burning out of his eyes. She felt the new power he had become possessed of. It seemed to radiate from him now as he sat looking at his wife. She told herself he had certainly learnt to hate.

'Now, my dear Grace,' he said in this quiet, controlled voice which was new and dangerous to her, 'let's talk about you for a change. We've hardly had a chance and you must have a great deal you want to tell me. About David Evers, for instance.

Why isn't he here at this moment? His ship's in harbour. Normally he would be, wouldn't he? Or is he keeping away because of me, do you think? I shouldn't have thought he was that sort of coward.'

'I don't know what you're getting at or what you're trying to say.'

'You understand perfectly. You don't want to discuss it now because *I* happened to have picked the time—not you.'

'Discuss what?'

She looked at him now with all her hackles up and for a moment or so he said nothing, as though he was thinking of how exactly to put it.

'Let me repeat what I said just now. One of the things I decided upon in Germany was a family. I need a son. I intend to have one. Any idea, therefore, that I shall set you free in order to marry Evers is doomed. I shall never agree.'

'What gives you the idea that I want to marry David or he me? I've never mentioned it before.'

'You mean how did I find out? Nicholas Pappadopoulos for one thing wrote me the facts in Germany; your own letters told me the rest.'

'What facts? What *is* this inquisition? What am I supposed to have done?'

'Oh! come, come, Grace. Don't be so arch. I don't blame you for having an affair with the gallant Commander. I'm merely telling you as plainly as I can that I do not intend to give you a divorce.'

There was another long pause.

'Do you seriously think you can hold me against my will—*make* me go to bed with you—*make* me bear your children? It's fantastic: monstrous.'

'But you're a Catholic, Grace,' he said softly, 'you married me in church—*your* Church.'

At that moment there was a knock at the door and a servant ushered in David. He walked over quickly to Grace saying:

'You didn't invite me but I thought I'd come anyway. I'm off to sea in an hour's time. Hallo, Lance, congratulations on your escape.'

Lance made no move to get up or to greet him.

'Congratulations on trying to make off with my wife. Isn't your own good enough any more?'

David stared at him and then quickly at Grace.

'He's just accused us of having an affair,' she said, 'I've been trying to point out. . . .'

'We have,' David said squarely. 'I'm very sorry it all had to happen behind your back. But there it is. It's happened. I won't sentimentalize about it. We want to be married.'

'Oh! well, that's splendid, isn't it?' Lance retorted with a short, contemptuous laugh, 'simple isn't it? You fall in love with someone else's wife: you don't want to sentimentalize: you just want to get married. Charming, I must say.'

'I'm sorry things should have gone the way they have,' David said after a pause, 'but I don't regret it for a moment. Neither does Grace. That's how we feel and talking sarcastically won't get us anywhere at all.'

'Talking in any way isn't going to get us anywhere. It's very simple, Evers. You want Grace and Grace is married to me. Well, you can't have her and that's the end of the discussion.'

Grace lit a cigarette and perched on the arm of a chair looking at Lance through the smoke. David was over by the window, his hands clasped behind his back in unconscious quarterdeck fashion. Lance stood with his back to the fireplace, his arms folded across his chest Napoleonically.

'You know, Lance,' Grace said eventually, 'you never have understood us Gibraltarians. You keep forgetting we were born on a rock. The Rock is there in everything we do or think or feel: it's a part of our lives. You've always discounted that fact. You've never thought it matters. I tell you, Lance, once a Rock Scorp makes up his mind there's nothing you can do to shake him. We know all about enduring a siege. Perhaps you know something about it too after being a prisoner of war. . . .' She shrugged her shoulders very slightly. 'Well, it happens to be here in my blood. That's what you're really up against, Lance—the Rock. I've told you once and now I'll tell you again. I love David and as soon as conditions allow, we're going to live together even if something or other prevents us from getting married. You'll never change that, however viciously you try. I hate doing it this way. I'm sorry you

[362]

should have come back to Gibraltar to such disagreeable news but you don't love me and I don't love you.' She went over to David and slipped her arm through his. 'There's something in every one of us that can recognize plain, simple goodness. Surely you see that, Lance, don't you? Goodness is the only ultimate virtue.'

There was another pause as Lance studied them, a supercilious smirk on his face.

'What hypocrites you are,' he said in the end and walked to the door, 'and how you delude yourselves. I shall go and have a bath, then I shall go out and probably get drunk. Commander Evers will proceed to sea in order to save us all from Hitler, and you, Grace, will go back to your funeral parlour in Spain. I shall ask to be sent home as soon as it's possible and I shall expect you to join me there. Other people know how to withstand a siege, Grace, besides the sacred inhabitants of this delectable, benighted Rock. Good night to you both.'

As the door closed behind him she clutched her arms round David, her head on his chest, the tears in her eyes. Neither of them spoke. There was nothing to be said: nothing to be done.

3

During the spring and summer of 1942 the war went more and more badly for the Allies. America was still busy making the vast change-over from peace to war. The Japanese had the initiative in the Pacific. Singapore had fallen. The battle-cruiser *Repulse* and the new battleship *Prince of Wales* had both been lost in a single day. The German advance into Russia continued and both Moscow and Stalingrad were besieged.

In the Mediterranean the initial advantages gained from German preoccupation in Russia were lost one by one. Benghazi which had been occupied by the Eighth Army on Christmas Eve was evacuated again at the end of January. Before June was out Tobruk, for so long a symbol of endurance like the Rock of Gibraltar, had fallen and by the 5th of July the Germans were only halted, for the moment it seemed, at El Alamein, a mere sixty miles from Alexandria.

Malta had the toughest time of all. The three cruisers of

Force K, the small squadron used to harry enemy shipping between Italy and North Africa, were all of them put out of action in one day by an unexpected mine-field—the *Neptune* being sunk with all hands and the other two cruisers *Aurora* and *Penelope* being damaged. By March the island was taking such a battering that all surface warships were withdrawn and a few weeks later, mainly because of a lack of shelter and of fuel, the submarines left as well.

In April Malta was uniquely awarded the George Cross in token of the tenacity and courage shown by the inhabitants. At the same time the aircraft-carriers H.M.S. *Eagle* and U.S.S. *Wasp* reinforced the island with forty-seven Spitfires. A week later every single one had been destroyed. By June the supply situation was serious and the desperate attempts to get convoys through reached a new intensity. Out of sixteen merchant ships attempting to relieve Malta in June exactly two got through. By August there remained but one single week's food supply in store.

In Gibraltar the threat of attack through Spain grew steadily stronger. Although the *Scharnhorst* and *Gneisenau* had escaped from Brest in February, making their dash home through the Channel, and were thus no longer the concern of Force H, the Battle of the Atlantic was now in spate. And this, too, was going badly against us. In January 1942 U-boats sank 320,000 tons of Allied shipping. In June this figure was 700,000 tons. Nor did Germany unduly suffer in the process with 140 operational submarines at sea, another 120 new ones coming into service and losses during those six months of exactly twenty-one boats. On the short view the outlook for the Allies was indeed grim.

Such then was the climate of the war while the United States gathered itself together for its first decisive blow in November of that year, a blow levered upon the port of Gibraltar and its new, tiny, grossly vulnerable airstrip.

In Gibraltar itself it seemed as though the occasional U-boat sunk, the occasional Italian aircraft destroyed during the first ten months of 1942 were scarcely visible pin-points of light in a wholly darkening scene. Back in England the Russian plight gave rise to a crescendo of agitation for a 'Second Front Now'.

It was vaguely but generally thought that this could only take place into France or the Low Countries and in a sense this public obsession made the keeping secret of Operation Torch somewhat easier. No one in their senses would have dreamt of a full-scale expedition to capture Morocco and Algeria. Indeed the Combined British and American Chiefs of Staff only agreed to this project as late in the year as July. Yet when Fortin was summoned back to England in August to be put in the picture and to render some practical advice, his instincts almost shouted at him that this was to be Gibraltar's greatest moment in the war and perhaps in the whole chequered history of the Rock. Without knowing it until now this was the point towards which they had all of them been working, the consummation— the apex of it all.

4

By August the Royal Air Force had come into its own in Gibraltar. Though primarily used by fighters, the runway was now long enough for a Liberator bomber to land and the internal balance of power in Gibraltar now rested on a tripod whose legs were all three Services. It was true that nests of Spanish machine-guns in their domed concrete covers dominated the airstrip from a distance of twenty yards. It was true that a belligerent Spain could have pulverized the Dockyard and the airstrip into uselessness within a matter of minutes—but Spain remained neutral and in the meantime the reception given to Italian reconnaissance grew hotter and hotter as the months went past.

Once again Gibraltar was bursting at the seams. There were still about fifteen hundred badly sub-standard houses in which human beings and rats vied with each other for accommodation, and in the previous year alone three hundred rooms had been lost through road widening or enemy bombs. It thus became less and less reasonable for Jaime to maintain the Line Wall Road house for himself alone and it had now been requisitioned for an R.A.F. mess. Jaime moved into Government House and, against his better judgment, allowed Grace and Rosita to stay on at San Roque. The Germans would come, he felt sure, and they would all be trapped, but his daughters separately and together had brought such pressure to bear on him that with Edie gone, he had given up fighting. Physically and mentally he was now a much older, slower man. Grace had taken her mother's place in the scheme of things and once again he did as he was told. Moreover a Spanish neighbour of theirs, the Marquis de Torre Cataldo, had fallen, hook, line and sinker for Rosita and both Jaime and Grace felt it would be a good thing if this interest was allowed to develop.

Lance had returned to England and now had an appointment at Combined Operations Headquarters. In the spring his father had died so that he was now Lord Pulborough and Grace, as forecast, his Lady. But Grace had not budged an inch in her determination to be free of him, to marry David and to remain within reach of Gibraltar. As the months went by, however, the practical difficulties of tidying up their private lives seemed to increase. Things were more involved all round. Everything took longer, people were more tired, things were in shorter supply. So, tacitly, the action she needed to take to get a divorce was pushed into the background and David and Grace simply lived together whenever they could. When *Firesprite* was docked and on short local spells of leave, David got out his plain-clothes and stayed at San Roque. Then they were man and wife for all practical purposes. Jaime shut his eyes to the questions which would have presented themselves so short a time ago and Rosita was firmly on their side.

With the exception of the Marquis de Torre Cataldo, local Spanish society, it is true, dropped the Barbarossas but this did not distress Jaime as it would have done Edie, and to Grace herself it was a blessing. She and David were very happy together. His own divorce had come through and, indeed, Pam had since married her Paymaster-Lieutenant. Only Lance now stood in their way and with that block of salt, as Grace called him, there was no prospect of change. But by August 1942 both Grace and David had somehow become used to this state of affairs. The attitude of the world no longer mattered. They clung more closely than ever to each other and when in August Grace knew she was going to have a baby, they were both profoundly delighted.

[366]

In August, with Egypt and Malta both in a critical condition, the Cabinet decided that at all costs Malta must be relieved, that everything was to be staked on getting through a
convoy from the west and for this purpose fourteen fast merchant ships, including an American tanker, the *Ohio*, were
gathered at Gibraltar. By now Operation Torch had been
decided upon as, too, had the timing of the great advance of
the Eighth Army from Egypt, which was to begin in October
with the battle of Alamein. But in August the Allies were
ready neither for Torch nor for Alamein and in the meantime
should Malta fall (one of the master-keys of the British Empire,
as Churchill had called it) this might well prejudice or, at any
rate, delay the other ventures. So Operation Pedestal was
authorized and put into effect. Operation Pedestal was the
August convoy through to Malta.

To get this convoy through, a force of two battleships, three
aircraft-carriers, seven cruisers and thirty-two destroyers was
assembled at Gibraltar, and on August 9th the convoy and its
huge escort sailed, fully aware of the hot Axis reception awaiting them in the Sicilian narrows.

David, of course, knew nothing of the North African landings then being planned. Even the idea of such an expedition
did not visit him, as they sailed along the Moroccan coast on
what up to now had always been the easy part of the trip. It
was fine August weather and the battleships *Nelson* and *Rodney*
with their sixteen-inch guns and their ponderous bulk gave a
splendidly solid appearance to the convoy. As usual *Firesprite*,
together with her old faithful companion the *Forthright*, was
screening ahead, her Asdics continuously searching below the
surface of the sea for the lurking U-boat. Nowadays, though,
it was never as simple as once it had been. Now the U-boats
came in packs. Now, while your attention was concentrated
upon one contact, others would suddenly attack. This was
what happened when the convoy was off Algiers. The aircraft-carrier *Eagle* was torpedoed while her sister carrier
Furious was in the process of flying off her Spitfires to Malta.
This was an ominous casualty, coming too soon and in the
wrong place. The real trouble still lay a day ahead. Then the
air attacks would begin.

Now, after three years of war during which he had been almost continuously at sea, David had a detachment in action akin to his uncle's sense of destiny. This isolation had been expensively acquired. He found now that he could divide himself into two—the body and the personality in its tin helmet and uniform, connected like a well-oiled mechanism to the bridge, the ship and the action then in progress: the inner part simply watching, knowing that what was happening to the husk was inevitable but, in a way, expendable. Sooner or later a bomb or a bullet or ultimately old age would seize on the outer and carry it away. But what happened then to the part that watched? Such trains of thought, as the bombs fell, the guns blazed away and the depth-charges exploded, he now found not only possible but indeed almost the only thing which kept him sure and balanced. It is not what you do but what you are and how you accept your life which alone matters, he kept reminding himself.

The next day, seven of the fourteen ships, two cruisers and a destroyer were sunk. In return thirty-nine enemy aircraft were shot down attacking the convoy and one Italian submarine was destroyed. The day after, two more cruisers and three more merchant ships, including the essential tanker *Ohio*, were damaged. Four gruelling days after leaving Gibraltar a bomb struck the *Forthright* at the base of her forward funnel, the ship blew up and almost instantly sank. There were no survivors.

The sudden loss of his old friend, Bill Downey, and the disappearance of their closest sister ship in just under a minute put the severest strain on David's detachment which it had yet undergone. Now, back in the pens at Gibraltar, there would be no more cheery insolence from the ship next door (Bill Downey had not been promoted Commander and probably never would have been): there would be no more alcoholic diversions at the Yacht Club and the Bristol Bar, no more of those inter-flotilla signals at which Downey excelled and which help to give destroyer life its particular flavour. A flash, a tremendous explosion and that was that. Well, he said to himself, as the convoy held on and the attacks continued, it was at least quick.

By now they were all exhausted. Four days and nights without sleep and daylight the next day, they well knew, would bring the most vicious attacks of all since thereafter what was left of the convoy would come under the Malta defences. David began counting up the number of times he had done this sort of club run before. They were changing in character as the months and the years went by. The early sense of adventure had gone. Now it was simply an ordeal. This was the grimmest so far—even the disastrous June convoy had not suffered such a sustained battering as this one. During daylight, attacks from the air were almost continuous. During the night there were the U-boat packs. Now another aircraft-carrier, the *Indomitable*, had been damaged, and the *Ohio* with her vital cargo of fuel slowed down to a dangerous crawl.

So now *Firesprite* was the only one of the original 28th Flotilla remaining afloat. In Norwegian waters, at Dunkirk and now on these agonizing convoys to Malta one by one they had gone. It was like the tolling of a bell—yet somehow through it all Bill Downey and he had survived. They had shrugged their shoulders and never brought it out into the open but both of them knew they had led charmed lives up to now. They had come through it all until now, until this last desperate convoy on the success of which the future of Malta depended. Well— there it was. There was not a soul in the convoy or its escort unaware of the dragon they were daunting. Everyone from the Admiral in the *Nelson* to the youngest stoker in *Firesprite* knew that it was the enemy's first interest to destroy them all, and that they had the almost absolute power necessary to carry out their will.

The *Ohio* with its aviation spirit now seemed to have become the symbol of the convoy and at dawn the next day, almost within sight of Malta, she was hit again from the air and completely stopped. Now she was a sitting target for the U-boats and *Firesprite* and two other destroyers slowly circled her to keep the contacts they could hear from time to time on their Asdics from coming up to periscope depth and attacking. Then as wave after wave of German aircraft pressed home their attacks, *Firesprite* was ordered to take the *Ohio* in tow and get her into Grand Harbour.

'It just needed that,' said Soakes, wiping his mouth with the back of his hand as he read the signal, 'tie us up to ten thousand flipping tons of flipping 100-octane fuel and we can kiss this flipping world farewell.'

'I don't suppose they're enjoying it much on board the *Ohio*,' said David sharply. 'Let's get a move on with that tow rope aft.'

Still murmuring Soakes disappeared angrily off the bridge. David reflected, as the guns opened up against another close attack, that he would never have had to use that tone of voice to Jimmy Allendale. Somehow that was the way the war was going. He had noticed it ashore in Gibraltar—the dumb insolence, the resentment, the sticking to the letter of the regulations, the eager crushing by sentries and military police of any extension of an officer's privileges. It was the beginning of the proletarian age and Soakes in his way, by lowering himself to a state of bloody-mindedness he should have been well above, was typical of that vast ugly mass that 'didn't see why'. There were times when David felt him to be more of a shop steward than a first lieutenant. He wanted to be rid of him but he could never quite justify taking any official action towards that end. As another stick of bombs fell round the ship he knew that there would now always be a Soakes for him to contend with— it was the way things were. It was something alien to the Navy David had grown up in, yet the type was here to stay. In fairness he had to admit that despite his unprepossessing manners Soakes was a hundred per cent loyal and efficient. He only wished he could like the man.

They took the *Ohio* in tow but the tanker was so badly damaged that she was difficult to control and the tow was parted three times before eventually, late in the afternoon of the 15th and to a ragged cheering which brought tears to the eyes, they got her into Grand Harbour, Valletta, with her precious cargo intact. Only five ships of the convoy had survived but those five ships contained food enough for four months and with the *Ohio* sufficient fuel to keep the air defences of Malta active and effective.

'Now that really is a shambles,' David remarked to Soakes, as they surveyed the ruined dockyard and the towering piles of yellowish dusty rubble which had been the surroundings to Grand Harbour. 'Poor old Malta! Poor old Valletta!'

But it was no time for hanging around. The job was done Thirty sacks of mail were taken aboard, delivered by a haggard working party from the St. Angelo. The entire stock of chocolate in *Firesprite*'s canteen was given by request of the ship's company for distribution to the wide-eyed children living in the burrows and the caves. The wardroom cleared out their wine store of whisky and gin as the officer's contribution to the beleaguered garrison. David had five minutes' conversation with his brother on the jetty, and then with a greater pull on the heart-strings than any of them cared to admit they turned in the harbour and set off back to Gibraltar, wondering as the figures in the rubble grew heroically smaller and the air attacks began once more whether they would any of them see Malta again.

XIX

THERE can be no real escape from a great event. Inevitably it creates its own emotional climate in which everyone concerned in any way in the crisis must live. It comes, it sucks people into its vortex, then like a tornado it moves on elsewhere or possibly disintegrates. It is invisible yet far more real and far more powerful than the human beings and their 'props' which it manipulates for its outward effect.

Such was Fortin's train of thought as the aircraft bringing him back from London after his first meeting with General Eisenhower circled the Rock and came in to land. This, he knew, would be the greatest test of detachment he had yet to undergo. Fortin had bought his self-control the hard way. Now there was something inside him, small but very strong, which could resist the effects of life, which could not only survive but was composed of energies from far beyond the level of life. To Fortin the soul was active and awake. This was the result of the work he had done on himself and he noticed that the power of this essence seemed to grow the greater the crisis it had to oppose.

But detachment depends upon seeing clearly what one has to separate from. Now, with the knowledge he had been given in London, he knew that the personal machine in which he lived, the small, severe compressed collection of personalities known as His Excellency the Governor and Commander-in-Chief of Gibraltar, would be completely involved, whatever the outcome might be, in Operation Torch—at that time the largest sea- and air-borne invasion the world had ever known.

And at that moment Fortin, alone on the Rock, knew what Operation Torch was going to entail and what it was designed to do. Only Fortin knew a little of the high-level wrangling which was still going on between the American Chiefs of Staff, with their Pacific preoccupations, and the British, harried by Russia to draw off German pressure that year in the west. Only Fortin knew that the raid into Dieppe which had just taken place had never been intended as anything but a large-scale diversion, an exploration in force where new types of landing-craft and techniques had been tested out and the enemy led to think that a bigger thrust on the same coast would be forth-coming before the winter arrived. Only Fortin knew some-thing of Operation Jupiter, the operation which was never done, the operation to capture the north of Norway and secure the Arctic convoy route. In Gibraltar at that time only Fortin knew how badly an invasion of North Africa could misfire and how disastrous the consequences were bound to be for the Rock.

The aircraft landed and Fortin noticed that even since he had been away the quantity of crated Spitfires had grown and how even now, in September, the number of fighters parked at the side of the runway must surely be attracting the attention of German Intelligence.

'It's impossible to disguise anything for long in Gibraltar,' he had told the American General and his staff at the conference in Norfolk House to which he had been summoned. 'Every move we make, every ship that arrives, every aircraft we un-crate is known and reported to Berlin. The most we can hope for is that we may be thought to be building up supplies for the relief of Malta. That makes sense after the mauling of the June and August convoys. If that rumour is carefully nurtured and possibly Dakar mentioned in the same breath, we may get away with the real destination.'

When, later that night in Gibraltar, he was briefing the Admiral, the Air-Marshal and the Deputy Fortress Comman-der, Fortin continued:

'The basic idea behind Torch is to get something for prac-tically nothing—as the Germans did in Norway. The French are thought to be ripe. The politicians maintain that if it's done at the right moment, we can occupy Morocco and Algeria almost without firing a shot. But the Americans must do it, not ourselves. The French have no bitter memories of the Americans. The Yanks didn't destroy their fleet at Oran. There's an American Ambassador at Vichy and another U.S. diplomat in Algiers. The British have to keep out of sight in the background. So we may find some of our assault troops in American uniform yet.'

'That's all very well,' the Admiral remarked, 'but what about

Gibraltar? The cat's going to be out of the bag if boat loads of Americans start staging through the Rock.'

'That was brought up too,' Fortin said. 'From that point of view it's all Alice-in-Wonderland. Just as some of us may be wearing U.S. uniform over there, so a certain number of American airmen may be here in British uniforms.'

The Air-Marshal snorted, as Fortin knew he would.

'That's higher lunacy of the highest order.'

'Nothing matters,' Fortin said, 'provided we can establish ourselves along the North African seaboard and secure Tunis as speedily as possible. The Americans think it can be pulled off without firing a shot but they want to do it all from Casablanca. They're scared of the Straits of Gibraltar.'

'Aren't we all?' the Admiral said dryly. 'How can it be practical without the harbours of Algiers and Oran?'

'Eisenhower knows that perfectly well. There's no division of opinion on that score in Norfolk House—it's only in Washington that the trouble starts. However no doubt Roosevelt and Churchill between them can settle that argument.'

As he mentioned the Prime Minister's name, Fortin recalled his two visits to Gibraltar the previous month on his way out to the famous Cairo and Moscow meetings. The condition of the Rock, its newly extended airstrip, its formidable anti-aircraft defence and the recently completed headquarters underneath the Rock itself had all been observed and inspected by the Prime Minister before Eisenhower had arrived in London. Churchill had an up-to-date picture of Gibraltar in his mind. In view of what could happen there was some comfort in that.

'If General Eisenhower is the Supreme Commander-in-Chief,' the Deputy Fortress Commander remarked, 'and he's going to run things initially from Gibraltar, does that make us all American citizens?'

Fortin smiled.

'Well, members of the same club perhaps,' he answered. 'It will result for a time in the unique spectacle of an American having command of a British colony. No one quite knows how that one is going to work out.'

'Personally,' said the Admiral, 'I happen to like Coca-Cola—provided there's enough rum in it.'

'And Eisenhower?' asked the Air-Marshal, 'what sort of man is he?'

Fortin looked round his inner cabinet before answering. This extraordinary situation with its invasion of their sovereignty would touch them all in a sensitive spot. These were all high officers with clear directives and they would obey to the end— but in a new event like this it was how they obeyed that was important.

'He has the full confidence of the American President and the British Prime Minister,' Fortin said. 'In the ultimate analysis that's what principally matters. Under his command will be British Admirals, Generals and Air-Marshals of much greater fighting experience than himself. Not a very easy state of affairs for him or for us. This is something which has never happened before. It's up to us to make it work. I can only say, for myself, that I came away without any qualms. He's not an arrogant man. He listens. He may not be fully aware of it himself, but Destiny put him there and Destiny will look after him till the job is done.'

There was a silence while each of them worked this out by his own lights.

'I should have thought a British officer with some actual war experience would have been much more to the point as Supremo,' the Air-Marshal opined. 'Not that I'm anti-Uncle Sam in any way.'

'This is basically an American expedition,' Fortin said sharply. 'The Americans are providing two-thirds of the men and material. They're doing this at the expense of the Pacific. In any case we're all in this together now. If Churchill and Roosevelt see eye to eye, it's up to us on our level not to let any out-of-date ideas or prejudices stand in the way. This joint expedition is something quite new. We *have* to make it work. And I can only repeat, this is a moment of destiny and Destiny always produces the men and the forces it needs. I am sure Eisenhower is one of those men.'

A little later in the discussion Fortin brought the focus back on to Gibraltar.

'The crux of it all lies in whether the enemy can guess our intentions. If we keep on piling up aircraft on the neutral ground,

at what stage does it become quite obvious that something is up
—something, that is, beyond reinforcements for Malta? The
Prime Minister wants a report from me as to how much these
preparations would appear to exceed those for a big Malta convoy. The Germans may start putting the heat on Spain any
time from now on, either to make us clear the neutral territory
or perhaps to have the use of the Valencia airfields for their
own aircraft. What steps can we take to keep down movement
on the airstrip and to camouflage our resources?'

As Fortin went on the majesty of this vast operation took
hold of his mind and lit up both him and his hearers. The
strategy of the war was normally none of Gibraltar's day-to-
day practical concern—their job was to run the Rock and keep
it in fighting trim—but now the idea of the North African invasion, upon the success of which the whole war would pivot,
suffused them all with a new and powerful light. The difficulties and dangers were seen to be immense. But they were
subordinate to the great original conception of the plan, a plan
which would set in motion an armada of 650 ships, and hundreds of thousands of men, an operation which would establish
a fusion between the United States and the British Empire
from which in many subtle senses there could be no going back.

'And Gibraltar,' Fortin concluded, 'is the main tent-pole for
this extraordinary circus, or the peg, if you like, upon which it
all hangs. The Americans are leery of plunging into the Mediterranean: they're not sure of the Straits of Gibraltar. Well
. . . if the Germans march into Spain there's nothing we can do
about that, except hold out and endure. If they don't come
though—if Spain stays neutral, as I think on balance she will—
then when the Torch is lit Gibraltar will be the strong arm
which holds it aloft. This will be the Rock's greatest moment
since 1781 when, you may remember, my distinguished pre-
decessor, General Eliott, crept out on the Spanish lines and in
one single night destroyed the work of two years' of siege. If
this North African surprise comes off it may shorten the war by
a year. I wish us all good luck.'

So the build-up in Gibraltar began. The stores and the
landing-craft, the petrol and the aircraft, the guns, the ammunition and the men all now began to form part of a new pat-

tern, the complex of energies drawn up under one huge umbrella known to the British and Americans as Operation Torch.

2

The maximum danger to the Rock was thought to be from D—2 Day until D+1. Then the airstrip would be crammed with every fighter that could be got on to it waiting for the capture of the Oran and Algiers airfields. If the Spanish batteries were to open up then, millions of pounds' worth of material and most of the Allied hopes would flash up in one magnificent conflagration. By November 8th, moreover, there would be over a million gallons of aviation spirit stowed in four-gallon drums wherever an open, empty space on the Rock could be found. A million gallons is a large quantity of fuel and the implications of a bomb dropped at random on Gibraltar nearly drove Hobart up the wall with anxiety. But for Hobart personally the end was in sight. At the beginning of 1943 he had been promised an appointment on the Joint Intelligence Staff in Washington, D.C. and the prospect of being reunited with Cornelia and the children enabled him virtually to do without sleep during these last critical weeks.

Neither Grace nor David knew what was up and therefore the fact that Lance had been appointed to the staff of the Naval Expeditionary Force had no significance. They could have no idea that within a few weeks Lance would again be in Gibraltar *en route* for Oran and that by some ghastly quirk of fate the communications unit of which he was to have command would take passage on D-Day in H.M.S. *Firesprite*.

So the Americans began to arrive. The advance staff was small but their influence soon began to be felt. Their outlook, methods and energy were all of a different quality and in the early days this could well have wrecked the alliance had not both Roosevelt and Churchill been like-minded and firm about the common aim.

In Gibraltar this integrating power was centred on Fortin. It was Fortin who kept in mind the purpose of it all. Down at the point, though, where plans are put into effect, the differences in technique called for the maximum tolerance and

[377]

understanding on both sides. Which side really knew the answer? In salvaging a port was it better to retrieve and repair as the British instinct decreed or blow up and build anew as the Americans preferred?

Even Grace saw it reflected in the matter of comforts and canteen supplies. The British signed, mustered and accounted for everything, the Americans ordered it up in bulk, dumped it and gave it away. To say that it was the difference between a poor and a rich economy: between a nation over three years at war and one not yet properly blooded was only to see it superficially. To say that the Americans were brash and ill-disciplined and the British unreceptive and arrogant was again only a partial and a negative view. To appreciate that there were now two entirely different energies in operation, each with its own voltage, each therefore working through its different human equipment in a different way was much nearer the mark. It was the quality of energy which mattered in the end, as France had found to her cost. Luckily these problems of harnessing the British and American forces, which were to flower in North Africa, hardly touched Gibraltar—yet those who dealt with the tiny nucleus of it all at the very start of the process could sense the dangers and attempt to deal with the responsibilities intelligently.

3

Since returning to England Lance had only written once to Grace. It urged her coldly and formally to come 'home' to England. It had the mark of having been concocted in a lawyer's office. Grace showed it to her father who advised her to ignore it and this she did. Edie's death and the conversation they had had in the car that afternoon had done something to Jaime. He never referred to either, yet he and Grace were now closer together than they had ever been before.

He did not press his two daughters to go to Madrid as he would once have done. He allowed the San Roque house to continue as before. He became in a wordless way and without losing dignity his daughters' servant as he had been Edie's but with Grace as matriarch the relationship was quieter and less

[378]

concerned with outward show than it had been when Edie was alive.

Both Grace and Rosita had been willed over £50,000 each from their mother. Since Lance had inherited only a mildewed estate in Bedfordshire from his father, together with a portfolio of devalued Argentine railway shares, it was small wonder, as Jaime remarked, that he urged Grace to return to England. A frigid heart was one thing—fifty thousand pounds another.

Meanwhile, as the Torch forces built up in England and America, there was something of a lull in the western Mediterranean. David found himself employed on anti-submarine patrols from the eastern reaches of Spain to the North African coast. But there were only the routine excitements of an Asdic contact or a suspicious merchant ship dodging the contraband control to fill up the long days at sea. That last August convoy to Malta had been some sort of peak on the graph of tension and nervous strain and now there was an intermission while the interest built up at the other end of the Mediterranean.

Then, close to midnight on the 23rd October 1942, the great battle of El Alamein opened with a barrage from over one thousand British guns. The North African landings lay two weeks ahead in time when this battle began, but by November the 6th, when the whole vast Torch armada was at sea, the Eighth Army had decisively broken Rommel's command, 30,000 prisoners were in the bag, 350 German and Italian tanks had been captured or destroyed, together with 400 guns. The advanced units of the Eighth Army had already passed Mersa Matruh while Operation Torch was still miraculously the best-kept secret of the war. Well might Churchill dub this victory the 'turning of the hinge of Fate', well might the bells ring out in England. Defeated in the east and deceived completely in the west the Germans and Italians were caught well off balance when, in the early hours of the 8th November, the largest combined expedition the world had seen descended upon Casablanca, Oran and Algiers. Operation Torch had begun.

4

During the week preceding the landings people poured into

Gibraltar. Each day ships or aircraft brought new personalities: organizations big and small ceased to be paragraphs in a paper plan but achieved, instead, their intended physical being. The assault and follow-up troops with their equipment were by now all on the high seas, sorted out into their different ships and convoys. They were not Gibraltar's concern. It was the staffs which seemed to collect in Gibraltar, ranging from that of the Supreme Commander-in-Chief, housed in Fortin's new headquarters under the Rock, to Lieutenant-Commander the Lord Pulborough's Advance Signals and Communications Unit No. 312 which was designed to be landed in a newly-captured port area and to operate on a self-contained basis among the ruins.

Lance himself arrived on the 3rd November, two days before General Eisenhower flew in and Fortin for a few days ceased to exercise his local sovereignty. But things were on the move and no one had any chance of 'bedding down and making things comfortable'. The Loretto Convent had been turned into a large dormitory and here Lance was accommodated. It was a far cry from the luxuries of the Mount and the Barbarossa mansion in the Line Wall Road.

Grace was astonished and dismayed to see him. This was a personal reaction but it linked up in her mind with the general uneasiness which the surrounding hustle and bustle engendered. By now it was quite obvious that something on a very big scale was brewing and she only half-believed the story, so carefully leaked for the benefit of German Intelligence that another all-out attempt to relieve Malta was to be made. This did not explain the Americans to her nor the diversity of small and special units for which her office was packing up comforts.

Lance's arrival, therefore, simply added to the puzzlement in her mind. This was nothing, though, to the shock sustained by the Commanding Officer, H.M.S. *Firesprite*, when he opened his Top Secret sealed Orders for Operation Torch and learnt that they would be taking part in the assault on Oran and moreover would be conveying there the gear and the personnel for No. 312 Advanced Signals Unit which was to be landed at the first opportunity in the harbour. It seemed to him that Fate was being needlessly tricky. To begin with he thought it had been deliberately engineered by Lance but when the latter came on board with his party, it was only too obvious that Lance, as well, had been taken by surprise and liked the prospect as little as he did. Luckily it would not be for long. Soakes was briefed to keep the noble Lord away from the bridge as much as he could. This, in fact, was not difficult since Lance showed every sign of wishing to avoid any contact between himself and David.

5

H.M.S. *Firesprite* formed part of the Centre Task Force whose job it was to land the U.S. 1st Division from forty-three carriers at three points—one at a little port called Arzeu to the east and the other two to the west of Oran. The covering forces were impressive. The battleship *Rodney*, wearing the Admiral's flag, the aircraft-carrier *Furious*, two escort carriers, the cruisers *Aurora* and *Jamaica*, thirteen destroyers and a large handful of lesser ships.

There was almost no opposition to the landings which took place between one and three o'clock on the morning of November 8th. Arzeu was soon captured and indeed the French Army proved to be, as forecast, friendly towards the Americans. As against this one positive fact, two more sinister ones revealed themselves. One was the weather which began to deteriorate almost as soon as the initial landings had been made: the other was the attitude of the French Navy which, whether to Americans or British, was implacably hostile.

It was indeed too much to ask of human nature for it to be otherwise. Two and a half years before, the British had destroyed the flower of the French Navy at Oran. Now the tragic attempt by two ex-U.S. coastguard cutters—the *Walney* and the *Hartland* to open the harbour of Oran fanned up all the latent resentment into a blaze of anger. Both ships were sunk, nearly all their crews and the special landing-parties on board being slaughtered. At the same time the fort above Mers-el-Kebir, the naval base just to the west of Oran, opened up a withering fire on any ship approaching the harbour.

It had been intended that *Firesprite* should follow in the two

U.S. cutters as soon as the way was clear. These orders were countermanded just in time and they then spent an anxious night patrolling off the harbour mouth waiting until either the Army captured the town or the sixteen-inch guns of H.M.S. *Rodney* could silence the fort.

It was a long night and during it the weather steadily worsened. Whilst they were used to this in *Firesprite*, the implications for the rest of the Torch armada were ominous. Once more it became a question of waiting. The minutes and the hours ticked away. David sat on the bridge staring moodily into the darkness. He could not get out of his mind the bizarre fact of Lance being on board, here on board his own ship, at a time like this and at about four-thirty in the morning, as if the thought had drawn them together, he suddenly became aware of Lance standing beside him on the bridge.

'Hallo, Lance.'

'Hallo, David.'

For a time neither of them spoke. There was no news and both were long past any inclination to chatter. Surprisingly enough David found he did not resent the other's presence on the bridge. In a way both of them were past emotion.

'Are your chaps being looked after all right?' David asked eventually.

'Yes, thanks. I've got most of them down in the wardroom flat.'

Another long silence ensued. But there was no awkwardness—no casting around for words.

'I hear you're divorced,' Lance said at last.

'Yes, I am.'

'I'm sorry to hear it.'

'Are you, Lance?'

Another lengthy silence fell upon them with only the noise of the wind and sea as background to their thoughts.

'She's not worth it, you know.'

'Perhaps not in your opinion.'

'But then if you love her—and you *do* love each other don't you?'

'I don't think I want to discuss it.'

'She'll change, you know, once she gets you in her power,'

Lance went on. 'I warn you—if she ever gets you where she got me then you'd better watch your step. There's a tramp element in both those girls—the piratical Barbarossas.'

'I don't agree and I don't want to discuss it.'

But there was no anger and scarcely even annoyance in the way he spoke. It was as though neither of them had enough energy for anger and this exchange was oddly matter-of-fact as the wind buffeted the bridge and the ship pitched and rolled beneath them and the night lay dark, dark about them.

'It's a long way to have come since Dartmouth,' Lance said eventually. 'Funny we didn't have any instinct about it when we were pink little cadets.'

'Hm!' He could not think of anything to say to that. There was another long pause, then Lance spoke again.

'You know the odd thing is I don't resent you any more. Even now when I know she's going to have a child of yours.'

'How did you know that?'

'She wrote and told me. I certainly minded then—but somehow now. . . .'

'In that case why don't you . . . ?' David began and then stopped. It was almost too casual, too matter-of-fact. Perhaps it was some sort of trap.

'I'm going to,' Lance went on as though finishing his thought, 'I'm through with it all. Now you can take her on. I'll set about a divorce as soon as I get back from this little business. I'll even wish you good luck. God knows you'll need it.'

David continued to stare out at the night, dully working out in his mind the implications of this sudden piece of good news. When he next turned his head to speak, he found he was once more alone. Lance had slipped away as quietly as he had come. David heaved a deep sigh. The longed-for freedom was now surprisingly in sight. Unpredictably, unexpectedly, out of the unending dark night they were all of them in, the freedom he and Grace had so desired was now promised. Why then did he feel so disturbed and ill-at-ease? What was causing this deeper apprehensiveness now making itself felt in his consciousness?

Abruptly he sent for the First Lieutenant and then turning the ship over to him, went down to his cabin for half an hour's

[383]

sleep. 'Sufficient unto the day is the evil thereof,' a voice in him murmured as the wind howled outside his scuttle and he lay down on his heaving bed, more puzzled than relieved by what had just happened.

In the morning there was half a gale blowing. To the east, Maison Blanche, the Algiers airport, was now in Allied hands and already fighters were landing there from Gibraltar. To the west, one of the Atlantic landings had been unopposed. At Casablanca itself, however, the French Navy with the battle-ship *Jean Bart's* fifteen-inch guns was contesting General Patton's forces as hotly as they were at Oran.

So it went on. All through the 8th and 9th November the fighting continued. By nightfall on the 8th the great harbour of Algiers had been won and transports were unloading inside its shelter as planned. At Oran, however, the situation had, if anything, worsened. During the day five French destroyers had sortied bravely against hopeless odds and had all been sunk or driven aground. This event had done nothing either to sweeten the French or to weaken the British resolve. Unloading from ocean-going transports into landing-craft had had to be abandoned because of the weather and the fort at Mers-el-Kebir was still making trouble.

Throughout the stormy night of the 8th–9th *Firesprite* in company with the other destroyers continued to patrol and wait outside the harbour. Lance sat dispirited in the wardroom, very occasionally coming up on the bridge to see what was going on. By this time he and his party should have been established ashore. He sat frowning and silent, lost in a private gloom.

The 9th November showed little improvement in the weather and an explosion from the port of Oran decided the Task Force Commander on another assault. It was essential to the overall plan that the port of Oran should be usable together with all its installations. This had been the point—and the gamble—of sending the *Walney* and the *Hartland* ahead of the main force. Highly trained anti-sabotage parties had been aboard both ships, their object being to prevent the blowing-up of cranes and jetties, and the blocking of the harbour.

But these parties had all been killed. Now as the time went by and Oran still remained in French hands, the chances of vindictive, desperate and ultimately pointless destruction increased. Midway through the morning of the 9th, therefore, *Firesprite* and another destroyer, the *Harpy*, were told to close the flagship and embark a stand-by assault force of Royal Marines. Another attempt on the harbour was to be made under cover of the *Rodney's* guns and of fighter protection from aircraft of the *Furious*.

As David and the Captain of *Harpy* were briefed in the Admiral's cabin in the *Rodney*, the Royal Marines were being put aboard the two destroyers together with their equipment. The prospect was grim. To land this party, both destroyers must get alongside a jetty. This in itself would be a feat. During the first assault everyone on the bridge of the *Walney* except the Captain had been killed by a single shell. To achieve their purpose, they would have to dare almost point-blank fire. The bombardment from the sea might help to neutralize the opposition, on the other hand it might merely make the reaction more vicious. The Marines were to seize key parts of the port and hold them intact until the French could be made to capitulate through common sense or *force majeure*. In the meantime, once the Marines had been landed, *Firesprite* and *Harpy* were to withdraw and then, perhaps, repeat the assault. The whole lash-up was what had long been known in the old 28th Flotilla as a 'posthumous V.C. party'.

The Admiral explained what he wanted. He explained coolly but understandingly that he had not ordered this desperate move but for the worsening weather and the passage of time. Oran had to be taken. The Army converging from east and west would, if all else failed, assault the town the next morning from the rear. But it was the harbour which was important—the harbour in a working condition must be secured with the utmost despatch. That, simply and daringly, was the job *Firesprite* and *Harpy* were to do. He wished them luck and a few minutes later both Captains were back aboard their respective destroyers briefing, in turn, their own ship's companies about the stark venture ahead.

Thirty minutes later the heavy ships of the force began their barrage and twenty minutes after that the two destroyers set off for the harbour mouth.

Back in Gibraltar the news of the North African landings spread like a heady scent at breakfast time on the 8th. It had been a troubled night. To begin with all had been quiet and Grace, across in San Roque, had slept till just before dawn. But then the Gibraltar A.A. barrage had suddenly sprung into life. From San Roque it was not always possible to know if bombs had been dropped, but on the Rock itself to hear the guns open up was both to relieve an almost unbearable tension and at the same time bring an instant awareness of the fact that this was the pinnacle of danger. The capture of the first North African airfield had yet to be announced and fourteen squadrons of fighters were packed like cigarettes in a box along Gibraltar's single airstrip waiting—waiting. The Rock was literally festooned with thousands of cans of 100-octane fuel. The situation resulting from the landings had yet to be known and assessed. An air-raid at this moment, therefore, was the one thing Gibraltar dreaded and the very last thing it wanted. Thus when the warning went it seemed as if every gun in Christendom had opened up.

But the aircraft were not hostile. This was a battalion of American parachute infantry being flown out from England direct to seize the airfields of Oran. Over Spain bad weather had scattered the force and some of the aircraft had homed on the Rock. They were strays. Luckily their pilots had the good sense to keep out of range of the barrage until they had got their bearings. Then they flew on to Morocco. The 'All Clear' sounded and with that scare the most critical night in Gibraltar's war came to an end.

From the moment Grace heard the news when she came in to work, she pestered her father, Hobart, Seale and the Admiral's secretary, who was a friend of hers, for more information especially of the Centre Task Force. Now that she knew what had happened, she gave way to the most fearful foreboding. It had never been as bad as this before. Nebulously groping about in her mind, praying and visualizing with an emotional ignorance what dangers David might be in, she went about her work in a trance of anxiety, listening to the

B.B.C., doodling on the blotting pad on her desk and fully prepared, at that moment, to sell her soul for news that he was safe. Then when the Admiral's secretary told her in an unguarded moment that Lance was also in *Firesprite* she felt as though she had been dealt a really giddying blow. She still suffered bouts of nausea, but that was nothing compared with the growing sickness in her heart which she now felt.

7

'Well, this is it,' David said to himself as the two little ships sped on towards Oran, 'this is the point of decision.' The approach to Oran was oddly like it had been two and a half years ago except that now it was winter, instead of summer, now the guns were blazing away instead of that appalling oppressive silence.

But the British guns stopped firing as they neared the entrance to the harbour. There was a high sea running and this threw them about a good deal. They rolled and pitched and the wind tore at the bridge screens as it had done for the last forty-eight hours. All this was very familiar. Nearer and nearer loomed the low cliffs behind Oran. The tension mounted. There was an ominous lack of reaction. Perhaps the French guns had now been neutralized—perhaps they had not. It was like stepping into the lair of a tiger you could not see but thought to be there waiting for you, poised and crouching.

With *Firesprite* ahead they passed through the broken boom, entered the harbour and began to turn towards the jetty. Then with a roar it began. Perhaps the French gunners had not believed their eyes. Perhaps the audacity of the two destroyers had taken them by surprise. Whatever had occasioned the pause it was now over. The torment had begun.

A few moments later a shell hit the water ahead of the ship, another skimmed over their heads passing between the bridge and the funnel, and then almost immediately there was a crunch and a shudder from aft. The ship continued on towards the jetty.

'Hit on the quarter-deck, sir,' the look-out yelled and a few seconds later a report came up the voice-pipe. 'Shell entered

the wardroom on the port side and exploded in the wardroom
flat.' That was where the bulk of Lance's party should have
been and as David took the ship nearer and nearer the jetty,
he thought for a second or two about what might have happened to them.

But there was no time for reflection. Too much was happening. Miraculously no damage had been done to *Firesprite's*
engine or boiler rooms. She could still manoeuvre and still fire
from her forward guns. She was thus able to continue on to
the jetty and in another few moments David had brought her
alongside with scarcely a bump.

At once the jetty seemed to be swarming with Royal
Marines, jumping off the ship, heaving their equipment ashore,
shouting, swearing and running along the jetty. There couldn't
have been that number of casualties in the wardroom flat,
judging by the number of men who poured out of the ship.
But there was no sign of Lance and he could only pick out a
few of the signalmen and telegraphists of No. 312 Advanced
Signals Unit. Yet things were happening at such speed that
only the most fleeting impression of anything could be gleaned.

'I believe we're out of range here, sir,' the Sub said to David
and indeed to begin with it did seem that the French guns
could not depress or traverse far enough to fire on them where
they were alongside the jetty. This illusion was fostered because out in the stream the unfortunate *Harpy* had been hit and
the French were concentrating on her, stopped as she was and
on fire in the middle of the harbour.

As the last of the landing-party left the ship, David toyed
with the idea of remaining alongside and giving close support
to the Marines. But this notion of security vanished as a shot
entered the base of the after-funnel causing a crash of wreckage.
It was time to be gone. Luckily the French rate of fire was slow
and as David went full-speed astern from the jetty they lost
their aim again. Indeed *Firesprite* had turned and was heading
out to sea before two more shells hit them, one forward by 'A'
gun and the other screaming its way into No. 1 boiler room,
tearing open a hole in the ship's side on the waterline through
which a small car could have been driven.

Firesprite was now wrecked forward, in the waist and aft.

'A' Gun was useless, No. 1 boiler room flooded and the ward-room an utter shambles. 'I can't reach the wardroom flat, sir,' the First Lieutenant reported, 'but most of the damage there seems to be above the waterline.'

In the meantime the ship could still steam and although listing badly, David managed to hold her on a steady course for the harbour mouth. 'B' Gun could still fire and for a time it looked as though she might get away with it.

But damage in an action at sea is rarely a static thing. A near miss, close to the hole already gashed in the ship's side, caused a further buckling and tearing of plates and then No. 2 boiler room was gone. By now they were just outside the harbour. Every movement the ship made in the high sea then running put an added strain on the bulkheads which remained.

Thus they were stopped, since there was now no steam and no electric or hydraulic power. They lay helpless in heavy weather outside a hostile port. At that moment a loud explosion came from inside the harbour. The fire had reached the *Harpy's* magazine and the ship had blown up. Now the shore batteries could concentrate on *Firesprite* and in a very short time she was again under fire.

The engine room itself had only been superficially damaged. But turbines need steam and they had lost all their steam, two out of the three boiler rooms being flooded and the third boiler being out. Communication with the engine room had to be by messenger since the telephones and voice-pipes had been cut. To David's demand to know if and when they could make steam, the Chief replied that they were shoring up the bulkhead in No. 3 boiler room and would know as soon as the leaks had been plugged and the boiler could be flashed up again. In the meantime would he oblige by stopping the ship from rolling and the French from making life so uncomfortable for them.

The *Rodney* as it happened did stop the shore batteries from paying any further attention to the stricken destroyer. Her huge salvoes began once more and this distraction coupled with poor visibility and high rolling seas caused the French to leave well alone. Moreover help was on the way. *Firesprite's* plight had been fully understood by the flag-ship and another destroyer came racing up to render assistance. This was H.M.S. *Hamilcar* and her Captain was none other than Jimmy Allendale, an astonishing fact made blasphemously clear to David as soon as a tow rope was passed and *Firesprite* began to be hauled out of range of the shore batteries.

As soon as he could David left the bridge to examine the damage for himself. The thought of Lance kept plaguing him. He climbed down the ladder to the upper deck and started picking his way aft. He was certain Lance had not landed with the remainder of his signals unit. Perhaps he'd been caught in the wardroom flat. It was where he was most likely to have been. As he worked his way aft, the First Lieutenant joined him. A piece of shrapnel had torn the side of his head and he was covered with blood.

'Are you all right, Number One?'

'Yes, sir, it's only a scratch. I was lucky.'

'What's the state of affairs?'

'I'm afraid it's a bit worse than I thought. I've counted three officers and over sixty men so far—all dead; about fifteen very badly wounded. The Doc was in the wardroom, Jevons was killed near the depth-charge rails on the quarter-deck and our passenger, Millingham. . . .'

'Where was he?' David interrupted impatiently.

'Coming up the ladder from the wardroom flat. There were six of them down there. It's the hell of a shambles.'

This proved to be a gross understatement. As David reached the gashed-open hole in the quarter-deck over the place where the wardroom and the wardroom flat had been, he felt as though he would retch up his guts. The mess was appalling. There were bits of flesh impaled grotesquely on jagged leaves of metal. There was a stench of explosive and of charred bodies and then as he peered down on the dark, smoking cavern below, he was struck by the most revolting spectacle he had seen in the whole of his life. Lance's head half-severed from the neck stared up at him dead and sightless. The face, those even, regular features, had miraculously not been touched and since the face was not distorted it might be presumed that death had come too quickly for him to have felt the agony, but the rest of his body, or what was left of it, was splayed out horizontally on the top of a metal locker, like a gutted fish on a slab, torn, bloody and very, very dead. For a moment David stared in absolute stillness at that face. He was overcome by a pity, a poignancy, a grief he could not contain. So that was how it ended. He was fascinated by that face as it was in death, that face he had known since they were boys together, the face of the man who had been his rival for so long, and which Grace had known so very intimately. Abruptly he turned away knowing that he could take no more at that time.

'I'm rigging up an emergency operating-theatre down on seventeen mess-deck,' the First Lieutenant said as they walked forward. David nodded, unable to speak. 'I've got one sick-berth attendant left and a leading-seaman to help him. . . .' The detailed report went on and David was grateful for the necessity of hearing it. It gave him time to recover. But he knew, as the First Lieutenant went on methodically listing the condition of the ship, that never for as long as he lived would he be free of that image he had just had forced into his consciousness.

'We'd better leave the quarter-deck as it is,' David said at last as he began to clamber up again to the bridge. 'Do what you can to help the Chief—we can't do much till there's some power in the ship.'

'Aye, aye, sir.'

'And get that "scratch" of yours seen to first of all, Number One.'

'Oh! I'm all right.'

'Do as I say. We're nowhere near out of the trouble.'

So David returned to the bridge while Soakes set about cleaning up the ship as best he could and the Chief sweated away repairing the machinery the ship had left. By now *Firesprite* was listing to port some twenty degrees and the effect of *Hamilcar's* towing was to cause the normal pounding of the sea to be dangerously increased. As soon as they were out of effective range of the shore batteries, therefore, the tow was slipped and way taken off the ship while work in the boiler room proceeded.

Firesprite had now become a liability to the Centre Task Force and would remain so until she could move under her own power again. For the present, however, as the Chief and his artificers worked away like demons in the rolling, pitching, torch-lit boiler room, wrenching out pipes, twisting, relaying and trying to make water- and steamtight joints to save the life of the ship, *Firesprite* was protected from submarine and aircraft attack by the rest of the Force. But their spirits were high. Moreover the Admiral had sent them a signal of congratulations in the strongest terms. Their action in landing the Marines, though not immediately effective, was to play an important part in the subsequent capitulation of Oran.

Three hours later the Chief asked David's permission to light up No. 3 boiler. Under normal circumstances one boiler would have given them steam enough for seventeen knots. When No. 3 was lit up, however, there was a silver nitrate 'cloud' in the feed-water gauge which showed that the fresh water essential to the boiler was now hopelessly contaminated with salt. Thus they had to drain out and start again, aided by fresh supplies from the *Hamilcar*. 'It hurts,' as Jimmy Allendale signalled, 'to be passing water to the old Firelighter. Can't you run her on gin?'

This took another two hours and by now the November day was already coming to an end. On the second attempt at flashing up, contamination was less and steam became available for the auxiliary machinery though not as yet sufficient to drive the main turbines. Like an invalid convalescing, additional muscles were again made to work. Continuously cursing but triumphant in the end, the Chief and the engine-room staff got the evaporators started so that *Firesprite* could now make from her own resources enough fresh water to compensate for losses and to provide steam for working the main engines.

All through the evening and halfway through the night they worked. *Rodney* took over the wounded but the dead had to be left where they were since in the high seas then running any movement not absolutely essential represented a danger and a waste of effort. Even when at last steam for the main engines was obtained, the possibility that *Firesprite* would have to be abandoned remained very present. It was still touch and go.

The next problem was to get her into a safe and friendly harbour. Oran is approximately the same distance from

Algiers as it is from Gibraltar. Therefore even though the port of Algiers was now in Allied hands there was no point in sending *Firesprite* to the east, and as soon as the screws began once more to turn she was ordered to Gibraltar at the best speed she could manage. At dawn on the 10th, therefore, alone and unescorted, *Firesprite* began the 300-mile journey back to the Rock, making good an estimated eight knots.

Throughout this time David, now ashen with fatigue, remained on the bridge except for two separated hours stretched out on his bunk when Soakes took over. This was the worst personal ordeal he had ever endured at sea. His ship was liable to sink under his feet at any moment, more than a third of his ship's company had been killed or wounded, Lance lay—but he did not dare let that picture form itself again in his mind—the Rock was nearly forty hours away under present weather conditions and represented at the start of the voyage an almost mythical haven at which to aim.

But the Rock which had seen them worked up and fully fledged as a young fighting ship two and a half years ago was now waiting to receive them back, battered, torn and scarcely afloat—the Rock was at the end of a long, long journey but it was attainable. With a little good fortune, with skill and attention, it could be reached and as hour after exhausting hour passed, as the wind howled and the waves smashed angrily against the twisted steel plates, this last voyage of the gallant little destroyer took on epic proportions.

From one point of view *Firesprite* had served her purpose and the job was done. One destroyer more or less would not affect the future of the Royal Navy, nor indeed of the war. If this, his first command were now to sink after her long and chequered story, it would at least save the dockyard a lot of trouble. But that was not how it seemed to David hunched up on the bridge. To David it was now a point of honour somehow or other to get this bruised collection of rivets back to Gibraltar in one piece and somewhere inside himself he knew that he would. But this was the certainty of faith—the evidence of things not seen. On the practical, sensual plane of what the eye saw and the racked ship endured, the chances were scarcely to be reckoned at all.

They began their journey at dawn on the 10th. There was thus no means of their knowing that later that same forenoon the French capitulated at Oran and the port became available for Allied use. Considerable damage had been done both by the French themselves and by the British bombardment but the Royal Marines put ashore by *Firesprite* had been able to hold intact two jetties alongside which the transports could unload. So the danger and the sacrifice had not been in vain and towards evening on the 10th, as they were overhauled by returning transports, they were surprised and encouraged when the ships' companies gathered on deck to cheer them as they passed. Help was offered but there was nothing practical that could be done and the little ship with her heavy list continued slowly on her way. Those who had heard the cheering and taken in the messages of goodwill from the transports they had spent so much of the war protecting, were left with a lump in their throats. Though help was never so very far away, the western Mediterranean seemed a very lonely place to a crippled destroyer.

There were submarines in the offing, but either *Firesprite* kept out of their tracks or they were after more valuable game and the night of the 10th–11th passed uneventfully with the weather moderating a little. Indeed as the day wore on the Chief was able proudly to beat ten knots out of the 'mechanical warming device' which was what he now called No. 3 boiler.

Their progress was followed from the air and by radar and plotted in the operations room both of the flag-ship and of Gibraltar. Indeed by noon on the 11th almost everyone in Gibraltar knew about *Firesprite* and was willing her hard to reach home safely.

At last, in the afternoon, the Rock itself hove in sight and David, with Soakes at his side, declared it to be the finest vision they had seen their whole lives. Presently the Chief, gaunt and hollow-eyed, made his way to the bridge and by the time the ship passed through the boom with the huge bulk of the Rock towering above them, the remaining officers not involved with jobs aft or on the fo'c'sle had wedged themselves somehow or other on the bridge at its dramatic angle. It was now evening and the Rock from behind a glowing black outline against the setting sun had again become the great friendly enveloping creature they had returned to so often before.

A tug helped them manœuvre slowly into harbour and they were directed first to their old berth alongside the pens. There, to the astonishment of everyone on board, was a band. There was also a really huge crowd of people on the jetty. The band began playing 'Rule Britannia' and the crowd was waving and cheering and some of the Wrens were crying.

'Is this really for *us*?' David murmured incredulously to the First Lieutenant. 'They must be expecting some other chaps?'

But it was no good looking over their shoulders. This was a homecoming and a welcome for them and for them alone. And this was as it should be. *Firesprite* was Gibraltar's Very Own ship and all that was left of the famous flotilla the Rock had once adopted. Her exploit at Oran had been a fitting climax to her career. Back in Gibraltar this had been noised abroad and it had caught the garrison's imagination. Both Fortin and the Admiral had readily agreed to Seale's suggestion that here was a moment calling for some public mark of respect. It was *Firesprite* that had landed the Royal Marines at Oran and the Royal Marines were as much part of Gibraltar as the Rock was of them. So it was a Royal Marine band that played them movingly into harbour, it was Lieutenant Seale, R.M., who had eagerly and proudly organized this reception—it was the Royal Marines who had pride of place—but when it came about, it began to look as though every inhabitant of the Rock itself had turned up spontaneously to see them come alongside, to watch their arrival.

As the ship was almost tenderly secured to the jetty, David could see his uncle, Jaime, Seale, the Admiral, Hobart and Grace all together in one group. They were all there—all there to do honour to the *Firesprite*. Though he was too tired now almost to feel, the tears sprang to his eyes as he saluted and acknowledged the lusty cheering of the crowd on the jetty which by now could be numbered in thousands with all the time fresh people running to join it, running to catch a first sight of the heroic little ship.

'Do ye know something, sir?' the Chief said in his brisk

Scottish voice, 'I believe Gibraltar was afraid we wouldn't come back. I think it scared them. They thought they might have to adopt some other inferior ship. But now they've seen us they can relax. They're safe. They've got us protecting them again.'

But David did not answer. He was watching Grace walking slowly with her father towards the gangway being placed aboard, Grace upon whom his whole life was now centred was there and would soon be in his arms. He lifted his hand to wave to her and his heart thudded dangerously as he saw her pause, smile a little uncertainly and then wave back. But it was at this moment that he knew things would never be as they had been before. His mind went back to that darkest of nights at Oran. It was as though Lance was now standing by his side ironically holding up his tired, heavy arm. 'Now you take her on,' a mocking voice said in his ear, 'I'll even wish you good luck. God knows you'll need it.' He shook his head violently. 'No—no—NO,' he said and from the sudden stir around him realized he had been talking aloud.

'Are you all right, sir?' Soakes asked him gruffly from behind the wad of bandages on his head. David nodded curtly in a way which precluded any further inquiries. He was aware that the tears were starting out of his eyes. He could not help it. This was the end of something, he knew not what. He took a deep breath and tried to regain control of himself. 'I've sort of come to terms with myself,' the voice said in his ear. 'Now it doesn't seem to matter any more.'

And perhaps it doesn't, he said to himself, as he left the bridge for the last time, lowering himself wearily down the ladder, making his way to what was left of the quarter-deck. Perhaps after all it really doesn't matter, he consoled himself as Lance's dead face again formed itself in his mind. This particular journey was over, a siege had been lifted and now there was to be a time for rejoicing and for rest. Lance was dead but he, David, was still alive. He must learn somehow to adjust, to come to terms with the time that now lay ahead.

As the November day turned swiftly into night the first lights began to twinkle above them on the Rock. They were home.